Shimeon took her by the shoulders, turned her to him, and gently lifted her face to his. He was staring at her, and she looked up into his eyes; but when he tried to draw her toward him and kiss her, she tensed and pulled away. His arms tightened.

"Poor thing, why are you so afraid?" he asked gently.

"Go away," she pleaded. "Please go away."

"I love you Berenice," he said softly. "I love you with all my heart."

"You fool, you fool," she whispered. "Don't you know who I am? I am the abomination of Israel—the whore of Herod—"

"I think I know you better than you know yourself," he said, drawing her to him. She took shelter in his arms, and then slowly, fearfully, she raised her face to look at him. . . . He kissed her. The fear was not yet gone, but she could control it, master it, and know the strange, hot wonderful fact of a man's kisses on her face. . . .

Agrippa's Daughter

Howard Fast

ace books

A Division of Charter Communications Inc.
A GROSSET & DUNLAP COMPANY
360 Park Avenue South
New York, New York 10010

AGRIPPA'S DAUGHTER

An ACE Book

By arrangement with Doubleday & Co., Inc.

First Ace Printing: May 1979

Published simultaneously in Canada

2 4 6 8 0 9 7 5 3 1
Manufactured in the United States of America

FOR BETTE

who has been with me through all,

the best and the worst

LIST OF PRINCIPAL CHARACTERS

Berenice Basagrippa Princess of Galilee (later queen of Chalcis)

Herod Agrippa Berenice's father, the king of Israel

Gabo Berenice's maid

Herod of Chalcis Berenice's first husband (also her uncle), king of the city of Chalcis in Lebanon

Agrippa Berenice's brother, king of Galilee

Polemon King of Cilicia, Berenice's second husband

Shimeon Bengamaliel Berenice's husband (third), grandson of Rabbi Hillel and prince of the Great Sanhedrin

Gamaliel Benhillel Shimeon's father, grandson of the founder of the House of Hillel

Gessius Florus A procurator of Judea

Titus Flavius Vespasianus Roman commander, subsequently, Emperor of Rome

Shimeon Bagiora War chief of the Sicarii

Cypros Berenice's mother

Drusilla Berenice's sister

Marcus Lysimachus Youngest son of alabarch of Alexandria

Alexander Lysimachus Alabarch of Alexandria

Germanicus Latus Legate in Palestine on trade mission for Claudius

Enoch Benaron Captain of the king's guard

Vibius Marsus Proconsul of Syria

Cuspius Fadus A procurator of Judea

Hyrcanus Berenice's elder son

Berenicianus Berenice's second son

Anat Beradin A merchant

Adam Benur Agrippa's armor-bearer

Gideon Benharmish Head of the House of Shlomo in Tiberias

Ishmael Barfabi High priest

Hillel Bengamaliel Shimeon's brother

Sarah   Shimeon's mother
Deborah   Hillel Bengamaliel's wife
Achon Baravrim   Grain engrosser at Syria
Ventidius Cumanus   A procurator of Judea
Joseph Benmattathias Hacohen   (Flavius Josephus) Jewish
   commander and historian
Ba'as Hacohen   Head of the House of Hakedron
Menahem Hacohen   A chief of the Sicarii
Jacobar Hacohen   Jewish banker
David Barona Purpureus   A wealthy Roman Jew

Agrippa's Daughter

PART ONE

BERENICE was sixteen years old when she witnessed her father's murder, and she watched the sequence of events that led to it with curious indifference. Since her father had embraced virtue and had hired an army of street singers to proclaim the fact that a saint dwelt among the living, Berenice had become conscious of him; she had become aware of him and curious about him, but her feelings toward him had not changed. As a child she had feared him; during the first years after puberty she had hated him; and finally indifference came. That was because it was not in her to go on hating; it took too great a toll of her. It was too destructive.

It was late spring; they were in Caesarea on the seacoast, and it should have been a cool and pleasant day. But the wind had backed upon itself during the night, and with morning, the slow, hot inland wind from the desert began to blow, crossing the hills of Low Galilee and rolling down on the seacoast like boiling oil. The wind blew evil, and everyone in Caesarea knew that it would be an evil day. Berenice knew it. She knew it in the hot, breathless, gasping morning, before the wind began to blow, and she was not afraid. Quite to the contrary, she was filled with anticipation, for some instinct told her that the evil was not directed toward her. Her whole family would be at the theater that day, and Berenice loved the theater.

So she dressed, quite deliberately, to greet evil and to blend evil with joy, in a cotton shift of blazing red, with an overdress of green. Her maid, a short, heavy-limbed, black-

3

haired, black-eyed, dark-skinned Benjaminite woman began to protest the combination of colors, but Berenice silenced her with a single glance. The Benjaminite's name had once been Leah, but Berenice detested the name Leah and forbade her to use it ever again, giving her instead the Idumean name of Gabo, which means the black sand mole. Gabo, as she was now called, was seventeen years old and had been body maid and of course chattel slave to Berenice for three years. When she had first appeared, Berenice had detested her and struck her upon the slightest provocation, sometimes with a short whip and sometimes with her hands. On occasion, more because of her own vexation than any sins of Gabo's, Berenice would beat her until the blood flowed. But as Berenice grew older, she found that a sharp glance or a cold word were as effective as a beating—and left her own soul untormented by the self-loathing and guilt that always followed one of her tantrums.

So now, a glance from Berenice was enough to make Gabo understand that her mistress was in no mood for arguments. It would be green and red, gold shoes, a gold sash for the waist, and a gold net for the hair. As a matter of fact, the colors became Berenice very well. At sixteen, she had reached her full growth, and she stood taller than most women of her time, with copper skin that glowed on the strong bones of her face. She had green eyes that became greener in juxtaposition to the sleeveless overdress, and the red of the shift went well with her coppery complexion and her auburn hair. She had the red-brown hair and the large bones of the Hasmoneans, large hands, long fingers, wide shoulders, and prominent cheekbones, planing down to a firm, clean-cut chin. Her mouth was too wide, her nose the high-bridged, arrogant Hasmonean nose, and nowhere upon her trace or evidence of the dark Idumean line—but she was now beginning to be beautiful. She had never been beautiful before. She had been a raw-boned, skinny, ugly, freckled child, and now she was a woman more strangely and differently attractive—to those who found her attractive—than any other in her father's kingdom. Her father was king. She was a princess.

She was also a queen, but the very thought of that was distasteful to her. As the scale of queens went and was weighed and counted, she was close to the bottom, queen of a tiny, unimportant and rather shabby little city in Lebanon called Chalcis. The king of Chalcis, her husband, was also her uncle; and this marriage with him her father had forced upon her only ten months before. This morning, when the hot wind started, she wished for the first time that her husband, her uncle, Herod of Chalcis, were here with her. He could not abide heat. Chalcis was pleasantly cool, one of its few virtues. It made her smile slightly as she thought of her husband breaking out all over with prickly heat and then the red heat irritation spreading over his bald skull.

"Gabo?" she said. Gabo was very quiet. She mistrusted her mistress's smile.

"Gabo, is it true that the spells made in Arad work—that they have power, effect, force—you know, you know?"

"I have never been in Arad, mistress."

"You're Benjamin. Why haven't you been there?"

"I was born in Betab, mistress, in Judea, where I was slave to your father's stablekeeper. Arad is an Idumean place," she ventured to instruct, her voice dying off with the awareness that she had dared to instruct.

"Idumea, Benjamin—black people, dirty people—I can't bear any of you. I told you to wash! I told you to wash every day! I told you to scrub that brown filth off your skin!"

"I do, I do," Gabo pleaded.

"I know what you do—rolling with everyone who crosses your path, like a little animal. How many yesterday? How many men did you have yesterday? How many?"

"Oh, none, none, none," Gabo pleaded.

"Big ones? Who was the biggest, Gabo?" Berenice's anger

vanished as she was caught up with the motion. "The longest? How long? Did you ever have one this long?" She spread her arms and Gabo burst out laughing.

Only with Gabo and with her brother; with all others, Berenice was on guard, tall, regal, witty on occasion, more often silent, never talkative and very often—for those who recognized it and knew—dangerous. Particularly, she herself knew that she was dangerous, a knowledge that had come to her concurrently with her ceasing to be afraid of her father. The first time she was master of a situation, she had the heady feeling of being drunk without incapacity—and thereafter a sense of the danger that accompanied the power. After that, it became easier and easier to master a situation—as this morning.

Whether he was at home in Galilee in his own city of Tiberias, or at the shore in Caesarea or in the hills of Jerusalem, Agrippa, Berenice's father, made a ceremony of meals and encouraged his family and friends to eat with him. Not that they were frequently together. This morning, for instance, his wife, Berenice's mother, Cypros, still lay in bed, sick, weaker each day, carried to the hot salt baths but deriving no strength from them. Berenice's sisters were both away with their husbands, Drusilla, the younger, in Commangene, and Mariamne in Alexandria; but her brother, Agrippa, was there—already in the breakfast room when Berenice entered, stuffing himself with figs, olives, cheese, and wine.

They breakfasted in the Greek manner—a little fruit, some olives, dry bread, and cold water—but Agrippa managed to turn the simple fare into a banquet. Yet Berenice observed that however much he ate, her long-legged, darkly handsome seventeen-year-old brother gained no weight, maintained his Apollo-like figure against all assaults—as if indeed bearing out the legend that the Herodian blood carried a devil's trace, like vinegar against decay.

6

He greeted Berenice with great mock ceremony, kissing her hand and offering her a fig, which she chewed absently while he told her what the day promised.

She only half listened, half heard; she had the gift of being able to compartmentalize her mind, to listen indifferently while she played with other thoughts, deaf with other problems, meanwhile sensuously enjoying the sweet juice of the wine-preserved fig. Agrippa, her brother, was telling her about the play that would be presented that afternoon—and at which their attendance was commanded—in honor of Agrippa, their father, to the glory of Claudius, the emperor, who was ostensibly the author.

"—which, to my way of thinking, is a rather disgusting fiction," Agrippa said. "It's perfectly natural, of course, that an emperor should be cock of the walk all over the place, but I think he should draw the line at plagiarism."

"It's no worse than taking the credit for victories he never won or for children he never birthed," Berenice said.

"You know, you have a peculiar turn of mind, sister—but it is worse. Somehow it's worse. Anyway, it's not military history Claudius dreams of making. He's a literary type, and somehow it is worse."

"Why? The real author is paid, and handsomely, too—which reminds me that I am poverty-stricken. Can I borrow?"

"You cannot," Agrippa answered firmly. "What do you spend your money on? Oh, look, Berenice, I don't want to be a swine about it, but this is a company of very talented Greeks from Colophon. Their girls have a reputation that has had me licking my lips for ages. And money buys—"

"You're an animal," Berenice said.

"Oh, yes—and let me tell you this, sister—"

He cut off whatever he had intended to say. Berenice thought that her father, Agrippa the king, had entered behind her, but when she turned around to greet him, she saw that it was only two priests, Phineas and Aaron by name, fat,

7

well-fed appurtenances to her father's court. They were most eager at mealtime. They bowed from the waist, holding in their white robes, and then hurried to the buffet. They broke the hard, dry circles of bread into bowls and then poured wine on it to soften it, and while the bread soaked up the wine, they took the edge off their hunger with figs and dates, stuffing their mouths full of the sweet fruit while they mumbled their greetings in Aramaic.

In Latin, Berenice said to her brother, "Do you know what I should do if I were king?"

"What, sister?"

"Geld every priest."

"Ahhah—and what makes you so sure that the fat little bastards know no Latin?"

"Look at them," Berenice smiled.

They smiled back. They were eating the wine-soaked bread now, but pouring honey over it first.

"Holy child," one of them managed to say to Berenice.

"Sacred child," mumbled the other, through his mouthful of food, managing to eat and talk simultaneously— "delight of God."

"Lovely creatures," said Berenice in Latin.

They swallowed their food so suddenly they almost choked. They gulped, swallowed, and turned out the linings of their sleeves to wipe their lips. They straightened, donned unctuousness, and held themselves in what they conceived of as dignity. They faced the length of the lovely room where breakfast food was laid out, a long room with one side open to the sea and walled off from the gardens below by a delightfully wrought cedar railing. Their ears were keen. They heard the steps of the approaching king and his attendants, or perhaps the ring of arms.

Berenice's father, Agrippa, was a bad man who had become a good man, an evil king who had become a saintly king; and like most converts to a new faith, he could become unbearable in its exercise, intolerable in his persuasion. Taken by a fit of saintliness, he could proceed to make the existence of those around him more burdensome than ever it was when he pursued the ways of evil. Having become conscious of the ways of the world and the older folk who managed it at a very early age, Berenice, though only sixteen, could remember the nonsaintly Agrippa. In fact, she could remember quite clearly his return from Jerusalem to Tiberias immediately after the transition.

As she heard it told, it had happened thus: Three years before, during Succoth, the harvest festival, King Agrippa put in an appearance at Jerusalem. The move was a calculated one and not without elements of danger. Caligula, the mad and sadistic Emperor of Rome, had been murdered—an act of charity which called forth the gratitude of all the Mediterranean world—and the gentle and scholarly Claudius had been made emperor in his place. Like many civilized and educated Romans, Claudius was a Judophile—and a friend to Agrippa in the bargain. With a large and generous gesture, he added to Agrippa's small holdings, in Galilee and on the coast, the large territories of Samaria and Judea, recreating by that action the great, united Israel of old and making Agrippa king over all of Palestine. Once again a Jewish king ruled over the ancient as well as the current lands of the Jews.

It was in the flush of this great gift, this splendid accolade by the Emperor of Rome, that Agrippa and his advisers came to the conclusion that he, Agrippa, must go to Jerusalem and appear before the Jewish masses, and confront them and somehow win them. Easier said than done. Agrippa was king over the Jewish lands, which was quite different and much less than being king over the Jews. He was still an evil king, the man the child of the wild youth, the man scheming, devising, murdering, living like a Gentile, raising his children to speak as fluently in Greek and Latin as in the Aramaic—the people's tongue in Israel—or the Hebrew, the holy tongue of the Book, of the Torah; raising them with the pagan ways and the pagan knowledge, contemptuous of the Law and what the Law meant to a Jew.

So it was no small thing for Agrippa to go to Jerusalem on the Feast of Succoth and to declare that he would take his place in front of the Temple, the Holy of Holies, and there, with the Torah in his arms, he would read as the Lord God Jehovah directed him to read, and let his fate and future be in the reading and in God's will—for no Roman emperor could make him king over the Jews, but only the Jews themselves.

Yet Agrippa knew that God is kinder to those willing to do some spadework on their own, and thus he pored through the Torah until he found a passage to his taste. It was not to the taste of his advisers, however, and they wailed that he was thrusting his head into the open mouth of the lion, verily the Lion of Judah, for the passage was an incitement that the Jews could not ignore.

"Or its reverse," Agrippa smiled. "Am I no Jew? Do I know nothing?"

It was the beginning of a reputation for courage as well as wisdom. Perhaps a million Jews were in Jerusalem for the Succoth, for the Feast of the Tabernacles—perhaps a million, perhaps half a million. Who knew? Who counted? But to Agrippa, king of the Jews, standing in front of the Temple, it was a revelation—more Jews than he had ever dreamed existed, a sea of Jewish faces in every direction as far as the eyes could reach, the temple courts filled with them, and the Jews packed on the walls of the Temple and in the streets beyond and on the roof tops—and all of them waiting for him to speak.

He had selected Deuteronomy 18:15; and with specific reason, for if a good part of his blood strain was from the Hasmoneans, the blood of Mattathias, the father of Judah Maccabeus, and of the line of kings he fathered, he also carried the blood of Herod the Idumean, Herod of the cursed memory; so what he did was no small thing. The parchment scroll of the Torah was open before him, and the priests had already unrolled it to Deuteronomy and the selection of his choice. Now they watched him carefully and thoughtfully, watched the crowd, too, as Agrippa read:

"Thou shalt definitely make him king over thee, whom the Lord thy God shall choose: one from among the brethren shalt thou make king over thee—"

A consummate actor? A priest wondered. But even Agrippa could not have answered that truly. The evil Agrippa was becoming the saintly Agrippa. It was happening before the eyes of thousands of Jews, for the king's voice broke, and the tears streamed down over his cheeks, and sobbing piteously, he cried out:

"One from among thy brethren shalt thou make king over thee; thou mayest not set a stranger over thee, who is not thy brother—

"Thou mayest not," Agrippa sobbed.

The first few ranks heard him. Perhaps a thousand heard him.

"What is he saying?"

"Why does he weep?"

"Who can hear?"

"What is he saying?"

The half a million voices of the crowd telegraphed, crisscrossed, back and forth, through the courts, through the streets, even down to the Lower City where the slaves and the unclean were gathered, the bearers of burdens, the camel drivers, the garbage collectors, the gravediggers and the ulcerated and the leprous—all of them united in that bond of curiosity that transcends everything, all of them pleading,

"What does the king say?"

From high above, from far away, from inside the walls of the Holy of Holies, from such a place as served them with death did they even touch its wall with one finger,

"He weeps."

That made no sense. "Why does the king weep?"

"He is cursed with Idumean blood. He is cursed with the curse of Herod. So he weeps."

Of course, that did make sense, even below, where the Idumean gravediggers and dung gatherers were gathered. But above, in the temple courtyard, where the king stood upon his platform with the scroll of the Torah open before him, the Jews facing him were moved and touched, and they cried out,

"No—no. You are our brother."

"I am not worthy," Agrippa wept.

"You are worthy. You are our brother."

And that cry was taken up, by rank after rank, until it swept across the whole city and even the unclean, a mile away, were screaming, until their throats ached,

"You are our brother! You are our brother!"

Praise God, a king and a saint!

So had Berenice heard it told, when her father returned to his own city of Tiberias from Jerusalem, now not only king over Palestine but over the Jews as well.

At the open archway to the breakfast room, two soldiers in brass, both of them tall, large-boned, dull-faced Galileans, took up their positions on either side of the doorway as Agrippa entered. Berenice studied him carefully—uncertain as to what his reaction to her presence would be. They were seeing each other now for the first time in six weeks, and he would be surprised. He had not known that she had decided to come to Caesarea, and she had arrived and gone to bed the evening before without seeing him. There would be no great flush of greeting or outpouring of emotion, but he might decide to be angry.

Berenice watched him for anger. She knew the signs. He was a large man, going to flesh and paunch in his middle years, a wide, heavy mouth under his small, trimmed beard, the nose red and swollen from too much wine and under his shaggy brows, the same translucent green eyes—implacable here—that were so extraordinary and captivating in Berenice. He swept the room with those eyes and they eliminated the priests as beyond notice or recognition, rested for a moment on his son, Agrippa, weighing him, accusing him, and then fixed on Berenice.

"Good morning, daughter," the king said.

She smiled in greeting and bowed deeply—as they all were bowing and scraping. He was angry. His voice trembled, as always when rage began to mount in him—and in response, Berenice moved toward control. She was not alarmed. Once she would have been terribly alarmed, but not now.

"You're a long way from Chalcis, daughter," the king said.

"I had to come a long way to be with you," she replied.

"And how am I to take that?"

"As a daughter's love."

"Oh?" He bridled his anger, watching her. Now he would trap her, he decided, and get to the bottom of this, whatever the bottom was. "Oh? And how did you leave Chalcis?"

"They talk of only one thing at Chalcis," she shrugged.

"Yes?"

"Of the good and saintly king who rules over the Jews."

He stared at her, frowning, and then shook his head. More and more, he sensed the growing maturity of her will and control. She could be lying now, mocking at him, deriding him—or telling the truth. The truth would be pleasant.

Berenice sensed now that even the possibility of gossip at so small and unimportant a place as Chalcis about the goodness of Agrippa was terribly important. Goodness was a drug he had begun to take only four years ago, but now he was an addict. He existed for goodness; he would kill, plot, lie, and scheme to uphold it—and nothing would stand in the way of the saintliness he proposed for himself. Toward that end, he would believe the unbelievable.

"What do they say at Chalcis, daughter?" he asked, watching her as he moved toward the buffet of food and took a handful of raisins and dates. The others watched too. Her brother, Agrippa, was chuckling inwardly at her pose. The two priests made note of what she was doing and were amazed that the king could not see through it.

"They tell a story. It's all over town. Everyone is telling it."

"What story?"

"Oh—" Berenice shrugged diffidently. "Probably something you forget a day after it happened. They say that you went out of Tiberias dressed as a common woodcutter, so that you might be among your people and feel them and know them, and presently you came to a woodcutter's hut, and he was poor because the arthritis was in his hands and fingers, so you gave him two pieces of gold, enough to last a year, but did not reveal yourself. And so you did with two other poor woodcutters. But then—then you came to a hut where the woodcutter and all his family were stricken with leprosy—"

Berenice was inventing as she went along, fashioning the story in a mixture of skill and contempt; and faltering for the moment at what a king in disguise might do at a hut of lepers—the more so since their Hasmonean blood was the holy priest's blood, and thus the injunction not to approach the unclean was strong upon them. The king was well aware of this, for since the beginning of his period of saintliness he had become stricter and stricter in his observance of the Law.

"Go on! Go on!" the king cried.

"Well—it was unclean, and even the ground all about for thirty paces in every direction was unclean, and who in the whole world does not know that the king of the Jews keeps the law? So as you stood there, your heart breaking with pity, but with no way to approach these sick and abhorrent people, an angel came down from heaven, and took the gold and gave it to the lepers and said to you, Blessed art thou, Agrippa, beloved King—"

Her voice trailed away as she finished the story, staring at her father, the king, with wide-open eyes. Suddenly, her brother was overcome with fear, and the two priests waited with satisfaction for the king's wrath to explode and destroy this arrogant, clever, and contemptuous princess, whom they hated so. But nothing exploded. Agrippa had stopped eating. He stood for a moment, the fruit in his hands, his eyes closed—and then he shook his head.

"Foolish child," he said. "Of course you know that the story is not true. An invention out of the whole cloth. The times have gone when angels descended to earth to intervene in the affairs of men. God leaves us to our own solutions, and the punishment is ours if we fail Him. But what interests me is that such a story should arise and get around. All over Chalcis, did you say?"

"If I heard it once, I heard it twenty times," Bernice replied.

"I should think my brother would have written concerning it."

"Only the very great take pleasure in the glory of others."

"Oh?" He had forgotten entirely his earlier irritation. Now he smiled at the manner in which she complimented herself and himself, the two bracketed.

"May I pour your wine, Father?" Berenice's brother asked brightly.

As the young Agrippa poured a goblet of wine for the older Agrippa, and then tasted it himself—for the king drank no wine that was not tasted by another—Berenice walked past the two fat priests, her back to the king for a moment, smiling at them scornfully, or, rather, grimacing at them the way a sixteen-year-old can grimace, and then turned to face her father. The king was further mollified by the fact that his son had acted as his taster. He looked with some pleasure now upon his two beautiful children, and, returning his look, Berenice said to herself,

"One day, my dear father, those fine green cat's eyes of yours will be dead, seeing nothing—but my own cat's eyes will be alive. Was it our dubious ancestor, King Solomon, who said that a live cat can look at a dead king—or was it a live dog?"

But her smile directed at her father was so sweet and gentle

15

that he was moved to say, "Your thoughts, my dear daughter?"

"Love and admiration are easy in thought—harder in speech."

"You've changed. Your months in Chalcis have improved you."

"Yes."

"A certain sweetness."

"I feel it too," she simpered.

"My brother's influence."

"But surely," she agreed.

"You see how wise I was, foolish child."

"So wise, yes," and she added silently, "I wish you were dead, damn you forever."

And he was before the day was over, causing Berenice to remember this incident and these thoughts; but in all truth causing her no more than a minimum of guilt.

"I have a remarkable memory," she told her brother then. "I remember things very clearly."

Until her first betrothal, Berenice paid little attention to her father, and he in turn took even less note of her. It might be said that he was absorbed. A young, handsome prince of the Herodian line, he was without realm except in a token sense, a tiny province of Galilee to substantiate his claims, but funds without limit. There were the endless attractions of Alexandria, Athens, and Rome for him to explore, and even simple, uninspired vice requires deadly concentration. That of course was before he became a saint. In his years of goodness—four of them, he had—he observed one day that Berenice, the child, had become a woman, that remarkable change that happens to young ladies at the age of thirteen or fourteen or fifteen, or even twelve. She was between fourteen and fifteen when King Agrippa made his observation, finding her tall, full-breasted, wide-hipped, and even attractive in a strange, outlandish way, with her freckled face, her coppery skin, her red hair, and her gleaming green eyes.

"Time for her to be married," Agrippa told his wife, Cypros.

"Time for her to have a little peace and pleasure first. She's only a child," Cypros retorted.

In his saintly stage at the time, Agrippa took a dim view of pleasure—which recalled his own past and the uneasiness that went with such recollection—and felt that Berenice was an object for his convenience and by no means for her own. However, when it came to the fact of marriage, it was not easy for Agrippa to make a choice. His one yardstick had become saintliness, and while there were good men in plenty in the ranks of Israel, he soon found that few of them were wellborn and even fewer were rich. If Agrippa was indifferent to the needs or desires of Berenice, he was by no means indifferent to her bloodlines; she could claim not only the Herodian and Hasmonean ancestry, but also the bloodline of King David and a trace of the Roman Julian Gens. There was the highest blood in Israel. Who will marry it?

His decision, finally was for a weak and ailing boy of sixteen called Marcus Lysimachus. He was the youngest son of Alexander Lysimachus, alabarch of Alexandria. Outside of Palestine, in what was known as the Diaspora, the largest and wealthiest community of Jews was in the city of Alexandria in Egypt. Here the Jews were a power unto themselves, inhabiting half the city, their houses the finest, their streets the broadest and grandest; and here, too, were their schools, colleges, their libraries, their theaters; and here lived not only the wealthiest merchants, but the most renowned scholars, poets, playwrights, and philosophers. Of these philosophers, one had become almost as famous as Plato in his own times; this was Philo—of whom it was said that not since Moses had a mortal man come so close to a knowledge and understanding of God.

Howsoever he achieved in the realms of theology and philosophy, in materialistic terms, Philo was enormously wealthy and influential and a part of one of the great Jewish families of the time. His brother, Alexander Lysimachus, was the titular head of this family, and alabarch as well—a word which meant "governor"—and lord over all the Jews and many of the Gentiles living on the Egyptian delta. It was his son, Marcus, whom Agrippa chose as a husband for his daughter, Berenice.

There were other families possessed of wordly goods who would have been eager for an alliance with the House of Herod and a marriage to King Agrippa's daughter, but the family of Lysimachus was saintly as well as rich. Philo's wife went unadorned, not even a gold clasp on her dress when she could have covered herself with diamonds, and, when asked why, retorted, "What jewels can match my husband's glory, which envelops me wherever I go." It was one of those childish, apocryphal tales told wherever there were Jews, just as they said of Alexander's wife that, secretly and covered with a cloak, she walked in the vile alleys to give charity to the beggars, and thus had sold all of her own jewels and the jewels of her sister-in-law as well. There was no need of the literal truth in such stories; the wealth of Lysimachus was such that he could feed all the beggars in Egypt and not have to pawn a jewel in the process; and such was their fame and power that after Agrippa had sent off his envoy, proposing a marriage between his daughter and Alexander's son, he was filled with uncertainties and doubts.

After all, King Agrippa was fifty-two years old at that time, two years before this last day in his life, and he had been saintly for only two of the fifty-two. For the other half century, he had been exactly what you would expect from the grandson of King Herod the Great. And Jews still uttered a curse and an invocation against the devil when Herod the Great's name was mentioned. So until he received a reply from Egypt, Agrippa reverted to being a surly, angry tyrant of a man.

In particular, he turned his anger against Berenice. He could anticipate precisely what would happen if Alexander Lysimachus rejected his proposal. Within weeks, the story would be all over the Roman Empire—how the king of the Jews had been scorned by the family of Lysimachus—and he would be held up to ridicule and become the butt of a new series of obscene stories.

Once Berenice ventured to speak to him unbidden, and he turned on her in fury and cried out, "Damn you filthy whelp—I ought to have you whipped, whipped and stoned!"

Since Berenice knew nothing at all of the preparation that had been undertaken, she was terrified and bewildered.

Finally, however, the answer came from Alexandria—penned in the fine, controlled hand of the alabarch himself. He was in receipt of the proposal of the most noble Agrippa, and he was highly conscious of what it meant to join one's own blood with the noble blood of the Hasmoneans—those jewels in the Crown of Judah—

Here Agrippa noticed but endured the fact that no mention was made of the Idumean blood of Herod but only of the blood strain of Mariamne, the wife of Herod and descendant of Mattathias the Hasmonean, who fathered the five great Maccabeans. This could be taken as a calculated insult; but it could also and more intelligently be accepted as a piece of thoughtful diplomacy, a polite pretext for creating no impediments to what was proposed. Once Agrippa would have burst forth in anger; now he went on reading with scarcely a tremor.

—jewels which, he might suggest in all modesty, would not be dimmed in such an alliance. He had heard much of the wit and beauty of Berenice, of her fair skin and red hair—the royal and priestly red hair that through the generations had marked the Tribe of Levi and the House of

19

Aaron—and he only hoped that she would not become impatient with his own son, good and gentle, but weak in body and given to illness—

Agrippa shrugged at this. A marriage was a marriage. Royal children were not like horses that you bought and sold and bred for strength and character.

Agrippa must understand, the alabarch went on—in all truth a gentle person himself—how much he loved his son, Marcus; and no words available to him would match the simple fact of bestowing his son in marriage to Berenice. No action either; but simply to indicate the love he knew he would bear for his daughter-in-law to be, he was sending King Agrippa a poor gift of two talents of gold and three of silver.

Even Agrippa was overwhelmed and awed by this princely—no kingly—sum, if indeed there were five kings in all the world who could gather such an amount together, much less be able to bestow it, not as a dowry but as a gesture of good will. Let him slight Agrippa's Herodian ancestors; at that price, Agrippa would renounce all connection with Herod.

He was a gay Agrippa then, smiling and gay, the cup of his fulfillment running over. Passing by the room where he was communicating the news to her mother, Berenice saw him doing a little jig of joy. Many years would pass before Berenice would come to fully comprehend the wilderness of space, time, and culture that divided the Herodian family from the line of Lysimachus. To her understanding at the time, she was noble born and this Marcus was a commoner—and not for her life could she grasp the subtleties of status that had been conferred upon her father and mother. So, passing by the room, she was halted; and in her father's command, there was a strange and disturbing note of tenderness:

"Berenice, my darling!"

She was not used to being addressed as darling. She halted warily at the doorway.

"Come in, darling," said her mother.

She took a few hesitant steps into the room. At fourteen, she was possessed of more wariness than poise.

"Wonderful news," her mother added, but a little less than overjoyed now that she was confronting her daughter—as if she suddenly realized that the child in front of her was a stranger.

"You are betrothed," her father announced. "We have made an alliance with one of the great Jewish families of all the world. We honor them and they honor us—which is precisely how these things should be."

Berenice heard, but nothing in her appearance changed, no expression on her face to replace the alert wariness. In her mind, she was dealing with what she had just heard, arranging the facts, gathering her own resources, such as they were. Vaguely and in the back of her being, there had been the knowledge that some day she would marry a man. Other knowledge went with that. Her brother, Agrippa, a year and a month older than she, was an able teacher—as were the slaves around the palace, who, in return for some small payment from her brother, would rut out a visual lesson in the perpetuation of the species. Her initial curiosity was wedded to distaste, but at no point in her life where curiosity could be satisfied did Berenice ever draw back. Many things motivated her, and not least among them the compulsion to know why, how and when.

Now, her mother and father had devised a new twist to her fate—and since nothing else of their devising was particularly delightful, this did not fill her with anticipation. She waited.

"Of course, I could have married you to some Gentile prince," Agrippa went on. "I could have enlarged my realm by half again—but what then? I am the keeper of the Law. I stand before the people as a saint stands before them. Marry you to a Gentile? But you may believe me that Jewish princes don't grow on trees—"

No muscle in Berenice's face moved.

"You don't seem very pleased."

"Whom am I betrothed to?" she asked.

"Marcus Lysimachus, son of the Alabarch Alexander, nephew of Philo, and only one of the richest young men on earth—that's all, only one of the richest—"

"I see," Berenice said, still unmoved.

Later, Berenice's mother, Cypros, said to her husband, "It seems a pity, such a child—"

"Child! The devil you say!" Agrippa retorted. "She's no child, not by a long measure. I just pray to the Lord God that she's a virgin."

Berenice was a virgin. Her brother, Agrippa, three cousins, and a young Roman princeling had all done their best to deflower her; but under her soft skin were muscles like steel, and wide-shouldered and long-limbed as she was, she was stronger than any of them. When the learned physicians from Alexandria came to examine her, they clucked with approval—and Berenice lay upon her back, hating them and all other men on earth. They examined her vagina and discussed her, and since this was entirely a part of the times, not only in Palestine but in a hundred other countries, she resented this hardly at all, but did resent violently that these common swine should touch her or lay hands on any part of her. And thinking at the same time that had she indeed been deflowered, what a damned outcast she would have been, spat upon by her own father and derided by every sot and whore and slave in Israel—thinking of this possibility which she had avoided simply by physical strength and willful purpose, she composed a thematic list of things she would inflict upon Agrippa, her brother, her cousins, and the Roman, if she ever saw him again. And that depended upon whether she ever saw Rome again, or whether she was intended for internment in Egypt, perpetual imprisonment behind the high garden walls of the home of an Alexandrian millionaire.

To Berenice, as to most Galilean Jews of her time—and she was a Galilean, firstly and basically—Egypt was less a geographical location than a moral abomination. All the glories of Alexandria, thrice repeated, the twin crowns of Judean and Greek culture, as it was put, impressed her not one whit. In so far as she knew, Egypt was the prison land, the abomination of abominations—the lowest step, whereas Rome was the highest; and she was being sold there for money; not to connect her with another royal bloodline, not to be the wife of some great king or prince—but to marry the son of a very rich man. The fact that her own morality was conditioned by Rome and the only slightly less refined practices of her native city, Tiberias, and was at best nothing to boast about, did nothing to change her attitude. It was an unsmiling, angry, hard-eyed princess that set off for Alexandria.

The alabarch of Alexandria had sent not only physicians and money, but a battalion of Greek troops, serving women, a great wheeled carriage for the Princess Berenice to ride in, wagonloads of gifts and twenty cavalrymen in shining brass armor as side riders. These cavalrymen were young Jewish boys of some of the best families in Alexandria, and while it was a great lark and treat for them to get a journey to distant Galilee at the expense of the alabarch, it was also a tribute to his influence that he was able to command them.

Though it was past the summer, the road down which they traveled from Tiberias to Caesarea, where they would take ship for Alexandria, was hot as the slope of a volcano, and inside the great covered carriage it was like a furnace. Berenice endured it long enough to get out of sight of Tiberias and for the procession to begin its climb out of the sunken pit of heat where the Sea of Galilee lay, and then she and Gabo climbed out of the wagon and leaped lightly to the ground. The Alexandrian serving women were afraid to follow her, and Berenice told them that they could suffocate and be damned so far as she was concerned. She herself was clad only in a white cotton undershift—cotton was more desirable, more expensive than silk then—and she kicked off her ornate sandals that she might walk comfortably barefoot.

At the sight of this, the alabarch's seneschals, who were in charge of the party, spurred their donkeys up to Berenice, voiced their horror shrilly, and pleaded with her to follow the dictates of modesty by returning to her carriage. She told them, in no uncertain terms, to go soak their heads in the waters of Galilee.

"But, Princess," they pleaded, "it is not fitting."

"And who are you wretched scribes to tell me what is or is not fitting?"

"We beg you, out of consideration for our noble master."

"I am less concerned for your noble master, as you put it," Berenice replied, "than I am for this wretched slave girl of mine. Far less. She, at least, helps me to wash and dress, but for your noble master, I am merchandise to be bought or sold. Well, I have been purchased, and there are my obligations to your noble master. Now get out of my sight!"

Dumfounded at this kind of response from a young lady of fifteen years, the seneschals retreated, but they were hardly mollified by her attitude, and they sedulously entered in their journals those actions of hers during the ensuing trip that they considered worthy of the alabarch's notice—which embraced almost all of her actions. Berenice was young enough to respond to handsome lads in brass armor, and the cavalrymen included some of the best-looking young Jews in Alexandria. They soon became her willing servants, admirers, suitors, and defenders; and for the time being she forgot her distaste for the opposite sex. Thus, the trip to Egypt turned out to be far more pleasant than she had ever imagined it might be.

But Egypt itself held none of the joys that might be anticipated in connection with a wedding or a bride. The great house of the alabarch was all that she could have expected, but the atmosphere was that of a tomb, and the man who greeted her was sunk in bereavement and despair. Berenice had steeled herself to despise all that she encountered in Egypt, but already, when she came to the palace of the alabarch, her adolescent arrogance had been dulled by the wide avenues, the splendid public buildings, and the magnificent monuments of Alexandria. Like all Greek cities, it gleamed with color, sang with the blues and greens and yellow and burning reds that covered every inch of stonework and brickwork; and through its boulevards swarmed the traffic of half a world—Romans and Greeks and Egyptians, black Nubians, hooded Arabians, Jews and Syrians and Gauls and Libyans and Parthians—a city so large and alive and noisy that by comparison her family's home seat of Tiberias was only a back-country village on the shore of an isolated highland lake.

So when she finally faced the alabarch, the edge had already been taken off her mettle, and she faced him soberly enough. She was well clad now, in silks and jewels, her hair gathered in a net of priceless pearls, her feet shod with golden sandals, and upon her rich red hair, a thin diadem with a lion rampant over a single ruby, this of gold, the lion of Judah, to seal her right to the Hasmonean blood and the Hasmonean line. Let it be Alexandria or Rome—still in all the world there was no bloodline as ancient as hers, no family so noble—who were kings when Rome was a village of mud and wattle huts. Perhaps the alabarch thought of this as he looked at her, no child this, but a woman of strange, almost bizarre beauty, thought of what might have been, wiping his eyes. He was a fine figure of a man, tall, wide-shouldered, erect, his beard white, his eyes piercing blue, as blue as the long robe he wore belted at the waist. He was a commanding figure with a commanding mind—a doer and leader, even as his brother Philo was a dreamer and a philosopher. His seneschals had come to him with their whining complaints of how she had behaved, what she had done, and he swept them away, crying out at them, "I care nothing for your damned spying! Bring the child to me!" So they had brought her to him, and now the Princess Berenice stood before him.

"My child, my daughter," he said hoarsely, fighting for control of himself. Still, Berenice did not understand, No one had told her. But she sensed that she had come into Alexandria in the presence of some enormous tragedy—as the alabarch went on, "And beautiful beyond all my imagining. Ah, what might have been." And as she stared at him, uncomprehendingly, "You see, my child, my son died this morning."

Still Berenice stared at him.

"My son, Marcus, your betrothed—he died."

And what was she in terms of all this? She didn't know. Was she saved? Or had she fought a battle to absolutely no purpose, a battle which she would have to fight again? She didn't know. And what was expected of her? Should she weep? Her husband to be was dead, but she had never seen him.

"Do you want to see him?" the alabarch asked gently.

"What is he asking me?" Berenice thought. "Do I want to see a corpse? Why should I want to see a corpse? I have seen corpses before. Why is this corpse any different?"

"If you are afraid, my dear?"

"Afraid?" she thought. "Afraid of what? Of a corpse? My dear man, you evidently have a strange notion of what it means to grow up as a princess in the House of Herod. I have seen men killed in front of my eyes. Yet I might confess that I have no desire to see this particularly corpse. Absolutely none."

But aloud she said nothing, only stared at the old man's grief-stricken face, and then finally nodded.

"Follow me, Berenice, my dear," he said.

She followed him through a number of rooms, past clusters of people who watched them in silence, and then into a candle-lit bedchamber, where the body was stretched out upon the bed and where a woman in black knelt by the bedside, sobbing, one of the boy's dead hands pressed against her cheek. Two girls lay crumped at the foot of the bed, and they too were sobbing, and at least a dozen other people were in the room, priests and physicians and womenservants, but they stood well back from the bed.

In the course of her life, Berenice would see many dreadful and heartbreaking things—but nothing that touched her so deeply and poignantly as the sight of the boy's mother with his dead hand pressed to her cheek. Why this was so, she did not know, but suddenly she was filled with nameless, meaningless grief of her own.

The alabarch led her to the bedside and uncovered his son's face, and Berenice saw the white, bloodless countenance of what appeared to be no more than a child, a little boy carved in candlewax—her husband to be, her bridegroom whom she would never address, never speak to, never touch, never kiss.

Suddenly, she was weeping. The alabarch's wife rose, went over to Berenice and took her in her arms.

"No, don't weep for him, my child," she whispered.

But Berenice wept for herself . . .

And then, later, months later at Tiberias, Berenice had to repeat it all for her father—who was thinking mainly of one thing, would Alexander want the money back? In his questioning of Berenice, he persisted on the question of the mood and attitude of the alabarch.

"He loved his son," Berenice said sullenly. "What shall I tell you about his attitude?"

"I don't give two damns about how he felt about his son!" Agrippa snorted. "How did he feel about the money?"

"I don't know how he felt about the money. And I don't care," Berenice said.

"Oh? You don't care! Only enough money to buy a kingdom, but you don't care! What do you care about? What did you care about during the weeks you stayed there?"

"Nothing," Berenice muttered.

"Then why did you stay?"

"I told you why I stayed. Because they begged me to. Because they loved me and wanted me to stay."

"Loved you? They never saw you before and they loved you? Is that what you're trying to tell me?"

"Yes."

"Well, I say you're a liar!"

"Agrippa," his wife begged him, "leave the child alone."

"I say she's a liar!" The king stormed, turning on his wife and demanding, "Is she or is she not a liar? Tell me that. Has she ever spoken the truth—since she was an infant? Ever?"

"Leave her be."

"Yes? Three weeks in the alabarch's house, and she never thought to ask him of the money?"

"No!" Berenice cried suddenly. "I do not think of money! I do not speak of money! I am a Hasmonean princess!"

"Oh!" cried Agrippa. "You tell that to me, your king, your father! I did not know you were a princess—a Hasmonean princess! Is that what they taught you in Alexandria?"

Berenice stared at him.

"And Herod's blood? Did you sell it to the alabarch?"

"I threw it to the swine," Berenice said deliberately—and then her father struck her, with all his strength across her face, so that she was flung back onto the floor, where she lay for a moment, bleeding from the nose. Then she pulled herself to her feet, turned her back on her mother and father, and left the room. She made no attempt to staunch the flow of blood from her nostrils, nor did she whimper or cry out.

"You shouldn't have done that," Cypros told her husband. "There was no need for it—no reason."

"You know," he said thoughtfully, his tension broken, his frustration released, "it occurs to me that the alabarch does not expect the money to have been returned. He must have taken a fancy to our Berenice. She won't be easily matched, now that she's a virgin no longer."

"How do you know?" his wife protested.

"How do I know? Don't be a fool. I'm a man. The alabarch is a man. He takes my daughter into his house. He has given me a fortune. I keep the fortune. He seeks for the fountain of youth where all old lechers seek it—in a woman's crotch. You know, my dear—I'd like to have the alabarch ask for his money. Damn me if I wouldn't, and I would teach him somthing about respect for a royal virgin. But I don't suppose anyone has to teach him anything. He knows that when you ride a new mare, you buy a saddle."

The alabarch never asked for the money to be returned, and Agrippa became increasingly convinced that his analysis was correct. While the money tempered his anger toward Berenice, he regarded her as a particular and puzzling problem, and of this she became increasingly aware; for regardless of the size of a palace, it holds no secrets from those who inhabit it. She would turn and see Agrippa staring at her, a brooding, faraway look in his eyes; and during those days, her brother said to her,

"So help me, Berenice, I do believe that he harbors lecherous designs toward you."

"Since he's your father," Berenice replied, "nothing he harbored would surprise me."

But she did not agree. He was in his saintly phase, and the years were catching up with him, and the look was not a look of lust. Berenice knew that. Love of money was crowding the love of women out of Agrippa's personality—the former not only less physically demanding upon a middle-aged man, but far more acceptable in the eyes of the country's population. Even a saint can be parsimonious, obeying King Solomon's injunction to heed the ways of the ant; but promiscuity stands in poorly with holiness.

One day, outside the door of their chamber, Berenice overheard her mother and father talking. Her father was in the process of complaining.

"No—I can't take the chance. Marry her off and then find out that she's been deflowered? And then have her flung back into my face, with all the world to know that she's a whore!"

"But you condemn her first," Cypros protested.

"What else? Have I no eyes? Am I a fool?"

His voice was beginning to shake with rage, and Cypros said soothingly, "I did not say that you were a fool, Agrippa. I know that you think about problems very brilliantly. In fact, you are the wisest man I know. But sometimes—well, I mean that if you are so upset over whether Berenice is a virgin or not, why not have the physicians to attend her—"

"And have it all over Tiberias the next day and all over Israel in a week? Have you ever met a doctor you can trust to keep his mouth shut? They are worse gossips than old women."

"Then what will you do?"

"Just leave it to me. I'll think of something."

He did. He summoned Berenice to his great, formal audience chamber and ordered them to be left alone. There was only one seat in the audience chamber, a polished wooden chair on a raised dais—where the king sat. He sat there now, clad—as he thought—simply in a white linen robe embroidered with gold thread, and on his head a golden skullcap—spun gold and silk—rather than a crown. He preferred it lately to a crown, and it was good for the street singers who cried his praise to let it be known that the king wore a skullcap as did any other Jew. In his years of piety he still allowed himself gold trappings—as a sign of royalty—but wore almost only white and on most occasions. In the face of that, and quite deliberately, Berenice wore a shift of lavender and an overdress of flaming orange. A slight smile of defiance on her face, she stood facing her father.

"Why do you dress like that?" he demanded. "To defy me?"

"To honor you," Berenice said softly.

"By dressing like a whore?"

"Does a whore dress this way?" Berenice sighed. "Then whores are wealthy. This is the most expensive dress I have ever owned."

"You are an abomination before my eyes!" Agrippa cried. "A stench unto my nostrils!"

His righteousness was growing in clichés. It bored Berenice. She was frightened, but she was also bored, and she asked Agrippa whether that was why he had called her in to him. "But it can't be," she added, looking about the big, empty chamber. "Why did you send them away?"

"I share my shame with no one."

Berenice yawned, and her father cried,

"God's curse on you! Yawn! Laugh! Sing! Sing! I wash my hands of it—of all of it. I am finished. Let another apologize for Berenice. I have given your hand in marriage." He flung his arms apart to signify the conclusion he had stated so firmly.

Berenice stared at him. Suddenly, her heart was like a lead weight—for she had expected nothing like this, and now she was afraid. And afraid, she whispered,

"Who? Who is my husband?"

"My brother," Agrippa said. "My brother, Herod, king of Chalcis."

Silence and no response at first, as Berenice attempted to re-create the words her father had just spoken, to put them together and make sense and reason out of them. Then she said,

"No. This is a ghastly joke. I deserve it. I know that I do. I'm sorry, my father, my king, my liege lord—I am sorry, I apologize, I abase myself. Forgive me." She came a step closer to Agrippa. "A joke? Humor? Should I laugh?"

"If you wish to laugh, laugh," Agrippa said.

"And you were not—"

"Of course. What I said I said. I have given you in marriage to my brother, Herod. Can you deserve better? He's a widower, a substantial and mature man—and king of Chalcis. He will treat you firmly but well—"

"An old man," Berenice whispered.

"Old? Come, daughter, you praise me poorly. He's a year younger than I am—and am I an old man? Hardly. In any case, he will be your husband and you will be his wife—"

She had never pleaded before, never begged before, never abased herself before, but now she was pleading that she was only fifteen years old—

"You're old enough to dance a jig and make the music too," Agrippa said sourly.

Now, on the day Agrippa was to die, a year after the two of them confronted each other in the empty audience room, a year after he had burned smiling horror into the fragile, fluttering soul of a fifteen-year-old girl who had never known a man and covered her horror of men with a veneer of little-girl strutting and boasting—a year after all this that same girl had played with his vanity and used his vanity, coldly—as cold as most of her actions were now. Her brother saluted her as they strolled in the gardens after the breakfast. He was absolutely delighted, as he told her, and said to her, "Oh, I don't hate him the way you do—not at all, but—"

"Don't you?" she interrupted. "Suppose you could kill him—"

"What a thing to suppose!"

"No, I don't mean that—not that at all, brother; because we're both civilized, aren't we? I mean that somewhere in us, there is a germ of human decency—"

"Where?" Agrippa grinned.

"I don't mean, kill him. But suppose you could interfere and prevent his death—would you?"

"I don't know," her brother said slowly and thoughtfully.

"There! And you say you don't hate him?"

"Not the way you do," Agrippa protested. "I mean—why should I? It's the difference between the son and the daughter, and if he's never shown me any love, he's never gone out of his way to be cruel to me."

"Because he's indifferent."

"Perhaps," Agrippa shrugged. "Perhaps you're right. But I love to see you handle him."

"Ah. I paid a price to learn that."

They paused in their stroll, and Agrippa turned to face his sister. "Why did you come here, Berenice?"

"To get away from Herod," she answered directly. "He's beginning to fear me. I work at that, and it's beginning to take hold. I have my own way—more and more—"

"You know, I was going to say it before, Berenice. I mean, out of admiration, really—that in spite of all your gabbling about being a Hasmonean, there's more of old Great-grandfather Herod in you than you care to acknowledge."

"How dare you!" she cried. "How dare you!"

"I didn't mean—"

"Don't ever say that to me again. Ever!"

"All right—never again," Agrippa agreed amiably. "Change the subject. Are you going to that stupid play?"

"Yes."

"Why?"

"I want to see these Greeks of yours. I want to see what's so erotic about them."

"No. Truly—why?"

Berenice shrugged.

"It will be hot as the very devil. And the play is a bore—three hours of it, written by father's dear friend, benefactor, and protector, the Emperor Claudius. Or ghost-written by some clever Greek. In any case, I am told that it's an utter bore. A melodrama would have been bad enough. This is a comedy—out of stale jokes and heavy-handed scholastic wit. God save us. Why don't we both go swimming?"

"I told Gabo I would take her," Berenice sighed.

"Gabo?"

"The little animal has never been in a theater. She pestered me until I agreed to take her."

"And that's it?"

Berenice shrugged.

"You know," her brother went on, "someday that hairy little toad will do you in. Those Benjaminites are all

33

murderers—I wouldn't have one near me. No, sir. Someday, she'll take a notion to cut your throat."

"And a good thing," Berenice nodded. "I've often had the same thought myself—but never enough guts to carry it off."

Cypros, Berenice's mother, lay dying slowly, and through this day and many days afterward she would continue to die. Her skin was almost as white as the counterpane, and her face was full of the empty frustration that appeared to grip every member of the House of Herod when he or she faced death. For she was cousin to Agrippa, her husband, and like him the grandchild of Herod. Once she had been a stately and strong woman—as Berenice could recall—but now, dying, she was weak and petulant, and she pleaded with Berenice, who stood by her bedside,

"Why doesn't he come to see me? All day yesterday he didn't come. Not once."

"Affairs of state," Berenice said. "After all, it's no small matter to be king over a realm like his." She hated to lie and she was a poor liar; lies flattened her rich voice; anyone who knew her knew when she was engaging in this careless kind of lying. "He rushed around—here—there—"

"Berenice, stop it!" her mother snapped.

"All right. What shall I tell you?"

"I don't know. I'm dying. Doesn't he care that I'm dying? I am so alone and so afraid—"

As young as she was, Berenice thought, "We are all dying—and who cares? Who can care?"

"What will you do when I'm gone?" Cypros cried plaintively. "What will all the children do?"

"We are not children now, Mother," said Berenice.

"I know him, and I soften his blows. He doesn't mean them. He rages and rants, and it means nothing, because inside he is like a saint. The people know it. They revere him. Don't they?"

"They revere him," said Berenice.

"Bring him to me, please," Cypros begged Berenice, beginning to weep, the tears flowing across her waxen cheeks. "Bring him to me. Berenice. He has forgotten. It slipped his mind. But remind him, and then he will come to me."

Agrippa had declared the day a holiday, and there was a distribution of bread and wine. In Caesarea, in the year forty-four of our era, only about a quarter of the population were Jewish. They disdained to accept the charity of Agrippa; they barred the doors to their houses and shuttered their windows and turned their backs on a Jewish king who dedicated a day to pagan practices and a pagan emperor who was worshipped as a god. Later in the day, they would have a perfect causative relationship between Agrippa's sin and his death—unperturbed by the fact that fifty-four years of variegated sinning preceding this day went unpunished by the Lord God. This was a culmination—which they accepted; although even this verdict was not accepted by the entire Jewish community. A good many of them considered Agrippa a good man and wept tears when he died—just as Jews all over Palestine rent their garments and wept when it became known that King Agrippa was no more. Thus in all justice it must be said that with Agrippa it was different than it had been with his grandfather Herod the Great. When Herod's time came and he lay dying, all the Jews in Israel smiled and poured libations of thankfulness. Songs of rejoicing were sung, and the Jews poured into the streets of their cities to embrace each other with the news that Herod lay dying. In fact, hearing these things, Herod toyed with the notion of executing the one hundred most respected and beloved men in Israel, so that when he was carried to his tomb, there would be tears in the land. Fortunately, he died too soon to put that notion into operation.

Agrippa knew that a king over Palestine ruled others than Jews—especially in cities the Romans had built, such as Caesarea, and if he provoked some of the Jews, by noontime the Greeks, Syrians, and Egyptians who lived in Caesarea were shouting his praises. The Gomesh-singers, survivors of the ancient cult in Philistia, were dancing through the streets, chanting choruses from the play, piping and wearing crowns of green leaves, drunk already; and from the windows of their room in the palace, Berenice and Gabo watched them. They were a lewd lot, the Gomesh-singers, the men pausing blatantly to urinate in full sight of the public, and the women dancing around the men, making lascivious gestures, baring their half-covered breasts and strutting erotically. The women wore stiff skirts and had their waists constricted very tightly under leather belts, in imitation of their ancestors who had come from ancient Crete in the half-forgotten past.

Gabo was shocked. At the age of seventeen she was intimate with every conceivable vice and perversion and accepted all of it as a part of her environment; but this open pagan ritual, on the streets of a Palestinian city, was new to her. She turned from the window, clucking in indignation, and told Berenice that in Jerusalem or in Mizpah or any other Jewish city, these heathen abominations would be torn limb from limb.

"Then you should be grateful that we are not in Jerusalem," Berenice said. "In Jerusalem there is no theater, and if not for this celebration here, how would a wretched little animal like you ever see the inside of a theater?"

"Is the theater like this?"

Berenice shrugged. "It could be. And even more so. I remember a comedy of Afranius when the actors performed intercourse openly—on the stage."

"Oh!" cried Gabo. "Oh! How terrible!"

"Why?"

"Don't you see that it's terrible? For a woman to subject herself to that—openly—"

"Foolish girl," Berenice said loftily, "no woman subjects herself to it. There are no women on the stage. The role of the woman is played by a man who wears woman's clothes and a mask."

36

"No?" Gabo gasped.

"Of course. You don't think everyone is as silly and narrow about these matters as Jews."

"But two men—"

"Yes, two men. You act as though this is new to you," Berenice said impatiently. "It's late, and I must dress."

"But openly—in sight of everyone—"

"You are impossible," Berenice snapped.

"But mistress," Gabo insisted, "your brother, the noble Agrippa, spoke of the women in the company. What—"

"Of course there are women. But not to appear on the stage. That wouldn't be proper. They are there for the pleasure of the men in the company—"

In time to come, in a tomorrow that was still many years away, Berenice would cease to mock at her father. She would come to understand that the "good" king is a thing that nature itself derides and deters—even as it would be a derision to all the natural laws of things for water to flow uphill. Her own people, the Jews, had suffered a thousand years of kings, and if one was wicked, the most cursory reading of history turned up another more wicked. And since iniquity is always unstable and risky, justice appears to be done in the end.

"Woe unto thee!" cried the prophets to their rulers, and time proved the logic of their predictions. No one stood up against time, and the good had only to wait patiently for the evil to be overthrown. Of course, they had to survive the period of waiting, and that took considerable talent—but a talent in which Jews were already incredibly experienced.

When Agrippa was struck down, the Jews gathered in the synagogues, not only to mourn the passing of a good king in the eyes of Israel, but to spell out the logic of God's justice. For of all things that were dear to them, the implacable justice of God was dearest. Thus, they totaled the score: was not the theater an obscenity? And was not the prince of darkness, the Emperor Claudius of Rome, an obscenity?

And was not the play he had written an obscenity? And were not the pagan players an obscenity? And was not the whole pagan city of Caesarea an obscenity? Proof begat proof, and if God forgave Agrippa much in his days of wickedness, He forgave him little in his days of holiness. For a contract made is not to be broken; and this was very much in the way of Jewish thought and very Jewish indeed.

But Berenice had yet to face herself as a Jew, and as superstitious as she was, she knew better than to place the death of her father as God's judgment. There were simply too many human beings who desired him dead, not wholly excluding herself and her brother. Yet there was no hatred in her today. She loved the kind of pagan holiday that turned into a citywide bacchanal, and she would dream of herself as a part of it, dancing in the streets, drunk with the wine of strangers, and giving herself with pleasure to what was no pleasure to her.

In reality, sex was a frozen lump in her heart and her groin; she was a combination of the pagan permissiveness and the Jewish priggishness and puritanism, and a product of a world in which these two outlooks were at merciless war. The tension of the two tore her gut into shreds and froze the shreds, and in a world where there was no word, place, or explanation for frigidity, she existed quite naturally in the jumble of discordant parts that comprised her personality.

When she faced her uncle, Herod of Chalcis, alone finally after the nightmare that was their wedding ceremony, she was rigid with horror, almost catatonic—a memory she deliberately evoked now in Caesarea as she dressed for the theater with Gabo's help and listened to the singing and music from the streets outside. He was a fat man, her Uncle Herod, to whom her father had married her in his senseless act of senseless revenge, a tall, fat man, almost dropsical in the thickness of his limbs, and now wrapped in a red robe and naked underneath as he faced her.

"Please—wait for tomorrow," she had managed to whisper.

He hardly knew her. Before their marriage, he had seen her three times, once when she was an infant months old, once when she was six, and again when she was ten. Now she had passed her fifteenth year, a grown woman, tall, wide-hipped, wide-shouldered, strange-looking, with her green eyes, her cat's eyes, and her red hair—strange, but beautiful, if this kind of thing was to one's taste. Fifty-two years old, Herod of Chalcis could not say truly whether she was or was not to his taste. He himself was an odd lot, graced with neither the bodily beauty nor the mental agility that marked the royal house of Israel. Subservient to the strong will of his brother, King Agrippa, he had agreed to the marriage. He did not enjoy the fact of being a widower, and of late he had become obsessed with the fear of impotence. While legend had it that a young virgin was proper medicine for the condition, surely youth was more important than virginity—and this niece of his was youthful indeed. Yet he was puzzled by the imploring terror in her eyes. He had been assured that she was deflowered and a practiced hand at the business of pleasing a man.

And now she begged him to wait for tomorrow.

Of course she was deceitful. He had asked a number of his brother's close advisers what was their opinion of the Princess Berenice. Along with labels of lechery, slyness, and prevarication, they had all agreed that she was generally deceitful. Herod of Chalcis was the kind of fool who goes through life determined and satisfied that no one else will make a fool of him.

He clutched Berenice in his arms. He was full of virility—throbbing with it. Impotence? He began to laugh with delight at his passion while he tore the clothes off his niece. He exhibited his own nakedness proudly, a fat, shapeless pile of a man, his own manhood protruding ridiculously from his folded layers of flesh, and when Berenice struggled screaming against him, he folded her under his great weight and size, enveloping her in his rolls of flesh, gasping and whimpering with his re-enforced masculine pride and delight— too carried away by his passion to have any sense of the girl under him—or what was happening to her.

Only after he stared foolishly at the pool of blood on the floor where he had flung her. "Have you never known a man before?" he asked her. "I am the first, Berenice?" He was prepared to swell and preen himself over the fact that he had taken a virgin—that all unbeknownst he had found this pure jewel in a supposedly rotten apple—when he saw her eyes. The green was veiled, like shore water, dark and cloudy and full of such cold, malignant hatred that his naked skin prickled, a flush of heat pouring sweat on his icy back in a reaction of fear, almost panic.

This, Berenice remembered now, remembered it all deliberately as she created for herself a fanciful role in the city's holiday, a fantasy of sex and excitement and freedom that excited her yet left her cold and unmoved—

The play was stiff, wooden, and quite dull, and nothing the company of Colophon Greeks were able to do could breathe any life into it. Two of the company spoke Latin poorly with an atrocious Ionian accent, and whenever one of these two had lines to speak, the audience roared with laughter and pelted him with fruit peelings and pits and bits of sausage. Even in a comedy, laughter at the wrong place can be destructive; and though the play was contrived as a comedy, it was not particularly funny. Writing in his formal, scholastic manner, Claudius had borrowed freely—if indeed the play actually was from his own hand—and had pasted together a series of contrived incidents. In a mythical country, a child is born to the king's wife. At precisely the same time, another child is born to the slave woman who tends the queen. Since the queen has no milk and a wet nurse is required, they choose the slave woman, and of course, she switches the infants so that her own blood may come into the throne. It was an ancient plot, and onto it was grafted a series of equally ancient plots, which unfolded with tedious predictability.

Berenice, with Gabo crouched at her feet, was seated toward the back of the royal pavilion, which contained places for about two dozen people in four terraces or steps, those of stone hollowed into shapes of chairs and cushioned for comfort. An awning stretched overhead provided shade. Only here and in the other pavilions was shade provided—otherwise the entire amphitheater lay open to the broiling rays of the midday sun. The emperor's pavilion was the same size as the royal pavilion and provided comfortable seating for those Roman functionaries in Caesarea who desired to see the current play. Today, the Legate Germanicus Latus, a fat, bald, good-natured Italian, was there with his wife and his three daughters and half a dozen people of his suite. Situated on an angle from the royal pavilion, they were able to smile and nod at the royal party. Latus was in Palestine on a trade mission for the emperor, and it would hardly do for him to miss an opening performance of his master's first theatrical effort. They were amply provided with buckets of iced wine, and they drank and smiled and bowed and stuffed themselves with fruit as the play went on.

Berenice and Gabo shared the back row of their pavilion with Berenice's brother, Agrippa, and a young palace page, Joseph Bennoch by name. In the row directly in front of them, three priests and a rather dubious woman of the court were seated. The next row was occupied by seneschals, advisers, more priests, and the palace steward. And in the front row, Agrippa sat with two young women he had favored lately. Two young men of good family shared seats to provide front and maintain the saintliness of the king's recent reputation.

Had this not been a command performance, with Claudius' reputation on stage, Berenice would have departed after a few minutes of the tedious nonsense. As it was, Agrippa had given orders that all gates to the theater be

closed, and the audience, most of whom were not even
provided with parasols against the sun, were forced to sit and
endure—a situation to which only a minority objected. The
others had come for a holiday and were ready to enjoy
anything on the stage. They had brought baskets of food and
bottles of wine, and they ate and drank and cheered the
players and mocked them and screamed with applause or
hissed with hatred—and became drunk and happy and occasionally violent, with no Jews present except the handful of
quality in the pavilions—no Jews to look down their noses
and despite the simple pleasures of plain people and thereby
spoil their fun and fulfillment. The Syrians and Levantine
Greeks and Egyptians and half-breed Philistines and Moabites and polyglot combinations of Persian, Parthian, Hittite,
Assyrian, Babylonian, Jebusites, Samaritans, Italians, and
even a sprinkling of Gauls, Spaniards, and Germans,
Phoenician seamen, Edomite longshoremen—and so many
others that a listing would be endless, Caesarea being perhaps
the most cosmopolitan of all seaports—all of them rocked
with pleasure, belched and farted at the actors, interrupted
them, pelted them, and generally took advantage of what
they sensed, even if they had not the taste to measure—that
this was a bad and tedious play and that the Jewish noblemen
in their gay pavilions would not interfere, so long as the
horseplay remained within the bounds of semi-order, which
meant anything less than a full-scale riot.

The heat increased as the play went on and with it Berenice's irritation. Were it not for the fact that Gabo appeared
to be absolutely enthralled as the story unfolded, Berenice
would have defied her father and forced her way out through
the guards. But she knew how long and eagerly Gabo had
looked forward to this, and she decided to endure it to the
end—a determination that made her glow with a sort of
virtuous self-approval.

Her brother, wiping his brow, observed that while he
perished of thirst, those Italian louts were drowning them-

selves in iced wine. He did not like Latus, whose low birth and business career—which had brought him to his present position, that of a very wealthy knight—he now recalled. "Trust his kind to have ice here," he said angrily—and Berenice felt, at that moment, a sense of annoyance. She might have articulated it by specifying that if one desired to be as much of a snob as her brother was, he should arm himself with more wit. Young Agrippa had qualities, but he was not clever.

Staring at Germanicus Latus, Berenice caught his eye. He smiled at her. He had that Italian gift of honoring a beautiful woman—or, more to the point, of being able to make a sixteen-year-old girl aware of the fact that she was beautiful and very much a woman. He made motions to show how devastated he was at the distance that separated them, and Berenice, in response, made motions of great thirst. She did not have to repeat the suggestion. He spread his arms in pseudo-tragic apology and issued quick orders to his servants. Meanwhile, King Agrippa's attention had been attracted, and Latus now made signs to beg his forgiveness. Now Berenice saw that her father had provided his own cool liquid refreshment. Only she and her brother, apparently, were not equipped to deal with their thirst.

Her brother sent Joseph Bennoch, the page, for the wine, which was in a glass beaker set in a wooden bucket of ice. The beaker was very large, holding at least a quart of liquid, and with the bucket and the ice made a weight under which the page staggered. As he brought it to their pavilion, Berenice's father watched, and Germanicus Latus made signs that the king was to have the first drink. "Ice? Isn't that ice in it? I thought I saw ice."

Berenice dipped into the bucket, found a piece of ice, and held it dripping. Several of the guests in the pavilion gathered around, for ice was no common thing here in Caesarea in the heat, and some of them had never seen a chunk of ice before. Ice was cut during the winter months on the high lakes in Lebanon and then packed in sawdust, to be sold through the hot months at fantastic prices, so much so that it was called, in the Aramaic, the language of Palestine, the gold that melts.

"Throw it here, child," Agrippa called in great good humor, his friends and advisers around him, and feeling more and more superior as he watched the Emperor Claudius' inept play unfold. For many years, he had been a close friend of the emperor, and there is a particular satisfaction in observing the literary cropper of a close friend.

The people around Berenice stood aside, and she threw the piece of ice to her father, who caught it deftly, grinning across the seats at Latus. "Old devil! Trust you to find ice! No ice in Caesarea for the king, but let a Roman set up court there, and there's ice and anything else he sets his mind to!"

Agrippa said this in Latin, a tongue he used as easily and readily as his native Aramaic, and the high-pitched, commanding tone of his voice drew the attention of the audience. The players paused in their scene, out of deference to the king, and Germanicus Latus shouted back.

"Which explains why we rule the earth, Your Majesty. I will find ice in Caesarea, water in the desert, and women of easy virtue in Jerusalem! Only command it!" The jest was not terribly witty, but it found its mark in the audience, sending those who understood Latin into peals of laughter and those who did not into a flurry of inquiry. King Agrippa smiled in appreciation. He did not think it worth the laughter, and in his present phase he had no desire to exhibit appreciation over a backhanded slur on Jerusalem.

Meanwhile, the king's beautifully wrought silver cup had been handed to his son, young Agrippa, who had poured about a third of the beaker of wine into it.

Afterward, Berenice was able to recall much of the history of the king's goblet during the next few moments. Out of the corner of her eye, she observed Agrippa the younger pouring the wine. He then handed the cup to the priest, Phineas, who started across the row of seats, only to be stopped by the king's seneschal, Herod-Kophas by name, and a fourth or fifth cousin in the royal family. The seneschal did a complete turn, hiding the cup for a moment, and then passed it to a scribe, who handed it to one of the young women who sat alongside of Agrippa the king. She made as to drink from it, but with mock severity, Agrippa clutched her wrist, took the cup, and, forgetting in the excitement and pleasure of the moment the function and duty of his royal taster, drained half the cup in one great swallow.

Berenice was watching her father. She remembered being suddenly thirsty at that moment and half reaching out to touch her brother's arm and ask him to pour a cup of wine for her, perhaps mixing it with some ice and water. But her gesture was halted midway, for suddenly her father rose to his feet, holding the silver cup of wine in front of him in one trembling hand. A hoarse, wordless cry came from his throat, choked out, gasped out—and then a shriller, louder cry of rage and pain, and then the heavy silver cup dropped with a crash from his hand, the hand remaining outstretched, the fingers curled.

The two girls with him began to scream. The play had stopped, and players and audience were staring at the stricken king. Voices stilled; conversation halted; smiles and laughter disappeared. Here and there, people in the audience were rising to their feet—that they might see better.

The king was swaying, a thick, branchless oak uprooted. People rushed toward him, but with a sweep of his arms he thrust them away. He tried to speak, but his throat tightened and closed around the words, and then he fell down. A few minutes later he was dead.

In the turmoil that followed Berenice remained strangely cool, collected, and aloof. While others reacted with panic, fear, total confusion, or the desperation of self-preservation, she kept her wits and prevented the singular tragedy of the king's death from turning into a much larger tragedy of riot and massacre. The role she played was a surprise, not only to others but to herself as well.

While a crowd quickly collected around the king's body, Berenice remained with her brother. She did not require confirmation of the fact that her father had been poisoned and was now dead. In such areas, her own experience and knowledge were conclusive; she had seen others die of the same poison, and she was not at this moment burdened with either grief or regret. Her brother was crouched rigidly over the bucket of wine and ice; horror, fear, and surprise held him, as it held the page, little Joseph Bennoch. As her brother straightened to move, Berenice had already removed the wine from the bucket. She dropped it, as by accident, and the glass beaker splintered as it crashed on the marble floor, sending the purple wine across the bright cushions and white stone. Her brother stared at her, his mouth forming the questions, "Why? Why?" To which she replied in a sibilant whisper, "Listen to me, now. What would you? If there was poison in the bottle, it was the hand of Rome. Or do you think Bennoch did it—a child? No, if there was poison there, it was Rome."

"But we'll never know now," he protested.

"Better never to know."

The audience was milling all over the theater now. Enoch Benaron, the captain of the king's guard, was in front of Agrippa now, informing him in an official sense that his father was dead. Otherse gathered behind Benaron, priests, seneschals, stewards—and the Jewish noblemen who were forcing their way from their own pavilions toward the royal box. Agrippa stared at them in bewilderment as Berenice whispered into his ear.

"Now you are king, brother. In the name of God, pull yourself together."

Enoch Benaron, a young Galilean with the hillman's hatred of pagans, told Agrippa that he had his men at every entrance to the theater, two thousand men, the king's men.

"Just give me the word," he begged Agrippa, "and I will teach this pagan filth to weep for a king's death. I will let them know how it feels when the king of the Jews is murdered. Just give me the word." He was choking with anger and sorrow; he had feelings about the dead Agrippa. The live Agrippa remained speechless, but Berenice cried.

"No! Have you lost your senses, Benaron? Now, I tell you this—if anything of the kind happens here in this theater or anywhere in Caesarea today, then we will hold you responsible. Do you understand, Benaron? Anything—street riots, massacres—any kind of bloodletting between Jews and pagans—you hear me?"

Her voice was shrill, high, and imperious, and Benaron nodded. She stared at him, and he faced up to her for a moment, and then bowed his head and then went down on one knee before her and her brother.

"Oh, get up," Berenice snapped. "Get up and keep order here and use your common sense. He died of poisoned wine—in a cup that was handed to him. They"—sweeping her arm at the audience—"did not kill him. Someone here in his own pavilion did, and whoever he is, God's finger will point to him. Now do what you have to do."

The sun was setting by the time they were back in the palace, the seventeen-year-old Agrippa, alone finally with his sixteen-year-old sister, Berenice, both of them exhausted from the pressure of events, the chaos that surrounds the death of a king, the near panic, the confusion and excitement, the hundred details thrust upon them suddenly—each a decision:

"The body—where shall we take the body?"

"Do we want embalmers? In this heat—"

"He desired to be buried in Galilee."

"His wife. The noble Cypros must be told."

"Have you informed Jerusalem?"

"His wife—"

"Will you send messages to Jerusalem?"

"Should there be a procession? If there is a procession, it must pass through Jerusalem."

Agrippa—the young Agrippa—was king. So everyone presumed, yet they addressed themselves to Berenice. Agrippa did not mind. Himself, he had no notion of what should or should not be done. Still dazed, he was taken to look at his father.

"Bear the body to the palace, of course," Berenice told them. Herod-Kophas was whimpering about litters—it would take so long to find a litter of proper size and dignity. "Oh, improvise something," Berenice said. "Can't any of you do anything?" At her elbow then was Germanicus Latus, the Roman: "I am yours to command," he whispered. "What a tragic day! What can I do to ease your suffering?" She shook her head hopelessly, while they continued to mill about her and about the body of the dead king.

She had to confront her mother alone. Her brother would not come with her, saying, "She will believe that I did it." "Of all the things to say!" Berenice burst out. "Never say that again—never suggest it! Never!" But she went alone to her mother's bedside and stood stiff and unmoved over the weeping Cypros, thinking to herself with abstract curiosity, "This woman loved him. She actually loved him."

"He was so good," Sypros said to her. "No one knew truly how good he was, how kind he was. He was misunderstood. He was so lonely and so misunderstood—"

There was nothing Berenice could say, so she stood woodenly and listened, without disagreeing.

"We will take his body to Jerusalem," Cypros whispered. "There must be a great procession —to do him honor."

"In this heat?" Berenice exclaimed.

"How dare you speak of heat!" Cypros cried out, suddenly regal and alive, pressing herself up from her bed. "Have the embalmers lay out his sweet body with pungent spices in a cedar coffin. Make the arrangements—" The effort exhausted her. White as a ghost, she lay back on her bed, staring at her daughter. "Ungrateful—ungrateful—he loved you."

Berenice could not tolerate another moment of it, and calling back the women in attendance, she left her mother and went to Agrippa. It was twilight. She and her brother stood alone in the long, open chamber where breakfast had been served that morning, only a few hours before, and they looked at each other, and finally Agrippa asked her how it had gone with his mother.

"As you might expect—"

"She took it poorly."

"I think she's dying," Berenice said flaty. "I don't think this will matter very much."

"How can you be so cold about it all?" Agrippa demanded.

"Cold? I'm neither warm nor cold," Berenice said testily. "I am trying to do what has to be done. I didn't love him. and I can't mourn him."

"He was the king," Agrippa said. "He had the power of life and death. He could have crushed us—he could have done what he willed with us—"

"He's dead," Berenice said sharply. "Pull yourself together. You are king now—with Rome's will. That's the point—how the Emperor Claudius will take this. I never quite understood how it was between him and father. Now Claudius and you—"

"I am the king," Agrippa nodded. "Strange. I try to feel it. There should be a difference—"

"If Claudius wills it," Berenice nodded.

"Still, I am king. I am king now." Agrippa cast about him, trying to pierce the gathering shadows. "Why don't they bring light?" He cried out for the lamp bearers, who came running, setting the flickering lights in their places around the room. Now the mourners were gathering in front of the palace, to bewail the passing of a king of the Jews who was like a saint. Berenice could hear their keening—and she knew that it would go on all night long.

"The least I can do is avenge him," Agrippa said.

"On whom?" Berenice asked.

"You spoke of the finger of God. Do you believe—"

"The finger of God, I have found," Berenice said, "moves in its own good time. What will it profit us to find the murderer?"

"What will it profit us?" Agrippa cried, aghast at her cold and practical attitude. "Is there no such thing as justice? Does a man murder a king and go unpunished? Does our own flesh and blood need no vengeance?"

"Our own flesh and blood is the last thing I am concerned about at this moment," Berenice said gently. "Think this through, brother. Try to see what we are getting into, before we step into to. Who could have poisoned the king? Think!"

"Any number of people," Agrippa replied.

"Hardly. I'll tell you who could have done it. Firstly, the Roman, Germanicus Latus—do we accuse him, break with Rome, kill a legate? And then what—war with Rome?"

"Why would Latus do it?"

"Hold on now," Berenice warned him. "I did not say that he did it. I said he could have. So could Joseph Bennoch. Do you suspect him? A child?"

"Not him," Agrippa agreed.

"So much if the poison was in the bottle. But if it was dropped into the cup, we have more possibilities—the priest, Phineas, the seneschal, Herod-Kophas, our cousin, the scribe, Joash, and that noble whore, Zipporah Basomen. Each of them held the cup for a moment; each of them had an opportunity. Well, whom do we accuse? Herod-Kophas? Why? What reason? Fifty others must die before he is in line for the throne. And if we accuse him, then we confess to the world that we murder each other. Who else? The scribe. Joash? He's a Pharisee—we accuse him and split the nation in two again. Pharisees on one side, Sadducees on the other? And why? What would it profit him? Or the girl. Do we accuse her and set a large and powerful family of Jews against us? But where is her motive? And lastly—the priest, Phineas, whom we both despise. He's lost his protector, his home, his hopes, his cushy post, and the bag of food he devours each day. Yes, we could find him and crucify him, and no one would complain very much—although I am sure he's halfway to Jerusalem by now, whipping some poor horse to death. No, he had no motive."

"Then who had a motive?" Agrippa asked.

"Only one of them," Berenice said. "The Roman."

"Surely you're not serious."

"Surely I am," Berenice said. "It neither profits nor hinders him to have the king dead, but he sent us the wine, and he serves his master, Claudius.

"Father's friend?"

"You think father had friends?" Berenice smiled.

The following day, just before the funerary procession left for Jerusalem, Germanicus Latus paid a formal call on Berenice, explaining that circumstances did not permit his making the journey to Jerusalem, much as he desired to. "For the king was my dear and beloved friend—as he was of all Romans—a brilliant and interesting man." Then Latus went on to say that he did not find the king's daughter less interesting or unusual. "They say you are only sixteen. Is this possible?" he asked Berenice.

"It is possible," Berenice smiled.

"I can hardly credit it. You will forgive me if I do not stress the matter of condolences. I don't imagine that you were too upset when the king died."

"He was my father," Berenice replied evenly.

"Of course. Of course. And I would be the last to belittle the bonds of blood. Nevertheless—"

He smiled and mopped his bare skull with a kerchief. His face was round and innocent as a child's, his dark eyes open and frank.

"Nevertheless—we attempt to understand each other."

"I always attempt to understand any representative of Rome's first citizen."

"Very nicely put, that," Latus nodded. "Hot here—I don't

know how you Galileans stand the heat of these coastal places. I much prefer your green hills."

"Thank you," Berenice smiled. "I too prefer the hills of Galilee to the coastal plain. But my father was here—"

"And where he was, his loyal daughter was," Latus nodded.

"If you wish to think of it in that way."

"Ah—yes, I suppose that I do. Your Latin is excellent, Queen Berenice."

"That's hardly surprising, since I spent a year in Rome as a child. Not that I remember too much, but the language is formed. I also had a Latin tutor as well as a Greek tutor."

"Amazing," Latus nodded, clasping his hands around his fat, protruding stomach. "Utterly amazing—the more so to such an ignoramus as myself. How many languages do you have, my dear?"

"Latin and Greek," Berenice replied dutifully, "and of course my native tongue, Aramaic. I also speak a little Egyptian—the patois—and naturally Hebrew, our holy tongue, in which our sacred books are written."

"Five languages," the Roman said, shaking his head in admiration. "A most astonishing woman, my dear. You don't mind if I address you as 'my dear.' I do hope you don't mind. I fully aware of your rank as queen of Chalcis and as the first princess of the ancient Hasmonean blood, but I am also fifty-three years old, and it is difficult for me not to think of a young girl of sixteen as my daughter. I have three daughters, you know."

"And I have a husband your age, as you also know." Berenice said engagingly. "So I do feel very comfortable with you, and I don't mind at all if you call me 'my dear,' or any other term that might strike your fancy."

"As I would a daughter."

"Naturally," Berenice nodded.

"And I would talk to you as I would to a daughter, You see, if you were my daughter, I would have to ask you why you disposed of the beaker of wine so quickly? It might have provided an interesting test."

"An accident," Berenice brushed the matter aside, as of no importance.

"Oh, no, no, no. Hardly an accident, my dear. Do you really think that I murdered your father?"

"The whole idea is monstrous," Berenice replied. "However, the captain of my father's guard, Enoch Benaron, has a short temper and an even shorter store of intelligence. He prefers action, as most stupid men do—and—"

"And a Roman legate might have been mistakenly killed. That would have been unfortunate."

"God help us, yes," Berenice whispered.

"But to you, my dear," Latus went on, "why should it mean anything to you, the queen of Chalcis? Rome would have punished this place. The legions would come and Roman justice would have come with them. But what skin off your back, if I may ask?"

"You forget that I am a Jew," Berenice said quietly.

"No, Oh no. That is something I never forget. No Jew allows anyone else ever to forget who he is."

"And a Hasmonean," Berenice added, nettled and trying to put down the Roman without revealing her irritation.

"Of course—but a moment ago, I reminded you of that. I am becoming quite an expert at Gentile-Jewish diplomacy, don't you think?"

"I hardly think one has to be an expert. We are plain folk."

"Oh no!" Latus burst into laughter. "Plain folk indeed, my dear! Never. You are frauds. Plain—no, you are complex to the point of bewilderment. You are all romantics, filled with illusions, and quite as dangerous as people with illusions can be. You worship a God who does not exist but who dwells in a temple that is empty, and you make virtue out of what is unpleasant and sin out of what is pleasant—and sages out of sixteen-year-old children who bear an international reputation for immorality and wantonness and proceed to behave

like combinations of vestal virgins and Latin tribunes, and so
help me, you do confuse a simple Italian peasant like myself.
You confuse me no end. But I am beginning to adore you,
and that is quite a dreadful thing when it happens to a fat,
bald man in his fifties. Perhaps because I am a Roman, and
thereby a little warier than your husband, I intend to discour-
age this tendency in myself. Do you hate me because you
believe that I killed your father?"

"I don't know who killed my father."

"Well, have it that way then."

"No, I don't hate you ate all," Berenice said. "As a matter
of fact, I find you very charming. Would you do something
for me?"

"I am at your service," he cried.

"Would you tell me whether the emperor will confirm my
brother, Agrippa, as king over all the Jews and over their
lands?"

"Ah—" He spread his thick, hamlike hands. "If the Jewish
succession could go to a woman, I might answer that more
easily."

"But it can go only to a man," Berenice said.

"Who knows, my dear? This morning, I sent a messenger
to Rome. It will taken him ten or eleven days to go, as much
to return—and time for the emperor to ponder the question.
In a month, we will know. Meanwhile, your brother is
as much king as anyone—and you—what are you, my
dear?"

"I wonder," Berenice said thoughtfully.

One other matter of importance happened before the
funeral procession left for Jerusalem. Enoch's soldiers discovered the priest Phineas trying to leave the city disguised as
an Egyptian bearer, a particularly nasty disguise for a Jewish
priest—as Agrippa pointed out informing his sister of the
event.

"What about him?" Berenice asked.

"I want to crucify the bastard. Anyway, someone must be
blamed and punished for the murder, and now that word is

around that Phineas disguised himself as an Egyptian, there won't be a shred of sympathy for him."

"That makes sense," Berenice agreed. "It's always best when someone is punished for something. People stop talking and speculating. But don't crucify him. Hang him."

"Why?" Agrippa protested. "I hate his guts. He always was an informer, a sniveling bearer of tales, a miserable and worthless glutton—"

"I know, I know. But it doesn't look too good for your first official act to be a crucifixion. It won't sit well with the Pharisees. Also, Phineas did not murder father."

"Then he'll hang," Agrippa shrugged.

"If you wish," Berenice said indifferently.

Jerusalem was a strange interval. It remembered Berenice, and in that way it evoked her memory and was thereby sentient. It lived and waited, something she would be aware of for years to come; and in her memory, she saw it both from above and from below. It was not the first time she had been to Jerusalem, but it was the first time in four years, and four years ago she had been only twelve. She had been a child, and now she was a woman.

She saw the city floating in the air. Without support it floated, the City of God pressed up by His holy breath, and it gleamed like silver and gold in the light of the morning sun. Was there ever such a sight? She was walking with Agrippa behind the dying Cypros, who was carried in a litter at the head of the procession, and, of like mind, they paused and stared.

The city was in two places at once; it was both above them and below them, here and now and once long ago and yet to be. Berenice could look down over its walls, and yet the city hung suspended in the sky. For once she was wordless, for seeing this city, she also saw a part of herself that she had been unaware of.

As the funeral procession approached close to the gates of Jerusalem, the people poured forth to greet the last remains of their dead king. Four years he had been king over them, and four years he had, so far as they knew, obeyed the injunctions of the Holy Torah. What else he was, they neither knew or cared; they understood only that the king of the Jews had passed away, and that this was a king who was like a saint.

So they rent their garments and poured dirt upon their heads. They cried out in grief—and then when they saw their queen lying in the litter, dying as all knew, and behind her, the brother and sister, Agrippa and Berenice, the living blood of the Maccabees, soon to be orphaned—when they saw all this, they silenced their cries of grief and stood and wept. More and more people came out of the city, hundreds and then thousands, and they stood, a wall of people along the road, weeping.

What prompted her to do it, she did not know, but now Berenice kicked off her sandals and walked barefoot in the dust. Seeing this, her brother did the same. She began to weep—not of her own volition, not out of grief or pain, but because the flow of emotion from the weeping thousands was so great she could not resist it. It made no difference that this rabble were the common glut of Jerusalem's streets—the Yisroel, as differentiated from the Levites, the priesthood, and the princely and noble families who claimed this or that spoonful of the blood of David, Mattathias, or Aaron—she became one with them, her heart wracked with a misery all the worse because it was nameless and without sorrow.

Outside the gates of the city, the procession halted—and there, too, halted the crowd, stretching away and covering the whole saddle of the hill the road topped, for this was Herod's Gate on the road from Samaria to Jericho, and the road to it only a dusty path off the main road. But it was Cypros' wish to enter the city here rather than through the great Damascus Gate, for Agrippa was of the House of Herod and the blood of Herod. She lay dying, and it was not for her to think now of her grandfather's sins. Let the same God punish Herod the Great who had made him king over Israel; but Herod's name and hand were on a gate into the city, and it was fitting that they enter there and that his grandson's body be symbolized there.

In front of the gate the high priest stood, the old man, Elionai, his snow-white beard falling to his waist, and he raised his arms for silence; and then when the silence came, he began to chant the prayer of the mourning:

"Glorified and made holy be the might name of Jehovah, everywhere on this earth which He has created as He willed it to be. Let His kingdom come in your lifetime, in your days, and soon—and thus in the days of the whole House of Israel! Oh, say ye Amen!"

"Amen" rose up from the thousands of throats.

The Aramaic chant was taken up by other thousands who crowded the city walls now:

"From holy heaven, peace, and life—for us! For all of Israel! Then say he Amen—"

In Jericho, deep down in the valley beyond the city, they heard the sound of that somber Amen.

Cypros remained in Jerusalem. She was dying, as she well knew, and she wanted to die there in Jerusalem where her last sight would be of the shining sun-drenched walls of the Temple. In any case, the climate at Jerusalem was cool and pleasant, far more comfortable and salubrious than the heat of the coastal plain; and certainly better than the oppressive heat on the shores of Lake Tiberias, the Sea of Galilee, where her home was. Part of the ancient palace of Simon Maccabeus was refurbished and furnished for her convenience, and there she was made as comfortable as possible, with her ladies to attend her. Berenice saw to these matters, not out of any sense of duty or affection, but because she had discovered that when she spoke or ordered or instructed, she was obeyed more readily than anyone else, including her brother—who was almost king of the Jews, Rome willing.

As for love of her mother or pity over her impending death, Berenice was devoid of both. Her father had been an impassable barrier to her mother, and Cypros herself had never successfully intervened to protect Berenice from the strong, violent, selfish man who had been her father. Although already in his tomb, Agrippa the elder remained alive in Berenice's mind. She would awaken by night, whimpering and sweating from a dream where she saw him and cringed before his will. She would see a man who resembled him on the street, and suddenly she would turn cold all over, her heart hammering with fear. How strange, she thought, that I should fear him more now that he is dead than I ever did when he was alive! Yet fear him she did—and she found herself avoiding Cypros, even to say farewell.

"Perhaps we should remain here with her?" Agrippa wondered. He had a certain affection for his mother. "We leave her and she dies—God won't forgive us for that."

"If you attempt to determine your actions by what God will or will not forgive you for, you will shortly go out of your mind. You will also betray everything the House of Herod has stood for," Berenice told him caustically. "You happen to be king—at least until Claudius wills otherwise, and your place is in the palace at Tiberias."

"I know," Agrippa sighed. He was seventeen, at least five years younger than his sister's sixteen.

"But do you know? I wonder. A government is not something you can carry around in a pouch. A government consists of lines of communication, ministers, ambassadors, an army, a navy, stewards, seneschals—and heaven knows what else—"

"God help me," Agrippa protested, "I don't know what to do or where to turn! Whom do I trust? They all come to me, morning, noon, and night, pleading for this and that post. They all want to advise me—and I hate and mistrust the lot of them. They were his men, and they hate me. If my brother was still alive, I'd be dead now—wouldn't I?"

"I suppose you would," Berenice nodded.

"Then whom to turn to?"

"Myself," Berenice smiled and as Agrippa continued to stare at her somberly, added, "or don't you trust me?"

"You're a girl—" Agrippa began.

"Ah, no—no, brother. Don't make that mistake. I tell you, no one will make that mistake again. Never! Now will you listen to me?"

Agrippa nodded.

"Good. Now we are going to return to Tiberias—now. Do you understand? This place is too big, too complex, full of too many parties and currents and plots and counterplots. God help us if we get caught up in any of those! In Tiberias, we are home, and the government is there—your government. There is only one thing to do before we leave here."

"And that?"

"The army. There are three thousand of the king's troops here. I want you to dismiss every captain—immediately— the captains of the fifties and the captains of the hundreds and the captains of the thousands. Dismiss them. Thank them. Give them some gold. But get rid of them, and that includes Benaron. All of them."

Agrippa shook his head slowly.

"Why? Are you afraid?"

"I suppose so," he replied miserably.

"Why? Why?"

"Damn it—look at me! They will. This boy, they'll say— this empty-headed kid. They're men. Some of them have been in the army a lifetime—"

"You're king," she interrupted, annoyed, provoked by his fear and his childishness. "Do you know what it means to be king?"

"Come with me," he begged her. "I tell you I can't do it alone—"

So Berenice went with him, stood beside him, and stared arrogantly at the bearded veterans who were told that their careers were over, that they were no longer a part of the armed forces of the king of the Jews.

Then she helped Agrippa to choose a new staff—very young men and Galileans for the most part. When she and her brother left Jerusalem the next day, the Jerusalem forces marched with them. Only the Levite temple guards remained to defend the city; but that troubled no one. The land was at peace.

The march of young King Agrippa and his sister, Berenice, from Jerusalem through Samaria and up into Galilee and Tiberias was a sort of triumphal procession; for even though the land was in mourning for the dead king, it was a joyous occasion to see these two fair children, his son and daughter, both of them as tall and beautiful as ancient legends come to life, the boy so slim and straight, his new beard light as down upon his cheeks and wearing no jewels or mark of rank over his dark cloak of mourning but only the felt cap of the Hasmoneans to show his ancestry and his noble bloodline, and the girl so tall and fair, her auburn hair flaming in the sunlight, her green eyes knowing and seeing with a sense of maturity and judgment beyond her sixteen years. They were a royal pair that delighted the simple country people—so much so that they were prepared to forget that Berenice was married to their dead king's despised brother, Herod of Chalcis.

And the reaction of these people in the little villages they passed through was equally gratifying to Berenice. She felt a sense of power, a sense of the necessity and purpose of her being and living and speaking and moving. For the first time, she began to value herself. She began to dream now of what might be when her brother, Agrippa, was confirmed in his kingship by the Romans—and more and more she became convinced that such confirmation would be forthcoming. Then no Herod of Chalcis would stand in her way—and for her and her brother nothing would be impossible.

As they marched into Samaria, Berenice remembered all

she had heard of the hostility of the Samaritans and their hatred of the Jews. While they marched now with an army, still the Samaritans could have closed the gates of their cities and barred the doors of their houses. Quite to the contrary, the gates and doors were wide open, and the Samaritans came by the thousands to cheer the young king and his sister and to throw flowers in their path. Elijah, high priest of the Samaritans, appeared in person at the gates of the city of Samaria. Surrounded by his own Levites—according to his own designation—he called down the blessing of the Almighty upon Agrippa and Berenice, and invoked for their future glory and success the Holy Tetragrammaton, pronouncing the name of God *Eyabe*, in the Samaritan fashion. The influential Pharisees with Berenice and Agrippa whispered to them that not in the past decade had a Samaritan priest pronounced the name of God aloud in the hearing of a Jew. The worship of the Samaritans was ridden with magic and Ashtart-practices, and they regarded the Tetragrammaton as a magic force and entity unto itself.

"Too long has brother torn at the throat of brother," the high priest intoned. "Then God sent us your saintly father, so that Jew and Samaritan might acknowledge the same king. The promise will fulfill itself in the children. Blessed be you, the seed of Mattathias. Blessed be the seed of Mattathias."

"Amen—amen," chanted the thousands who listened, Jewish soldiers and Samaritan peasants.

And then there was cooking and eating, the Samaritan girls giving their own personal welcome to the Jewish soldiers, so tall and brave in their shining armor—

There too, that night, a young captain of a thousand, Samuel Beneli by name drunk, full of high spirits with the celebration of the afternoon, pushed his way into Berenice's tent, told her that he admired and loved her, and attempted to kiss her. He had been prepared for a number of reactions, but hardly for the cold loathing with which his advances were received. When he persisted, she struck him over the head with a clay water jug. Then she called the guard and ordered Beneli bound to a post and whipped. They gave him a hundred lashes, and then Berenice ordered that he remain bound to the post for the remainder of the night. In the morning he was dead.

The following day, Gabo, Berenice's body maid, attempted to run away. Berenice sent horsemen after her and had her brought back.

"The next time," Berenice said to her, "you will feel the whip yourself, Gabo."

Agrippa made no comment at all; but he looked at his sister strangely, as if he had not actually seen her before.

Gabo, weeping, crawled on her belly toward Berenice. The sight of her sickened Berenice. Gabo rubbed her face in the dust of the tent floor.

"Oh, stop that!" Berenice cried. "For heaven's sake, look at yourself! You're a sight, and not a pleasant one."

"You are going to kill me," Gabo whined.

"What?"

"You are going to kill me. I don't want to die. What have I done that I should die?"

"Who said I'm going to kill you?" Berenice demanded wearily.

"Everyone says so."

"You will kill me—the way you killed Beneli."

"Do they now," Berenice whispered, rising and standing over the girl. "And what else do they say, Gabo."

"Nothing else—"

"What else?"

"Nothing else. I swear to you, mistress. I swear—"

"Don't swear! My anger is enough! Do you want God's anger too?"

"No—no," Gabo begged her.

"Then tell me the truth. What else do they say?"

"Must I tell you? You will tear my tongue out. Is that right? I don't say these things. Others say them."

"I know that," Berenice said more gently. "I know that, foolish girl. No harm will come to you. I give you my royal word. Now tell me what else they say."

"They say that you killed your husband, King Herod, and that is why he is not with you."

"Ha! The fools! You saw my husband alive and well when we left Chalcis. Didn't you?"

"I did, yes, I did."

"Do you tell them that?"

"They think I lie for you," Gabo said.

"And what else?"

"I can't—"

"Oh, but you will, Gabo," said Berenice, "or I will be angry. Do you want me to be angry?"

"No, mistress. Oh no—I don't want you to be angry. But what can I do? I am caught in the middle."

"Just tell me the truth and no harm will come to you," Berenice said coldly. "But no more of this. Get up off the ground and tell me the truth."

Gabo rose to a sitting position and said, "They are saying that you killed your father, that you murdered him, so that your brother could be king—"

When the great procession of the young King Agrippa and his sister, his advisers, courtiers, and various and sundry appurtenances of his deceased father came finally into Galilee, Berenice felt at last a degree of peace. Here she would not be carried in a litter but walked in the dust of the road, seeing, feeling, remembering. Seemingly it was not a matter of months but lifetimes since she had been here; and as she climbed onto the high ridges where the cool, clean winds blew and where the air was sweetened by the delicious scent of the cedars, she felt that her heart would burst with joy. Joy or ecstasy of any kind was so infrequent in her existence, so strange to her, that the sense of it was overwhelming, almost terrifying, filling her with disturbing awareness and doubts and guilts that tore her ego into shreds.

Barefood, she walked with her head bent to hide the tears; and when she looked up and saw the blue distances of the land, the vista of mountains and more mountains and still more mountains, north to Lebanon and beyond, without boundary or measure, she wanted to cry aloud for the sheer joy of being alive. But that she could not do; even if she were along, it would have been impossible to her; but she was not alone, and with every good thought there was another thought; that such and such was what they said of Berenice, queen of Chalcis, what they all said, the soldiers in their shining armor, the people of the king's suite, the Galilean peasants who came running from their houses and villages to cheer the king, everyone, everyone. Even herself; she was the prisoner of herself, free only to despise herself.

Gabo awoke one night to hear her mistress sobbing. For hours Gabo lay awake, listening to the soft sobbing of Berenice.

Her brother told her that the family of Beneli would want blood money.

"Then give them blood money," Berenice said. "I would give them nothing, but if you want to keep peace with them, give them blood money."

"I'm king for three days, and already demands for blood money—"

"Do you know what Beneli did?" Berenice asked him.

"I know."

"Then why the whimpers? Do you want me to go away? Do you want me back in Chalcis?"

His reaction was terror. He pleaded.

"All right," she said.

"Don't leave me, Berenice. You're the only one who ever loved me—the only one I trust. You're the only friend I have in the world. If you go away—"

"I'll be with you as long as you need me," she told him, irritated by his insistence.

"I can't be king without you," he said. "I won't. King over

the Jews—God help me, do you know what that is? I don't
want it. I'm not Herod. I'm not Agrippa either."

"You are Agrippa," she said gently. "Be tall and strong.
And don't be afraid."

So she began the making of a crutch out of herself. It was
true that she loved him. The two of them, brother and sister
hae a strange mutual trust, a need for each other. In a way
that only they understood, it was both of them against the
whole world. Berenice was his mother. She had been his
mother for as long as she could remember—

Galilee made her weep. Whenever she loved, there was
hatred. She turned love into a barb to rake her own skin. But
in Galilee she was also home.

Thus they finished their journey and came to Tiberias.

The Sea of Galilee, or the Lake of Gennesaret as it was
called by some, or Lake Tiberias as it was called by others,
was deep in a hollow of Galilee, deep in a pocket of the
mountains, over six hundred feet below sea level, the River
Jordan flowing into it in the north and out of it in the south,
and all around it the high, forested hills. As a result of the
strange location of this lake and the cleft valleys through
which the River Jordan entered and left it, weather conditions there were treacherous and unpredictable, with heavy,
hot calms followed by wild windstorms, that turned the
placid surface of the lake into a raging inferno. In the sum-
mertime, the heat in the hollow lake valley could become so
oppressive as to be unbearable; on the other hand, the winter
weather was mild and delightful.

Perhaps it was this delightful winter climate, as well as the
fact that for the past two hundred years a steady stream of Jews
had left the dry valleys of their native Judea to settle among
the mountains of Galilee, that had induced Herod-Antipas
to build a city in Galilee that would be the capital of the
Jewish state. For one thing, not only had the constant influx
of Jews into Galilee turned it into the most populous area in

Palestine—so far as Jews were concerned—but it was an area with a traditional and ancient love for the Masmonean bloodline. It was there that the patriarch Mattathias and his five sons had fled at the inception of the Great Agrarian War of the Jews, two centuries before; there in Galilee he found shelter and hiding places, and when at last he liberated the Temple in Jerusalem and cleansed it, the entire Jewish population of Galilee left their homes and marched to Jerusalem to do honor to the Maccabees and to God. All of this population were participants in the war and they were few enough to enter Jerusalem as a group; but since then, the population had increased perhaps a hundred times.

And for another thing, Herod-Antipas was the son of Herod the Great, and no son of Herod the Great could live in peace at Jerusalem, where every stone, every street, every building was a concrete reminder of the unspeakable cruelties and abominations of his father. In Galilee they were farther away, quicker to forget and forgive; so it was in Galilee, on the shores of Lake Tiberias, the Herod-Antipas build his city.

Ground had been broken for the city only three years before Berenice was born, and the walls and many of the streets and buildings were completed a year later. So when Berenice and her brother returned there from Jerusalem and Caesarea, the city of Tiberias was only eighteen years old; yet to Berenice it had been there always—her own always, for here she was born, and in Tiberias were the first things upon which her eyes had ever rested. Yet even though she knew no time when Tiberias had not been, she could remember that in her childhood scaffolding still stood around half of the buildings, and she could well remember the Greek architects and engineers who were everywhere around the half-completed palace—big, black-bearded men who swung her up in their arms, gently corrected her childish Greek, and fed her insatiable curiosity with bits and pieces of that incredible web of promontories, mountains, and islands that were the world of Greece. Tiberias was named for the Emperor of Rome, but it rose from the hand of Jew and Greek, and just as she learned to read and write, the child Berenice learned that the beauty and thought of the world were the products of Jew and Greek—the iron fist, the product of Rome.

As with so many Jewish children of that time, Greece was a wonderland and a fairyland, a land of all dreams, myths and possibilities for Berenice; and like other Jewish children, she knew that Jew and Spartan were blood brother to each other, the king of the Spartans bound to the king of the Jews in eternal fealty. Of course, both nations were vassal to Rome, and of ancient Sparta only a shadow remained, yet Berenice knew the story of the seven hundred Spartan mercenaries who had deserted the cause of the Syrian emperor during the Great Agrarian War and had gone over to the banner of Judah ben Mattathias the Maccabee; and how their commander, Laetus, and Judah had mixed blood and sworn eternal love and friendship. As the Greek engineers explained to the child Berenice, this put Lacedaemonian blood in her veins—mixed blood being as true and lasting as natural blood—and made her a princess of Sparta as well as Judea. They made a game of this, bowing and saluting her royally whenever they met her, and of course she giggled with delight; but sometimes the Greeks would turn somber, remembering too much, for Sparta was no more, as so much of Greece was no more.

But they built Herod-Antipas a noble city on the shores of the Sea of Galilee. This they could do as no one else on earth could—certainly not the Jews, to whom the whole notion of building a city where an empty field had been before was incredible. The Jewish cities were as old as time. No one had built them; they had always been there, and when the first Jew set foot in Israel, there were cities already at Jerusalem, at Jericho, at Gibeon and Shechem and Bethlehem and all the other places where the Jewish cities stand. But here these Greek engineers, with four thousand Jewish and heathen workmen, laid out walls and streets and buildings and dug the foundations for all. In that digging, they uncovered an ancient graveyard, the burying place of some forgotten people who had lived here before Jew or Canaanite; but the Jewish workers threw down their tools and said that they were cursed and the city was cursed—thus to disturb the dead. Others said it was the eternal curse laid upon Herod the Great and all of his seed forever. Herod-Antipas had to go to Jerusalem and seek the intervention of the high priest before the work could go on. Though people continued to say that the city was an unclean place, Jews began to flock there even before the walls were completed. While its buildings were still cloaked in wooden scaffolds, Tiberias became a center of crafts and trade. There flocked the finest craftsmen and artists in Israel, Jew and Greek, and there, too, merchants and bankers and grain dealers and cloth dealers. The fish from the entire lake were smoked and salted and dried there and shipped everywhere, even to Rome. A major road was built north across the ridges to Chalcis; another major road south; and still a third road westward to the sea.

Nineteen years before, an empty pasture. Now, as Berenice had heard said, one need only wait at Tiberias and the whole world would come there and pass by.

In Tiberias, as in the other cities of Israel, the prophet was unmolested. Berenice's great-grandfather Herod the Great had not, however, been one to honor custom; and he killed prophets with as little unease as he experienced with ordinary murders. However, his children and their children had made a point of assuring the inviolability of those whose speech was inspired. Not that these were the true prophets; only time could tell who was true and who was false; but these lean, skin-clad men carried on a very old tradition. In the market places of the cities, they called down the wrath of God on the sinner, and they spelled out the sins of the mighty. One of them, Joshua by name, stood in the great central market place of Tiberias the day after young King Agrippa had returned to his city and denounced the king and his sister. Berenice in particular was his target. A crowd gathered to hear his version of how she had whipped to death a young soldier of Israel, of her incest—so he alleged—with her brother Agrippa; of how she had mocked God in the Temple at Jerusalem; and of how in all likelihood she herself was responsible for the death of her father.

The accusations were brought to Berenice word by word, and she sat and pleaded for herself. "These things," her brother said, "are nothing and less than nothing."

"Stop him," she begged her brother, but this he refused.

"No," he said, "I will not raise my hand against a prophet. No." They sat in the royal palace—yet isolated and more alone than ever before. In a curious sense, they were like two children as they wandered through the place, no one to fear now, no one to stop them, no one for them to account to. They were the masters.

At times, they were petulant as children. The city was governed in a practical sense by a council of ten elders, over whom there was an archon, Isaac Benabram, an old man who had worked with the original builders of the city. Now the council and the archon sat and waited for the king to address them; but Agrippa and Berenice played a game of losing themselves in the warren of the palace. The seneschals searched for the king, while he and his sister crept down a winding staircase to a little bathing pavilion on the shore of the lake. They had never known this pavilion existed. When darkness came, they plunged into the warm waters of the lake and swam a great distance out from the shore.

Lying there in the water, treading water easily, for she had learned to swim when she learned to walk, watching the lights of Tiberias through the darkness, Berenice said to her brother,

"I think, the way I feel now—I think this is what is meant by the word happiness."

"I hate that city," Agrippa said.

"Don't you want to be king?"

"No," Agrippa said.

"But you must be king. You know that, don't you?"

"I know it," Agrippa said.

Berenice let him be king. She found another role for herself. While Agrippa sat upon his throne, trying to grope with the formality of judgment and decision, Berenice found herself pressed into a particular role—that of minister of all things without a portfolio in any. In other words, people came to her, and suddenly a sixteen-year-old girl found herself in a position of power and decision. She welcomed it.

Five days after they returned to Tiberias, Berenice's husband, Herod of Chalcis, put in an appearance. Word came ahead of him, and Berenice and Agrippa knew that he was coming. They set a watch upon the walls, and the moment Herod's party came into sight they ordered the gates ot Tiberias closed. This was a deliberate and calculated insult, and not one without risk. Chalcis was not a great city like Rome or Jerusalem, but neither was it of no consequence, and if Herod now came to pay his respects to his brother's memory with only two hundred horsemen in brazen armor, it was worth remembering that he could put several thousand in the field if he had to. Chalcis, which lay eighty miles to the north of Tiberias, on the slopes of the Valley of Mizpah, was the ancient capital of Iturea, and while most of the population of the city were heathen, a key section of the nobility were Jewish, wealthy and powerful Jews with strong and influential connections at the Temple in Jerusalem. They might not love their King Herod, but neither would they relish calculated insults to him by the boy and girl in Tiberias.

The boy and girl, Agrippa and Berenice, stood on the wall over the gate staring at Herod, who, seated upon his horse, looked up at them with growing rage. A heavy, red-faced, thick-necked man, he had come in some magnificence the long distance from Chalcis, journeying for six days along wretched mountain roads—for apart from the few roads the Romans had built on the seacoast, there were no surfaced roads anywhere in Palestine. He had brought with him two hundred armored horsemen, half of them provided with new gold-plated helms for the occasion, over twenty men and women of his court, at least a hundred slaves of both sexes, and more than a hundred pack animals and two-wheeled baggage carts. Now this whole vast procession sprawled in front of the city wall, the noise of the animals mingling with grunts of annoyance and disbelief and shrill questions as to what this was all about; and over everything, the hoarse voice of Herod shouting at his child bride.

"Now, devil take me, what is this? What are you two up to? Open the gates! Do you hear me—open the gates!"

The commotion and shouting and nickering of the horses brought people running from everywhere in the city, and very shortly the walls were packed with the citizens of Tiberias, all of them grinning and enjoying a good show, and all of them suddenly partisan; for while they had no particular position concerning Herod of Chalcis, he was trying to enter their city, and they were naturally on the side of whoever was keeping him out.

His patience exhausted, Herod seized a spear from one of his horsemen and, reversing it, pounded with the butt end upon the gates, roaring,

"Open, do you hear me—you bitch! I come to do honor to my dead brother! Open!"

From the top of the wall Berenice regarded him impassively, and her brother said to her, "He's likely to get a stroke if he carries on like that. I never realized what a fat and choleric old gentleman he is. He must be the very devil in bed, sister."

Berenice made no reply to this, and Agrippa said,

"He makes me nervous with all that pounding and shouting."

"When he excites himself, he tends to lose control," Berenice nodded.

Suddenly, Herod flung the spear away from him and took several deep breaths. Then he said to his wife, "Very well, Berenice, I think this has gone far enough. Are you going to open the gates and let us come into the city?"

"I don't think so," Berenice answered.

"Why? Have you lost your senses?"

By now the children of the city, who were the natural keepers of the postern gates, had opened these small doors and poured out to scream their own insults at the column from Chalcis and to pelt the horses with pebbles. The armed guards shouted vituperation at the children, and the children gave it back two for one. Herod attempted to be heard above all this, but much of what he said, Berenice missed entirely. He spoke first about wifely duty.

"You should be ashamed to call me your wife," Berenice said. "I'm young enough to be your granddaughter."

"What?"

"Your granddaughter."

"What about my granddaughter?"

"Go home. You bore me. You tire me."

"Hire thee?"

"Tire me."

The walls roared with laughter.

"My brother is dead. You cannot deny me the funeral blessing."

"Mourn him at home."

"What?"

"Go away!" the seventeen-year-old king shouted.

"You must obey me! You are my wife!" he shouted.

Yawning, Berenice turned away. "Come, brother," she said to Agrippa. "I am tired of playing games with that fat old man."

But Herod refused to return to Chalcis until he had been admitted to the city, and he said that if Berenice and Agrippa kept the gates closed again him, he would send envoys to

Rome to plead his case with the Emperor Claudius himself. He made his camp on the shore of the lake, about half a mile from the city; and from the high windows of the palace, Berenice could see him standing before his striped tent and glaring at Tiberias.

She had never played with dolls, as other children do, or with a doll's house or with any of the toys of childhood, for indeed her childhood came and went, leaving neither an interval of time nor memories. Now she played a wonderful, endlessly complex, and exciting game—the game of force-behind-the-throne—with all the great area of Palestine as her toy. And indeed, it was, after Rome, the largest and richest land of the ancient world. Stretching from the desert in the south to what was once Phoenicia in the north, and including part of old Phoenicia and part of Iturea, it included Galilee, Bashan, Samaria, Judea, Idumea, and Peraea—with limited dominion beyond its borders over what was left of the ancient Trans-Jordanic peoples, the Edomites and the Moabites and the Ammonites. All of this vast area was placed under the scepter of the dead Agrippa by his friends, the Emperor of Rome. Now, with its population of twenty diverse and fractious peoples, it would have fragmented and torn itself to shreds overnight, were it not for the invisible but memorable power of Rome. The two strange children in Tiberias were less rulers than reminders.

But to Berenice, for this short interval, it appeared that she ruled, that she governed, that she moved the pawns of power. In almost every case of decision, her brother Agrippa did as she advised him to. All sorts of people—soldiers and merchants and priests and Bedouin chieftains and petty lords and archons of this city and that city and ethnarchs of this district and that district and rabbis and Levites—all of these flocked to Tiberias during the first days of Agrippa's rule, and less to see the king than his beautiful, green-eyed sister who was already the most discussed woman in Israel.

Among these visitors was a Alexandrian Jew named Philo,

and when Berenice heard that he was in the city, she ordered that he be presented to her immediately. There was brought to her then a tall, thin man of sixty-four years, his hair and beard snow-white, his eyes deep blue, a simple white robe as his costume, and his bare feet as a symbol of mourning. He smiled at her warmly and then bent and kissed her hand. Then she had a chair brought for him and a tray of fresh fruit and wines. He in turn could not take his eyes from her.

"Is this then," he finally said, "the child who was brought to us in Alexandria—the frightened child who knew not what fate awaited her among the barbarians? Do you remember me, Berenice? I am Philo, who would have been your uncle had that poor lad, my nephew, lived. The Alabarch Alexander is my brother. Surely you remember?"

"Could I forget?" Berenice smiled. "And if I should forget—would not the whole world know? For who is there in the world who has not heard of Philo, who is for our time Plato and Socrates and Euripides too. You see, I am not entirely the ignorant little savage my reputation presents. I have not read everything you have written, but I have read the *Metaphysics* and *The Journey* and parts of the *Persecutions*—"

"No savage, my dear," Philo said. "I knew a little girl who was charming beyond her realization. I find a woman of grace and beauty, of whom the whole world talks."

"Of the monster Berenice!"

"Oh, no—no," replied Philo. "There are no monsters in my world, my dear—only men and women striving with uncertainty and ignorance and driven and compelled to the actions they take. Men are poor judges, and if they judge what we call evil, they must also perforce judge what we call good. That is why when news came to us at Alexandria that the great King Agrippa was dead, it was decided that I would journey here to Tiberias and present the condolences of myself and my brother and the whole community of Jews at Alexandria to yourself and your brother. For even though death intervened, we are knit together by ties of betrothal. It was perhaps too boastful a dream that we entertained—that our house would be knit to the House of Herod and the House of Mattathias, to create for all the Jews such a royal family as the old Greeks dreamed about when they speculated on the role of the philosopher kings. Too boastful a dream, too vainglorious, I think; for who are we to say what the future will bring? But in any case, there are ties—and in Alexandria we wept for your father. The synagogues were full, and the whole people prayed to God that He be gentle and understanding with the soul of your royal father—such children are we that we ask God to be gentle."

Berenice did not know how to answer him. His guileless face and his clear blue eyes rejected the polite commonplaces that she would ordinarily have spoken.

"My father," she began—

"I know more of your father than you might imagine, Berenice, but I judge him within a context. There are many easier matters than to be king. Four years he ruled over Israel, and in those four years he allowed us our pride. Our pride is very important to us. So important that we accept the hatred and envy of millions rather than part with a shred of it."

"Did he?" Berenice wondered. Awed at first at having the living legend of Jewish philosophy before her, this tall, white-bearded Jew of Alexandria, who had the power of a prince without domain, whose family was reputed to be one of the three richest in all the world—awed at first, she was irritated now, provoked, and childishly unable to contain her irritation and annoyance. Somehow, she could accept praise of her father from others; not from this man. "I don't think you knew him. Not at all."

"Perhaps."

"Do you know who my husband is?"

"Herod of Chalcis," Philo nodded.

"That's my heritage from my father—"

"I know what you feel."

"That and the blood of Herod."

"There's no curse in the blood of Herod, Berenice."

"Please, leave me now," she said to Philo. "My brother and I will both talk to you later. Now I am tired."

He took his departure gracefully and without offense. When he had gone, Berenice covered her face with her hands, her body wracked with hard, dry sobs.

Philo remained four days in Tiberias, and during that time he was constantly with either Berenice or Agrippa. Both of them remembered those days, for it was the last time Philo came to Palestine. Three months after he returned to Alexandria, he was dead. But the memory of his being with her was a good thing for Berenice, the memory of his calm and his dispassionate view of events being an antidote to her depressions during the following years.

The very day after Philo left Tiberias, Vibius Marsus arrived. Vibius Marsus was proconsul of Syria, and at that time the most powerful and important representative of Rome in the Near East. From his headquarters in Damascus, he kept his finger on the pulse of the entire Jewish world—Marsus being one of those perceptive Romans who realized that in all of its history, Rome had faced only two real threats, two powers that might have destroyed her. The first was Carthage, and the second was Jerusalem. But just as Carthage was more than the single city, so was Jerusalem, and from Damascus to Alexandria there was no city in which the Jews were not the pivotal force, the nucleus of wealth, culture, and power. Recently Marsus had been to Rome, and the Emperor Claudius had said to him, "These Jews will eat us yet, Marsus." "Unless they eat each other," Marsus had replied. He was in Rome when the news of Agrippa's death reached that city, and the emperor had called him and had said to him, "The time has come for Jew to eat Jew, Marsus." That same day, Vibius Marsus left Rome, and twelve hours later he was on a fast galley bound for Palestine and Caesarea.

In Caesarea, he spent a few hours talking to Germanicus Latus, and then Marsus set off for Tiberias, himself and his secretary and two Roman soldiers. He left behind him in Caesarea a man who had traveled with him all the way from Rome, a man called Cuspius Fadus.

So to Berenice these two events were connected. Philo went back to Alexandria and to his death, and Vibius Marsus came to Tiberias, riding on a large black horse, two mounted soldiers and his secretary behind him. Before he left, Philo bid Berenice farewell, telling her,

"My child, let Berenice judge Berenice."

"What do you mean?" Berenice wanted to know.

"Think about it enough and you will realize what I mean. Have you ever tried to love?"

"Oh? Is it something you attempt, like jumping? Or do you study it, like Greek grammar?"

"I think both. Open your heart, Berenice. You have become a woman of great beauty and keen mind, and you are a queen of Israel. I think Israel has waited for a woman like yourself."

"Why?" Berenice asked directly, irritated as always by poetic obscuration.

"I don't know," Philo replied slowly. "This is only something I feel."

The Roman, Vibius Marsus, spoke flatly and his words were plain enough. He was the very opposite of Philo, a short, black-haired, dark-eyed and heavily muscled man of about fifty. His body was covered with thick, curling black hair, and, unlike a Greek or a Jew, he made no attempt to conceal this, either by shaving his limbs, or by long sleeves or high hose. He was one of those Romans who made a face and cult of simplicity, a brown, short-sleeved shirt, a leather kilt, and plain, heavy-duty army shoes. His hair was clipped short in the fashion of the time at Rome, and his shaved beard gave his broad face a blue sheen. His simple virtues did not, however, bespeak a Spartan existence, and he took for

77

granted the banquet Agrippa served for him and the erotic dances by nude men and women that followed. He ate hugely, drank enough to get quite drunk, and in his drunkenness spun a parable for the edification of Agrippa and Berenice.

"A Jew, a Greek, a Roman, an Egyptian, and a Gaul were in a ship on the Mediterranean," he told them thickly, "when a great storm arose. A very large storm, believe me. The Greek was the captain of the ship. The Jew was the supercargo. As captain, the Greek decided that the gods must be mollified and the ship lightened, and the Jew, even though he did not believe in the gods, agreed with the Greek. Knowing that a Roman recognized his duty, the Greek pointed to the Roman, who shouted his praise of Caesar and leaped overboard. But still the ship was in danger, and now the Greek pointed to an Egyptian. Egyptians are exceedingly religious folk, with a great sense of justice. So the Egyptian cried out, Praise Pharaoh—and overboard he went. Still the ship foundered, and now the Greek looked at the Gaul. The Gauls do proper reverence to the gods, and overboard he went, leaving just the Jew and the Greek. Well, now, the Greek cried out, the fools are dead. Let's get this ship in to shore."

Both Agrippa and Berenice laughed dutifully, but neither of them considered the story to be particularly funny.

"Jew and Greek," muttered the proconsul. "I have governed Syria for a dozen years, but still I cannot afford parties like this, food like this, girls like this—"

"Whatever girl you desire," Agrippa said, "is yours. One girl or all of them—as your heart desires, Vibius Marsus."

"I'm old enough to be your grandfather," the proconsul said. "But you will give me girls, will you?"

"As you wish," Agrippa nodded; but Vibius Marsus was staring at Berenice now. His stare, frank, sensual, and uninhibited, did not disturb her. Men had stared at her like that since her breasts budded, since the narrowing of her waist and the widening of her hips proclaimed the fact that she was becoming a woman, and she had survived the two or three post-puberty years of her life in contest and struggle with men. Blocked in so much of her relationship with men, she was driven by no compelling wants or desires; and most men, after their first reaction to her ruddy, green-eyed beauty, sensed the lack of warmth or desire. Vibius Marsus was too drunk to sense it now, and he told Agrippa plainly enough what he wanted.

The boy had to control himself and to struggle for such control, his dark face hardening and becoming like a Greek player's mask over the somber holes of his eyes. That a Roman could fail to understand what it meant to bear the bloodlines of the Hasmonean and Herodian houses was possible, even natural; for in Berenice's mind, the Romans were a mongrel race who substituted adoption for natural birth and wove out of the whole cloth a fiction of ancient family and descent that the whole world smiled at; but for a Roman diplomat to fail to realize what it meant to be a princess of the Jewish royal house, out of the oldest descent and people on earth—this was unforgivable. With anyone else, Agrippa's dagger would have exacted proper payment, and he would have been justified; but no rules applied to the Romans—just as no custom or dignity was valued by them. Agrippa controlled himself, as so many other kings had controlled themselves when faced by Roman proconsuls; he ignored what was said; and he directed Marsus' attention to one of the dancing girls.

"I spoke of your sister," the Roman said.

"Did you?" Berenice asked in faultless Latin, her voice as sweet as honey and as cold as ice. "How very droll. You have an excellent sense of humor, Proconsul Marsus. I shall have an occasion soon to send a message to the Emperor Claudius, acknowledging his grief over my father's death, and in that message I will be sure to convey the delicate and irreproachable sentiments with which you have honored me tonight. I'm sure the emperor will be amused." Berenice rose then and added, "And now I am quite tired. I am sure you will forgive me if I retire."

The following morning, Vibius Marsus asked for an appointment with Berenice. He made his request through ordinary channels—that is, his secretary requested it of Berenice's secretary, and his name was entered on the calendar of her day. At about an hour before noon he entered the room where she received people who sought her out. She sat at a table with paper and pen in front of her. She wore a green shift with an overdress of russet brown and, quite deliberately, sandals with an inch of heel. As the Roman entered, Berenice rose, ignoring his protests, came around the table, and greeted him with warmth and charm, as if nothing at all had happened the evening before. In her heels, she was a full three inches taller than the Roman, a tall, coolly possessed, and arresting figure of a woman, her clothes hanging splendidly from her wide shoulders, her hair gathered on her head in the Greek fashion, and her rather large, high-bridged nose and wide mouth accenting her manner of pleasant aloofness. That she was only sixteen years old appeared as impossible to the Roman as it had appeared so many others—and like so many others, sober now, he was abashed in her presence.

"About last night—" he began.

"We have both forgotten about last night, have we not, Vibius Marsus?" she said smilingly. "Whatever I said, it was certainly more foolish than anything you said—so let us agree that nothing was said."

"That is very kind of you," the Roman nodded.

"And charitable of you. Pray, sit down—please?" She took his hand quite naturally, leading him to a chair, where he seated himself. But he never took his eyes off her.

"It's true," he nodded.

"What is true, Proconsul?"

"What they say of you."

"And what do they say of me, Proconsul?"

"That you were never a child and that your years are many times sixteen. Are you a witch, lady?"

"Oh, hardly, Vibius Marsus," Berenice laughed. "And I can see that you don't know the meaning of that word among our people, or you would not have asked me what no Jew would dare to ask me."

"If I have offended you again—"

"No. No. It is a confusion in words. To the Roman, the Latin word *saga* means simply a woman who pracies the art of *magicus*—or as you would call such a man, a *magus*. But to us, to the Jews, the same word would mean a temple prostitute, one who served the mother-god, Ashtoreth— there is a temple in Rome to her honor, but there she is called Astarte—and such worship is giving of herself to all men who come, so that even if she is a princess, any can lie with her—of any race or age, so long as they would serve the mother. To us, this is an abomination and a horror, a debasement, and in our holy scroll of the Law, which we call the Torah, it is written, 'Thou shalt now allow a witch to live.' So you see, when you call me a witch, I'm not flattered."

"Then I humbly apologize. But I have seen these temples of Ashtoreth in the mountains of Phoenicia, only a few miles to the north of here."

"And gone to them too," Berenice said to herself, "for there never was an Italian who wouldn't go half a hundred miles out of his way to lie with the witches," But aloud, shrugging slightly, she said, "The Phoenicians make much of what they call live-and-let-live. They are a tired people, obsessed by their ancient greatness and tolerant of their present wretchedness. Their ignorant peasants support the temples and send their daughters to whore for their mother-god, and their noblemen send gifts to our Temple in Jerusalem and journey there to do homage to the only true

God. But even so, they can stand only in the court of the Gentiles, for though they are circumcised, they remain unclean. They are tolerant. I don't think Romans approve of tolerance, and we Jews are hardly what you would call a tolerant people."

"I agree with that," the Roman nodded.

"Then perhaps we have some common ground, Proconsul, in spite of all the fingers pointed at our differences."

"Perhaps. And may I ask, my lady, how it is that you and your brother talk Latin as if you were born to it? Greek I would understand, for you Jews make a fetish of the Greek tongue, but you hate and despise Latin as much as you hate and fear Romans, in spite of our common tolerance."

"You are quite a man, Proconsul," Berenice nodded. "I would not want you for an enemy. May we stop fencing and be friends?"

"You are fencing, my dear. I am only defending myself in my poor, cloddish Italian manner. I shall be delighted to be your friend, and if I were twenty years young, I would see half the world in flames before I surrendered the right to be your lover. But Antony went through all that—and unlike the Egyptians, the Jews will not permit a woman to reign over them. Rome can be thankful for that. And you have not answered my question."

"My brother and I lived in Rome when we were children. I don't remember the moment, but I have been told that your emperor had me on his knee. I was very small then, and he was not yet emperor."

"Indeed. Yes, the emperor loves your house—and I am sure that he loved you, as he did your noble father."

"Did he indeed, Proconsul," Berenice said quietly, "I am curious to know why, if he loved Agrippa, my father, he had him murdered?"

"By all the gods," the Roman burst out, "you have a damned loose way of speech, my lady!"

"And I have been told only that Romans were practical people, frank, forthright, and realistic in all their approaches. But these walls have no ears, Vibius Marsus. And see how this chamber is built, so vast in size, with rich hangings on every wall to muffle the sound. Who can hear us? And who can approach to hearing distance without being seen by us? I do not speak in hatred or out of need for vengeance. It is surely no secret to you that I did not love my father, and that he in turn shed few tears over my own sorrows. As a matter of fact, I was aware from the very beginning that Germanicus Latus put the poison in the wine that he sent to my father to drink. It was not a clever assassination—not subtle or well thought out—and only a series of accidents in the transmission of the wine caused the suspicion to be directed elsewhere, to myself among others."

"I was informed that a Jewish priest confessed to the murder and was appropriately hanged by your brother," the Roman said evenly.

"Oh, come, Proconsul. You know that there is nothing so unsettling to a people as an unpunished crime. Crime and punishment, the two arms on the scale of society. Balance them, and the society persists in good order. Unbalance them and you have confusion."

"You grow on me, my Jewish princess," Marsus said coldly and evenly. "I constantly underestimate you. I keep recollecting that you are only sixteen years old. Tell me, how old was Cleopatra when she first ensnared Caesar?"

"Possibly my age," Berenice yawned. "I never admired her. Like most Egyptians, I think she was stupid. Also, Proconsul, I have no intentions of even attempting to ensnare you. I watched my father's murder. I am not guessing as to who was responsible. I know. I am only trying to understand why—if the Emperor Claudius loved him."

"He loved him, and, mind you, I agree with nothing you have said except that. How well did you know your father?"

"Not well. Even the child who loves his father knows him poorly, and I did not love Agrippa."

"You are cold as ice, aren't you?" the Roman observed. "I was told Jews burned hotly."

"I don't burn at all, and as for what was between my father and me—I don't think that is pertinent to our conversation, Proconsul. Say I did know him, in your sense."

"Then you did not know his ambitions."

"I knew what he wanted."

"Yes?"

"Money."

"Oh? Is it as simple as that, Princess? Let me tell you this. Your father and Claudius were very close, as close as two men can be, and just between us, the emperor owed him a good deal. Agrippa's support during the few critical hours before and after Claudius became emperor was not to be dismissed. It was in return for this that the emperor gave your father suzerainty over such an area as no Jewish king ruled since the days of your King Solomon. He was more than a king then, your father. Ruling from Chalcis in the north to Idumea in the south, he held sway over enough nations and cities to be thought of as some eastern emperor. In return— what?"

His voice had hardened, and suddenly Berenice saw and understood the whole pattern of his being there, of the concretization of his role into the drunken bout of the night before, and now of his decision to talk with her rather than Agrippa.

Slowly Berenice said, "My father was a good king. He kept the Law. The people loved him—" Strangely, she had no sense of lying or pretending. Too late—and with the knowledge that it is always too late—she had a sense of her father and herself and the interconnected meaning of both of them on the stage of the world. And because she was Berenice, she was also able to sense the grandeur of the process of their downfall. She waited as the Roman snapped,

"Loved him indeed! I tell you, lady, the Jewish mind is one no normal person can ever cope with. Claudius gave your father an empire, and Agrippa's first action was to rebuild the outer walls of Jerusalem. I traveled down from

Damascus to watch what he was doing, and then I wrote to the emperor and told him that Agrippa was making Jerusalem impregnable. Against whom?"

Berenice sat silently, watching him.

"Against whom?" the Roman shouted.

"I hear you, Proconsul."

"Claudius ordered him to stop. He disobeyed the emperor. Then I was instructed to inform him personally that if he laid one more stone on that damned wall it would mean war with Rome. Then he stopped, full of smiles and humble apologies. He was fortifying the wall against the Parthians, as he put it, in case it should enter their heads to travel a thousand miles and attack Jerusalem. He was building a bulwark for Rome. Lies. Pretenses. Everything except the truth—that he was no sooner king than he began to build for the day when he could challenge Rome. The Jewish disease, my dear lady—or is it the Jewish insanity?"

"That was almost four years ago," Berenice replied evenly.

"Yes. And when one thing failed, another was attempted. Your father had an agile mind. A year or so ago I was informed that twelve princes and kings were either on their way to Tiberias or here already—twelve, every petty monarch in the area, the king of Seleucia and the prince of Antioch and the king of Sidon and the king of Cappadocia and the two supposed royal brothers of Sparta, who still pretend that they are a people and a nation, and all the rest of your petty lords—here and with their noses in a heady Jewish brew they were cooking up. I came here alone. They were meeting here in this room where we are sitting, and I pushed your guards aside and walked through that door and faced them and told them to go home. I came with no legions, no guards, just myself—and I told them there would be no conspiracies, no alliances against Rome. I told them to go home, and like whipped dogs, they went."

Berenice sat in silence now.

"It was almost six months before I could go to Rome and

discuss these matters with the emperor. While I was there, another matter came to my attention, and I brought it before the emperor. Your father, Agrippa, was hoarding money, hoarding it and collecting it and making loans wherever there was a Jewish community—from one end of the earth to the other. And do you know why?"

"He always loved money," Berenice whispered.

"How wrong you are, my dear. He despised money. He spent millions in his youth. Money ran through his fingers like water. Do you know why he became a miser? Because he had decided to hire one hundred thousand mercenary troops for his war with Rome. He was a remarkable man. Singleminded. Give me a good man who gains power and becomes evil. That is both natural and inevitable, and it can be dealt with. But save me from the sinner who gains power and becomes a saint! The emperor and I discussed the matter, and it was his opinion that your father had overstepped the bounds of both wisdom and gratitude. But then he died, and the problem was solved."

"What do you intend for my brother?" Berenice asked softly.

"The emperor is not ungenerous, and he remembers your father with warmth. Your brother will continue to be king over this city of Tiberias, and his domain will include a few hundred square miles of Galilee, roughly an area within ten miles of the lake. If he fulfills his duties loyally, the emperor will perhaps reward him additionally in the future. But so far as the Jews are concerned, the emperor is determined that your father shall be remembered as the last king. There will be no more Jewish kings over what you people call Israel and what we call Palestine. As far as that is concerned, the House of Herod and the House of Mattathias can look only to the past. Instead, the emperor has appointed a procurator over Judea. His name is Cuspius Fadus. He traveled with me from Rome, and he is now in Caesarea, organizing his government before he proceeds to Jerusalem."

Somber, rigid, her green eyes hooded and withdrawn, Berenice sat without speaking. She was cold and numb inside, and her thoughts were slow, sluggish, and weary.

"It will take a little time to get used to this," the Roman nodded. "I imagine it means a great disappointment for you—and even more so for your brother. But you are still the queen of Chalcis and Agrippa is still king—even if only of a small part of his father's domain. Tiberias is a rich and beautiful city, and the countryside here is fertile and productive. Not all of us can be emperors. I advise you and your brother to make the best of what you have, and to consider yourselves fortunate. Honor Rome—and Rome will honor you."

Berenice and Agrippa ate their dinner alone, the two of them silent for the most part. When they spoke, it was to no great point, and only once did Agrippa even mention the possibility of a difference with Rome's opinion.

"War with Rome?" Berenice said. "But those who go to war with Rome are destroyed—"

"I know." Miserably.

"We were told that our father was a saint. You and I—"

"I know."

"We are not saints."

"No, I suppose not."

"In fact," said Berenice, "I am not sure that anyone cares a great deal about us. There would be no great mourning in Israel if we were dead."

Agrippa nodded.

"War? No one would go to war for us. Let's face that, brother. That's the plain truth of it. The fact of it is that a couple of enterprising Jews would just as soon put a knife in our backs and sell the remains to Rome. That makes more sense than war, and there's a profit in it."

"Still, I was king for a while—twenty-three days to be exact."

"You are still king of Tiberias."

Agrippa smiled plaintively. "You know the old man, Isaac Benabram?"

"The archon of the city?"

"Yes. I asked him whether he needed help. He smiled at me as if I was some sort of half-wit. I asked about a royal court. Don't trouble yourself, my son, he said to me."

"Still, it's better than Chalcis," Berenice said.

"Will you go back to Chalcis now?"

"What else can I do?" Berenice said. "Brother—the plain rotten truth of it is that I am pregnant. And it's his child—the child of that fat lout, sitting in his tent alongside the city. Where else do I go? I thought once that power and glory would solve everything. But the Roman removed our power and glory, and a war between Tiberias and Chalcis would not be entertaining, much less plausible. I'll go back to Chalcis, brother."

Berenice sent for her husband. Instead of Herod's response in person, a messenger from him appeared, bearing a note which said, "My loyal and faithful wife: I am here in my tent, and I shall await your arrival with pleasure and eagerness. If you are not here in twenty-four hours, a messenger will go to Chalcis, with orders for my entire army to join me here. The army of Chalcis is neither very large nor particularly frightening, but I believe it is sufficient to cope with Tiberias. And since more of my soldiers are not Jewish than Jewish, they will no doubt take pleasure in spelling out, on the streets, building, and people of Tiberias, an understandable resentment and envy which they display toward Jews. This would be regrettable to us, who as Jews should express no desire for a massacre of our own people; but hardly regrettable to my good friends and allies, the Romans. Vibius Marsus, who was kind enough to repeat to me the substance of his instructions to you, has already indicated that if I were forced to undertake a just attack upon Tiberias, in defense of my rights and honor, he would be pleased to supply me with sufficient siege engines to break down your walls. So, my good wife, knowing your reputation for clear thinking and logical action, I shall expect you at my tent. And soon."

Berenice showed the message to Agrippa, who began to tremble with anger as he read it. "The bastard!" he cried. "The lousy, rotten, degraded bastard! Some day I will gut him! By the Holy Name of God, I swear that! I'll cut upon that fat belly of his while he's alive and feeling and pull out his guts with my own hands—"

"Easy, brother—easy," Berenice begged him. "He is merely displaying a proper Herodian attitude—"

"What will you do?"

"Do I have a choice? I will go to him, of course."

"Suppose we called his bluff. Would he dare? Would he actually attack Tiberias?"

"He would—and the proconsul would help him."

"And no one would come to our aid?"

"Who? Who, brother? They would say, Let the Herodian dogs destroy each other. And they would be right. Anyway, the days are gone when nations went to war over a woman's desire to avoid her husband. This is not Troy, and my glutton of a husband is no Agamemnon, and Jews do not make war unless their pride or their religion is offended. No, Agrippa. I will go."

And with that, Berenice sought out Gabo and put her to packing the three enormous chests that held her wardrobe. A few hours later, she was ready to leave. Tiberias was not a large city, and word had already gotten around that Berenice was returning to the fat Herod of Chalcis. It was also commonly known by now that the Emperor Claudius had shattered the great Jewish kingdom and reconstituted it as a group of minor Roman provinces. A new procurator was on his way to Judea in the south, as as for Agrippa Benagrippa, their seventeen-year-old monarch, he was king of Tiberias and no more than that. So when Berenice emerged from the palace, followed by Gabo, a dozen men of arms assigned by her brother to accompany her, and slaves bearing her great clothes chests, the streets were crowded with men, women, and children; for there is nothing more delightful than to see the mighty come a cropper. Some were silent out of a decent respect for the daughter of dead Agrippa; but others could not resist the temptation to hoot, whistle, and spit in contempt. As one old woman put it, "Whore—go to your husband instead of your brother!" If they could have devised a worse charge than incest, they would have hurled it at her. Some did, considering patricide the deadlier of the two sins. But there were others who watched her silently as she walked by—she would not be carried in a litter or hide her face—and said to themselves that never before had a woman of such beauty or such grace walked on the soil of Israel.

Herod, her husband, waited for her inside his tent. He stood there, enveloped head to foot in a long robe of white and gold, his face murderously grim, nor did he say anything as she entered and faced him. He had rehearsed his response a hundred times, and he knew that if she made one single, simple gesture of contrition, his anger would melt away. But she did not. She only regarded him silently and steadily, her green eyes fixed on his face, her mouth moving in the slightest gesture of contempt—yet enough to explode his hair-trigger wrath.

The blow he struck caught her on the side of her head and felled her the way the slaughterer fells an ox. First Herod feared he had killed her. Then he saw her move.

Her head exploding with pain, her mind reeling, bleeding from both nostrils, Berenice forced herself to her feet, stood swaying a moment, and then stepped back from her husband as he came to offer his hand.

"You struck your blow, Herod," she managed to say.

He was shaking himself now, and he began to plead an apology.

"Be quiet," she whispered.

The force of her personality as she stood there, her face

and dress splotched with the blood that ran from her nostrils, was such as to meet him physically. He recoiled from her. He reached out his hands, as if to touch and help her, but lacked the courage to make the physical contact, and as he stood there like that Berenice whispered,

"If you strike me again, ever, Herod, I will kill you. Do you understand?"

Her green eyes commanded the situation. He tried to face her look, and could not.

"Do you understand, Herod?"

Miserably, he nodded.

"I go to my own tent now," she said, "and I will not be disturbed again tonight."

So she had won. How she had won, Herod did not know. He still had the soldiers, the support of Rome, the power and the clenched fist, but the contest was to Berenice. He had nothing.

PART TWO

In the forty-eighth year of our era, four years after Berenice had walked out of the gates of Tiberias and into the tent of her husband, Herod of Chalcis, she wrote a long letter to her brother, King Agrippa of Tiberias, and dispatched it to him by messenger.

Greetings and respect to you, my brother Agrippa, she wrote, Tetrarch of Galilee and King of Tiberias—I bow to you and wish you good health and peace. I send you this message because there is no one here for me to turn to; and out of the emptiness in my heart, I turn to you.

This morning, just at the rising of the dawn, my son Hyrcanus died. He was not yet four years old, and he was my first-born. It is now seven weeks since his father, Herod, went to his death, and eleven weeks since I lost my other son, Berenicianus, who had not yet reached his third year. Was ever a mother so bereft as I? Here I have not yet reached my twenty-first year, and all the issue of my blood has perished.

He was sleeping in my bed last night, and I think the heat of his poor fever-wracked little body awakened me. When I awoke, it appeared to be in the full darkness of the night, but when I drew back the bed curtains, I saw that the gray breath of dawn was on the world. I reached out to touch my son and to feel of his fever, and my first reaction was that the fever had broken and that his skin was cooling naturally under my touch. But only for a moment did I have that good hope; then the awful fear entered me. I touched him, but he did not respond. I raised his eyelid, and it remained up. Oh, was there ever so sorry a woman as I!

I screamed out in my fear and agony, and immediately all sorts of these cursed servants who surround me came running, my handmaidens, my body maidens, and Gabo of course, and the seneschals who hover all over the place and even sleep with an ear to the door, as the saying has it—and of course the physicians. God's anger take these physicians for the rotten, lying, and ignorant crew that they are! But they preen themselves even more than the priests do, and this Avram Benrubin pushed to the bed to touch and handle my son—may he rest in peace, poor withered little thing that he was—and said in those pious, unctuous tones they assume,

"The bad humors have overtaken him and consumed him, and thus his soul is fled, O my lady."

"You have consumed him with your ignorance!" I shouted out, for I have such a temper, as well you know. "There is death in your touch, you lousy, lying physician who is no physician at all!"

They have grown bold, my brother. They all grow bold and they feel confident; for now they speak of me that I am Herod the Great come to life again, not in greatness but in the monstrousness of my actions; and they are certain to make my actions to fit. They will have it that I murdered my husband, Herod, even though every doctor who came by his side saw how the evil tumor within him swelled out his belly, until it was so huge he could barely walk, as if he was with some devil's child. Night after night, he lay awake in such pain that even my own hate for him and for his actions against me was quelled, and truly I pitied him; but still they would have it that I was the cause of his death. And then, to plunge the knife even deeper into my heart, they began the gossip that I had destroyed my own son Berenicianus, that precious and beautiful child—that I had wrung his neck, so that my first-born, Hyrcanus, would have no one to challenge his claim to the throne of Chalcis. Fools with small and evil minds! A thousand thrones like this wretched seat of Chalcis would I give to spare either of my children a moment of pain—yet such is the talk that goes about of me; and with such talk they grow bold.

This physician, Avram Benrubin, he dared to face me over my child's body, and gesturing and posturing, he cried out that this was God's judgment upon me for my wickedness. Yet I did nothing to him for saying this incredible thing—and of course it is all over the city now, that the God of the Jews struck down the first-born child of the Jew queen. As much as you may chafe, my brother, over the smallness of your place there in Galilee, at least it is a Jewish city that you rule; so if you are hated for being the House of Herod, you are not additionally hated for being a Jew.

But I must go back to my sorrows and my loss this morning. They took away the body of my son to prepare it for burial, and then Gabo helped me to dress. She desired me to eat, but I could not think of food or touch food, and I went instead to that lovely room in the palace, which you have admired, and which we call the music room, since when the wandering singers come to Chalcis, we gather there to hear them. I went there because it has that mosaic wall of Abraham preparing to sacrifice his first-born son to the Lord God, and I thought that the picture would comfort me. Here in Chalcis, it is easier to have pictures on the walls than in a city like Tiberias, where every Pharisee considers it his duty to denounce an image as an abomination.

I sat in the music room on a bench, and my grief lay upon me like a robe heavier than my shoulders could bear—and the more I sat there, the more it seemed to me that I was guilty of doing awful harm to my son.

About a week ago, when Hyrcanus first took sick and the fever first came upon him, there came to the palace a Rabbi Ezra, who is known in Chalcis for his laying on of hands. I know that this laying on of hands is all over the country and that the ignorant believe in it, but when this Rabbi Ezra said that he could cure my son, I had him driven away. How can I explain why? To me there was something dreadful in this dirty, mumbling old man telling me that he could cure my child, and I told myself that never, so long as I lived, would he lay hands upon my child.

Now my child is dead.

I have paused in my writing, my brother, and night has fallen. I called for light, and now by the light of lamps, I continue—and I try to find the thread and lament of my thoughts; hard, indeed, so many are the lamentations that fill my heart. I have a picture constantly before my eyes— of that mosaic wall in the music room, Abraham with his knife poised above the prone and bound body of his son, Isaac. But God stayed his hand—

I do not know how I have lived through today, my brother. On a day of my life when above all things I need a little love, a feeling of warmth from even a single human being—on such a day there was nothing but the hatred and suspicion and contempt that surrounds me.

And in the very midst of all this, there came a message from the Emperor Claudius in Rome. I am sure that by now a similar message has been conveyed to you. The emperor greets me and consoles me for the loss of my husband. Evidently, the loss of my son has not been brought to the attention of the emperor—or perhaps in Rome they do not brood over such matters. In any case, the emperor states that out of love and respect for the House of Herod, he is present-ing the city of Chalcis to you, my brother. Let me make two things clear. Firstly, you know of my love for you. You are the only person in our family who has not shown hatred and contempt for me. Even on her deathbed, my mother did not ask for me, but only for my sisters, who are married to heathens, and those same sisters add fuel to the fires of falsehood circulated about me. So I must stress how precious you are to me, and I can only take joy in the enlargement of your realm. Secondly, I have no desire to be queen here in

Chalcis. This place is hateful to me, and the only pleasure I found in the royal title was that it afforded me a certain dignity and protection. But now that is taken from me, and I am only the king's sister. This I do not resent, but neither do I desire to live on here in my loneliness.

Please, dear brother, I beg you to send for me and to invite me to live with you in Tiberias. For all that I have lived only twenty years, I nevertheless feel the burden of them and the weight of time. I ask nothing now but to be allowed to live in peace in Tiberias, where there are at least a few memorish that I cherish.

I await your reply,

your sister, BERENICE.

Agrippa, Tetarch of Galilee and King of Tiberias and Chalcis: to his sister Berenice:

I greet you and console you. Who is to know the ways of the Lord God? He giveth and He taketh away, blessed be the Name of the Lord. Yet I would have gutted that physician. I trust none of that whole fraternity, and as for the laying on of hands, I would forbid it were it not for the way the ignorant have embraced it. I had a doctor in to examine pains in my rectum, and after he had given me three powders intended to cure me but which only plagued me worse, I had thirty stripes applied to his back—the better for him to understand his art.

My heart goes out to you, my sister. What can I say to ease your suffering? Yet when you tell me that you must come here to me at Tiberias, I must warn you that you would not be well advised. The wells of hatred and malice do not only deepen at Chalcis. They look at me and ask, "Why has he not taken a wife?" And others say, "It is unnatural in the House of Herod for a prince to live like an Essene. Therefore, this Agrippa practices his abominations in secret."

A deputation of three came to me from Jerusalem, two of

them priests and the third one of those cursed Pharisees from the Sanhedrin, and they wanted to know why I consort with my sister, as a man does with his wife, and why I called down the wrath of God?

I managed to stifle my anger and point out to them that while I was here in Tiberias, my sister Berenice was far away in Chalcis.

"So how do I consort with her?" I demanded of them.

"By going secretly to Chalcis."

"I have not gone to Chalcis these many years. You know of the bitter feeling that existed between myself and my uncle, Herod of Chalcis. Unless I went there in great force to make war upon him, I would not leave there alive. So how do you tell me that I go secretly to Chalcis?"

"So we have been told."

"By whom? Who tells these tales?"

"And Herod of Chalcis is dead."

"Yes—and my sister's heart is also dead, for she has not taken off the veils of mourning for even a day."

"Yet it is told that you consort with her."

"Lies!"

"Truth or lies, this is an abomination and we bring you warning. These are not the days of your ancestor, Herod the Great. If you call down the wrath of God upon Israel, then that wrath will consume you."

It was a very thinly disguised warning, my sister. What am I to do? They are making a religion out of hatred of the House of Herod, and believe me, the Emperor Claudius will encourage it and give me no sustenance whatsoever. It has always been the way of Rome to split a land and then play one part of a people against another. And there are so many plots and counterplots around me that my head spins.

This act of Claudius of making me King of Chalcis as well as this, my own city, was calculated in that same Roman manner. He makes me king now over a city of the heathen, where they have no love for a Jew and have had a bellyful of

Herod and the House of Herod. He knows that sooner or later, I will have trouble in Chalcis, and that this will weaken me in terms of Israel.

So, my sister, I beg you to remain in Chalcis for the time being, but to know that Tiberias is your home always. Your palace stands untouched. I think you would be wise to send here from Chalcis gold and jewels for your security, but to remain there yourself until we put to rest these cursed slanders that are spoken of us.

AGRIPPA, KING OF TIBERIAS.

From Berenice, widow of the King of Chalcis, to my brother, Agrippa, King of Tiberias and Chalcis:

I greet you and salute you—and for this long silence of mine, I tender my apology. It is five weeks since I received your letter, but during those five weeks I lived with despair and misery. I saw no one but my stewards and my maid, Gabo; I sat in my rooms and I walked in my garden. I am afraid that I ate too little, for my flesh has fallen away, and when I look into my mirror and see the flesh stretched so tightly over the bones of my face, I am not quick to recognize myself.

I was in a condition where I had neither interest nor excitement in anything the world held. I existed in a sort of torpor, from which nothing seemed able to arouse me. Then two days ago, there came to the palace two Persian magicians who said they had heard of the queen's misery and heartsickness, and that they possessed spells and amulets which would raise up her soul and bring her great happiness and forgetfulness of her miseries. Ordinarily, I would have had them scourged away, for I despise those practitioners in magic who bring only promises and never fulfillment. But now I was too sunk in my sorrows to take any action against them, and when my seneschal urged me to see them, I made no protest. They were two men of middle age with fat stomachs and long hair and beards, their pride, combed and brushed and preened constantly, egotistical and strutting fat men who first elicited from me a promise to pay them one hundred shekels of gold—and then proceeded to make their spells and conjurations. Of course, it was to no point or purpose, and I had them seized. They screamed and pleaded and reminded me of my promise to pay them. So I had the gold measured out for them, and then I brought in barbers and had them both shaved, not only their hair and beards and eyebrows, but I had them stripped to nakedness and shaved as clean as newborn babes around their maleness. Then, still naked, their hands full of the money paid to them, they were ejected from the palace and told not to halt until they were beyond the gates of Chalcis.

I was cruel to them, brother, for indeed the sight of these two naked, shaven, big-bellied magicians, with their fat pink rumps, and their money clutched against their breasts set me to laughing as I have not laughed for years—truly, I became weak with laughter, which shows that even the most fraudulent magic will work if only one gives it full opportunity.

I have a letter from the Emperor Claudius, inviting me to Rome—but I have no desire to go. Truth be told, I am tired to death of living among the heathen, and my heart longs for my own people and for the green hills of Galilee. Tell me that I can come back to Israel and Tiberias, and I will be forever indebted to you.

Your sister, BERENICE.

King Agrippa, to his sister Berenice:

I have been discussing our problem with my two seneschals, Joseph Bendavid and Oman Bensimon. Knowing you, my sister, and your attitude toward those who cling to courts and fawn on kings and abase themselves that they may creep into positions of power, I am sure that you will despise the advice of these men, as you do the men. But I cannot carry on alone. I sometimes wonder why men like our grandfather fought and killed and lied and murdered to cling to this crown; but power must have been a disease with them—as it surely was with our Jewish kings for a thousand years now. When I read in the Scriptures of the history of our bloodline, I am past surprise or awe at the murderous passions of men. Our sister, Drusilla, only sixteen now and married to Epiphanes, hired three men to discuss with them the possibility of poisoning me—or such was the story that one of the three sold to Bensimon, or such is Bensimon's declaration to me. Who is to be believed? I put the man to death, and then for three nights I could not sleep. Can you be a king and not take life? But what if you cannot take life and sleep too? So, you see, I must have advisers—I must have people to help me.

The opinion of Bendavid and Bensimon is that you must take another husband. As they point out, you are not yet twenty-one years old, and your reputation as a woman of beauty and wit has extended as far as Rome; and I think you will agree that sooner or later you would have to come to such a decision.

They won me over to their point of view without too much argument; for I can see that there is no alternative to such a course; but when it came down to cases and finding the proper husband for you, well, that was another matter and by no means simple. There are at least five great Jewish families with eligible sons, the House of Avram, the House of Phaedocieus, the House of Laeterus, the House of Shimma, and the House of Cunniea. Two of these claim the blood of David, and one of them, Shimma, is a priestly house. But except for Shimma, they are all Pharisee houses, and if we were to make a union with a family of Pharisees, it would open me up to hate and mistrust on the part of the House of

Zadok—who, as you know, control the Temple and have nothing but hatred and contempt for the Pharisees. The very thought of a break with the Temple makes every important citizen here in Tiberias shudder; but on the other hand, the son of Shimma is only eleven years old—and it would be two years before any marriage could be consummated, even if we could persuade the house to allow the boy to marry a woman so much older.

On the other hand, there are several royal families connected to us by blood or marriage—but I will not force you into any position as second or third wife.

However, a most interesting thing has occurred—a matter I have refrained from conveying to you until now. It concerns Polemon, king of Cilicia, who came here to Tiberias with Anat Beradin, the wool merchant. Beradin controls the wool trade all the way eastward to Parthia, and he is the titular head of the Jewish community in Tarsus and almost as important and wealthy as the alabarch of Alexandria. You know of the increasing importance of Tiberias as a manufacturing center for the dyeing and weaving of woolen cloth. This trade in wool began under our father, who was a close friend of Beradin, and now Beradin has shown interest and affection for me and for our house, a thing none too common among these wealthy Pharisee marchants.

Polemon himself, the king of Cilicia, is a heathen, but as you know, his own city of Tarsus has a large and powerful Jewish population, as have Zephyrion and Taurus-Amanus, the other important cities of Cilicia. Polemon depends upon Jews for stewards, seneschals, and for officers in his army—as well as for direction in foreign trade, and there has been a good deal of intermarriage between the noble families of Cilicia and the Jewish families.

Now I do not know whether you have ever looked upon Polemon, but he is a well-set, tall, healthy, and decently educated man in his middle forties; and he has looked upon you. He saw you several times, but first at the wedding feast after your marriage to Herod, and the most recent time was when he was passing through Chalcis. There it seems that out of respect for your grief, no celebration for him was made, but your seneschal took him to dinner in the palace, and before dinner he stood at a balcony looking down upon a little garden where you sat in your grief.

He claims that he first lost his heart to you when he saw you four years ago at the wedding, and he says that his love is constant and increasing, so that he cannot eat or sleep or have any peace for desire of you.

I put it to him that this made a strange kind of approach, seeing that he already had a wife. But he told me that she tired him and he was ready to put her aside, and that he had already spoken to what passes for the high priest at Tarsus in terms of a religious dissolution of his marriage. He asked me whether you would be badly affected if his wife were to die inadvertently. I replied that not only would you react poorly to this, but that it would only add flames to the talk that already circulates around you and myself and our house. I must say that he is unaffected by this talk.

Beradin urges the marriage, for he sees it leading to a very considerable union of kingdoms to the north of Israel—either in favor of our house or controlled by our house. For myself, I am not ambitious, but such a marriage would mean that you could spend at least the best part of each year at Tiberias. Beradin is building a villa on the lake, not far from the city, and Polemon proposes to build for himself a small winter palace there, so that you need never be out of sight of the place you love so much. I admire this thoughtfulness.

Berenice, to her brother, King Agrippa:

I send this by postrider, that you may tell the king of Cilica that all his hopes and aspirations are pointless and senseless. Oh, but I am sick to death of your aging men who dream of flinging their youth in the crotch of a young woman! I know your Polemon, and I want no part of him—and inform him that he need not murder his wife for me. Tell him that I am dry and cold and that my seed is gone and used up, and that death goes with me wherever I go. It will not be too far from the truth either.

Nor will I marry a heathen. I have no desire ever to marry again, but should it come about, I will marry only a Jew.

Agrippa, King of Tiberias and Chalcis, to his sister Berenice:

I tell you, sister, that you misjudge Polemon. You misjudge his quality and you misjudge his love.

When I brought to him the news that you would only marry a Jew, I thought that would be the end of it. But no—Polemon put off his departure for Tarsus and remained here, and after three days of brooding over the matter, he announced to me that he must become a Jew.

Upon hearing this, I took council with Bendavid and Bensimon, who agreed that the wisest things to do would be to send word of what Polemon proposed to Vibius Marsus, the proconsul of Syria. That is, we could not regard this simply as a religious or even as a medical question—in terms of the proposed circumcision—when above all it becomes a political matter. I know that we foster the illusion that we are our are own masters, yet when it comes to basic things, it is Rome that must decide whether a Jewish king should sit on the throne of Cilicia. However, it worked out well enough, for Vibius Marsus took a light view of the matter, saying that so far as he was concerned, Polemon could cut off his hand or his head as well as his foreskin—Rome being less concerned with the religion of its vassals than with their loyalty. It would seem that Polemon has proven his loyalty, for when Marsus charged his brother, Cheleth, with plotting against Rome, Polemon tried him and hanged him—that is, his brother Cheleth of course and not the proconsul. So Vibius Marsus put no barriers in our way.

However, Anat Beradin implored me to make plain to Polemon what risks he faced—medically speaking, that is. It is one thing to be circumcised as an infant and it is something else entirely to undergo this in the middle years after the age of forty. At that age, it can be particularly painful and severe. There have been many cases of infection—some leading to death. In still other cases, the man undergoing the operation has bled to death. And in still other cases, the result of such circumcision in the later years has been impotence equal to that which accompanies gelding. There is no need to bore you with these details, but I do think you should realize what this man faced—as I tried to make him realize.

But no—no, nothing would give him pause.

"At least go back to Tarsus and have the operation there," I begged him, but he protested that there was no Jewish surgeon in Tarsus who would dare to circumcise him, for fear of reprisal his family might take. Well, you may believe, my sister, that I had some of the same forebodings, and no desire for him to die on my hands and leave me with a bloodfeud.

When I set out to find a doctor, my fears were confirmed, for I discovered that no physician in Tiberias would operate on him. Again, I begged him to return to Tarsus, where at least he would be surrounded by his loved ones; but he only replied that his loved ones would seize such an opportunity to poison him and claim that he died of the circumcision. What choice had I? Could I cast him out?

At last we found a doctor, but under curious circumstances. I was informed that a young man who had studied medicine in Athens and also in Ephesus under the great masters there, was staying with some relatives in Tiberias. These were of the House of Shlomo, a family of some consequence, with fishing rights here in the lake, and with twelve fishing vessels and a smokehouse at Dora, a fishing village to the north of Caesarea. They are a family of Israelites, apparently with no priestly or Levite blood, but very wealthy and influential with the Romans; for they have served as army chandlers for over a generation. They have over twenty retainers here in their house in Tiberias, and they are not a house that I desire to offend. I learned that the name of this physician was Shimeon Bengamaliel, out of the line of Hillel and three generations of Jewish physicians. Like the House of Shlomo, they have neither priestly nor noble blood and make no claim of descent, but they are as coolly proud and independent as if they were out of the direct line of David and Zadok combined.

I go into this in such detail in order to demonstrate the lengths to which I went to satisfy Polemon—and so you may realize that I do not consider any of this to be a light matter. I sent for this Shimeon by royal messenger, but instead of his appearing as any sensible man would—having indicated that I awaited him—he sent me a message informing me that he awaited me in the House of Shlomo, and that I was entirely welcome there. I must say that since I have come into this throne built of twigs and this empty crown, I have endured insults in plenty, but not one that I remember as gratuitous as this. What was I to do? What would you have done, my sister? Send soldiers to drag him forth and scourge him? But this would have turned against me not only the House of Shlomo but every Pharisee house of wealth and distinction in Galilee—perhaps in Israel, if word got around. For only consider how the insult was couched—as a perfectly calm and reasonable invitation. Could I ignore it? Then I had this vexatious problem of Polemon on my hands again— and how to solve it? Summon him again and be insulted again? I saw no point in that.

I discussed the matter with Anat Beradin, for these merchant families are thick as thieves, and this man Beradin appears to be incredibly well informed. Beradin agreed that this young physician should be our first choice. He explained that this man was out of the House of Hillel—which is a name we have known, but only to curse. That is because the priests are at great odds with this house, and Beradin claims that much they say of the house and of its founder, Hillel—

who died about forty years ago—is false. I was taken aback to discover—again according to Beradin—that the doctrines of this house have penetrated to every corner of the earth, wherever Jews are, and that these same doctrines are known, discussed, and tossed about by the lowest Jews—bearers, and laborers, and peasants. How then that I remain so ignorant of even the tenor of this teaching? We are not scholars, but among the countless slanders hurled against us has never been that of ignorance. With you, when we were children, we spent endless dreary hours with the philosophers as well as the Law—page after page of Plato committed to memory, heaven help us, not to mention our endless hours with the Torah. Well, I put this to Beradin, who was in no way surprised and who explained that these teachings of the House of Hillel were a Pharisee business and regarded as the prating of ignorance by those of noble blood. Quite naturally they would form no part of our education.

At the same time, Beradin made plain to me how widely these strange teachings had penetrated among the people. He told me how the House of Hillel sent a son of each generation to study with the finest Greek physicians and how this son would train others to the profession, here in Israel. Without going into the complexities of this, let me say that Beradin felt that since Shimeon Bengamaliel was here in Tiberias, only he must perform the operation—so that not only would Polemon become Jewish, but in the most blessed fashion.

This still left his insult to the crown.

"Turn it on its head," Beradin told me. "At long last, let it be said that a royal member of the House of Herod went of his own will to speak with a member of the House of Hillel. You have no idea what the effect of this will be."

I did not leap with joy at the suggestion, and I pointed out to Beradin that this kind of consorting with every dubious element, whether they called themselves Pharisees or Hillelites, could only lose me support among the Noble families. It was his opinion, however, that I had far less support from that quarter than I imagined.

"It is not my place to advise you, Agrippa Benagrippa," he said to me, speaking out arrogantly enough, for he is one of those little men who have come up in the world by their own force of character, and he esteems himself well indeed. "You have advisers. But simply let me say that they have not kept you well informed. There are new currents in Israel—and many a great family today that carries no drop of noble or priestly blood. They are not to be ignored, for in all truth they outnumber your noble families. Your nobility clings to its landed estates and traces its lineage over and over and piles up its little hoard of gold pieces and dreams of the old Hasmonean days—but believe me, young man, those days are gone forever and will never return. There is a new Jew today. He has sailed his ships everywhere in the world. He has driven his camel caravans across desert and mountain. He buys silk from the Chinese and cotton from the Ganges people; he trades both for the tin in Cornwall, and that he ships to Egypt, where he buys wheat to be unloaded at the mouth of the River Tiber. Your noble families still venerate the Temple and its priesthood above all else, but there are synagogues in every city of the world, and to the Jews who worship in these synagoguges the Temple is only a word or a dream, but the doctrine of Hillel is very real indeed. In these communities, they no longer ask whether a man is of Israelite or Levite blood, whether he is out of the House of David or the House of Zadok, whether he has a fifth cousin who is a blood Kohan—no, they ask little and they care less. A man is what the power and wealth of his house make him—and many such could buy and sell your tetrarchate here in Galilee. So put less stock in these so-called 'noblemen' who give their petty support to your house, and think about what is new in the world."

I considered what he said. Believe me, sister, it is no easy matter to sort out this advice from that advice and to make sense of two sage pieces of counsel, each of them opposed to the other. But the upshot of this thing was that I decided to swallow my pride and go to speak with this Shimeon Bengamaliel. I tell you in all detail what followed then; and I tell it to you bluntly and plainly:

I went alone to the House of Shlomo—that is, alone except for my armor-bearer, who is one of those oversized Galilean hulks, with a neck as thick as my waist and a little bit of brains in his fists. His name is Adam Benur, and he is a holy terror in an argument, and as large and ugly as he is, less of an attention-gatherer than a troop of armed guards. The House of Shlomo is outside of the city walls, one of those large villas built directly on the lake, with a stepped terrace down to the lake, built of pink stone fetched here all the way from Megiddo. Believe me, they do themselves well, these fishermen. I was greeted by the head of the house, Gideon Benharmish—they have gone back to the old Hebrew names, these newly rich Israelites—a tall, soft-spoken man in his fifties, and well-mannered for a merchant. Servants all over the place. The master, his wife, his relatives—no lack of respect, believe me—bowing and scraping and honored beyond their ability to express. Of course, they would never have had the courage to demand that I come here. That was the doing of this Shimeon, who is only a few years older than I, certainly. They greeted even my horse as if it was of royal blood, and took big Adam off to sit in the kitchen and fill his belly, an honored guest on his own terms.

Shimeon himself stood somewhat aloof, back and away from the immediate family—so that I was there for a while before they presented him to me. He is a big man, a full head taller than I am, broad, dark-eyed, with a close-cropped black beard. He was dressed very simply but presentably in sandals, the latest style of white linen trousers, cut just below the knee, and a sleeveless coat of white linen that revealed a pair of large and muscular arms, too large and muscular, it appeared to me, for a physician and a scholar. Like the stricter Pharisees, he wore no ornaments or colors, but he is no ascetic. At the magnificent table they spread, he ate as well as any and better than most.

He bowed to me and did me honor, at which I expressed

surprise, and then he explained, "I honor the House of Mattathias. I am told that your sister puts herself forward as a Hasmonean."

"We have every right to do so," I said, "by the line of my great-grandmother Mariamne, who was herself the granddaughter of Hyrcanus, and thus out of the true Maccabee blood and line."

He smiled at my protestations, as if they amused him, and said that here in the House of Shlomo, as in his own house, they had too much work to do to bother about their pedigrees. But some of this attitude is merely bragging, for I am given to understand that he is the grandson of the sage Hillel, an immigrant from Babylon who was the founder of his house, and as proud as a peacock of this short line and descent. In any case, he was pleasant enough, and I think we became friends of a sort. I did not have to explain concerning the slanders that are circulated about us. He had heard them, and he was contemptuous of people who slander others. Then I explained to him the circumstances of Polemon's relationship to you.

"So he desires to become a Jew," Shimeon said.

"Exactly. We need a surgeon of skill and importance. Polemon can pay whatever fee you ask."

"Has it never occurred to Polemon that there's more to being a Jew than having one's foreskin chopped off?"

"Come, come," I reminded him. "Every day, thousands of infants are born into this world, and they become Jews willy-nilly, simply by having their foreskins chopped, as you put it. Polemon is a king. Surely, he can become Jewish by doing the same thing at great cost of pain and risk."

"That's a hard argument to meet," Shimeon nodded, smiling.

"It appears to amuse you."

"It does. From what you have told me, Queen Berenice has no desire to marry this Polemon."

"She can be persuaded."

"Why?"

"I told you why. Either you will do the operation—or we shall find another."

"Oh, I will do it," Shimeon said. "Have no fear of that. Even if it's a sort of lopsided Jew that I am making, I will do the making. There's supposed to be some virtue in it, although why there should be at the news of one more Jew in this sorry world is more than I pretend to understand. How old are you, Lord Agrippa?"

I was pleased that he used "Adon" as a title for me. Too many did not. Nor was he being cynical. I could see that he liked me.

"Twenty-one years," I answered.

"Ah. That is young, isn't it? I suppose one becomes a king when one does, not by choice or training."

"I never thought of it that way. But you're right."

"You know," he said, "I will be creating another Jewish king with this operation. Don't you mind?"

"Not at all," I shrugged.

"Your great-grandfather—no, even your father would have seen me in hell before I was prompted to create royal Jews."

"I am afraid I lack the lusts of either the Herods or the Hasmoneans," I shrugged. "Being king is not something that delights me. I suppose I have small character and little ambition."

"You have a sense of humor, my lord, and that delights me."

So, you see, sister, we became friends, and tomorrow Polemon subjects to Shimeon's knife. I pray you to send me your consent by return messenger.

From Berenice to her brother, Agrippa:

I do not know what to say. The days and weeks and months pass, and I feel more and more like some animal creature enclosed in a box. However I turn, there is no way out.

Always I have taken a husband or betrothed because it was necessary or expedient. My father married me to his brother because, as he had it, I was a whore. Now I cannot go near the place I was born or the brother of my flesh because all the wagging, evil tongues in the land will have it that we lie together. My brother Agrippa—what am I to do? I am lost, and there is no way for me to find myself.

Agrippa to his sister Berenice:

I am sending for you. I am sending a troop of horse and a gift from Polemon. This is a scarf, measuring two feet in width and seven feet in length, and the whole surface is covered with pearls that have been sewn to it—over two thousand pearls. It is said to be very valuable. Beradin, who has excellent connections with the pearl dealers in the Far East, has been after me to sell it, since according to him the pearl market is at its height today. He feels that if the money is invested in the glassworks at Tyre, it can be doubled within a year. He says that the gesture of presenting the scarf to you is typical of Polemon. I gather from Beradin that financially, Polemon leaves something to be desired, but the advantages of a union with him far outweigh such disadvantages. In any case, the disposal of the scarf is a worthy gesture.

I am amazed at the grasp of matters financial by people like Beradin or the men of the House of Shlomo. Their knowledge fairly makes my head spin, but as Beradin puts it, it is more important for a king to know the assets and resources of his neighbors than the size of their armies. He has persuaded me to put funds into the wool trade, and already I can see profits that amaze me.

But that is off the point, is it not? I am writing to tell you that Shimeon Bengamaliel has successfully completed his operation on the king of Cilicia, and that for the past two weeks Polemon has been recuperating very nicely.

We postponed the operation until Polemon's uncle and two of his seneschals could come to Tiberias—a considerable journey, as you know, from Cilicia. Along with myself, Beradin, and others, they witnessed the operation. The operation itself is no great problem for a skilled surgeon, and in this case it took only a few minutes. Not only is Shimeon very clever at his work, but he makes a fetish of cleanliness, being of the school of Hippocrates, which holds that cleanliness is a bar against infection. He uses wine as wash water—which most of our Jewish surgeons do—but he also heats his instruments and then cools them. In this case, he used a copper plate almost identical to that which the Mohel uses for infants, except that it was somewhat larger to accommodate the manhood of Poleman—such manood being of normal size, a reassuring fact in itself. The plate has a slit, and after the foreskin is properly inserted in this slit, the surgeon removes it with three quick cuts. The wine is poured upon it and the cut member is packed with wadding to halt the bleeding.

I must say that Polemon took it very well, not crying out except for a single squeal when the first cut was made; and all the people watching applauded him and said that he had shown a very kingly spirit indeed. Yet I must say that I am quite grateful that my own circumcision took place in my infancy.

The following day, some slight infection set in, and for three days thereafter Polemon had a fever. I was very uneasy lest he should become really ill and die in Tiberias—something that could only lead to endless political complications. But he overcame the infection and now he is completely healed and healthy.

He looks forward to your arrival as eagerly as I do, my sister. I await you. Our separation has been too long.

PART THREE

An old man with a limp, a withered arm, and a tattered gray beard was called Rabbi Gershon—a title which no one questioned too stringently. He had the freedom of the palace for alms, as certain other beggars did, providing that they were old and unobtrusive and appeared infrequently enough to avoid being nuisances. Berenice met him in the hallway, as she was entering her chamber, and when he asked for alms, Bago appeared to chase him away.

"Let him be," Berenice said, going into her bag and finding a gold piece that she dropped into his outstretched hand.

"Gold!" Gabo exclaimed. Her eyes were wide as saucers.

"You made a mistake, my lady, Berenice," said the old man.

"Why?"

"Gold. Just as that Benjaminite says—her eyes are ready to fall out of her head. I thank you with all my heart, and I bow to you and kneel to you—if I may, figuratively—my arthritis being what it is, if I did get down on my knees there is no telling when I would get up again."

"I didn't make a mistake," Berenice said. "I have plenty of gold. It is nothing."

"But one does not give gold to a beggar," Rabbi Gershon insisted.

"You are a most obstinate old man, aren't you? And how did you know that my maidservant here is a Benjaminite?"

"Oh? It's simple—dark skin, crafty as a jackal at night,

shies away like a wild animal—but very clever if they are educated." He bit at the gold piece with his yellow fangs.

"Don't you believe my gold is gold?" Berenice asked.

"You I believe, my lady. This is simply the reaction to the world I live in—a world full of thieves and connivers. You—I ask for God's blessing on you. God keep you, back here in the land of your fathers in this good place, Tiberias. May the Lord God Almighty bless you and make your womb ripe and fruitful and your years prosperous."

"And you would call down such a blessing upon the infamous Berenice?"

"May my tongue wither before I repeat such a term," the old man said. "God bless you."

In her chamber, Berenice said to Gabo, "That was very nice of him."

"So would I for a gold piece."

"You're not a rabbi—not even a self-styled one. You are a bothersome girl who never bathes enough—and you'd better bathe today because you are beginning to smell ripe. Anyway, whether a gold piece purchased it or not—"

"A gold piece," said Gabo. "Enough to keep a family for a year!"

Looking at her brother, Agrippa, king of Tiberias and king of Chalcis, king of some Jews and some Gentiles, Berenice decided that he had changed very little in five years. He was almost twenty-two years old now, but he was as slender and boyish as at seventeen, his head covered with dark ringlets of hair, his beard short and softly curled, his face the long-suffering face of a put-upon young man—a face without too much strength or ambition. He was like his face too—as if all the fierce, unspeakably cruel ambition and lust for power that had marked the Hasmonean and Herodian lines with a brand of infamy that all of time would never erase had washed out in him, the last male of his line; leaving him serenely unassuming and unperturbed by either ambition or overwhelming desire. People were always struck by his diffidence. He had a sort of stammer that was not a stammer; and if he were not a king—and not simply a king but the last of the most famous royal house in all the world of his age—he would have been occupied with an endless series of apologies. He disliked anger and scenes charged with emotion, so that even now, when his patience was near the breaking point, he resisted the temptation to shout at his sister.

And it was a matter of patience rather than anger, for Agrippa could never face his sister and be angry. Berenice was the most wonderful and improbable creature in his environment. If the charges of incest constantly flung at his sister and himself were blatantly false, there was nevertheless truth in the fact that he adored her; and now he tried to be reasonable rather than rigid.

"My dear," he said to Berenice, "you must admit that all this puts me in the most ridiculous position imaginable."

"I admit nothing of the sort," Berenice replied. She was very fond of Agrippa, but in the relationship between them she was the mother and he was the child. More than that filled her with anxiety and horror, for in the dark, tangled web that spelled out her relationship to sex and womanhood, the very thought of incest was like a knife into her heart. She had lost two children. Agrippa was her surviving child; she humored him as one would a child.

"Oh, come now," Agrippa said. "Just look at the thing from my point of view, Berenice. Or from anyone's point of view. From Chalcis, you wrote to me, agreeing to marry poor Polemon—"

"I will not have you call him 'poor Polemon,' " Berenice interrupted. "Poor nothing of the sort! He is a large, grown man who has had three wives before me and more women than King Solomon. He is a lecher and a pig—and I think something of a homosexual, too, with this great need of his to prove that he is one huge penis from head to foot—"

"That's putting it much too strongly, and you know it," Agrippa said. "The fact remains that you did agree to marry him. You accepted his gifts. You allowed me to bring the high priest here from Jerusalem, and you went through with the ceremony. You married the man. You must face that—you married the man. And then you promptly turned your back on him, retired here to your chambers—and here you have been for the past five days."

"I changed my mind." Berenice shrugged.

"You haven't even kissed him."

"I changed my mind. I have no desire to kiss him, now or ever."

"Berenice—you don't seem to understand. He underwent a circumcision for you."

"I am thoroughly bored with that circumcision of his. The truth is that I couldn't care less if they had castrated him. Brother—I am bored with Polemon, his circumcision, his so-called love, and most of all with his whining. Why doesn't he go back to Cilicia and leave us along?"

"You know why he doesn't. Because you are his wife."

"Well, I have no intention of continuing in that function. I told that high priest of yours that I wanted the marriage dissolved."

"He can't just dissolve the marriage," Agrippa protested.

"He certainly can. He's the high priest. He can do anything he desires to do, and if he doesn't do it, we can make certain that he does not remain as high priest."

"We had reasons for this," Agrippa began miserably, but Berenice interrupted him again and asked, "Why don't you get married, brother?"

"Me?"

"Yes—you, brother."

At that point, he threw up his arms and stalked out of her chamber.

She lay down in her chambers. She said to Gabo, "Do you

understand, I will see no one. No reason, no person. No one." She couldn't bear the light that poured in through the windows. "Draw the blinds," she said to Gabo. The darkness was better. She lay in the darkness and allowed sorrow and self-pity to engulf her. Gabo tiptoed out of the room, and when Berenice knew that she was alone, she allowed herself to weep. She wept for a while, and then her hand went to the table by her couch and fumbled here and there until her fingers closed over a small, razor-sharp dagger. But the dagger was no good. Her thoughts of suicide were always ridiculous. She could not even begin the process of bringing them to consummation.

"Because I am a Jew!" she cried angrily. "The most cursed, wretched, miserable Jew that ever lived. The pagans can die as easily and effortlessly as they live—"

She hurled the dagger across the room. She put her face into the pillow—already moist from tears—and remembered her wedding to Polemon. All through it, she had been securely wrapped in a spell, a charm, a witch's robe; she had walked as confidently and omnipotently as a little girl; and she had been as witless as a person asleep or unconscious. Why? she asked herself now. What had happened to her? Do cattle go to slaughter that way, lost in an idiot dream? And then, already her husband, he had bent to kiss her and she had smelled the appalling foul odor of his breath. He had a bad tooth that had abscessed, and the smell from his mouth was the smell of death stinking and decaying in the hot sun; it exploded her into wakefulness, and she fled. Had anything like this ever happened—in all the history of kings and princesses and weddings—a woman wed to a king, who then was bending to kiss her when she fled? She fled through them all—through the grandees of Cilicia, the noble and the rich who were not so noble of Tiberias, the barons of Galilee, the great landowners of Judea, there by royal invitation, the Jewish merchant-princes of Chalcis, the Syrian-Greek dukes, the Phoenician shipowners, the Roman tax farmers

and bureaucrats and administrators, the Alexandrian aes-
thetes, heirs of the greatest of Jewish houses, the Idumean
chieftains in their black and white striped robes, all of them,
like all noble Idumeans, tracing some weary, tenuous blood
connection to Antipater, the founder of the House of Herod,
the Samaritan priests and petty kings and poverty-stricken,
illiterate gentry, making their own tiresome claim to the
blood of David and the House of David—all of these and so
many others, and through them Berenice fled to be away
from that hateful smell of death and decay, emanating from
this strange, fleshy, loose-lipped man who, through some
dim process of memory, she could remember as having
married. Long ago? No, the wedding words were still linger-
ing in the air as she fled, and the wedding guests stood aside.
No one dared put out a hand to halt her or interfere with her
progress. This was Berenice, who was already more of a
legend than reality, clad now in shining white, glittering
white, white silk sewn with pearls and diamonds and even
tiny rubies where the red sheen flickered about her
shoulders—so beautiful that poor Polemon choked with
emotion at his first sight of her in her wedding finery; and
swore a vow to his pagan gods, still remembered, that he
would not only have his wife put to death, but three concubines to whom he still clung—so that he could come clean
and unhindered and pure to this radiant vision of loveliness.
But the radiant vision of loveliness fled from the palace as if
all the hounds of hell pursued her and through the guards
outside, tearing away the long skeins of priceless cloth that
impeded her progress.

Through the streets she fled, into dark alleys, and then
through a postern gate which she wrenched open. All behind
her she left a trail of silks and pearls and diamonds and rubies
and gold clasps and gold pins and broken bracelets and beads
from snapped strings—even the pearl-and-diamond-
encrusted slippers which she wore; and finally, barefoot and
naked, she found the shore of the lake and almost without

hesitating in her wild pace plunged into the warm, sweet water.

Ah—what peace this was, what delight, what sweet and gentle relaxation, what safety, what security there in the black and good waters of Gennesaret! This was her mother and her mother's womb, and with the perfect freedom of nakedness she swam as easily and noiselessly as some great fish—long, smooth strokes, and behind her the web of her rich red hair undulating and floating on the water. Once she turned on her back to look at Tiberias, at the flickering lights of the city, and she listened to the frantic shouting and watched the waving torches. Let them find her here! Let them look on the lake! God was on the lake. Was there not a rabbi once, as she heard it told, who had walked on the waters of the lake? The lake was filled with magic.

She would swim and swim until all her strength was gone, and then she would give herself to the lake. Gennesaret would take her into its warm bosom. Down, down, down, into the deep darkness of eternity. But an hour later, far out on the lake, weary to exhaustion, she found the will to live too much for her, too much for Gennesaret—and swimming slowly, floating, resting, her long copper-skinned body a water thing, a part of the lake and the water, she made her way back. She swam back to the landing where she and Agrippa had played as children and dragged herself out onto the cool stone slab of the dock and lay there panting, whimpering—until she was strong enough to creep through their secret passages to her chambers. The corridors to the chambers were dark. She felt her way. She found her bed and crawled into it, and a moment later she was asleep.

She was awakened once for a moment by Gabo's sobbing joy; then she slept again.

The high priest at that time was Ishmael Barfabi, a pompous, strutting little man. Young Agrippa's advisers had persuaded him to appoint Ishmael because of the priest's connections with the wealthy and powerful Jerusalem House of Homash—and Agrippa himself could readily understand the need for strong connections in Judea. Not only were the Jews of Judea uneasy and resentful under the heel of the Roman procurator who governed the land, but they had never fully given their hearts to the House of Herod, even when Agrippa's father became a saint of sorts. When the marriage of Berenice to Polemon was announced, opinion was mixed in Jerusalem. Some were flattered that Agrippa would have the ceremony performed by no other than the high priest; others—especially among the highly orthodox—felt that it was rather abject and tasteless, if not blasphemous, for the high priest to go off to Galilee to marry the widow of an incestuous uncle-niece relationship to a heathen. The high priest, however, did as he was told, and he had appeared at the wedding in the full costume of office, purple robe with its hem of golden bells, the pomegranate tassels, the glittering Ephod, the breastplate set with rubies and diamonds, and his great *miznefit* of hammered gold, towering up a foot above his head.

When he wore these ancient and holy vestments in the Temple at Jerusalem, there was no one to observe him but other priests and pious Jews. Here, however, he was the focus for the eyes of all the noble blood and less noble wealth of the Middle East, and he strutted like a little popinjay. A year later he died of snake bite, and this unfortunate accident convinced people that Nehushtan, the ancient serpent-god, had destroyed him for his sins. But this night, when Berenice fled from the man to whom he had duly wedded her, Barfabi felt that the disgrace had descended squarely upon his own shoulders, turning his moment of glory into a beginning of ridicule. He would be remembered as the priest who had driven the bride away from the altar. Or would they say, beware of Barfabi—whom he marries is instantaneously divorced? In any case, when Berenice summoned him the following day, he went to her chambers stiff as a ramrod with irritation and bruised pride. There was a crowd around the door to her chambers, at least twenty men and women who desired to see her but who remained at a safe distance because the door was guarded by the oversized Adam Benur, who had switched his allegiance from Agrippa to Berenice. This had been a simple matter for Berenice, who had smiled upon the overmuscled Galilean soldier and won his undying loyalty; but others put it down to witchcraft and spells—which was the simplest way to explain Berenice.

Benur allowed Barfabi through the door, and then Gabo took him to Berenice's bedroom, where she lay upon her couch with a saffron-colored robe wrapped around her, her red hair loose and cast over her pillow like a splash of honey. Seeing her half-bare legs and her naked feet, Barfabi began to mutter prayers and invocations against the whores of the mother-god, only to be interrupted by Berenice who exclaimed angrily.

"How dare you spout that nonsense—what is your name?—Ishmael, isn't it?"

"I am the high priest, madam!" he cried.

"I know exactly what you are, little man—and if you repeat one more word of that stupid invocation about prostitutes and temples, I will call in that oversized soldier who stands in front of my door, and I will have him put you across his knee and spank you until you are unable to sit down for a week."

"You wouldn't dare!" Barfabi squealed.

"But wouldn't I! Don't you put on airs for me. I know exactly what your family paid my brother's seneschals for your office, and there are plenty of other priests who are cheaper and more amiable. Now will you behave?"

Breathing deeply, chewing his lower lip in rage, clenching his trembling fists, Barfabi calculated the chances of opposing the queen and then abandoned them. He let out his breath slowly and nodded.

"Good. Now I want you to annul my marriage to King Polemon."

"I can't."

"Of course you can," Berenice said, sitting up now and facing him. "And you will."

"But an annullment can proceed only out of specific cause. That is the Law. Can I change the Law?"

"Is deception specific cause?"

"What deception?"

"Polemon claimed to be a Jew."

"He became a Jew."

"Nonsense," Berenice declared. "He was circumcised by some Pharisee physician, which meant nothing. In his heart, he remained an idol worshiper."

"I shall have to .question him," the high priest said warily.

"You will do nothing of the kind. You will annul the marriage. Otherwise, we will find a high priest who is amiable and intelligent as well as pious. Do you understand me?"

He stared at this tall, lean, and beautiful women who sat on the couch facing him, and he asked himself, Who can go against a witch or a devil?

"I understand you," he said.

"And do not think that you can turn my brother against me, Barfabi. You are not strong enough for intrigue—nor wise enough."

But nothing changed the fact that this was certainly the strangest marriage and the juiciest bit of gossip in the entire world—as the world was at that time. In his report to the Emperor Claudius, Cuspius Fadus, the procurator of Judea, said among other things: "While there is precious little of what we would call entertainment in a Jewish world, all of what passes for polite society here is titillated with the astonishing marriage of Queen Berenice, the daughter of your friend Agrippa and sister to the present tetrarch of Galilee. You will recall that she was formerly married to Herod of Chalcis, who was old enough to be her grandfather, and there is some rumor of a previous marriage to the son of the alabarch of Alexandria—who possesses some rank or role or situation in the unfathomable web of Jewish nobility, if you can call it that. Anyway, both the Alexandrian and the king of Chalcis died mysteriously, as did Berenice's two sons; and I would hardly think that anyone would look forward to an alliance with her. But apparently this Polemon, who is titular king of old Cilicia, and to whom we permit a palace and certain ceremonies in Tarsus, has a suicidal bent. He fell madly in love with Berenice, submitted himself to having his foreskin hacked away in this nasty Jewish rite of circumcision, became Jewish, and then was married to Berenice. But no sooner was the ceremony completed than Berenice up and fled. All that wedding night they hunted vainly for her, and finally old Polemon had to go to bed with no other company than his truncated penis. Now I hear that Berenice has ordered the wedding dissolved. Whatever her virtues or vices, we should be grateful for the diversions she provides—"

If all of this and a thousand comments like it were *sotto voce,* the whispers still penetrated to the palace. Berenice heard and knew. She locked her doors and fortified herself behind them. The last person she saw for a long while, except her brother, was Anat Beradin, the wool merchant. He pleaded for an audience, sent messages importuning her, pleading for five minutes of her time. Finally she consented to see him without even knowing why she consented; and when he confronted her, her rigid form, her face like stone, and her stony silence, he was at a loss. He had believed that he could reach her, but once he began to speak, he realized that she was unreachable.

"To be a Jew," he began, "is either a blessing or a curse or both, but in any case, something we are born with, like a sixth finger or a clubfoot, but invisible, or maybe a coat of many colors such as Joseph wore, but also invisible. However, one of the first things one learns in the school of being a

Jew is that the Almighty—who does most things humorously—made the Jew indivisible. A Roman beggar or a Roman knight can do unspeakable things, and this reflects not one whit upon the basic character and reputation of Rome, just as an Egyptian can be a thief—as so many of them are—without shaking the innate dignity of Egypt. But let a Jewish woodcutter or a Jewish ditchdigger take an action that is indefensible or shocking, and immediately the entire community of the Jew is tried, found guilty, slandered, and condemned—"

He was watching Berenice for anger, irritation, recognition—but she yawned as if she had heard nothing and asked him whether that was all?

"Could I simply say this—my lady, Berenice: that in Polemon we have a curious thing—by which I mean something that is not obvious. He may appear obvious, crude by our standards, dull as a Jew measures intelligence, and very much a figurehead maintained by Rome, without either prestige or power. But his line is a very ancient one—not of blood do I speak here, but of the continuity that we call Cilicia. When David Benjesse of the blessed memory was king over all of Israel, there were princes in Cilicia who sent gifts to Jerusalem out of respect for the Almighty, and even a thousand years ago Jews dwelt in Tarsus and others of their cities, Corycos, where we built a synagogue when every hand was lifted against us, Anas—as you surely know. What you have done to Polemon is not merely cruel—"

She awakened to his words then. She stood up, her green eyes flaming in rage, and cried, "How dare you! Enough! I have listened enough! Leave me now!"

When he tried to speak again, Berenice shouted, "Don't tempt me, you fool!"

Then Anat Beradin realized suddenly how close to death he was. Step by step, he backed away from this enraged woman who was like a Greek fury with her great height, her wide shoulders and her long red hair—he backed away until he could feel the door behind him; and then he turned and fled through the door.

For the next week, Berenice would see no one. Behind the barred doors of her chambers, she sat in an enormous silence, where she existed without desire or regret. Sometimes she would go a whole day without food or drink. Again, in response to Gabo's pleading, she would have a few figs, dates, some olives. Whether she ate or not was of little moment to her. In a time when the depths of depression were widespread but little understood, her soul had been seized by evil spirits. She had lost all desire to live, to eat, to move, or to speak to members of her own species. Sometimes she paced her room, back and forth, back and forth—like a caged animal. Other times she sat motionless.

She had warned Gabo to speak to no one about her, but after eight days had gone by, eight days during which everyone was turned away from her door, Gabo disobeyed her and went to the king and said to him,

"I think my mistress is dying."

"What?"

"Slowly, slowly, Lord Agrippa. Not today or tomorrow—but surely she is dying. I have seen people die like that in the desert in the south. An evil spirit embraces their soul—"

"I have no desire to hear about your Benjaminite superstitions, and if my sister is dying she is certainly vigorous enough about keeping the sanctity of her chamber. I will go to see her."

"The marriage is dissolved," Agrippa said to Berenice sitting in her bedroom where the air was thick with scent and dead and stale, where the only light trickled in through the blinds and drapes. "That is what you wanted, isn't it?" He peered at her face through the gloom. "Well, I have done what you wished. I am even ready to confess that I was wrong. The marriage should never have been arranged, and that stupid ox, Polemon, should never have been permitted to have his penis bobbed." Still, he searched for some expression on the face, some angle that would reveal her. "Why do you keep the blinds closed, the drapes drawn? How can you sit in this darkness?"

"I prefer to," Berenice answered dully.

"Well, do you blame me, sister?" Agrippa demanded of her. "It's true that for a while I found myself acting like our father. Royal blood is a disease, I suppose. But watching poor Polemon was like looking into a mirror. He's not really a king, you know, but only by the sufferance of the Romans—"

"Poor Polemon, poor Polemon—I am sick to death of poor Polemon, and if that's all you have to say, brother, go away and leave me alone."

"No—please, Berenice, I just used the expression. He's a slob. That's a nasty word, but what else? Some men are slobs by nature—that's what Polemon is."

"Yes," Berenice cried, "poor Polemon, who had two wives murdered and was ready to murder the third and who put his own brother to death so that he could crawl to the Romans and say, love me, love me—poor Polemon!"

"Devil take me!" Agrippa cried in despair. "I did not come here to talk about Polemon, but since you have brought it up, your might as well know. The marriage was dissolved before Barfabi left for Jerusalem, and Polemon has gone back to Tarsus. He was filled with empty threats about coming back here with fifty thousand horsemen and turning Tiberias down over my head—which is utter nonsense. He can't muster ten horsemen without the specific consent of Vibius Marsus, although he can make it uncomfortable for the Jews in Tarsus. Well, I began all this by pointing to him as an example of myself, because my little throne is as fraudulent as his. I am a king by consent of the Romans—and all in all I suppose I am no happier than you are. Happiness has never been a strong family trait of either the Herods or the Hasmoneans. So what do you accomplish, Berenice, by sulking here in this dark and airless room?"

"Leave me alone."

"That's just it, Berenice, if I leave you alone—"

"Oh no—no more speeches, brother. Leave me alone. Just get out of here and leave me alone."

So Agrippa left, and three more days went by and he heard, outside of his throne room the high-pitched, nasal Aramaic bleat of Gabo the Benjaminite—cursing his door guards and demanding to see the king.

"Have them let her in," Agrippa told his seneschal, Bensimon. "They know she comes from my sister. Why haven't they the sense to let her in without all this screaming and whining?"

Gabo said much the same thing. "Do I want to assassinate you, my lord, Agrippa?" she demanded. "Do I want to waste your time with idle gossip? Isn't it plain to those stupid Galileans of yours that I am handmaiden to your sister, and if I come to you, come I must?"

"All right, Gabo," replied Agrippa. "What now?"

"Now she lies on her couch in darkness, staring at nothing, hearing nothing, and she does not eat or drink—and she is going to die. She is going to die."

Then, out of sheer desperation, Agrippa sent to the House of Shlomo for the physician, Shimeon Bengamaliel. He sent a messenger to say that if it was necessary, he, Agrippa, would come personally. Gideon Benharmish, as the head of the house, came personally to the palace to tell Agrippa that the message had been accepted and that a rider had gone to fetch Shimeon. "He will come here," Benharmish assured Agrippa. "You have my word for that."

His word was good, and the following morning, a few hours after sunrise, Shimeon Bengamaliel appeared at the palace and was taken directly to Agrippa. Always considerate of his guests, Agrippa had bread and fruit and wine placed before Shimeon, and only after the doctor had eaten did he speak of his own problems. As he spoke, he watched Shimeon carefully and curiously, trying to guess the reactions of this tall, wide-shouldered Pharisee. On his own part, Shimeon studied the king, thinking to himself that while it made some sense to employ him as a surgeon for a heathen, it made none at all to consult him in regard to the infamous Berenice.

Agrippa anticipated that. "I can guess what you think of my sister—" he began.

"Only what all Israel thinks of her."

"Ah—well, that is not even diplomatic," Agrippa sighed, "and all of Israel can be wrong—terribly wrong."

"I have an open mind," Shimeon said seriously.

"Do you? I know that is a Pharisee attitude, and I wonder how much truth there is in it. Remember, Shimeon Bengamaliel, that I was taught, as a child, that the Pharisees are the servants of the devil—and the House of Hillel the abode of wickedness itself—"

Shimeon had to smile.

"It amuses you? Right, wrong—slander, truth—did it ever occur to you that we, my sister and myself, that we are slandered, that we might be something other than the monsters we are depicted?"

"That has occurred to me," Shimeon nodded.

"Oh? Do you know that when a Jewish mother in Judea desires to discipline her child, she says, 'Behave or Berenice will get you!' Amusing, isn't it? My sister is twenty years old—two months remain before her twenty-first birthday— and she lives with the knowledge that this is common. There isn't a Jew in Palestine who isn't certain that she murdered our father, even though we saw the murder done with our own eyes by a Roman knight called Germanicus Latus. You have heard that she murdered the son of the Alabarch Alexander?"

"I have heard that," Shimeon nodded.

"He was dead when she was brought to look at him for the first time—she was a child of fourteen then. Shall I go on?"

"No," Shimeon said decisively. "Do not defend your sister to me. I am a doctor, not a judge—and I presume that you summoned me as a physician. Although, why me I do not know."

"I believe in you as a physician," Agrippa said. "I love my sister—not as the filth that is spoken would have it, but because we never had more than each other, if you can understand that. Now she is dying. I don't want her to die."

"Dying? Of what disease? What are her symptoms?"

Agrippa told him—and Shimeon shook his head uneasily. "No," he said, "I am not the one you want. I'm no rabbi or magician, and I do not practice the laying on of hands. In our house, in the House of Hillel, we look upon such things with distaste and suspicion—but neither do I believe that a doctor can cure a sickness of the soul."

"Then she will die," Agrippa said miserably. "She will not tolerate the laying on of the hands—she will die first."

There was a long silence then, while Shimeon stared at the table which held his breakfast food and toyed with the bag of instruments that hung from his waist. Agrippa, his eyes closed, listened to the faint clink of the tools as they were moved one against the other. Then he opened his eyes to meet the eyes of the Pharisee. Shimeon nodded.

"I will see her. I will do what I can."

Then Agrippa took Shimeon Bengamaliel to Berenice's chambers, where Benur stood guard; and where he pointed out to Benur that since Queen Berenice was sick, a physician was needed.

"I am sworn to die here for her, if need be," Benur said to Shimeon.

"Yes, yes, I know that," Agrippa said imiatiently. "But right now the necessity is not for anyone to die for my sister but simply to permit her to be treated by a competent physician and get well. This is Shimeon Bengamaliel, the physician. When he goes in there, my sister, who has a ready temper, may not welcome him. Nevertheless, he must go to her and treat her. Do you understand, Adam?"

The huge man nodded.

"Even if she calls out, you are not to go to her or interfere in any way."

"Oh no. No. My life is hers, to defend her."

"But before her life can be adequately defended, she has to get better. This is the doctor. He must treat her. And furthermore, I command you to keep your nose out of the chambers. I am the king—"

Long years afterward, Berenice would think back to the time when she saw Shimeon Bengamaliel for the first time, and sometimes she would smile in the reflection of her memory and sometimes she would weep. It was the beginning. Before that, there was only confusion and pain, and then one day she lay on her bed and she knew that she was dying. Her room was in darkness, but the darkness in her soul was much deeper. Seh was removed from all the world. She was alone, and she was sinking into an inescapable pit. Each day she sank deeper into that pit, and each day she cared less. The only escape was to care—but she cared for nothing. Her hands were the hands of death; whatever she touched died; whatever she cared for died; so now she cared for nothing and she touched nothing, and she was dying.

Only it took a long time to die.

Then, as she lay in the darkness dying, the interference began. It began as a glare of light, and as much as she clenched her eyelids against it, it increased, and with it noise and action of various sorts.

Whereupon she opened her eyes and realized that a man was in her chamber, a very tall, wide-shouldered man, clad in sandals, white linen trousers, and a sleeveless white coat. He was a madman, and he went about his work as a madman would. He tore down her drapes, thee beautiful, priceless drapes of linen dyed purple and lined with wool, the linen embroidered with gold and silver thread until it was heavy as metal, the woolen lining sewn all over with sequins, so that when the drapes turned or fluttered the sun would reflect as from diamonds; and these drapes he ripped violently from their supports, rended them when they resisted his large and powerful hands, and cast them aside. Then, behind the drapes, he attacked the blinds, made of cane woven cunningly together, and these he ripped down and flung aside, allowing great, terrifying slabs of yellow sunlight into the room.

It was true that Berenice was dying and as a dying woman set no great store by drapes or blinds; but as the queen of Chalcis and the first princess of the Jews, she reacted to what was certainly the worst instance of *lèse majesté* she had ever encountered. She was weak and without strength, yet by sheer force of will she managed to find her feet, stood wavering, and cried out for the madman to stop and cease and desist with his madness. He paid no attention to her. He was now engaged in tearing down a set of portieres that separated this, her bedchamber, from her sitting room. The portieres were hung from a huge brass rod set into a molding over the side doorway, but under the strength of the madman the brass rod bent and then came down with a wild crash.

"Stop it! Stop it!" cried Berenice.

As if she did not exist, he strode into her sitting room and ripped away the drapes that concealed a long balcony that looked out over Gennesaret, as the Romans called it. Behind these drapes were more cane blinds, and as he began to tear them loose, the tall, red-headed woman he had been observing out of the corners of his eyes flung herself upon him. Without pausing in his work, he shook her off, and such was the force with which he shrugged her away that she tripped over the tangle of drapes and sprawled upon the floor. As she rolled over, her long legs exposed, he glanced with satisfaction on her shapely nakedness and then returned to the work of destroying the cane blinds. She screamed. She screamed tentatively—and then several times with vigor. The big man in white paid no attention to her, and no one else came to her aid.

She now dragged at the huge brass curtain rod, hoping to

free it as a weapon, and had just pulled it loose when the blinds fell and a mighty ocean of yellow sunlight poured into the room. Blinking and blinded, she swung the brass pole at the madman, who caught it and took it away from her.

"You will die for this!" she cried. "You will die! You will die!"

"That's better," replied the madman throwing the brass pole out into the lake and grasping the shaking, furious Berenice by the arms.

"Let go of me!"

"I think now you can rest. At least the air is breathable, and there's enough light to cheer one a bit."

"Let go of me!"

"In a moment. Back to bed now."

"How dare you? Let go of me! Who are you?"

He lifted her in his arms now, as easily as one lifts an infant, and for all her frustrated rage, she could not help but react to the way she was lifted from the ground and cradled in the big man's arms. Like all very tall women, she had substituted the dream for the fact of being cradled in a man's arms. No one had ever picked her up like this; it was unthinkable and impossible.

"I am your physician," he answered her.

"Put me down!"

"In a moment—in your bed." And he bent over her bed and laid her there as easily and gently as he would a doll or a tiny child. "There."

She lay there a moment and stared at him, her green eyes blazing, her loose red hair framing her magnificent head, the coppery skin so pale now and drawn so tightly over the high cheekbones. As Shimeon watched her, he wondered whether this was indeed the most beautiful woman in Israel, as some said, or perhaps only the most devilish. He had no set opinion, and he clung rigidly and intelligently to his own objectivity. He would attempt to cure her; only that.

"My physician," she whispered in scorn. "You will be no

one's physician. For the first fifty lashes you will feel pain and scream and plead. Then you will feel nothing.

"Gabo!" she cried.

And then when nothing happened, "Adam! Adam Benur!"

And when still nothing happened, at the top of her lungs, "Adam Benur!"

"You will only strain your throat and hurt your voice screaming like that," Shimeon said gently. "Your brother, the king, sent them both away. At first, we attempted to make the big man understand and help me, but he's not very intelligent, is he?"

She bit her lips and said nothing.

"So for today, we sent him away with Gabo. No one is within call now. No one but you and me. And I don't think it's good for you to threaten me with hideous deaths. In the first place, I don't believe you would carry out such threats, and in the second place, the whole process is not constructive. You are sick. I want to heal you."

"Sick? I am not sick!"

"No? Then why did you lie here in the darkness and alone, day after day?"

Again, she retreated into silence, and he went on, in brisk professional tones, "Since I do not practice the laying on of hands, I can't put this at the devil's doorstep. Perhaps the evil spirits have taken hold of your soul; I cannot say there is no truth in that sort of thing, although in Greece, where I studied medicine, they reject it entirely. Since I must treat you in the Greek manner, I would say that other factors are responsible, a sluggish digestion, insufficient exercise, and a certain amount of guilt for your treatment of Polemon and others. I will prescribe a physic and a good tonic for the blood, and of course sunlight and fresh air."

This flat statement on his part struck Berenice as being so bald and droll, and Shimeon stood so large and boyish over her couch that she had to resist an inclination to smile. Her anger washed away. She found herself asking his name.

"Shimeon Bengamaliel."

"Oh. Then you—"

"Yes. Exactly. I bobbed your husband—or erstwhile husband—and thereby got you into this mess, so it is only fair that I should try to get you out of it."

"What did you say?"

"Getting you into this—"

"No, the word you used. Bobbed—"

Shimeon shrugged.

"And my brother sent you here? Truly?"

"He loves you," Shimeon said. "Do you imagine that he wants to see you die?"

"And the drapes," she cried, desperately eager for some reason not to talk about her brother and herself, "you have ruined them. Do you know what such drapes cost?"

"You are dying—so why should the cost of some drapes matter?"

"I am not dying."

"You were, weren't you?"

"No."

"Then you take from me all the joy of curing you."

"Bobbed Polemon—"

"I should have refused."

"Why?" Berenice demanded.

"Well, look what I started. Heaven knows where it will end!"

"Am I really sick?" she asked suddenly.

"I think that is for you to decide, my lady."

"Oh?"

"How do you feel? Does the light bother you now?"

"The blinds too. Just look at this room—as if barbarians had been at work in it. But that's because you're a Pharisee—you don't care about anything beautiful, do you, or any refinements—anything Greek is an abomination to you."

"Oh no, Queen Berenice," Shimeon said. "Not at all. You must remember that I was educated in Greece, and as far as speech is concerned, I suppose my Greek is better than my Hebrew."

"Still, Pharisees are no better than barbarians—"

"I suppose some of us are and some of us aren't."

"The blinds too. Did you have to tear down the blinds?"

"To let light in and to let air in, you see, Queen Berenice—"

"Why do you call me Queen Berenice?"

"Well, your title," Shimeon began, when she interrupted again, "I don't like to be called that—oh, not at all. It makes me feel like an old woman. How old do you think I am?"

"Eighteen? Nineteen?"

She knew he was acting, teasing, pretending, manipulating—yet in some way she was delighted, and it was against every inclination in her to be delighted. The memory of the depression hung over her, like the sick aftermath of a headache, and she found it incredible that she should be lying here, sprawled on her bed in the blazing sunlight, with this tall, wide-shouldered physician beside her bed. Seeking for the misery of only moments ago, she was unable to find it or re-experience it, and she asked him desperately,

"Did you lay hands on me?"

He shook his head quite seriously. "It is not done in our house."

"Then what lifted the devils from my heart?"

"Who knows," Shimeon shrugged, "if indeed your sickness was of devils. The Greeks call it simply the heaviness of heart; yet unless the heart is lightened the patient will die—or lose his mind. Sometimes there is a moment of enough, enough sorrow and guilt and heartache, and then this terrible weight lifts of itself. Do you feel that—a weight lifted from your heart?"

Berenice nodded.

"And you will let me take your pulse now?"

"Why?"

"Why? What do you mean, why? I only want to count your heartbeat."

"Why? No other physician does it."

Shimeon took a tiny sand glass and placed it on the bed. "I measure your pulse against this," he explained, his voice deep, matter-of-fact, and comforting. "Twelve to eighteen is normal. More or less is cause for concern. With the very old, it is less, but if you were with fever sickness, it would be more."

"How much more?"

"Shall I tell you all my art? Well, over eighteen would be alarming—over twenty and you would be a sick woman, believe me." He took her wrist as he spoke, not as anyone had ever taken it, but with a firm, assured grasp, his second finger seeking the pulse, finding it and remaining there with a steady, soft pressure.

"And am I sick?"

"No—but neither are you well. What have you had to eat today?"

"Nothing."

"Why?"

"I felt no hunger—no desire for food—" Berenice said.

"More than that. It was ashes in your mouth."

"How do you know?"

"Ah—well, how I know is not important. Will you try to eat now if I prescribe for you?"

"What?"

"Wheat mush with butter?"

She made a face.

"It's good, quite good—very tasty. I want you to eat it and then sleep, and I'll see you again tomorrow."

She slept and woke in the hour of dawn. When she had been a child, she had slept like this. It was the peaceful, gentle sleep of childhood. When she was a child, she had awakened like this, at the hour of dawn, with the sweet dawn wind making music in the dry fronds of the palms that grew by the shore of the lake—and in her nostrils the smell of the lake, the wet, remembered smell of Gennesaret. Other things were remembered, too, the sound of the fishermen splashing as they walked their boats into the deep water, the creak of their oars, their sing-song blessing as they went out on their day's work, "Blessed are Thou, O Lord our God, King of the Universe, who maketh the fish to swim in the deeps." The morning birds sang with their chanting. No doubt, on the hilltops there was sunlight already, but in the deep, below sealevel hollow where the lake lay, the shadow was as dark as ink—as dark as the purple ink which the Tyreans extract from the mollusks on their shore and use to dye the robes of emperors and the drapes of queens. But the drapes lay folded by one wall, the blinds stacked by another, and the windows were wide open as the mad Pharisee said they must be; and half awake, Berenice thought of this strange man, so violent in his cures, so positive in his knowledge. He was like the Greek engineers of her childhood, and with their mathematics and angles and their sines and cosines, of whom it was whispered that they worshiped no other gods than their mathematics and had no other religion than the truth, of which they were always quite certain. They called themselves Stoics, and Berenice had only a most confused notion of what a Stoic was, and as she realized now, an equally inadequate notion of what a Pharisee was.

They were setting the nets for tomorrow and gathering in the nets of the day before. In her mind's eye, Berenice could see the silver fish flopping and twisting; and she threw her bedclothes aside and ran to the balcony—but the mist lay upon the lake, and she could see nothing. But in her nostrils was the smell of charcoal burning as all over Tiberias the fires were lit to cook the gruel and take the chill out of the morning air, and from the city side came the call of the bakers, "My bread is fresh—who buys my bread?" It was a song as old as time, four notes descending, four notes ascending. Berenice remembered it from when she was a child, and then she had an old nurse who said that in her own childhood, in the ancient city of Gadara, the song was the same, the bakers taking their flat, tortillalike breads quick from the red-hot oven, piling them on a wooden plank, and the going from house to house through the streets in the dawning, who buys my bread? Oh, was there ever anything so delicious as that bread, with a lump of sweet butter melted upon it, a bit of rock salt, and then all of it, dripping aroma and goodness, conveyed to the mouth? Was there ever such goodness, hot bread and butter and cold buttermilk to wash it down?

"Gabo!" she cried. "Gabo!" And then ran to her chest of jewels and gold to find a coin. A tiny silver coin called spaeta. And as Gabo came running in, rubbing her eyes, Berenice told her,

"Go and buy bread from the street vendor!"

"From the street vendor?"

"Yes, from the street vendor."

"But, mistress, they will be baking in the palace—"

"From the street vendor," Berenice repeated, allowing a note of warning to creep into her voice. "And cover it to keep it warm. And on the way back, bring sweet butter and buttermilk."

She had a vast appetite this morning, did Berenice, a savage hunger on top of all the days she had gone without touching food, and she ate and ate of the hot bread and the sweet butter—until at last she was satisfied, full of the swelling sensation of good food, the satisfaction of being awake and alive and replete.

By noontime, she was impatient, striding back and forth, dressed and then undressed and in bed, and then dressed again, and snapping at Gabo.

"Where is he?"

"Who, mistress?"

"The physician, stupid girl. Am I not sick? Or am I

well—and no physician is needed? Or does no one care? Well, I'll teach them to care! Go to my brother! Tell him that the physician is a liar—that he said he would come—and now? Where is he? Go to my brother!"

Gabo fled, and Berenice's voice whipped her back.

"Where are you going?"

"To your brother, the king."

"To my brother, the king. To my brother, the king," Berenice said, "Have you no sense?"

And then, in midafternoon, he came; and for all that she had steeled and lectured herself against it, Berenice burst out angrily,

"Where were you?"

He looked at her curiously, and then he shook his head.

"And what does that mean?" she demanded.

"Only that you have a vile temper."

"Oh—how dare you?" she cried. "Devil take you—who do you think you are to talk to me like that!"

"I know who I am," he answered gently. "Who you are, my lady, is another matter entirely—and perhaps something known to neither of us. You are beautiful beyond belief—but what does it signify? There must be a reflection of that beauty somewhere in your spirit, but if there is, you hide it well."

She stared at him, tears welling into her eyes in spite of herself, suddenly at a loss for words; and then she walked over to her bed, dropped onto it, and said bleakly, "You didn't have to say that to me. The whole world says it to me. You didn't have to say it to me. I am sick. I am your patient, and you are a physician."

"What do you mean, the whole world says it to you?" he asked softly.

"As if you don't know what the world says—Berenice the monster, the murderer, the embodiment of evil—" Her voice trailed away, and she sat like a little girl, her hands in her lap.

"And are you all that, Berenice?"

"I can't defend myself. I don't know how."

"But you know what you are?"

"No," she replied woefully. "I don't."

He gave her no sympathy, and she did not know how to ask for any. In all her life, she had never asked for sympathy or quarter. He was kind and gentle in his motions and aloof. He took her pulse, felt her forehead, and gave her a small bottle of powder, a measure of which she was to take each day in water.

"You are much better today," he told her gravely.

"What do you mean?"

"I only mean that you are better."

"I need a physician. Can't you see that I am ill?"

"I will come again tomorrow," he said. "Meanwhile, I don't want you to lie in bed. Go and walk in the garden. The gardens in this palace are beautiful. When you walk by on the street side, there is only the blank wall, but in here you have your own wonderland. You should be happy here."

"You are so clever, Pharisee," said Berenice. "Do you think there is happiness to be found in gardens? Or in anything else inside of a palace?"

"I wouldn't know, my lady, having never lived in a palace. But to us who see the palace from the outside it is quite glamorous, you may be sure. Also, I no more enjoy your calling me Pharisee than you do my calling you Queen Berenice."

"But you are a Pharisee," Berenice said pettishly.

"In a matter of speaking, yes. I suppose you could say that we of the House of Hillel are close to the thinking of the Pharisees—still not so close as you might imagine. We are of our own, for what it is worth—"

"What is your own?"

"People come to us for teaching—and if it is a matter of teaching, how can I explain it in a word? But you know my name—Shimeon Bengamaliel. Gamaliel, Shimeon, and

146

Hillel—three generations of the names of our house; I bear two of them—"

"I don't know what you are talking about," she interrupted.

He shrugged. "I'll come tomorrow."

He left her frustrated and angered, but she obeyed him and walked in the gardens. The seneschals and stewards and ladies of the court came to congratulate her on her recovery—and she knew how they would go back to their own circle of gossip—"I saw her in the garden. Disturbed? Hardly, my dear. Nothing disturbs Berenice. If you had done away with your own father, not to mention the children, would anything disturb you?"—She nodded and smiled—"I don't believe she was every sick."—She picked a pink blossom and put it in her hair.

Then they said, "Look at her—flowers in her hair." And someone else, being told of it, would wonder why she did not dance. The dance of Berenice then, they decided, could replace the dance of death that they practiced in Tyre on suitable occasions.

But to this, Berenice was indifferent, being fascinated by a process within her. She recalled an instance as a child when she had watched a cocoon break open and the butterfly emerge, and she remembered that she had wondered then whether the cocoon has knowledge of what it might be. Childishly and sentimentally, she envisioned herself as the creature in the cocoon and enveloped herself in an aura of pleasure and well-being—and yet she was unaware that she loved a man; and when the whole of the next day passed without his putting in an appearance, her warmth cooled and her frustration fanned a rage that left no room for love. Another day, and he came in the morning, and her welcome to him was harsh and imperious.

"Where were you yesterday?"

"A woman was dying. I eased her pain a little," he said.

"A young woman? What sort of woman?"

"She's dead."

"Best for her. How dared you not to come?"

"You are something," he sighed. "You are indeed."

"What do you mean by that?"

"How would it help for me to try to tell you? How do you feel today?"

"I feel that I would like to see you hanged by your heels and drawn—drawn with your guts hanging out!"

"Oh?" He reached for her hand to take her pulse.

"I don't need you!" she cried, pulling her hand away. "I don't want you. I am cured. Get out of here!"

He stared at her for a while; then he shook his head and said to her, "There is so much hate that it baffles me. The Almighty favored you, as few woman are favored, a strong and healthy body, and great beauty, and a mind. I am told that you have a keen, a discerning mind. And with that, riches, position, power—yet out of it all, you distill only hatred." He stood over her now as she sat on her couch. "Yes—I think you are cured, as cured as you will ever be, God help you." He turned his back on her and walked from the room.

After a moment, she lay down on the couch and began to weep. Never before had she wept like this, her whole body wracked with sobs. Indeed, never before had she actually wept. It was a new accomplishment.

The weeks passed, and gradually the scandal created by the curious circumstances of Berenice's marriage to Polemon and the subsequent annulment by the high priest ceased to be a prime topic of conversation in Jewish circles. Not that it was forgotten, but other matters pressed to the fore. Cuspius Fadus, the new procurator of Judea, demonstrated how little he understood Jews by forcing his way into the outer court of the Temple and demanding the custody of the high priest's robes. It was an infantile plan for control of the Jews, and while Ishmael Barfabi might be corrupt in other matters, in the face of this pagan affront to his faith, he bared his breast, called his Levite spearmen to die by his side, and faced the Romans. Within hours, all of Jerusalem was up in arms, and every Jew had a weapon in hand, if no more than a knife or a club. In the face of overwhelming force, Fadus backed down but sent to Caesarea for his legions. Meanwhile, the more sober heads among the population of Jerusalem sent postriders to Galilee for the young King Agrippa. Agrippa rode two horses to death to reach Jerusalem, where he argued, pleaded, promised, and cozened with the procurator. Fadus agreed to preserve the status quo until word came from Rome—to which city Agrippa had already sent a committee and a petition. Delighted with the way the young man had handled the situation, the Emperor Claudius supported him. Agrippa was invited by the priesthood to read from the Torah in the public assembly in Jerusalem, and for the occasion he chose Genesis 44:18, namely:

"Then Judah came near unto him and said, O my lord, let thy servant, I pray thee, speak a word in my lord's ears, and let not thine anger burn against thy servant; for thou art even as Pharaoh."

It was a brilliant choice, and if the masses of people in Jerusalem failed to comprehend this, nevertheless the educated people of the upper classes were delighted and hailed Agrippa as a young Solomon come to judgment. Hearing pleasant accolades bestowed upon him, he forgot his sister for the moment.

She, meanwhile, had her own problems and torments to deal with, and when she could stand it no longer, when her stomach was empty and aching with loneliness and want, she went to Oman Bensimon, the old seneschal to her brother the king, and said to him,

"Tell me of the House of Hillel, and where is it and what is it?"

The old man, no fool, studied her shrewdly, and put in his demurral almost legalistically, informing her that between the House of Herod and the House of Hillel, there was a gap as wide as the ocean and as deep as the pit of the Dead Sea.

"Is it blood debt?" Berenice asked. "Is it for blood let that there is blood due in payment?"

"Strangely enough, not at all," answered old Bensimon. "For in all the generations of your house, my lady, no hand was ever raised against one of the House of Hillel. Not even by your royal great-grandfather Herod the Great. For it is told that when he lay dying, knowing that in all the world no man or woman or child would shed a tear for him, he called his advisers to him and asked how he could die and have all Israel weep for him? Ah, they answered, that is very simple indeed, for all you have to do, mighty king, is to have the Rabbi Hillel put to death when you feel your own death upon you. They were right. But do you know, Queen Berenice, he would not do this—"

"Why?" Berenice demanded. "Was he afraid of Hillel?"

"Yes."

"I don't believe that at all," she said.

"No? Who knows?" the old man shrugged. "That was half a century ago—"

"And when Hillel died," Berenice demanded, "did all of Israel weep?"

"Where there were Jews, they wept," the old man replied softly.

"I don't believe that Herod was afraid of him."

"Who knows? Hillel was a saint. Kings fear saints."

"That is nonsense," Berenice declared. "There are no saints today. It is like the voice of God. The rabbis would tell me how God spoke to Moses, to Aaron and Joshua and Gideon and David—and all the others. But who has heard the voice of God today? Did Hillel hear the voice of God?"

"You would make me a student of Hillel," the old man shrugged. "I am a seneschal in the House of Herod—so obviously not even a admirer of Hillel, and poorly informed, most poorly informed, Queen Berenice. But so far as my small knowledge goes—mostly hearsay—the Rabbi Hillel never claimed to have heard the voice of God."

"Of course not. But still you haven't told me why we are so apart."

"Hillel and Herod are apart. That's the way it is. Why is the mountain high and the sea low? Because the Almighty willed it to be so."

"I resent your talking to me as if I were either a child or a halfwit," Berenice said. "It is even possible that an old and trusted seneschal might regret making sport with me."

"Ah, my lady," pleaded the old man, "I beg your pardon. Humbly—but as God is my witness, what can I say to you? The House of Hillel is anathema to the House of Herod. Thus it has been; thus it will be. I did not make it so; it is simply the natural order of things."

"I see. And tell me Oman, where is their place?"

"Their place?"

"Their house, their seat—where does one go to find the House of Hillel? Or do they hide?"

"They don't hide. Why should they hide? No one has ever raised a hand against them, not the kings or the Zealots or the Romans or the pagans—no, they have nothing to fear, and they live in peace. Not far from Tiberias, either. When you go out of the main gate and take the road to the sea, there is an hour's walk, and then another road branching off to the right. Not a very good road, but ten or fifteen minutes of walking on it will bring you to the House of Hillel."

"You appear to know the way very well indeed," said Berenice.

"Ah—" The old man spread his arms. "One hears everything."

In the old tales, it was said that this was the first time Berenice had walked upon the roads of Israel; but that is an effect-saying, and a good deal of nonsense, too. Perhaps if Berenice had been a Judean princess, raised behind the walls of Herod's palace in Jericho, which contained many of the features of an oriental seraglio, the story might have held some truth; but she had grown up in Galilee, where there were few great houses and fewer harems, where as a child she ran free as an animal in the forest and swam free as a fish in the lake, and where her Greek teachers made a fetish of the body in its use and function. So she was no stranger to the roads, which were not hard surfaced and mathematically precise Roman highways but rather deeply rutted cart tracks and mountain trails.

She dressed for the road, plain leather sandals, a shift of white linen in a coarse peasant weave, and such a gray overdress as could be found on ten thousand women on any day in Galilee, and she set out by herself, telling no one where she was off to. She washed her face clean of any trace of paint, lip rouge, or eye shadow and bound her hair in a kerchief, so that none of its rich red color showed—and then there were only the green eyes to identify her. Yet with hair hidden and her dress so plain and common, no one recognized her or bothered to give her a second glance of recognition—although many a man turned to look again at her face and try to catch a bit more of ankle and leg than the long shift revealed. That was something else. She was another woman in the streets of Tiberias, taller than most and well worth a bit of scrutiny; but no more than that. She walked through the early morning crowds with a comfortable feeling of invisibility, and even the guards at the open gate, grinning with appreciation, made no more of her. As a princess, her particular crown was the red hair. She was "the red one." She wore a crown of blood, as they would have it, and since people had seen her for the most part from a distance, they had seen only that.

She walked on. She had said to herself that an hour of walking would be nothing, but in time her legs became weary. She had been too long away from walking, too long away from exercise of any kind, and too long away from the road to remember the fine dust that soon covered her feet and laid its thin skin upon her hands and face too, so that when the sweat came, it grimed her. She didn't care. The Princess Berenice, queen of Chalcis, was left behind. At least for the moment, she was free, and she breathed her freedom with pleasure as the life of the road eddied about her. This was the main road to the sea, and she had forgotten the life and motion and color of such a road. A camel caravan of plodding, stinking, loud-farting beasts passed her, its Arab drivers cursing and grunting as they prodded the stupid beasts. Again, a flock of sheep washed about her, one big ewe treading on her foot and causing her to cry out with pain. The shepherds, two long-boned and beardless boys of fourteen or so, grinned at her plight and were bold enough to try an obscene remark or two. An old woman heard them and went into the flock and after them with her stick, and the boys fled away, laughing. Again, a Roman party on horseback thundered by, on their way from Caesarea to their watering place on Semanhenitis, deliberately going into a gallop at the sight of a Jewish woman on the road; and then a cluster of Zealots, those grim and savage religious warriors of the northern hills, looking after the Romans with hatred, their hands on their knives and bows, their leader asking her,

"Did you take any hurt from those swine, missy?"

Berenice smiled and shook her head, looking at them with curiosity. So these were the Zealots, of whom one heard more and more these days! You didn't see them in the cities—at least not this kind, such tall, lean, wild-looking men, their feet bare and hardened to the road, their trousers dirty and ragged, and over their shirts, instead of a jacket or coat, the short, sleeveless vests with the long fringes, one blue thread hanging from each corner, that were like a uniform to them. They carried the curved, razor-sharp knives that had almost religious significance in their ranks, and of the seven that were here, four had bows and quivers of arrows. The bows were of laminated horn, made in Persia but sold widely and used widely in Israel, and the arrows were cedar shafts, dove-feathered and armed with business-like iron heads. They wore their hair long and braided, as the Nazarites did, but unlike the Nazarites, they clipped their beards short in the Hasmonean fashion and wore upon their heads the jaunty cap of the Hasmoneans.

Unbathed as they were from year's end to year's end, Berenice could smell their strong, rank, and masculine odor. They worked intermittently as farm laborers, as tinkers and carpenters, but only intermittently, preferring, as she had heard, to take their living out of highway robbery, preying out of preference upon Arab and Syrian merchants. Berenice stared at them with such interest and delight that one of them asked,

"Have you never seen the like of us before, missy?"

Another said, "We should have sent a shaft or two after those Latin bastards."

"Their time will come."

"More to the point are the camels. Have you seen them, missy—loaded camels with Arab drivers? We have been following their turds on the road."

"Back half an hour from here," Berenice nodded.

"Devil take us, they'll be in Tiberias by now."

"Tomorrow's another day. Patience—there's the virtue."

Berenice asked them about the House of Hillel.

"Oh," said their leader, a tall, lean man, blue-eyed and blond, his fierce, hooked nose, hatched face, and pale coloring testifying to Kohan blood, "so that is where you're bound, missy. Well, it's the times, isn't it? Find a woman with a face and bosom worth looking at, and she with Hillel. Just walk up the road and turn right."

They left her then, striding through the dust that still hung where the Roman horses had sprayed it, their hands on their knives, their rank smell dangling behind them. Berenice went on, and a hundred paces further she turned right on a narrow path that wound through a grove of sweet-smelling cedar. For half a mile the path continued in forest, and then it crested a hill to reveal below a fertile valley, in the center of which was a large country villa surrounded by low farm walls, stone cottages, and rich fields of wheat and barley. Dividing the fields were lines of olive trees, heavy with their burden of fruit, fig trees, plum trees, and here and there a spreading of ancient live oak, the sacred terebinth, which the people of Galilee had worshiped as gods in the olden times. On the slopes of the hills around the valley, flocks of sheep and goats grazed. Men in white trousers, bare to the waist but shaded from the sun by wide-brimmed straw hats, worked the fields with hoes, chopping weeds and loosening soil—and all in all, it was as rich and peaceful and bucolic a scene as Berenice had ever witnessed. A little stream ran through the bottom of the valley, and women were washing clothes there—singing as they worked, and faintly the sound of the song came to Berenice where she stood on the lip of the valley.

"So this is the House of Hillel," she thought, as she walked down the path toward the villa. "They do themselves well for saints. A king could hardly want more." Yet she admitted to herself that most kings did, asking herself what she had expected—was it a monastery such as the Essenes built in the burning desert on the shores of the Dead Sea? But these people of Hillel were not Essenes, not monks, not fanatics, not Nazarites—and certainly not Zealots. Since to Berenice they were summed up in the tall, wide-shouldered person of Shimeon Bengamaliel, Berenice was certain of what they were not, but most uncertain of what they were. For his essence was not that of a Pharisee or a Sadducee, not of Roman or Greek—but of a Jew in a way that was new and different to her, a kind of Jew apart from the Jews she had known, the Latin-aping nobility, the syncophants of the king's court and circle, the merchants and servants and slaves, the farmers and the fishermen of the lake, the professional soldiers, the sons of the good families in their burnished armor with the fancy manners copied from the Romans, the Levites, the Kohanim or priests—apart from all of these yet connected with them.

Thinking this and that and to no great end, she walked down into the valley toward the villa. What she would do there, and what she would say, how she would introduce herself and whether she would—of this she had no clear notion; any more than she had an explanation of her own presence in her sweat-soaked shift with her dust-covered feet. But certainly this was not a place that would press for explanations—that at least she knew about the House of Hillel—and being tired, dry, and desperately eager to sit down, she walked toward the open gates of the courtyard wall that surrounded the villa.

Outside the wall, there was a well and a cistern, with dry gourds for dippers. She drank and quenched her thirst, listening meanwhile to the sound of voices—young voices that piped up for answers. It was the sound of a class in progress, and, drawn by curiosity, she walked slowly through the gates into the courtyard—which was not unlike any other courtyard or barnyard of a great country villa in Galilee, open stables to one side, an enclosed herb garden on the other, and a wall and gateway on the side where she had entered. The fourth side of the enclosure was the back of the villa itself, kitchen and workrooms where the grapes were pressed for the wine and the olives for the oil, and where wheat was ground into flour, where chickens were plucked and cleaned, and where the fresh fruit was sliced and set out to dry. She could see men and women working in the sheds and kitchens, but her immediate attention was drawn to a great, spreading terebinth tree, which towered up higher than the roof of the villa and cast its great umbrella of shade over more than a third of the yard. Underneath this tree, in its cool shadows, there sat upon the ground at least forty or fifty boys between the ages of ten and sixteen—and among them, here and there, mature men, middle-aged men, and one or two very old men. A little apart from them and behind them, but still in the shelter of the tree, there was a cluster of about a dozen women and girls, some of the girls very small and nestling in the laps of their mothers.

In front of this group, a tall man paced back and forth, and in the first moment Berenice thought it was Shimeon Ben-gamaliel himself, so great was the likeness of movement and feature. A second glance told her it was another, a teacher here, talking and gesturing as he paced. Behind him there was a wooden table, and on it a jug of water, a cup, and an open scroll that was apparently a Torah. He gestured toward this as he talked and managed to notice Berenice out of the corner of an eye and nod at her without breaking his speech. The nod said, be welcome and sit down and stay if you wish. She stood a moment at the edge of the shade, and then sank down to the ground, her legs bent under her, the shade cool and pleasant after the morning in the sun. She was tired, and it was good to rest there.

"The Law," the teacher was saying, tapping his finger on the open scroll. "Why are we called the People of the Law?"

A skinny, freckled boy of fourteen or so rose up, cleared his throat, and said it was because Jews reverenced the Law above life itself.

"That's mighty peculiar," the teacher said. He looked at the boy; the boy looked at him. Faintly, from the distance came the sound of the women singing at the brookside as they washed clothes. Insects hummed and danced in the hot sunlight, outside the shade of the terebinth tree. It occurred to Berenice that this was a mighty peculiar school.

"I don't know how to reverence anything above life itself," said the teacher, after a few moments, "I don't mean that it isn't a good idea. It sounds attractive. I just don't know how. Do you, Abram?"

"I would die for the Torah," the skinny boy persisted.

"I am sure you would—but it's not a particularly engaging thought when there is so much to live for. Or is it? I have been thinking all morning about going fishing. You die—no more fishing. Never again. That's bleak, don't you agree?"

A little ripple of laughter among the others; no immediate reply from Abram; and, on Berenice's part, an increasing conviction that this was a very strange school indeed.

"What is the Law?" the teacher asked.

"The Torah."

"What is the Torah?"

"The Pentateuch—namely, Genesis, Exodus, Leviticus, Numbers, and Deuteronomy. The five books of the Law, which were written by the hand of Moses and inspired by the breath of the Almighty Himself."

The teacher, who continued to pace, took a deep breath and observed that he had gotten more than he had bargained for. "Sit down, Abram," he said. He tapped the scroll now. "I only desired to elicit the fact that the Torah is a book—an excellent and singular book—but still that, a book. These are recent observations, I will admit. In the time of my grandfather Hillel, of the blessed memory, who began this school here, the Torah was considered to be much more, treated as a force of magic, as a living thing—almost as the flesh of the Almighty Himself. Hillel was impatient with that kind of thinking, as you know." He pointed to another boy, "David—do you know the story of the pagan who came to Hillel to study the Law?"

David rose, scratched his head, and piped up that he did know the story. They all knew the story, except for Berenice; and this was very apparent to her.

"Tell it to us, and we'll pick at it a bit," the teacher said.

"From Parthia came the pagan," David began, "a long distance—"

"How long, David?" the teacher interrupted. "Philosophy is never the worse for the injection of some of the exactitude of geography."

"Thirty days' journey?" David asked tentatively.

"On foot? On a camel? On a horse? Hardly very exact.

Suppose we say three hundred parasangs, as the Persians measure it. As it is told, he was from Hecatompylos, in the heart of Parthia. Go on."

"He traveled this long distance," said David, "that he might become a Jew, and he sought out the Rabbi Hillel and said to him, 'I would study the Law, Rabbi Hillel, that I may become a Jew and know the Almighty as the one God.' To this, Hillel replied, 'Then I will teach you the Law. This is the Law, namely, Love thy neighbor as thyself. This is the whole Law. All the rest is commentary.' "

"Oh? Well," the teacher said, "I have heard this little tale a thousand times, yet I never hear it but it puzzles me. Thus. The Law is the Torah, yet Hillel made of it a commentary on a single injunction, Love thy neighbor as thyself. If that is the Law, then surely it is more important than the commentary. The substance must precede the commentary. And the substance must exist, even without the commentary—"

A middle-aged man arose, cleared his throat several times, and apologized for his temerity as well as his presence. He was a well-dressed, well-set man—as he explained it, a dealer in mother-of-pearl and other shell products, and on his way from his home in Damascus to the shell market at Tyre. It had been a privilege—to which he had looked forward for years—to see with his own eyes the place where the saintly Hillel had spent his last years, and an honor to sit among the students of Hillel's school, if only for an hour or two. Pardon him then for his daring to disagree; yet if you take away from a Jew his right to disagree, what is left to him?

"What, indeed?" the teacher smiled.

"So, Rabbi—" began the merchant from Damascus, but was stopped with an admonition that they in the House of Hillel used the term rabbi most sparingly. "My name is Hillel Bengamaliel," the teacher explained, "but I am no rabbi. The title is a high one in our house—"

The Jew from Damascus spread his hands in acknowledgment and addressed the teacher with the formal *Adon*, or as My Lord Hillel, the son of Gamaliel—stating that as this famous tale of the first Hillel was told in the synagogues of Damascus, the instructions of HIllel to the pagan from Parthia were somewhat different.

"Thus is it said in Damascus," said the traveler meekly, "that Hillel said to the pagan, 'Do not unto others as you wouldst not have them do unto you. This is the whole Law, and the rest is commentary.' "

"Indeed," agreed the teacher. "Yes indeed—so it is said, and that is unquestionably true."

"And the other?"

"Also true."

"But how can both be true?" the merchant pleaded in despair. "If one is the whole Law, then how can the other be the whole Law?"

"If they are the same?" He waited. The boy, David, sat down, and then the merchant seated himself.

"Do not unto others," he said thoughtfully. "Thus we have the negative. Love they neighbor—the positive; the two are contained."

The traveler shook his head slightly. The teacher went on, "Not quickly, but brood over it somewhat. It was my notion to talk to the children about the reaction to Hillel's action. Oh yes—some storms burst around his head, and there came to him from Jerusalem a group of learned Pharisees and scholars. They said to Hillel, 'Do you deny that the Almighty is in the Torah?' To which Hillel answered, 'The Almighty is everywhere.' But that was hardly enough, and the learned men demanded to know whether Hillel denied that God inspired the Torah. 'There is no great book which the Almighty has not inspired,' Hillel replied. He was not being clever. Hillel was never clever—yes, perhaps the wisest man in all the world, but never clever. He did not have the gift for that. Then the scholars demanded of him, 'Do you deny that the Torah is from the hand of Moses, may his name be remembered forever?' 'Could a Jew deny this?' Hillel asked, and then they said to him, 'Will you admit that the Torah is sacred and holy?' He admitted it, and then they charged him, 'But you state that it is commentary. What is more holy than the Law?' 'Many things,' Hillel replied. 'The Almighty is holier—and my child, too, for if I put the Law in flames, the Almighty would forgive me, but if I offered my child to the flames, He would never forgive me. And I will tell you something else,' Hillel said. 'Love is holier than the Law—' " The teacher paused, poured himself a cup of water, and drank.

"They were upset, those scholars," he continued. "They cried, 'What has Hillel done with God?' 'Is God so ineffectual that I could do this or that with Him?' Hillel replied."

"Zeno!" the merchant from Damascus snorted. "Did I come to the House of Hillel to hear the preachments of Zeno?"

"Oh no—no," the teacher said gently. "We are no Stoics here, and neither was the Rabbi Hillel. For the Stoics said that man can only live in the grandeur of a hero, facing his own fate, his own meaningless existence, recognizing it and living without fear of it. He preached that the good man was the wise man; but Hillel preached that the good man was he who loved his fellow man; and where the Stoics said there was no God but the cold rationale of nature and substance and being, Hillel said that the Almighty Himself is the author of all of nature and being. The Greeks would like God to be reason, but without love reason has no compassion. When the Pharisees demanded that Hillel define God, he did not retreat into a philosophical hole, as does the good Philo of Alexandria, who is entranced with the unknowability of God. These are the games of clever men. The Rabbi Hillel was not clever, only wise, and he said that the nature of God was love; the being of God compassion."

He drank water again and then said to the traveler from Damascus, "Stay with us a little. There is so much more—and so many loopholes in what I said that we can spend hours

plugging them. We talk a great deal at this school, but we also
learn a little—" As he spoke, he walked toward the merchant,
his voice dropping so that Berenice could no longer hear
what he said. The school, meanwhile, broke up into clusters
of men and boys, some in hot discussion, and then the
clusters began to coalesce around Hillel Bengamaliel. For
some reason, it reminded Berenice of her readings in Plato,
and she found herself thinking that the school of Socrates in
Athens could not have been too different from this. As the
others rose from the ground, she did, too, brushing the dust
off her dress. The woman with two small children, a dark-
eyed and comely woman, walked by, nodding at her and
smiling slightly. No one asked her who she was or why she
was there; and all in all, it appeared to be a place where any
and all were welcome and where any and all came.

Now, household slaves or servants—it was difficult for
Berenice to determine their status, so easy was their manner
and so readily did they talk to others—were bringing tables
and benches from the sheds to the shade of the great oak tree
and setting them up for the midday meal. The tables con-
sisted of planks laced onto crosspieces and set on sawhorses,
and the benches were of the simplest kind, but four long
tables were set up with space enough for half a hundred
people to eat. Some of the boys remained; others exploded
into freedom and ran whooping from the courtyard; and still
others went to the tables with their own packages of food.
Nothing seemed to be planned or ordered, yet everything
took place with dispatch and organization. A stream of
people were coming through the courtyard gate—field hands
burnt by the sun and glistening with the sweat of their work;
shepherds; the women whom Berenice had seen washing
clothes in the stream, now carrying huge baskets of wash
balanced on their heads; house-maids bowed with the weight
of fresh-water buckets; and strangely enough, two of the lean,
hard, and dirty bandits whom she had met in the band of
Zealots earlier this day—neither swaggering nor diffident,

but coming matter-of-factly to take their places at the table.

The tables were no longer empty. A stream of slaves brought an unending stream of edibles from the kitchen— platters of cucumbers and leeks, great bowls of fruit, trays piled high with smoked fish, bowls of dates and figs and grapes and olives and onions, and warm, sweet-smelling stacks of the round, pancakelike bread—and wine and water.

Standing, watching, Berenice told herself that not even a king, not even her brother could set such a table as a matter of routine, probably day in and day out. What then, she wondered, was this strange House of Hillel, nestling here in this fruitful valley only a few miles from Tiberias?

As if to answer Berenice's question, a man appeared whom she recognized, Shimeon, standing at a door to the house across the yard and looking at the people clustered around the tree. At his left there was a middle-aged woman, her gray hair piled upon her head, giving the impression of even more height than was actually hers. At his right, a thin man coming into his older years, gray beard streaked with white, the man himself clad in an ankle-length gown of blue linen, cut fully and belted in the Babylonian manner; and this man was talking to Shimeon as they walked out of the house and across the yard to the tree. Almost at the tree and already in the shade, Shimeon looked up from the commanding position of his height and saw her. Then he whispered something to the man and woman, left them, walked around the cluster of tables, where people were already eating, and directly over to Berenice—the surprise and disbelief on his face replaced now by very real delight; yet he did not take her hand or reach out to her. He stood before her with diffidence, no longer the doctora at his patient's bed; and it was more than this difference in him that Berenice felt, rather a difference that pervaded him, his manner, his being. He examined her with his eyes as a man examines a woman, her dusty feet, her stained clothes, and the kerchief wrapped tightly to conceal her torrent of auburn hair.

"How long have you been here, my lady?" he asked her.

"Perhaps an hour."

"Then forgive me for my failings as a host."

"It was a good hour. I sat at the edge of the school and I listened."

"There's a fate, for there's nothing in the world charms my brother Hillel like the sound of his own voice. Come—please." He led her to one side, where there was an old mounting bench, and then he motioned to a slave and told him to bring a basin and water. He knelt in front of Berenice as he unbuckled her sandals.

"Shouldn't you be there?" Berenice asked, nodding at the tables.

"There—you mean to eat? No, no—I hold with my blessed mentor, Hippocrates, that three quarters of the physical evils that beset mankind flow from eating too much, not too little. But they will be at it for a while, and there is food enough. When the House of Hillel dines, the world stands still." The slaves returned with the water now, and Shimeon poured it into the basin and began to wash Berenice's feet.

More times than she could count she had had her feet washed, but never exactly like this, so easily and spontaneously and with hands that rippled the whole fiber of her body whenever they touched her. She could have closed her eyes and said—as she thought—go on like this and wash them for ever and ever, and wash away everything that hurts and exacerbates and torments and shames, and leave them clean and leave me clean—but these were thoughts out of the strangeness of the occasion, and to feel something one had never felt before can be more disquieting than anything else. As he washed her feet, Shimeon told her of his amazement when he first saw her, yet he had recognized her immediately—

"Which," he said, "is rather strange, because you look different."

"Because my hair is covered?"

"No. No—I think—you will be angry if I say it?" He had to talk loudly to be heard over the babble of voices from the tables.

"Nothing could make me angry here."

"Well, that's it," Shimeon nodded.

"I don't understand."

"There's no hate, no anger. You were always angry. Such anger! If it were not blasphemous to think of the Almighty as a woman, I would say it reminded me of the stories in the Torah—when God explodes in anger at Moses."

He added, grinning, "That was very regal anger—if you know what I mean?"

"I don't know whether you're mocking me or praising me or scolding me."

"Not scolding you—" He dried her feet with linen napkins. "Mockery and praise—yes, that's the due of a queen—"

"And yet you're not surprised to find me here?" Berenice said.

"Surprised? No. Perhaps in our ego, we have come to believe that the whole world will come to the House of Hillel—sooner or later. And there is some truth in that. Here have come kings and procurators and proconsuls and tetrarchs and alabarchs and princes and priests—and heaven knows what other titles. And most go away disappointed that what they have heard so much of is merely a Galilean farmhouse, a country villa, and far from the largest in Galilee. Are you disappointed, Queen Berenice—no, I did not mean to call you that."

"I don't understand this place," she replied. "Will you call me Berenice? I will call you Shimeon, and we will be friends. I never had a friend. Will you be my friend, Shimeon?"

"If you wish—and what is not to be understood here, Berenice?"

"Just"—her sandals buckled on, her feet cool and clean, she dipped a linen napkin into the water and washed her face and hands—"all of this," she said. "What is it? What are you? You are not a sect—not a party. In one breath you will link yourselves with the Pharisees, and in the next breath you denounce them. You appear to be without weapon and without rancor, and I see no soldiers anywhere, no arms; yet those two Zealots who came in here to your table as if it were at their hearth and home and under their own rooftree—they're as hard-bitten and bloody-minded a pair of bandits as I have ever seen, and I saw them on the road this morning where they and their comrades were cursing the fate that led them to miss an Arab caravan—which they would have looted, and murdered too—"

"The Zealots come here," Shimeon nodded. "Why not? They have no homes, many of them, no land, no rooftree, and here they can sit an hour in peace and fill their bellies. Does that hurt anyone?"

"Hurt? I don't understand you. Your brother preaches a God of love and compassion—"

"As we all do."

—"and decries the Torah—"

"No," Shimeon smiled, "we honor the Torah, but we honor people more—is that mysterious?"

"But all of this"—she waved at the tables, suddenly very hungry with the hot smell of broken bread everywhere now—"what does it mean?"

"People are hungry, and they are fed. Thus it must be at the House of Hillel," said Shimeon. "And when it cannot be this way, the House of Hillel will crumble."

"But this? Oh, I have heard about the Essenes and their monasteries in the desert by the Dead Sea—but they are holy men, and their common table is an altar to God, and they take no wives but eat their crust of bread and drink their cup of water—"

"And they live in poverty and filth, and they exalt filth and worship poverty, and they hate women and fear women, and their holiness can be measured by the smell and their piousness by the shout of doom that arises from their grim and ugly nests—and the more they suffer, the larger their pride; and if a wise man or a learned man, an engineer or an architect or a doctor should come among them, they sould scourge him out like a pestilence. They fear knowledge and they love ignorance; they whip each other the better to glorify the Almighty, and they go on long fasts, until they look like famine victims, and for this they ask God's approval—oh, tell me, Berenice, do you admire them?"

"They are fanatics," Berenice said, "but they are holy men."

"Ha—that I should hear Berenice Basagrippa parroting phrases. Holy men indeed!"

"And how do you honor the Almighty?" Berenice asked.

"As men should, I think. There is no hatred in the House of Hillel. In the Torah, it says that the Almighty made man in His own image, so to us the body of man is holy—the superb and supreme work of God. To allow a fellow man among us to go unfed is sinful. To hate Jew or Gentile is sinful—and these things we eschew—as we do the bearing of arms, and if need be, we will die before we raise a hand against a fellow man. We hold that the love of a man for a woman and of a woman for a man is holy and perfect—and we work to understand the meaning of love and compassion, so we can practice both. We are Jews—but no Gentile has ever been turned away from the House of Hillel, and many come here. But enough of this schooling and preaching—come with me, Berenice, and meet my father and mother and the others of my family."

The torrent of words and the passion implicit amazed Berenice, and she said nothing as he took her hand and led her toward the tables. Indeed, there was nothing she could think of that must be said. The whole world was new, and this was either a madhouse or a dream—and it was more likely a madhouse, since Berenice had never been one to stumble over the difference between dreams and reality; and if it were that, its inhabitants were well chosen, for this physician had been mad in the beginning when he tore down the drapes and blinds in her chambers and roared out his intolerant theories of medicine and health. Then he had spoken around her and now he spoke to her, but his words were no more sensible in terms of the plain world of wealth and manners and ambition in which she spent her life.

"And thieves come here," she managed to say finally.

"Thieves, murderers, sinners, and even some saints, and devils too—and this, Berenice, is my kinblood, my father, Gamaliel the son of Hillel the Babylonian, who was the founder of our house." He bowed, an older man than she had suspected from the distance, courtly, gentle, his twinkling blue eyes hidden under shaggy white brows. He had been watching her and now he regarded her shrewdly, as he broke a piece of bread, dipped it in salt, and offered it to her.

"Take our bread from my hand and honor me, my child," he said. She took the bread. "Eat, please. I have hoped that my son would bring a woman to our table, but one so beautiful—"

She munched the bread. "This is my mother, Sarah," Shimeon said, watching with pleasure the way Berenice's strong white teeth chewed so hungrily at the salted bread.

"Welcome and peace—but I look deeper than my husband for beauty."

"And to you, peace," Berenice replied. "If I have beauty, it has brought me no happiness. Your bread is good, and blessed is the house where the bread of the earth is savored."

The old man chuckled with pleasure, and Shimeon introduced her to his brother, "Hillel, my brother—he teaches of wisdom and confusion, and he will make you believe that the two are identical—as perhaps they are."

"We teach, we learn, and we practice medicine," the old man shrugged.

"I saw her," Hillel nodded. "As she came in through the gate. You are a tall woman, and striking—"

"Thank you."

Shimeon was introducing his sister-in-law now. "Deborah."

"Bas Shaba," she named her house. "We are from across the river in the Land of Gad. I have been his wife nine years, yet I am a stranger here."

"What nonsense," Hillel declared.

"Will you bare you head?" Sarah, the mother, asked. "Or must you keep it covered?"

"My head?" Berenice asked, confused a moment.

"You have beautiful eyes," Deborah said. They were as simple and direct in their observations as children. "Your eyes remind me of Berenice, the queen of shame, may God spare her His anger." And then she realized what she had said and whom she was talking to, even before Berenice untied the kerchief to reveal the red braids.

"I have eaten your bread," she said in a hoarse whisper, and then her voice choked in her throat and she started away, the tears flowing down her cheeks. Sarah, the mother embraced her. Not for a moment had Berenice dreamed that there would be such strength in the old woman.

"Let me go," Berenice cried chokingly.

"No, no," Sarah said woefully. "Sooner would I go myself and never lay eyes on this goodly house again. No, because if you go in your grief at our cruelty and obtuseness, then this house is worthless and will soon crumble. Let it be ashes."

Then Berenice stood still, unresisting, and Gamaliel, the son of Hillel, said to her, "Honor us and break your fast here. There is good food and good wine on our table."

But Shimeon said nothing, only watching her through narrowed eyes; and through the cloak of self-pity that covered her the way it covers a little girl, she was aware of this.

Sitting by her side at the table a while later, the old man, the father, Gamaliel, was explaining his years and how Shimeon was the last child of his loins. There had been a bewildering array of daughters and grandchildren and great-grandchildren—so that Berenice was utterly confused—and most of them speechless anyway as they faced this strange-looking green-eyed woman with her two plaits of red hair, who was queen of Chalcis, but to the child's geography, having never seen another queen, was the queen of queens, queen of the Jews and perhaps the Gentiles too, and at the same time Berenice the infamous and frightful. The father linked their houses through marriage, but the thread was very thin.

"More to the point," he told her, "I knew your Great-grandfather Herod the Great. He came here, you know—here to our house to visit my father, Hillel, and they stood face to face, and my father Hillel welcomed him. Then a saint welcomes a devil? Herod asked. He was no fool, be sure of that, my child, but a big, handsome man of great personal beauty, and my father said to him, If I measure your deviltry by my own saintliness, my own reputation to the man I actually am—well, I can say that the reports on both sides are vastly exaggereated. Herod roared with laughter—he was a clever man, may the Almighty hold his poor twisted soul gently and kindly, but my father was a wise man, and we are great ones here to put cleverness on one side of a knife edge and wisdom on the other. So he broke bread with us and took our salt right here, under this terebinth tree, did your blood ancestor—and young as I was, I felt the curse it was for a man to be a king—"

"But how can it be?" Berenice insisted. "Why did I never know? I live a few miles away, and all that I heard of the House of Hillel was mockery and distortion."

"Because your father feared us and his father feared us—and because here was something they feared but could not destroy. And then, already in your father's time, Berenice, he saw that neither the kingly House of Herod nor the kingly House of Mattathias nor the Romans would decide the fate of Israel and the fate of Jewry the world over—God help me, perhaps even the fate of the world itself; no, neither of these." He paused and nodded at the Zealots, who ate silently at another table. "Them—or ourselves. There is the fate of Israel. Either the House of Shammai"—he dropped his voice—"whose tool is the sword and the spear, and whose preacher is the Zealot; or the House of Hillel, whose tool is love and whose preacher is the physician. Wherever there are Jews today, wherever there is a synagogue, from the Ganges River to the coast of Cornwall, Israel is divided between our two houses—and in all things Shammai and Hillel differ."

Berenice resisted it; the whole flow of forces, as presented by this old man, made no sense to her. She was no stranger to politics. Still an infant, she had sucked the pap of politics and power, and all her growing years it had been in her house what talk of weather, clothes, and food is in another. The House of Herod lived and breathed the politics of cities and nations, the force of armies, the lust of princes—and she knew power. Or at least she believed she she did; and to Berenice power was money and resources, gold and iron and copper and wheat, mercenaries and ships of war and walled cities, taxes and imposts and tithes—these were the blood and substance of power, and not an old Jewish philosopher sitting under an oak tree and talking of love and compassion.

On the other side of her, Shimeon watched her. "He is comparing me with the women here," she thought with irritation. "Why doesn't he say anything?"

Gamaliel, the father, nodded. Her understood her, strangely enough. "Ten years ago, my dear," he said. "you were a little girl, and in all the hills there were not enough Zealots to fill a synagogue. Now they number thousands— and tomorrow?"

"They are bandits, fanatics, of no consequence. A troop of our horse guard would sweep them out of Galilee," Berenice said.

One of the Zealots paused in his eating and glanced at her. Had he overheard her? No—he was too far away.

"I would be slow to try," Shimeon's brother said thoughtfully.

"What we are—how that must puzzle you," the old man

said. "But it must, my child—I mean no mockery. I am still a Jew, and I talk to the last of the Hasmoneans. Should I not venerate you?"

Berenice shook her head dumbly. She had never known people like these. When she most needed to rage and defy, they took all the wind out of her sails and left her only with the curious glow of their affection.

"But what is a Jew?" he went on. "We of the House of Hillel explain ourselves in this way: that the only difference between the Jew and the Gentile is an awareness. Such is the meaning of the *covenant* we have with God, and for more than half a hundred years, we have taught this creed here at this house under this oak tree—and from here our teachings have traced their way all over the world. Do you know, we here estimate that since the death of my beloved father, may he rest in peace, nearly a million of the goyim have become Jews. Do you know what that means? You saw what King Polemon went through with his circumcision—think of half a million circumcisions. Such is the belief and need that we have engendered among mankind—such is the power of compassion. Have we an argument with Herod? With Rome? With Egypt? I think not. There are only two mighty forces in the Almighty's world today—Rome and Judaism. If the House of Hillel prevails, Judaism will win. But those—"

Again, he looked at the Zealots. "Yes, our doors are open to the members of the House of Shammai. We turn no one away—but to them we are an abomination. They dare not lift a hand against us, because the people love us too much; but they preach their own creed. Every Roman must die, they cry. Every goy is accursed. No Jew must eat with a Gentile, talk to a Gentile, trade with a Gentile, shelter under the same roof with a Gentile. We must build a wall between ourselves and the world, and we must fast out those who came to us because they saw that what we have is good. Deep in the South, the House of Shammai has taken to monasteries and thrust away women. They have embraced a fanatical madness, which they call the Law, and they hide in the heat and misery of their caves and crannies. But here in the North, they live for war and dream of war—and each day there are more of them. For they offer the young man a dream of power and glory and a return to the ancient days of greatness—which were only days of sorrow—"

Abruptly, the old man finished. "I talk too much. It is a disease of the old—"

The day was a dream, unreal, an eternity of slow movement. Later, she was weary, and Deborah took her into the house. The rooms were large and simple and cooled by ceiling-high vents through which a cool breeze blew, a miracle of engineering through an analysis of air currents. The walls were limed white, and the furniture was plain, simple, and in good taste. She lay down on a bed and scarcely had closed her eyes but she was asleep. She was nursed in the bosom of a mother; she was rocked in a cradle; she was secure; she was like a lamb, and the Lord was her shepherd. She dreamed of the House of Hillel, where they had been waiting for her. In her dream, someone said, "Cometh now the queen of the Jews." The voices were all raised in a mighty hallelujah, and she walked among throngs of people.

She was awakened by a boy's clear, pure alto voice, ringing like a glass bell tapped, singing:

"Hear, O Israel! The Lord is our God! The Lord is one!"

It was the call to prayer before sundown. Rubbing her eyes, she went to the window of the shadow-full room and looked out into the courtyard. The boy was a lad of thirteen or so. He stood in the shadows on a two-wheeled cart, his hands cupped, singing again in his trilling and pure alto:

"Hear, O Israel! The Lord is our God—"

Had she ever heard anything so beautiful? She didn't know, and she looked up at the deep blue sky over Galilee, the hillside hiding the sun already; and below her the courtyard was filling with people—men from the fields and men

173

from the house and the school and travelers from the road who had paced their journey so that they might partake of the evening prayer here at the House of Hillel—a few at first and then more and more, the courtyard filling. It was full when she came down from the room and out past the kitchen. They were roasing lamb now. Were the fires never cold in these kitchens?

The old man, the father, walked through the courtyard, which was filled now with people. They opened a path for him, and he walked like some Bedouin memory, covered head to foot in a great stripped prayer-shawl, and near the two-wheeled cart he stood on a platform of bricks and chanted from the Hundredth Psalm: "The Lord is good. His mercy is everlasting. His truth shall endure forever."

Thus the service began.

Shimeon walked back to Tiberias with her. A golden moon had come up over the hills, and in its light they walked without haste and at first in silence. Berenice was thinking of a good many things, and it occurred to her that Shimeon also had one or two matters on his mind, and when finally she spoke it had to be at least in a measure of derision—"For I know something of people, too," she said, "and the world is what it is, more or less the open gut of a stuck pig."

"That's one way to look at it," he agreed.

"Is there another way? Is that the Garden of Eden back here?"

"No—only a farm."

"No hate, jealousy, lust in the House of Hillel?"

"Yes—all the things that human beings edify themselves with. We only try not to make it admirable."

"Then where and precisely how did this house come into being? Didn't I hear the stories of Hillel, the ragged boy from Babylon? But now poverty is forgotten, isn't it?"

"We make no virtue of poverty," Shimeon shrugged. "There are the sects of Shammai that do, but we see no benediction in hunger or degradation."

"And your wealth—property, cattle, food—where does the food come from?" she demanded stridently.

"Berenice," he said, "we are no threat to you or your house. People give us food—as they gave us land and the house—so that the school may exist and that there be a place of Hillel. My grandfather never asked, but neither did he refuse what was given. Why do you want to doubt us and hate us?"

"Why should I hate you?" she shrugged.

Shimeon made no answer to that, and they walked on in silence; but things gnawed at her and irritated her, and finally she burst out, "You know how you make me feel?—like a barbarian—and all that honey flow of sanctimonious talk of love! Oh, you make me sick with it!"

Still no answer from Shimeon, and she quickened her pace. But a little while later he asked her why.

"Why what?"

"Why do we make you sick with our talk?"

"Because it's a lie."

"In our teachings, all lies contain an element of truth—"

"I really couldn't care less about what you teach, and I don't think I want to talk about it."

So again they walked on in silence, and presently she felt his hand touching her, the back of his hand brushing the back of hers, and she began to tighten like a wild animal aware of danger. Then he took her hand. She did not draw it away, but it lay limp. She was tight and tense, and her fear had no point of origin.

At the city gates the soldiers on guard were in a tight group in the shadows, their deep voices mingled with the laughter of girls. There was precious little attempt at military standards in Tiberias. No enemy threatened them, and to the north and to the south the Roman legions guarded the frontiers. Berenice's head was covered again, and no one recognized her. They walked on to the palace, and then when Shimeon would have left her, she clung to him for a moment, explaining that he must look at the lake from the palace landing. "On a night like this, the lake is the most beautiful thing in the world." But he said simply, "I think that on a night like this, you are the most beautiful thing in the world." And to that she did not react, only to wonder vaguely what he meant and why he had said something of that sort. She began to talk quickly once they were on the stone landing, telling him how as children she and her brother, Agrippa, lived in the lake. "There is an old story that under Geshur—that's the old, old name for the lake and for the land to the east of here—there is an entire city, and people live there, and we believed that one day they would catch us and take us down there—"

Out on the lake, the fishermen were at work with torches. The light of their torches glittered on the lake, and faintly came the sound of their voices.

—"but you're not listening."

"I was watching the fishermen, Berenice." He took her by her shoulders, turned her to him, and gently lifted her face to his. She found herself thinking how odd it was that a man should be so much taller than she, but otherwise had no reaction. He was staring at her, and she looked up into his eyes; but when he tried to draw her toward him and kiss her, she tensed and pulled away. His arms tightened. She struggled and then struck him across the cheek with all her strength.

"Poor thing—why are you so afraid?" he asked gently. Then he let go of her, and she sank down on the warm stone of the landing. He knelt on one knee next to her, and she would not look at him, covering her face with her hands.

"Are you always afraid?" he asked her.

She nodded, screaming inside of herself for him to go away, "Leave me, leave me, leave me!" But this silently.

"Always afraid—of course."

"Go away," she whispered, pleading with him, begging him. "Go away and leave me alone."

"And then, Berenice? What then? A whole life as empty as a dry gourd?"

"It was always empty."

"That doesn't mean it always will be empty. Take your hands away from your face, Berenice. Uncover it." Her hands fell, and then he reached out and drew her to her feet, rising himself and then standing before her. "Do I mean you harm? Hurt?"

"You have a wife," she pleaded, feeling her own inner defenses crumble, feeling panic beat at her heart in compulsive and frightful waves.

"I have no wife," Shimeon answered. "I was married once, Berenice. My wife died. I was a physician, and I couldn't save her. I have no wife. I am twenty-eight years old now—four years since my wife died, and I have kissed no other woman and loved no other woman. I love you, Berenice. I love you with all my heart, and when I close my eyes, I see you clearly as when they are open."

"You fool, you fool," she found herself whimpering, "Don't you know who I am? I am the abomination of Israel—the whore of Herod—"

"I think I know you better than you know yourself."

"I am no good for any man—"

"Let me decide," he said softly, drawing her to him, and after resisting a moment, she buried her face in the coarse linen of his coat, savoring the smell of him, the hard, firm front of him, the rocklike strength of him. The waves of panic beat more slowly now. His arms around her were like two walls. She took shelter there, and then slowly, fearfully, she raised her face to look at him. Then he kissed her. The fear was not yet gone, but she could control it, master it, and know the strange, hot wonderful fact of a man's kisses on her face. It was the first time.

Vibius Marsus, proconsul of Syria, came down from Damascus, bringing with him Achon Baravrim, a withered, tight-mouthed Jew who was grain engrosser for the whole of Syria and possessed of very considerable power. By prearrangement, Ventidius Cumanus, the new procurator of Judea, was at Tiberias to meet him. They met together with King Agrippa.

It was always a tense time in Tiberias when one or another of the Roman governors came there to visit. Not only was Tiberias more Jewish than Jerusalem, having been built by Jews where there was no city before, but on any day its streets would be host to ten or ten hundred Zealots, angry, well-armed devotees of the House of Shammai. The Roman guards who accompanied the governors moved carefully through the streets of Tiberias, never a legionary alone but always three or four or ten of them clustered warily together. Today they were even warier than usual, and there were no smiles for them in the streets. Ventidius Cumanus, the new procurator, was a gross, self-indulgent, and stupid man, with a large belly, a pimpled face, and the conviction—born out of ignorance and belief in the current anti-Semitic mores of the time—that the Jews worshiped nothing and were rejected of all the gods. In a matter of months he had made himself the most hated procurator in the history of the Roman occupation; and the fact that he had arrived in Tiberias to meet with Vibius Marsus and the grain engrosser did nothing to soften his reputation. All grain engrossers, partially because they were so influential in fixing the price of the crop and partially because they worked hand in glove with the Romans, were feared and hated by the people. Whatever Rome conquered was added to her rapacious, insatiable, and expanding breadbasket, and grain was the blood flow of the Empire.

The meeting took place in Agrippa's throne room, and in addition to the two Romans and the grain engrosser, Bendavid and Bensimon were present, and Anat Beradim too, the wood merchant who had become very close to the young king. Agrippa spared no effort to make his Roman guests at home, the best food, the best fruit, the best wine, ices and sweetmeats and various appetizing delicacies brought from places as far away as China. The meeting went well, but he could not keep his sister out of it, and finally the Romans demanded that she be present. Agrippa sent for her.

Anticipating that she would be sent for, Berenice had dressed carefully, an overdress of green silk to set off her incredible eyes and a net of sewn pearls and tiny bits of jade for her hot auburn hair. The hair was braided and gathered in a bun at the base of her neck; and she came into the room where they were with such poise and assurance that even the Romans were taken aback; and before anyone spoke, she said to Vibius Marsus,

"Last week, I sent a letter to your emperor, may he know many good days, and I told him of your earnestness. I also told him that I measured every action by his image—"

That it was a lie Vibius Marsus took for granted; but no one was ever certain that Berenice was lying, and even when certain, men thought twice before challenging her. Marsus noticed a difference about her—but he could not put his finger on it. What gossip had he heard?—that she had taken to the House of Hillel or was in the process of an affair with some scion of the house? As many years as he had spent in Jewish lands, Vibius Marsus was still confused by the intricate schematics of their class structure and nobility—the Gen Hacohen, the House of David, the line of Mattathias Hacohen, the House of Mattathias, the line of Hasmonea, the Gen Halevi, the House of Herod, the line of Elisha, the Gen Hagershon—one could go on and on, but unless one were born a Jew, one could never unravel or make sense of their relationships—yet it was still inconceivable that there could be a union between the House of Herod and the House of Hillel. Although in all truth, this Agrippa was as un-Herodian as any human being could be.

"My dear," Agrippa said, appreciative of her gentle manner of taking the wind out of their sails, "this is Achon

Baravrim—may there be peace between our houses—of Damascus, who is grain engrosser there."

Berenice nodded at Ventidius Cumanus and smiled at Anat Beradim. The tight, dried-up Achon Baravrim was conscious of her snub but undisturbed by it. He was a grain engrosser, a Samaritan-Israelite by ancestry, and the grandson of a slave; and thereby he was used to snubs, expected them from royalty and nobility, expected and received respect from crowned rulers of cities and states, was very rich and quite satisfied to be by birth the lowest of the low.

"Our city is honored by your presence," Berenice said to all of them.

"We are honored by your beauty," Ventidius Cumanus replied. He was attempting manners. Romans were intensely conscious of a lack of manners on their part, and of late they had gone in for polite phraseology, which ill became them. It was un-Roman. Vibius Marsus frowned and made it plain that he bore no love for his fellow citizen and would grovel to no one to ape a despised Easterner, and he said to Berenice,

"Queen Berenice, suppose we come to the point. There is no need to preface our language with a study of politics. We are all well versed, and I don't have to expound on the relationship between Roman power and bread."

"I like your clear and sensible approach to things," Berenice acknowledged, smiling. "But I can't believe that a convocation on this level and of this importance was called simply because I decided to give bread to the hungry of Tiberias."

"Of all Galilee is nearer the truth," the grain engrosser snapped.

"To whosoever is hungry," Berenice shrugged. "I do not inquire for his home, his house, his place of birth or his birth. If he desires bread, he may have bread. And whose affair is that, may I ask? I buy the bread. I pay for it with my own money."

"Bread is always Rome's affair," Marsus said reasonably.

"And in Rome do the hungry die of their hunger? Or are they given bread?"

"That is the Roman way."

"It is also the Jewish way," Berenice countered, smiling.

"Sister," said Agrippa, "I am here as a neutral, so to speak. I never questioned your decision to give bread to the hungry. I neither agreed nor disagreed. Not long ago, you were sick; now you are well—and that is enough for me. If you desire to give bread away—"

"Who can afford to give bread away?" the grain engrosser cried.

"Little man," Berenice said ominously, "don't interrupt my brother when he speaks. My brother is king—and you are here purely by sufferance, as any other Samaritan would be. So take heed."

He bristled and spluttered, but Agrippa calmed him. "My sister can afford it," Agrippa said. "She is a very rich woman—possibly the richest woman in Israel, so have no qualms about what she can afford."

"It corrupts the people!" Baravrim said.

"Starvation corrupts more stringently, believe me," Berenice said.

"Why not to the point?" Vibius Marsus demanded. "And the point is simply this—is this Rome's bread that you are buying for your dole, Queen Berenice?"

"Is there a shortage of bread in Rome?"

"That is neither here nor there. I understand that you approached Baravrim here for grain, and that he refused to sell—because to sell would have cut into supplies earmarked for Roman consumption—"

"He lies," Berenice said indifferently. "He's a dirty little swine, you know—"

"I will not stand this!" Baravrim cried shrilly. "I will not be insulted by this Jezebel! I will not—"

—"and he was perfectly willing to sell me all the grain I required at twice the price the Parthians were paying him—"

Suddenly Baravrim was quiet, and the quiet enveloped the room, and all Berenice heard was the hoarse breathing of the men, and then the voice of Marsus, almost offhand, "Is that true, Baravrim?"

"Lies, lies, lie," whimpered the little man.

"I will find out, for course."

"A few bushels a month—"

"Nearer twenty thousand bushels a month," Berenice said.

Agrippa pointed to the guards at the door and then to the grain engrosser. "Take him away," he said, and then began an apology to Vibius Marsus. "I don't want to hear it," the Roman said. "You knew it as little as I did." Berenice watched him inquiringly, and Marsus said, "All right—do as you please."

"Will you sell me grain in Damascus?"

"We will sell you grain in Damascus," Marsus sighed.

But now Berenice lived in a lopsided world that no longer smacked of reason or familiarity. A long stone house was built outside of Tiberias for the milling of flour, and in the bakers' quarters of Tiberias the ovens were never cold. Such was the activity of the ovens that where there had been one charcoal burner before, now there were three, and where there had been one baker, now there were half a dozen. The prosperity of the city increased, and the hungry were fed, and although she never advertised it, the knowledge of Berenice's role spread about. There was no hunger in Galilee because Berenice fed the hungry, and even in Samaria, where the crops had been poor, the word was spoken, and skinny, half-starving Samaritans dared the roads of Galilee and the hatred of the Zealots to share in the bread that was baked in Tiberias. That the people have short memories and fickle emotions was not a surprise to Berenice; yesterday, she had been the whore of the ages, the abomination of abominations, the shameful bitch of the House of Herod. A mouthful of well-baked bread disposed of the Herodian side of her ancestry, and now she became Berenice the Hasmonean, the good queen of mercy.

And outside of the gates of Tiberias, the Romans crucified the grain engrosser, Achon Baravrim. When the court was convened, Agrippa, as king of Galilee and Chalcis, had to preside and sit in judgment, but Vibius Marsus made it plain what the verdict must be. In the whole world, Rome had only one military enemy. There was only one nation contemptuous enough to defy Rome, adroit enough to baffle Rome, and nimble enough to bring disaster to every Roman army sent against it—and that was Parthia, with its thousands of marvelous horsemen; and as he sat in judgment Agrippa remembered how he and Berenice had whispered of the possibility of uniting Parthia and Israel—and wiping out the power of Rome forever. They were scarcely more than children then, and childlike they were mouthing his father's dream. Today Agrippa sent Baravrim to his death; and seeing the little man hanging from the crucifix, Berenice was suddenly sickened, nauseated by the whole spectacle and her part in it as well. She shared none of the joy of the population of Tiberias, who came to the crucifix and spat at the grain engrosser, symbol of all they hated and feared, and when they cheered her as she passed through the gate, she felt a sense of shame—or rather a confusion of shame.

She had given the people bread because she felt, for the first time in her life, an irresistible compulsion to give. She was full and flowing over with her fullness, and she had to share it and let it pour out of her. She had no desire to be the good queen of mercy, and she took no great satisfaction from it. The gesture she made had been a small one and no great effort—to issue orders that grain should be milled and bread baked.

She had also killed a man, indirectly yet deliberately; and with equal deliberation and indirectness, she had sat in judgment upon him. Even though he was a hated grain engrosser, she slept less well. Lying awake in the dark, she was moved to ask the Almighty for forgiveness. It was the second time in her life that Berenice had pleaded for anything.

Most of her meetings with Shimeon took place at the House of Shlomo in Tiberias. On her own part, she would have had him to the palace, paraded him there, flaunted him there—or anywhere else that was hers—but he was not a man to be paraded or flaunted. He did not come to her; she came to him. He would come and he would go. His profession took him to many places; he would be gone a day, a week, or a month, and then a messenger would come to the palace from the House of Shlomo, with word that Queen Berenice was expected. Never did old Gideon Benharmish, head of the house, allow the respect due her to falter. The old man, like the crucified grain engrosser, was an Israelite without blood or rank or ancient family, and for all his wealth and power, he bowed low to Berenice when she entered his house, addressing her as Queen Berenice Basagrippa Hacohen, honoring both her bloodlines in the most formal of formal greeting, and said: "Peace be upon you and your House and all your ancestors, may they dwell in peace alongside of the Almighty." He had a manner more courtly than many a prince even though in all likelihood he came from Samaritan blood, and the doors of his house were not only open, but frequently entered.

In the large, open dining room and patio of the House of Shlomo, a room that extended down to the lake in broad marble steps and was furnished exquisitely, one was likely to find the most interesting as well as the most important people of the Middle Eastern world. It might be the high priest of Jerusalem, passing through Galilee, the proconsul of Syria, the alabarch of Antioch, or Rabbi Barlazen or Rabbi Ish Kemel, or the shriveled Indian philosopher, Budikka, who had come from the Ganges to spend his last years in Caesarea, waiting for a wise king on a white horse to ride by and tell him the secret of eternity, or Mika Benyosha, who preached the gospel of Rabbi Joshua, who had been crucified outside of Jerusalem a decade and a half past, or a Greek teacher-philosopher or architect or engineer, or a Babylonian seer, or a Phoenician sea captain to enthrall all present with the wonders of Africa or the British Isles, or any one of a hundred Jews who commanded the far-flung trade routes of the whole known world and had their clerks and account books in places as far separated as Ireland and China. Or it might be any one of a number of people of Galilee, as, for example, Shimeon of the House of Hillel or Agrippa of the House or Herod or his sister Berenice.

It might well be Shimeon and Berenice, for they were together there more and more, and no one questioned the relationship between them; and even Berenice's brother, the young King Agrippa, accepted the fact that his beloved and wonderful sister—as he saw her—had finally given her heart to a man.

But in so far as Berenice herself was concerned, it was her whole life and being. She was twenty-three years old now, a late age for a woman to taste love for the first time; and in those days even later. She did not simply fall in love; she became a creature of love; she lived for it. She bowed her head to emotional storms that ripped her through and through, as if she were staked out as a lightning rod in some vast electrical storm. She lay awake and wept out nights, but her superb health masked it, and she glowed with a beauty that was breath-taking. People who saw her for the first time would gaze entranced, forgotten of courtesy—and yet she was impervious to this. She had created a new world, in the center of which was Shimeon Bengamaliel. She listened to all he said, forcing herself to comprehend and accept; she bound herself in iron bands of control, holding in check her imperious nature, her violent temper; and even more than that, she fought the battle with her own terror of men and sex.

She won her battle. It came when she was out on the lake

with Shimeon, he paddling a flat wooden skiff and herself sprawled on a floor of cushions and a mat, her face on a level with his foot, touching his foot, spelling out sinews and toes with her fingernail. Then he put the paddle aside and lay down next to her, his dark eyes so close that she could see her own reflection in them—and then he made love to her. She was afraid. She lay there, her wild green eyes hooded with terror, stiff, uncomprehending, unresponding—yet holding herself while his hands and his voice softened her, so that it appeared to her that she melted little by little, melted under some kind of dark sun, until the flame entered her and she was burning and writhing and screaming her pain and agony and fierce joy—and then dissolving onto a long, gentle, and endless incline. Not only had this never happened before, but not in her wildest dreams had she ever believed that such a thing could happen—yes, to animals and to people like Gabo, her slave, and to the whores and concubines of the court—but not to Berenice—

Night fell, and she threw off her clothes and slipped over the side of the boat into the water. Shimeon could not swim—a thing that amazed her—and she said she would teach him, but he shook his head, staring puzzled and with wonder at this long-limbed, tawny woman, whose coppery skin flashed with the joy and ease of one born to the water—

"Help me in!" she cried. She was shameless. She curled naked at the bottom of the boat, while he looked at her in amazement. "Do you still love me, Shimeon?" she asked him. "When I am no queen—but like this, and wanton? You're ashamed, aren't you?"

He nodded.

"You're such a big, stupid trained bear. Laugh. Laugh at me. Oh, you're so much the Jew!"

"You're the most beautiful woman on earth," he replied finally. "You're not real, and I think you are part devil, but I would cut out my heart for you."

"What a thing to say!" she cried, laughing at him. "Like

your entire family, you are probably very wise but not at all clever—and I have absolutely no use for your heart if you cut it out."

"And if it stays here?"

"Then I want it for myself—forever."

Such a thing had to be talked about. It was too rare, too juicy with fascination, too improbable to be avoided; and from Phrygia to Alexandria, through that half of the world which was a domain of Jewish lands, Jewish cities, Jewish enclaves, and Gentiles who noted every move that the Jews made—all through that area the romance between Shimeon Bengamaliel and Berenice Basagrippa was observed and dwelt upon. The she-devil, the whore-of-Babylon, had ensnared the scion of the House of Saints; and since the House of Hillel was a little less than wholly admired by Jewish wealth and nobility, it was an unexpected but welcome opportunity to undercut what the Hillelites stood for. In the synagogues of Galilee where the House of Shammai dominated, Zealot preachers made the most of this union of so-called goodness with the devil.

"Be ye warned!" they cried out.

But the bread that Berenice gave away was real, and the taste of it lingered. Her brother Agrippa was thankful for the process of the bread when he called her in to him and asked her,

"How long do you expect to continue with this, Berenice?"

"Forever."

"Come now," Agrippa smiled. "There is no forever—which you know as well as I do."

"I love him, brother. He's the only man I ever loved—yes, yourself, as they say, but you are my brother whatever they say. He is a man and my lover."

"He is also from Hillel—a physician without a shekel to his name."

This kind of talk bored Berenice. She endured it because

her brother was king, but her mind was a wall against far more powerful men than her brother, and she reminded him that by now he should know her well enough to forego such arguments.

"Still, he's a pauper," Agrippa insisted, feeling that this was basic, and that since the House of Herod had not yet produced anyone indifferent to money, it was unlikely that Berenice would be the first.

"I have enough money for both of us," Berenice shrugged.

"And you intend to marry him?"

"If he will have me," Berenice said.

Yet, to her profound annoyance, Shimeon raised some of the same arguments: pointing out to her that she was rich almost beyond one's ability to comprehend. They were at the House of Shlomo—seven weeks had passed since the incident in the boat—and Shimeon told Berenice he was going away.

"Where?" she asked.

"To Ezion Geber."

"Why?"

"Because I must go," he said simply. "The plague is there, and the physicians who were there are dead."

"And if you are dead?"

He shrugged. "That's my life. I chose it."

"And my life? What is my life, Shimeon Bengamaliel? Did I choose it? Or did the Almighty say to me, Bitch—be born on earth and let earth be cursed with you!"

"No, don't talk like that," he begged her.

"Why? Because I blaspheme?"

"Against yourself, my beloved."

"How dare you call me that now!" she cried. "Beloved!" Her eyes flashed scorn and rage. "By what right?"

"I love you—or does that mean nothing?" Shimeon demanded.

"Love? Such love is worthless!"

"What then?" he demanded desperately. "What can you

ask of me? I am a pauper. I have the clothes on my back and the surgeon's tools in my bag, and there is all that I have in the world. Even the great House of Hillel is not ours in your sense. We don't own it—we occupy it—if God wills it. So how do you measure yourself against me? You have a palace in Chalcis, a palace in Tiberias, a great palace in Caesarea—and I have even heard that the palace of the Hasmoneans in Jerusalem is yours, left to you by your grandmother. You have a villa here on the lake that you never set foot in, a villa on the Waters of Merom, a villa on the sea at Tyre—and a villa in Rome, too, I am told. They say that half the property in Chalcis is yours, the ironworks outside of Chalcis, over a thousand slaves, a farm of horses near Meggido, and twelve plantations of olive trees and perhaps ten hundred talents of gold and silver to satisfy your whims—"

"What are you?" she demanded scornfully. "A clerk? I had heard told that you are a physician—but I find that you have more skill in the counting of money and the keeping of books than a battery of Egyptian scribes." She said this and watched his face redden, and as he shook his head, so desperately and dumbly, she almost pitied him.

"You are richer than Claudius Germanicus, who is Emperor of Rome, and you mock and sneer at me—"

"Then what is it, physician?" she spat out at him. "Do you know as little about women as I do about men?"

Finally he took her in his arms—when she had reached the point of doubt that caused her to wonder whether she had gone too far and provoked him out of her reach. Because all through it, she was saying to herself, "I will not live without him, but neither will he die without me. We do both together."

Many years later, Berenice was to remember this vow of hers.

A most unusual meeting was held by King Agrippa in his

palace in Tiberias. For one thing, Gamaliel Benhillel, the old man, the father, the son of the saintly Hillel himself and the patriarch of the house—and thus, in the eyes of hundreds of thousands of Jews, the patriarch of all Jewry—this Gamaliel came to Agrippa's house, the House of Herod and discussed the union of Shimeon and Berenice. The king and the patriarch sat with Gideon Benharmish, Anat Beradin, Joseph Bendavid, and Oman Bensimon—all of them except Agrippa men of their declining years with long memories and the strange consciousness that finally saint and devil were joined, the House of Hillel to the House of Herod, which had already been joined to the House of David and the House of Mattathias, so that one out of this union would carry not only the blood of kings and wise men, but could style himself *Hacohen*, out of a bloodline that led without break—as they calculated such things—to Moses the prophet and beloved of the Almighty and to Aaron his brother. It was a strange occasion, an awesome occasion, and a quiet one—for while the step proposed by the two lovers was almost mysterious in its significance it was also ominous in its political implications. Would it make an unhealable rift between the Jews of Judea in the South and those of Galilee in the North? Would the Jews of the South, who so revered the House of Hillel, curse Agrippa in that he had fostered this? Would the Zealots, who feared and hated the House of Hillel, curse Agrippa for selling their birthright? And how would the Romans react?

"It is very complicated," Agrippa sighed, and thus caused Beradin to remark,

"You will find, my dear boy, that nothing pertaining to Jewish politics or philosophy is ever simple and nothing so uncomplicated that a sage can unravel it."

Yet with all the talk, doubt, and discussion, they could not set aside the will of two strong-willed people. They could only make of the marriage, for the time being, a sort of secret—a secret that many would know but would nevertheless hide in itself.

Thus the marriage took place very quietly at the House of
Hillel, with no more than half a hundred people present,
including the slaves of the house. Standing next to her
brother, Berenice had to reflect on how strange this was
compared to the somber dignity of the alabarch's household
in Alexandria, where death had come before her, or to the
wild splendor of the festivities at Chalcis, when Herod of
Chalcis took her in marriage. But that was of no consequence, and those incidents were buried so deeply, so
vaguely in her memory that they might indeed never have
happened. Now it was her own father-in-law, the rabbi and
patriarch, who said,

"Thus the Almighty wills it, that the two of flesh become
the one of flesh, the two of thought become the one of
thought, the two of blood become the one of blood, for the
blood is the life and the life is unto Yaweh, the Lord God of
Hosts." The very ancient ceremony was in a sing-song
Aramaic. "Where is the contract?" the old man asked.

The contract was brought. Berenice stood with her back to
Shimeon's back; she could feel his firm buttocks pressed
against her, and she began to tremble with desire for him.
Three veils covered her face, and her breath was hot and
heavy under the cloth.

"Oh, give the dowry," chanted Agrippa, feeling foolish
that he should be speaking the words of an old man. "Give
me comfort for my last years. Give me bread for my hungry
days. Give me shelter from the hot sun. Give me a black
goatskin tent to shelter me."

"Give him the dowry!" cried the Cohen or priest, who
stood by in the name of his line.

"Thou takest what is best his, the doe of his flock, the
virgin ewe, the unopened passage, the sweetness of the
crotch, the host for thy manhood, the host for the parts where
the covenent is reckoned."

This section was in Hebrew, and Berenice began to fidget
with irritation and impatience. Why all this nonsense about
virginity? They were no longer in the desert, and neither was

one old, grizzled, dirty sheik trading wives and dowries with another. She was hot. She wanted it over with.

"My dowry is little," Shimeon said.

"Mine is in fullness," said Agrippa.

Then Agrippa knelt and put his name on the contract, which was stretched out on the floor, a long scroll of parchment covered with archaic Hebrew. Then the patriarch knelt and put his name to it. It was rolled up. Berenice was escorted out to the bath, where she would be washed again, and Shimeon held out a great silver goblet for the wine to be poured. The goblet was passed around and each man present drank from it, the women having gone away with Berenice to the bath. The old patriarch wept in joy, and he went to Agrippa and kissed him upon the mouth.

"Be blessed in your stewardship, my son," he said. "Israel has a king both good and gentle, and my house is blessed with such a queen as we have not known since the days of Esther."

Then lamps were lit on the tables under the terebinth tree, and the feasting began. Berenice watched from the window of the bride's room—where she waited for Shimeon Bengamaliel, her husband.

Berenice had not been to Jerusalem since the death of her father, seven years before; and this time it was not to go into the city and focus upon herself the attention and delay and gossip consequent to her recent marriage, but only because the city lay on the road from Tiberias to Ezion Geber. She had been to Jerusalem as a child, and Shimeon had been there many times; and Shimeon could comprehend why she liked it so little. Jerusalem was a cold city. Unlike Tiberias or Caesarea, it had no parks, no groves of trees, no places where travelers could sit in the shade of growing things, no fountains, no gardens with shrubs and sculpture. It was a city of brick and stone, of flat slab and cobbled pavement. The great houses of the city sheltered themselves behind blank walls; they hid their warmth behind expressionless faces; they were defenses against hate and bloodletting, even as the city was in itself a series of defenses—perhaps the mightiest combination of natural and man-made defenses in all the ancient world, tier upon tier of wall and fortress mounting up to the height where the Temple itself stood, a tall, hard-edged building, whose sheer walls elicited awe rather than admiration.

Approaching the city from the west, so that they might go around it to the southern suburb where their destination, the House of Hakedron, stood, Berenice and Shimeon passed through the Valley of Hinnom. In other cities forms of garbage collection and disposal had been set up by Berenice's father, Agrippa I, but such was the enormous size of Jerusalem and so quick its rate of growth and expansion and so violently independent its groupings, tribes, classes, and priestly sects, that no successful means of garbage disposal had ever been inaugurated. Instead, filth, refuse, and garbage were dumped into the Valley of Hinnom. Each day, thousands of animals and birds were brought to the Temple by pious Jews and offered to the priests for sacrifice. The animals were slaughtered and gutted, and there flowed from the Temple to the Valley of Hinnom an unending stream of baskets filled with the entrails of these offerings. The meat was sold by the priests—and eaten by them too—but when one or another of twenty-one ancient totemic taboos appeared in the entrails, the meat was discarded, as were the haunches of certain animals, the heads and feet of the birds, the feet of the animals with cloven hoofs, and the skins of those animals sold as meat without offering. All of this was dumped in Hinnom, as was the garbage of the city, the dead and unclean animals of the city, the night soil of much of the poor population, and all too frequently the body of some poor devil dead of violence or disease and too forgotten or poor to have anyone who would purchase burial.

The road through this valley to the south suburb cut a considerable distance off the journey, and Berenice and

Shimeon decided to go this way in spite of the horror of the place, which was frequently called Gehenna—so that they might reach shelter before sundown. Berenice, Shimeon, the huge Adam Benur, who accompanied them as armorbearer and servant, and Gabo—all covered mouths and noses with clots saturated in perfume; but smell was only part of this place. There were human creatures prowling in the mounds of flesh and garbage, wild dogs and jackals, hundreds of black vultures—and robbers and killers, the cast-out and excommunicated of the city. Mostly, as a result of the prevailing wind, the frightful odor was not smelled in Jerusalem; but there were times when the wind changed and covered the city with a hot effusion of horror. Now, for half an hour, Berenice and her party rode through this horror, and the only word spoken was by Shimeon, who said in a sort of desperation,

"Still, this high place above us is holy."

They rode quickly there, and soon had turned to the south of the city, where the air became sweet and the city hung in the late golden sunlight like an unreal thing, like a dream. The House of Hakedron, where they would stay the night, had its gate open, awaiting them, and they turned into the courtyard weary and relieved. Slaves, alert and waiting for them, seized their horses, helped them to dismount, and brought them foaming goblets of ice-cold wine and water—and beyond the slaves, at the door to the house itself, their hosts waited.

The head of the house was a strange and very old man, who called himself Ba'as Hacohen. He was enormously rich and powerful—as he would perforce have to be to maintain his great residence outside of and unprotected by the walls of Jerusalem—in a land where every kind of bandit and thief abounded—Jebusites, the decadent remnants of the ancients who had once occupied the city; Zealots, bitter, resentful as they hunted Romans and Egyptians; and the dreaded and terrible Sicarii, a murder-sect of the Zealots whom even the Zealots feared, conscienceless men who were professional assassins, who solved all problems with murder, and who, armed with Roman short-swords that they concealed under their dirty jackets, struck swiftly and silently. Along with these, the Edomites, Arab half-Jews, bitter and dispossessed, who would periodically raid out of the badlands to the south. No, life to the south of Jerusalem was not relished by ordinary people, but Ba'as Hacohen was far from ordinary.

For one thing, it was said that he was well over a hundred years old; and this was something that Berenice could believe, seeing the incredible network of wrinkles that covered his face, his skin, like dried and ancient parchment; and to lend proof to his claim, there were four generations of his descendants waiting with him to greet the travelers. A thousand legends were told about this man, the Ba'as Adon, that he had once been high priest in the Temple, that he had been a captain of captains under Herod the Great, that once, dying, they brought him to Hillel the Good, who made a strange pact with the prophet Elijah, that the Ba'as Hacohen would live a year of atonement for every wrong he had done—but this of course was nonsense, legends, old wives' tales. He was a great priestly prince, the Ba'as Adon, with much wealth in gold and silver and diamonds. The tale was told that he had ransacked the temple treasury once, carrying away his vast wealth under the wing and protection of Herod, or perhaps under Herod's father, Antipater, which would have made him well over a hundred years; but the plain truth was that he had once held leases to copper mines near Elat and a monopoly of the tin trade with the Tyreans, who brought the tin from Cornwall in far-away Britain, and that shrewdly conducting this and other trade, he had piled up wealth in good measure. At one point in his life, while the Sage Hillel still lived, the Ba'as Adon had been converted to support the House of Hillel, and in this he had never wavered. Now he received the grandson of his beloved teacher and rabbi as a guest in his house for the first time—and no effort was spared to make the occasion memorable.

A table was set to awe even Berenice. There were singers

from Crete, dancers from the Ganges River, and a clever juggler from Alexandria. Over eighty men and women sat to table, for in the manner of the Hillelites, the sexes were mixed—and in the same manner, there was neither drunkenness nor overeating. The old man, sitting beside Berenice, wiped his eyes with his napkin, tried to control his emotion, and told her what it meant to his old heart to see the two houses of Herod and Hillel finally united.

"You have heard that I was high priest, my child—so it was, so it was, long, long ago and almost at the beginning of time, when Herod your great-grandfather was king over Israel—oh, the measure of his wickedness!—and the good and saintly Hillel was king over the hearts of good men. I knew them both, may they rest in peace, the evil with the good, for who but the Almighty ever truly knows of an absence of goodness? For sitting here now, in the long overdue twilight, I seem to sense the pattern of the Almighty's working, the meaning of His design, that He forgive me and have mercy upon me, for He does not take kindly to our knowledge of His ways—yet I see a glimmer of the morning sun which, like Moses, was to be denied to me—a glimmer of brave and glorious future Israel—no, the whole world might know. For you, who are Queen Esther born again—you will sit with your husband on a throne mightier than any, any—I was talking of thrones, was I not—and the throne of Herod was four cubits tall, with cherubim for him to lay his hands upon—" His voice wandered away. In spite of the heat, he was wrapped in a striped woolen cloak, and he held it tightly around him, shivering a little—

In bed that night, Berenice clutched Shimeon, whispering to him that she was afraid. "So much afraid, Shimeon. The Angel of Death is in this house. I am afraid to fall asleep."

But he soothed her, and at last she slept.

They took the road south from Jerusalem, their way being by Bethlehem to Hebron and from thence to Beersheba. But above Hebron, they passed through Betab, the tiny Benjamite village where Gabo was born. She rode through with her face covered, for the air was dry as a shard and hot as fire. "Your birthplace," Berenice reminded her, and Gabo said, "Curses on my birthplace. I never want to see this land again." On their left lay the awful wildnerness of Judea, with its stark and precipitious cliff faces, its slashed, ocher-colored wadis that were clefts into the belly of hell, at the bottom of which lay the Dead Salt Sea. The burning, dry air was filled with a powdery dust that forced its way into every wrinkle and fold of skin and eyes, and the travelers mostly rode with their faces covered and often with their eyes closed, leaving it to the small, nimble-footed Lebanese ponies who had carried them from Galilee to find their own way. For Berenice, every step of the way was discomfort and bodily indignity, the heat—so different from the green coolness of her native land—the dust, the great empty spaces of the badland rock desert, the sheer cliffs, the dust, the misery of the few tiny villages they passed through, the skinny goats seeking fodder where a lizard would starve to death, and always the imminence of danger. Yet it was what she wanted and what she had sought, and she would not complain. She had said that she would follow Shimeon to hell—and this was precisely what had occurred.

Below Hebron, in the Land of Idumea, they came across a camel caravan that had been attacked. The camels had been led away, except for one that was gutted and dead, but seven of the drivers lay dead along the road and the eighth moaned in agony and bled out his life. Shimeon dismounted and did what he could for the poor man, binding his wounds, stopping the flow of blood, and giving him water. They remained with him for an hour, until he died. The desert floor was too stony for burial, but Shimeon explained to Berenice that sooner or later—certainly in the next few days—the local people would find the bodies and bury them. Looking around the wasteland where they were Berenice found it hard to conceive that there were local people of any kind. Her ancestors on the Herodian side of her bloodline were Idumeans, and she shivered to think that they had an origin in this rocky wasteland where no blade of grass grew.

They went on. In Beersheba, the local inn was a pesthole, stinking to the sky of urine and human and animal waste; so they passed it by and pitched a tent in the open. On a striped Bedouin blanket, Berenice lay in the arms of her husband, with the glittering, star-strewed desert sky like a bowl above them. She watched the lines of flame left by the meteorites and told Shimeon that each one marked a visit to earth from the Angel of Death, Malak Hamashhit, who always kept one corner of one eye fixed upon Jerusalem, for while it was necessary to bring death to the Gentiles as well, the Malak Hamashhit did not like the Jews to forget him even for a moment.

"Which only goes to prove," she went on, "what a provoking race we are. Others desire a large share of what is good, and we can't rest unless we have the lion's share of what is bad."

"All very profound, my darling," Shimeon agreed, "but I have seen too many die from too many earthly causes to put much stock in your Malak Hamashhit—who is no different from all the other kings of the underworld, Egyptian, Syrian, Greek and so forth. As for those streaks up there, the Greeks teach that they are bits of burning iron falling from the sky, and when I was a student there, I saw one of those fragments—"

"You are too Greek and too rational for me." He took her in his arms, and she said, "Except to come here. What is rational in that?"

The next day, they left the main road and took the track to the southeast that led to Ezion Geber. They left before dawn, but by midday it was too hot to travel, and they lay for shelter and rest in the shade of an overhanging rock crag. By midafternoon they traveled again, and now they rode past the ruins of an ancient city of great size. Berenice wondered whether it might be the legendary Sodom, but Shimeon pointed out that those old cities that the Torah told about were far to the north. This might well be a forgotten city of the Amalekites or the Edomites.

The day afterward they were halted and surrounded by a mixed band of Sicarii and Idumeans, about two dozen of them, well mounted and well armed. Shimeon warned Adam to make no hostile move, Neither he nor Adam had arms in sight. Berenice had a sudden wave of terror as the band of highwaymen came sweeping down on them, screaming and hooting; and she took great pride in the fact that Shimeon sat his horse calmly, waiting without any apparent alarm. Gabo began to scream and plead, but a sharp blow across her face by Berenice put an end to this. Berenice sensed that the situation had to be controlled—that if it got out of control it would be very dangerous for all of them, and she sat motionless while the robbers closed in on them, handled their horses and clothes and trapping.

"Who are you and where from and where to?" their leader spat at Shimeon.

"A physician, out of Galilee. This is my wife—and these two are our slaves."

Berenice, her hair hidden, her face covered with dust, provoked no recognition—nor was she apparently desirable, her frame too big and bony, the ridges of her face too marked. They were handled and questioned, and then the leader of the band complained of a wearing pain in his gut. Did he have purges with him?

They dismounted, as did the robbers, and Adam unpacked Shimeon's stock of medicine. Shimeon examined the man with the pain in the belly, and prescribed a mixture of dried hemp and dwa leaf, both to be burned and breathed as incense. As he told Berenice later, the man had a lump the size of a melon in his gut, a tumor that would kill him in no great time ahead. Another robber had a festering thigh wound, and Shimeon cleaned it and put a drain into it. He lanced boils, cleaned cankers, and cut away an ingrown toenail; and stifling her disgust at the filthy condition of the robbers—they never washed, and their odor was unbearable—Berenice managed to help him and work with him.

He finished with the band, and they gave him three gold coins for his efforts—which he gravely accepted. The robbers guided them to a sheltered camping place, an abandoned building of stone, all that was left of an ancient fortress—and the following day, Berenice saw the slag heaps of Ezion Geber in the distance.

Many years after this, Titus, who was to be Emperor of Rome, asked Berenice what had moved Shimeon to go to Ezion Geber, and she replied that he had gone because there was no physician there and one was needed.

"Why?" Titus insisted, and Berenice replied, "Because people were dying." "But people die everywhere." It was not to be explained. You are married and you take a bride to such a place; and afterward Berenice remembered this as a happy time, a strangely and improbably happy time. "We took our honeymoon in hell," she said to her brother afterward. "I have married a very strange man indeed, but that does not change the fact that he is the man for me, the only man I have had any happiness from."

A hard-faced Jew, Smah Barachad, commanded the soldiers at Ezion Geber. There had been a hundred and twelve soldiers, but now fully half of them were dead. The overseers were Egypto-Arabs from the Sinai Peninsula, degraded and illiterate brutes who boasted in their slovenly Aramaic of some kind of bastard descent from the Tribe of Ken, and thereby from the mythical ancestor, Jethro, the father-in-law of Moses; but in all truth they were nameless bastards out of nowhere, sadistic, lustful the way animals are lustful, and utterly without mercy. There had been almost three hundred of them, but they too had been cut down by disease, as had been their brothel of women, slaves, cast-outs—anything they could lay hands on with name or shape of woman to it. But the worst toll the plague had taken was among the slaves—of whom there had been over six thousand. Now only two thousand were left.

Berenice had never been to a mine before. She had seen field slaves and house slaves, but never these blind and twisted and fleshless mockeries of men that crawled each day like animals into their black tunnels to emerge dragging baskets of copper ore, to return again, to die in their tunnels, to come out and thrash and twist and beat themselves in a lust for suicide but without the strength for suicide. They were naked, covered with a crust of filth, covered with their own feces dried and caked on them, elbow and knee black with festering callus, bearded, long-haired, bereft of language, whimpering and groaning instead of speaking—

"Dogs," said Smah Barachad. "Lazy, dirty dogs. Soon they'll all be dead." He was content with the situation and resented Shimeon's presence there. He had first call on the property of the soldiers and overseers who died and a firm belief that he would outlive all of them. Eventually Shimeon and Adam Benur buried him. A plain young soldier, a boy with a hard stomach and a harder constitution, got his money.

After the first night there, Shimeon said to Berenice, "You had better go back to the north with Gabo and Adam."

"Why?" Berenice asked him.

"This is no place for you."

"For you?"

Shimeon shrugged. "I must—"

"Well, I don't think you must," Berenice interrupted. "You can't cure anyone. None of you physicians can, and they will die anyway. But while you are here, I intend to remain here with you—and at least I will come to understand you. I don't now."

"This will disgust you—"

"I don't disgust easily," Berenice said.

"And turn you against me."

"Not because you are noble," Berenice smiled, "but only because you are stupid. It's stupidity that I cannot abide."

Yet she bore everything else, and strangely enough, she was not unhappy. When Smah Barachad made advances toward her, she told him matter-of-factly that other men had died for the same thing and that forewarned was forearmed. He did not know who she was, but something in her unlikely green eyes convinced him that she was telling the truth. She got along with the worst as well as the best. The overseers she treated with haughty disdain and aloofness; the Jewish soldiers directly and with no affectation or flirtatiousness; and the slaves with a controlled pity and tenderness that was the constant amazement and wonder of Shimeon Bengamaliel. Perhaps even more amazed was Berenice, for she found herself doing things that would have been inconceivable—and no need to force herself, and no horror when she cradled the lice-ridden head of a dying slave against her breast, and no disgust at smells that would have sent her fainting once, smells and filth and the bony, hideous remnants of human bodies. Shimeon tried to keep her away from his work, and she said to him, "There's no other alternative to madness here. If you lose me as a worker, then you lose a mistress too." "You are a queen." "Oh, you poor fool! Do you bring a queen here?" she demanded. He taught her then, and she learned how to dress wounds, how to clean open sores, how to set broken bones, and how to minister to the dying. She lost weight. The dry air dehydrated her, and though her youthful skin was stretched tight against her face bones, it retained its elasticity and vitality. In fact, all of her was vitality—a combination of spirit and strength such as Shimeon had never believed possible in a woman; and when Gabo came down with the same hellish disease that was raging in the mines, a flush at first, and then sores all over the body, and then raging fever and most often death, Berenice

nursed her through, tended her as gently and carefully as she
would have tended her own child.

At night, she lay in Shimeon's great arms, and she knew
more happiness than she had ever know before. They remained forty-one days at Ezion Geber, until the plague had
burned itself out. Smah Barachad, the hard-faced, hard-
souled Jewish mercenary was not the only one who died
there. Gabo recovered, but there in the desert they buried the
big Galilean Adam Benur. Berenice wept like a child. It was
not hard now. Ezion Geber had been an education in grief;
she had learned to weep as the world weeps.

Dying, Adam Benur had named her and called her by title
and position, while many others stood around and listened.
This did not change things, for her identity was already
suspected. She could not work here and keep her crown of
red hair hidden, and with her red hair and pale green eyes she
was as much a feature of the land as any mark of wood or
stone. News has wings, and the word has wings. She was
Berenice of the bread, which she had given to the poor and
the hungry in Tiberias; and the slaves, who had learned to die
without pleading, groveled before her and pleaded for life
and freedom. She wept and turned to Shimeon:

"What can I do?"

"You must decide that, my beloved."

"There are half a million slaves in Israel. Did I do it? Did I
enslave them? And where does the Torah say that this is
wrong?"

Shimeon shook his head.

"Are there no slaves in the House of Hillel?" she cried.

"There are—yes, God help me, there are, and this is the
shape of the world, Berenice. We change the world a little,
but slowly, slowly."

"Then what should I do? Tell me, Shimeon."

She was treating a slave who pleaded with her, and when
she shook her head mutely, he took a sliver of stone he had

concealed about his person and plunged it into his heart. He was only a boy—no more than fourteen or fifteen years old—a Jewish boy, as Berenice could see from his nakedness. He was skin and bones, as unkempt as an animal, and he had pleaded with her for life and freedom and accepted death instead.

The owner of the mines, Salam Baryusuf, a very rich Idumean, made one of his rare visits to the mine. He came in rage with thirty soldiers, for word had come to him that there were people at his mine planting seeds of discontent among his slaves and overseers; but his rage passed away when he realized that two of the most famous people in Israel were facing him, and that they had been working for weeks to save the lives of his slaves and soldiers and overseers. In the face of Berenice, he became obsequious. He humbled himself, apologized for the conditions at the mine, explained that while these mines were fruitful in the ancient days of King Solomon, they had by now been worked to death. In fact, as he explained it, the mines were practically an institution for maintaining the lives of his slaves.

"I will buy the mines from you," Berenice said suddenly. "The mines and the slaves. Set me a price."

Shimeon was no less stunned than Baryusuf. The Idumean stroked his beard with a trembling hand, muttered, calculated. It was true that the mines were worked out. They brought barely a profit, but did the Jewish woman know that? How could she? The other was a physician and out of the House of Hillel—and they were alien to all things practical. He asked for a million shekels. Berenice did not laugh. "You belittle me," she said softly. "Perhaps you forget who I am. Have you heard about my anger?" The Idumean glanced about nervously. He knew that they had come here with a single male servant, whom they had buried already. He had his soldiers and his overseers. Why should he be afraid? Yet he was afraid, and he muttered that Bernice should make him an offer.

"I will pay you ten thousand shekels," she said.

He whined, pleaded, protested, wrung his hands in despair, and finally the sale was completed for fifteen thousand shekels, and Berenice wrote him a draft on Jacobar Hacohen, who was her banker in Jerusalem. The soldiers were sent away with Baryusuf, the overseers discharged, the slaves freed—for whatever they could do with freedom, broken and mentally ruined as they were. They wandered off northward. The wind was blowing sand, and already some of the shaft openings were silting up. Berenice had no desire to work the mine. A year from now, sand would have disguised all entrances to it . . .

She and Gabo and Shimeon rode away from the place. Shimeon said little. As his wife learned about him, so was he learning about Berenice.

But the word travels on wings, and when they reached Hebron, the people of the town flocked around Berenice, pleading to touch her, to kiss the hem of a garment, begging her to lay hands upon their afflictions. Their sick came to them, and Shimeon did what he could. Berenice took a child that was strangling from an asthmatic attack and gave him mouth-to-mouth respiration, as Shimeon had taught her. Word sped that she had brought one back from the dead.

As they rode out of there, Shimeon, "You may find, my beloved, that it is harder to be a saint than a devil."

Berenice was not disposed to laugh. "My father discovered that, may he rest in peace," she said. "But he was a saint who hated too much. Do you hate, Shimeon?"

He thought for a while before he shook his head.

"And with me," Berenice nodded. "What has happened to me, Shimeon? I berated the Idumean—I didn't hate him or fear him."

In Bethlehem they stayed with one Meneleus Hamoser, who was a follower of Hillel and who begged Shimeon to preach a sermon at the synagogue. Shimeon disliked preaching intensely, yet he agreed; but the matter was taken out of his hands. When word spread through Bethlehem that Berenice was there, the crowd around the House of Hamoser became so thick that it would have been impossible to break through to the synagogue. The people pleaded for a sight of her, and when at least she came and stood upon the roof of the house, they lapsed into silence, although some of them wept.

There was a bath here, and Berenice was able to soak in hot water until the grime was cleansed away. Her body was as lean as a boy's, her breasts reduced in size, her long-limbed tightness like that of a girl in her teens. She had to ask herself her age—twenty-three?—twenty-four?

At dinner that evening, Hamoser said to her, "You must accept the fact, Queen Berenice, that you are deeply loved. It does not matter that people are fickle. They are quite earnest in their love of you."

"I tell her that," Shimeon nodded.

Berenice shrugged and said that it mattered very little. Her indifference was not a pose. It was very real. She did what she had to do. She had no sense of what it meant to be loved by a great many.

"And here in Israel," Hamoser went on, "it is a very new phenomenon. In fact, when I think back to our history, the only other heroic and independent figure of womanhood is Deborah—and that was very long ago, when our ancestors still worshiped the mother."

"Esther?" Shimeon wondered. "But little proof there—"

"None to speak of," Hamoser nodded, a studious man who was proud of his scholarship. "Esther is unquestionably apocryphal, a splendid invention called to life when Israel had need of her. But this—this thing of Queen Berenice—"

"How can you talk about me like that, myself sitting here?" Berenice cried. "Anyway, it's nonsense that you talk!"

And she stalked out of the room in anger.

Yet somehow the slaves released at Ezion Geber had made their way to Jerusalem, and the word was in Jerusalem.

Shimeon and Berenice had decided that they would not go into Jerusalem, switching from their former plan to spend a day or two in Berenice's villa there, enjoying the good weather and the cool winds on the high places. Now, at Berenice's urging, they were to pass by quickly and make straightaway for Galilee, but the word was before them and the road was packed with thousands of people. Curiosity brought Ventidius Cumanus, the new procurator, down from the city to invite them to be his guests at his palace in the city, and with him was a legion of the Romans, holding the crowd back from the road and cursing them in Latin. Berenice thanked him but explained that they had decided to return to Galilee. "Surely," he said, gesturing at the crowd, "they don't expect bread from you." And added mockingly, "You are not planning to feed all of Jerusalem—or are you?" "Hardly," Berenice replied flatly, and when the procurator wanted to know by what other virtue she was the beloved of the crowd, Berenice murmured the old proverb about short explanations being suited for fools. "I don't think you are a fool, Procurator," she said.

Later, Shimeon pointed out that she had taken a long chance in insulting the procurator.

"I hardly think he knew," Berenice said. "He's a fool and a wretched person. I will not mind my words with such people."

"Yes," Shimeon agreed, "I don't suppose that you will— and for my part, I have married a most unusual woman. Don't you think?"

"No more unusual than the man I married," replied Berenice.

"I suppose," Berenice said to Shimeon, after they were back in Tiberias, just the two of them alone, sprawled on the bed in her chamber, the same bed to which she as a patient had summoned her husband, "that I will get used to this sort of thing. It appears to run in my family, for my father also became a saint of sorts. He died for his trouble, and in short order. Do you suppose that is what fate has in store for me?"

"I hope not," Shimeon smiled.

"Why do crowds have such short memories? Do you suppose they have really forgotten how much they hated me?"

"Did they hate you?" Shimeon wondered. "Or had they manufactured their own demon out of the whole cloth? That's the thing to know. You are someone, Berenice, my beloved—and I don't know that there ever was anyone just like you. You did some remarkable things. You fed them. That alone is basic. They were hungry, and you fed them."

"Out of pride and vanity," she said indifferently.

"Yes?" She watched him as he studied her keenly; and she reflected that you never really know about a man who was wise without being clever. "Perhaps," he admitted. "Or perhaps not."

"Yes and no," she said, "which is spoken like a rabbi."

"Oh? By the way, I noticed that Gabo is pregnant. Is she married? I never asked you."

"She's no more married than with previous pregnancies."

"Then this isn't the first?"

"The fourth," Berenice told him.

"Really? What happens to the children?"

"Well, what should happen to them?" Berenice demanded with some asperity. "Don't look at me like that. I did not eat them. They're growing up like little animals in the corridors of this palace—which is a very large place."

Shimeon breathed deeply and said, "I mentioned that you fed them. And then you went to the South with me. They were sick and you healed them—"

"I find this kind of talk tiresome."

"Of course," Shimeon continued, "such an attitude on your part is a fraud. You don't find it tiresome at all. I think you enjoy the role—and in good time, you will be all saint and forget that you were ever part devil at all."

"And will you love me then, Shimeon?" she asked.

"I don't know."

PART FOUR

Berenice emerged from the entranceway to her palace and stood looking at the vista of hills, misty valleys, and blue sky. The view was excellent from here, and dramatic too; for immediately in front of her were the deep shadows cast by the looming structure of the Temple and its walled courts; and beyond that, the spread of height and distance. Her grandmother had chosen well to build a palace here, on the mighty, upthrust shoulder of Jerusalem. The very sense of the place renewed you, and Berenice could understand why, in the olden times, all of these high places were considered sacred to the gods—in the old, old times, when the people knew other gods besides Yaweh.

The air was clear, cool and sweet as wine—as it so often was in the early hours of the morning in Jerusalem. Rarely did the weather disappoint one here. It was almost fifteen years since she and Shimeon had taken to the habit of spending the warmest months of the year in Jerusalem, to escape the cloying heat of the lake bowl at Tiberias, and bit by bit she had come to love and feel this city. For all of its cold and forbidding aspect, its stone streets, stone walls, stone elevations, mighty stone staircases, and cobbled roads, it was a thing of purpose and emotion, alive in its own strange way. It was not soft and limpid and tropical, as was Tiberias, nor did it have any of the planned and mathematical construction of Caesarea; it had grown almost at random through countless ages; its streets twisted and curled and tunneled. Walls paralleled walls; old walls and new walls, old cities and

211

new cities; stone faces on stone faces, but no sculpture anywhere and very little color. Berenice could remember her first sight of Athens, the incredible, living, vibrating color of the city—walls of blue and yellow and green and hot red, but nowhere a bit of white stone, everything painted, every bit of sculpture painted so skillfully that frequently one would mistake sculptured stone for the living flesh. But here in Jerusalem stone was left unpainted, white limestone, gray granite, red and yellow marble, blue sandstone—vast, cold, natural faces of rock that were alive only when they caught the evening sunset or the morning sunrise. The whole city existed for a purpose, not as Rome existed to rule the world, not as Athens existed to excite the envy of the world and to weep for days that were no more, not as Alexandria existed to house the wealth or knowledge of the world—but for a purpose specific and singular, to support the Temple of Yaweh; and in some strange and intangible manner the city fulfilled its purpose. Even Shimeon, who never had felt too warmly toward Jerusalem, would admit that it was in a sense the footstool of the Almighty—and never did Berenice walk through its streets without some awareness of that.

And she loved to walk in its streets, dropping from level to level, or climbing toward the sky with that tightness of the chest, that panting for breath that was peculiar to Jerusalem. To walk in its streets each morning and each evening had become ritual for her and for Shimeon over the years. They enjoyed such walks, and as the years passed without any quickening in Berenice's womb, without any pregnant life for the one man she had loved, both she and Shimeon substituted each other for the children they would not have. They moved closer and closer to each other, closer than they were aware of. When they walked, hand in hand, people looked at them and nodded. It was a familiar sight.

He would have been with her this morning, but the Sanhedrin had convened in emergency session at the moment of dawn, and a messenger had come for Shimeon while it was still dark. She woke to see him as a dark, shapeless figure in the night, and then to feel the touch of his kiss as he whispered to her that he must go. "With God—with the Almighty," she said to him. They both knew what it presaged; his father, the old man, the patriarch of the House of Hillel had been dead a year now, and his brother Hillel was the head of the house. One or the other—Hillel or Shimeon, was in line for the curious title of *nashi*, which in ancient times had been translated as prince, but which now referred to the man elected to sit at the head of the council of seventy-one, or the Great Sanhedrin of Israel. His father —Shimeon's father, Gamaliel—had been the first of the nashis; and now a war had been fought in the council between the House of Shammai and the House of Hillel. Victory or defeat; or a laying aside of arms? Now they had convened again in the dark hours of the morning, and Berenice was left to walk alone.

Old Shupa, the doorkeeper, bowed to her and commented on the quality of the morning. "It will be a good morning for us," he said—"or so I feel, lady."

"God willing." Berenice nodded.

A good morning, Berenice thought. So many mornings had been good mornings; and even with all the trouble on the land, they had been years, easy years that slid away leaving only a good sense of warmth. Was she old? Was thirty-eight old? A hand went up to touch the underside of her chin. The flesh was firm there. A few additional pounds of weight covered her thighs and bust, but her body was still firm and strong, her breasts round and upright. In her dark moments—she had never cast them aside entirely— Shimeon would say, "Is that to fear, beloved, to grow old in the sight of the Almighty?" Then the magic of her youth was as simple as that, she told herself, and these were no thoughts for so clean and lovely a day as this. On such a day, one lives and tastes and smells, and she was so much alive today. She

213

had known it the moment she awakened and had dressed herself in a shift of pale blue—the priestly color, the color she was entitled to wear for the blood of Aaron in her veins—and an overdress of mustard-yellow. Her red hair—still with no gray thread—was caught in a gold-netted coif on her head, adding to her height. The only jewel she wore was a diamond clasp upon her breast.

By the time Berenice had come to the edge of the great Upper City Market, with her great-grandfather's palace binding the farther edge of it, and all around it the homes of the wealthy and fashionable and noble Judeans, the city was alive and stirring, and at least a dozen men and women had paused to greet her. Now, as she entered the Upper Market from one side, the morning relief of the Roman guard on its way to the temple area entered upon the other. There were twenty legionaries, a standard-bearer, an officer, and a musician of sorts who sounded periodic blasts upon a long, straight horn called a tuba. Of the many aspects of the Roman occupation hated by the Jews, the tuba was not least.

Berenice walked across the square as if the Roman detail did not exist, looking straight ahead of her; but midway she heard the centurion give a sharp order to halt and stand at attention; and then, leaving his detail in the middle of the square, he came to Berenice, who paused a moment; he bowed low, and he introduced himself as Casper Ventix, explaining that he had seen her three times and was so enchanted by her appearance that he could not resist this opportunity to make her acquaintance. He also could not resist the opportunity to drop the fact that he was related to Nero, the emperor—by marriage rather than by blood, and distantly, but nevertheless related. He was a young man, a few years less than thirty, good-looking in the dark Italian manner, and about three inches shorter than Berenice.

"You have made my acquaintance," Berenice nodded coldly. He had addressed her in bad Aramaic; she replied in perfect Latin. He switched to Latin that was not nearly so good to explain that he was an admirer.

"And what do you admire?" Berenice asked. "There is so much to admire in Jerusalem—particularly our manners, which are rather formal. We do not press our presence upon strangers."

She turned away from him then, and the young officer stood for a moment before he turned back to his men. They were grinning. He swore at them and barked his orders. "All in good time," he said quietly to himself.

Berenice walked on toward the broad staircase that led from the Upper Market to the Lower City, past a stream of water-carriers and vendors of fresh vegetables and charcoal. A man who had been watching the whole encounter now crossed the square and fell into step beside her. He was a very tall, good-looking young man in his late twenties—large-boned, with a high-ridged hawk nose, a pair of dark, narrow, and shrewd eyes, and a russet beard clipped close. He wore an ankle-length sleeveless robe of position, with a pale blue sash of fine silk, specifying to both his wealth and his priestly blood. A tiny symbolic dagger, hanging from his robe, attested to his military inclination, while a six-pointed star upon the hilt reminded gently of his pretensions to royal blood. He was a man full of reminders and pretensions, and Berenice had met him upon two previous occasions—once as a guest in her house. He was a man of wit and brilliance, very young, but promising much in many directions. He was also, Berenice felt, frequently unbearable in his didactic certainties. His name was Joseph Benmattathias Hacohen; he had spent time in Rome; he spoke a fair Latin and wrote the language fluently, and when he wrote in Latin he styled himself Josephus.

Walking next to Berenice, he greeted her with great formality. There was nothing as elegant or as conscious of itself as an upper-class Jew—no one more eager to contrast a fluidity of manners with a rigidity of premise and notion. He greeted her, apologized for his intrusion, and asked whether he might walk with her.

"If you wish," she shrugged. "We walk a good distance in

the morning, my husband and myself, to the Fountain Gate and then perhaps to the House Gate and up the steep steps. There are many people who dislike the climb."

"I assure you that I enjoy the climb," Joseph said. "Perhaps you will find me amusing."

"Perhaps."

"Or even informative. I beg the opportunity. I have never seen you without your husband before—"

"Then you watch me?" Berenice asked. It was hard to be angry with Joseph Benmattathias. He was nakedly opportunistic, but he made no secret of it; he was as nakedly ambitious. Had he seen her walk by alone and not seized this opportunity, he would have never forgiven himself; but Berenice knew this and he was aware that she knew.

"When I see you, I watch you, Queen Berenice," he replied. "Like all young, male Jews, I am in love with you."

"What nonsense—and rather insulting too! Only my age makes you bold enough to say such a thing. If I were ten years younger, you would bite your tongue."

"I am ready to bite it to shreds now." He spread his hands. "When I saw that wretched little Roman preening himself in front of you, I bit my lips until I felt the taste of blood in my mouth. It's there now. Yet it was too evident that you despised him."

"Indeed?"

"Oh, yes. Yes, indeed, my lady."

"You miss very little."

"I try to miss nothing."

"I don't care for men like that," Berenice said slowly. "I don't like centurions. They are a dirty breed. But I admire Rome."

"Oh? And might I ask why?"

"Do you admire Rome, Joseph?"

"They have many qualities I admire."

"As I do. Order and stability—" She spoke in generalities, realizing as she spoke that she was uncertain about Joseph

Benmattathias. He nodded soberly at her answer, however, and took her arm to help her down five steps hewn from the naked rock.

"Our city leaves much to be desired. And does the nashi share your opinion of Rome?"

"The nashi?"

"Your husband."

"Why do you call him the nashi?"

Joseph shrugged expressively. "Everyone knows—am I to think that the cleverest woman in Jerusalem remains ignorant?"

"You risk a good deal with that kind of flattery."

"And I gain a good deal. Let us accept the fact that we have certain things in common."

"Such as?"

"Such as a hatred for senseless destruction and a taste for civilization."

"Because we are Jews?" Berenice asked. "Or because we admire Rome?"

"Perhaps we admire certain qualities in Rome only because we are Jews—just as our being Jews makes us the implacable enemies of other qualities that Rome embraces."

"Such as?"

"A witless, aimless, and pointless universe," Joseph replied surprisingly. "Because I am brash, my lady, don't mistake me for a fool. I am very young by the lights of some and profoundly old by the lights of others. Right now, the Great Sanhedrin is placing the crown of nashi upon your husband. The fact that the crown is only symbolic does not make him less the head of all Israel. He is that, and they had no other choice than to confirm it. There is only himself and his brother left out of the bloodline of Hillel the Good, and his brother is a scholar and a teacher. We want a man of iron."

"And you think that my husband is a man of iron?"

They had dropped down from the Upper City to the Lower

City, steps and steep streets and twisting pavement, and now they stopped for a moment in the wide Square of the Jebusites, where there was an open water gutter where women knelt and washed clothes. There were a stone bench and an olive tree fighting for life in this wilderness of man-hewn stone.

"We can sit here a moment," Berenice said, sinking down onto the bench.

"Yes—yes." He was self-conscious with his fine robe. The bench was dirty. "Yes, I will tell you what I think," he said, his pretensions forgotten for the moment, all of him absorbed in what he was formulating. "I think this, Queen Berenice. I think that the struggle is not between Jew and Roman but between Hillel and Shammai." He nodded at a little cluster of lean, hard-faced, and ragged Jews making their way across the square. For all of their stained and torn clothes, they walked easily and warily, their hands hidden in their linen vests, long blue threads trailing from the corners of their garments. "Sicarii," he said softly. "There is Shammai—"

"And where is Hillel?" Berenice wondered.

"There." Nodding at the women washing their clothes. "Hillel is life and Shammai is death. I despise the ignorant old men who cover their foolishness by talking in riddles. I am not talking in riddles. I talk of life and death. Everything we Jews do, we do to the extreme. We have become enamored of life, and thereby we are enamored of death. We love the sword and we hate the sword. We will use it or eschew it. Think of your own father. Claudius gave him everything—all that a Jewish king could desire and a realm as large as any Jewish king ever ruled before—yet your father had to plot war against Rome. Was there ever such a people as ourselves? We are a nation split in two—and where do the two connect? The House of Hillel says, Thou shalt not kill—and nothing—nothing justifies the taking of human life. Life is God and God is life. Will you do away with the Almighty?" His voice rose. Never had Berenice dreamed that this controlled and aloof young man could thus be carried away. "And what does the House of Shammai say?" he went on. "Death—the meaning of life. By death, life is made pure!"

She touched the dagger that hung from his sash. "Then why do you wear this?"

"Because we are all like that," he answered moodily. "Shammai and Hillel, inside of us—"

Eight days after this, Berenice gave a reception for the members of the Great Sanhedrin. They had voted Shimeon the nashi, sitting in continuous session for almost seven hours, in the Hall of Hewn Stone in the Temple. Then, when the final ballot had been cast and this man, a common Israelite with no drop of priestly blood or royal blood in his veins, had been named the prince in judgment over all of Israel, even over King Agrippa in the North, the members of the Sanhedrin walked with slow pace into the innermost sanctum of the Holy of Holies, the sanctuary of the Almighty Himself. They walked between two lines of Levites, who held flaming torches to light their way, the Levites resplendent in their blue and orange trappings, the members of the Sanhedrin wrapped plainly in black and white striped robes, a symbol of the desert costume and the tents where the legendary patriarchs meted out the first justice. Phinehas Benhavta, the high priest just appointed by the Sanhedrin, had dressed himself entirely in white, as a priest would on the Day of Atonement, and as the Sanhedrin entered the Holy of Holies, he chanted the ancient unity. Then Shimeon prostrated himself before Phinehas, who anointed him.

No woman had ever seen such a ceremony, and Berenice listened, fascinated, as Shimeon repeated the steps of the process. Berenice felt herself swelling with pride and had to hold back from a desire to touch Shimeon's face as he spoke, to caress his hands. "This is the man who chose me," she kept repeating to herself. Her eyes were wet, yet she laughed with delight, and Shimeon said, "There's no credit or virtue

on my part. It had to be either the blood of Hillel or
Shammai—and they chose Hillel. God be praised."

"And what will the Zealots do?" Berenice asked.

"I don't know—no one knows. We will wait and see, and
meanwhile, they have asked me to hold a reception—for the
Romans as well as our own."

It was the event of the season in Jerusalem, and over four
hundred guests appeared to pay their respects to Shimeon
Bengamaliel—among them one Menahem Hacohen, a tall,
exceedingly thin yet handsome man, who was the leader of
the Sicarii. He was dressed all in pale blue, but soberly, with
no ornament of gold or silver visible, and after he had bowed
to Shimeon, he said softly, "We are both Jews. I will remember that. Will you, Bengamaliel?"

Who had invited him, or whether he had been invited at
all, Shimeon did not know; and as for Berenice, she had her
hands full; by the time the reception was over, Shimeon had
forgotten about Menahem. Berenice, on her part, had a
hundred other matters to be concerned about, the summon-
ing of the guests in the very short time allowed—only enough
time to send postriders to Galilee and have at least a token
representation from there—the balance of the guests, who
would include not only a handful of the leading Romans in
Jerusalem and in Caesarea as well, but Pharisees and Sadducees, Hillelites and Shammaites, Zealots and
Herodians—a mixture that could only resolve itself under
the masterly control of a particular hostess, and perhaps no
other hostess than Berenice. Food had to be planned for and
purchased, musicians provided, prejudices shelved for the
moment at least—and in the end guests greeted and handled
and directed. And all of it on top of the fact that Judea was on
edge.

It was more than two decades since Berenice's father had
been murdered at Caesarea—and that meant two decades of
Roman occupation and rule in Judea and thereby in
Jerusalem. Berenice thought of this as she placed at the head

of her list of guests the name of Gessius Florus, the current procurator of Judea. She had known a great many procurators since that day of her father's death, seven in all to be exact, and all alike in their compulsive, corroding greed for money. No, there was one exception to that—Tiberius Julius, who was an apostate Jew and nephew to the Alabarch Alexander and to Philo, both of them dead these many years. Yet suppose the sickly boy in Alexandria had survived and she had married him? What would the shape of the world be to her now? She shook loose from these fruitless thoughts. The fact of the matter was that a procurator was a procurator, as if shaken from a mold—self-made petty slave traders and business men of Rome, who bought their appointment from the emperor and then proceeded to regard Judea as one great tax farm. Why, she wondered, did no one ever equate Rome with money? Why all the splendid words to disguise one plain fact—that she had never known a Roman who did not want money more than anything else in the world? Well, here was her list, and on top of it, Gessius Florus, a short, plump man of fifty-two, with a protruding belly the size of a large melon. Was he worse than the others? Or was it her imagination? Fadus, the first of them, hated fanatics. How can you govern Jews and hate fanatics? There was a single day when he crucified one hundred and twelve of the immersers, who were doing no more than baptizing themselves in the River Jordan. The second procurator, Tiberius Julius the apostate, would take a father who had broken the law and execute the sons. The third one, Ventidius Cumanus, had provoked a minor civil war between Samaritans and Jews in Samaria—so that two branches of the same folk killed and killed until the streets of every Samaritan city ran with blood. That was when Berenice and Shimeon had gone to Rome to plead for his removal; and Berenice remembered well how the Emperor Claudius had listened to her and wept as the daughter of his old friend told of what took place in Samaria. Cumanus was removed and replaced with Felix, who wanted only money, and after him, Festus, who wanted even more money, and then Albinus, who was half insane in his lust for money, and now at last Gessius Florus, who, it was said, had taken a sacred oath before every god he encountered, including Yaweh, that he would not leave Judea until he had amassed one hundred talents[1] in gold, which would make him the most successful administrator in the History of Roman administrators.

Berenice studied his name thoughtfully as she wrote it. After a manner, he would be the guest of honor. He was in residence in Caesarea, but he would cheerfully come to Jerusalem. Two motives would bring him: suspicion and greed.

Gessius Florus said to Berenice, speaking Latin, for his Greek was embarrassingly bad and he could not speak a word of Hebrew or Aramaic, "This would do you credit in Rome, you know. Fine affair—fine party. And the wine—excellent wine."

"We Jews pride ourselves on our wine, and of course we are honored to have the procurator as our guest."

"And may I remark upon your beauty? This we do not have in Rome—beauty, yes, but not Berenice."

"I admire Rome, both its strong men and its beautiful women."

She passed him on then. Personally, she had to greet hundreds of guests, remember them or recognize them, and say the right thing in the most suitable language to each of them—for while the occasion was in honor of the nashi, no guest came without the anticipation of seeing Berenice. The past fifteen years had turned her into a legend—the mother symbol that the Jews yearned for so passionately, the dim yet fervent memory of Ashtarte whom they had worshiped once in legendary past, before the fierce and commanding figure of Yaweh had forbidden them to whore after the fertility

[1]About four million dollars in today's currency.

images. Yet again and again, they would create a mother for Israel, were she Sarah or Rachel or Esther—or now Berenice. They had made a saint of Berenice. Had not the Almighty Himself chosen her? Did she change? Did she grow older? Did her beauty wither or become less? Was there ever a streak of gray or white in the red flame of her hair—the blooded hair where the finger of the Almighty touches the seed of Aaron?

"No," said old Anat Beradin, who had journeyed down from Galilee to be here, "no, my child—time has exempted you. We grow old, we wither, we die, but Berenice does not change."

"Berenice gets old and still and tired," she told him. "And God bless you for coming. It's good to see old friends. We have been too long here, and my heart yearns for my homeland."

"As we yearn for you. Is your brother here?"

"He's in Alexandria, and he did not dare leave now. Kings or nashis or Sanhedrins—we all exist by virtue of the bankers in Alexandria—and between the banks and the Romans, well—"

She greeted Shimeon's brother, Hillel, Britannicus Galul, the new proconsul from Damascus, Atak Phen, the Egyptian shipping lord, whose fleet of wheat barges poured an unending stream of grain into Rome; she greeted the old, old man, Isaac Benabram, the archon of her own Tiberias, and young Rabbi Tava, only nineteen years old, She greeted the members of the Sanhedrin, fighting desperately to control the sequence of names.

Seeing her, watching her, so tall and calmly gracious, struck again for the thousandth time by her strange, breathtaking beauty, Shimeon made his way toward her. In all the chaos of the growing, articulating, swirling party, he had to touch her and confirm her reality.

Also moving toward Berenice, Joseph Benmattathias was intercepted by the Procurator Florus, who said that he heard a great deal about him, "Fine expectations from so young a man," Florus nodded. "They tell me you intend to write a history."

"When I find time. Not for a good many years, I expect."

"Well, we don't want it to be a one-sided thing. do we? Rome thinks well of those who respect Rome. Come to me when the time is at hand. I can be of help to you."

"I will remember that," Joseph said.

"Odd though—"

"Yes?"

"One doesn't expect history from a Jew. From a Greek, yes—and a Roman. But a Jew?"

"What does one expect from a Jew?"

"Business, you know. You are a nation of merchants. The hand out all the time, you know. That's why you are all so improbably rich. Go anywhere—anywhere in the world, and you find your rich Jew."

"We are merchants," Joseph nodded. "I can't deny that. Your emperors wear the purple because Jews crush the shell and extract the dye, and because Jewish ships bring the dye to Thrace to dye the cotton there, and other Jews buy the cotton cloth in Egypt. By virtue of the same, your silk tunic exists because Jewish caravans trade between here and Cathay, and the beautiful bronze clasp you wear, with the hawk emblazoned on it, exists because a Jewish trading station and synagogue had flourished in Cornwall for a hundred years before ever a Roman set foot in Britain, and because Jewish supercargoes directed Phoenician shipping into the tin trade before certain other peoples ever learned that bronze was an alloy of copper and tin. We create wealth, my dear procurator; we don't steal it."

Florus reddened, sought for some clever rejoinder, and then simply said, "Meaning what precisely?"

"No meanings are really precise," Joseph replied, shrugging and turning away. One of the Sanhedrin, who had overheard, remarked that it did not help anything at this moment to make worse enemies of men like Florus, and

Joseph replied that anyone in Rome with an ounce of sophistication detested Florus, who was nobody.

"But nobody can do damage, and we are a long way from Rome," the member of the Sanhedrin pointed out.

The object of their discussion was getting drunk and being mollified by the charms of a number of Jewish ladies, who made a great deal of him. All things noted, he remained the ranking Roman in Judea. The fact that he was a knight, a member of the merchant class and no more, meant little to Jerusalem society, since to the Jews the patterns of Roman quality and nobility were incomprehensible—just as the Jewish bloodlines, traced so matter-of-factly for twelve hundred years into the past, were meaningless to the Romans. Ventix, the centurion who was related to the emperor's family, commented on the procurator's behavior, but Berenice would venture no opinions. "He is my guest. I desire him to be happy." "And myself?" Ventix demanded. He reached out to touch her breast, and as she evaded him, she could not control the flash of anger that crossed her face. Neither could the young man fail to notice it. His own rage and frustration churned in his stomach. The popular bon mot of Rome held that the Jews were unique in that you had to hate the men as much as you loved the women. He was ready to accept what they said about Jewish women, but there was only one woman he had eyes for, and she turned her back on him simply and deliberately.

In the course of the evening, a tall, lean man dressed in pale blue—and Casper Ventix realized only later that this was most likely Menahem Hacohen, the infamous leader of the dreaded Sicarii—stopped by the young centurion and said, "I saw you with the Queen Berenice."

"Did you? And just how does it concern you?" The centurion was a little drunk by now.

"I am concerned as a Jew is concerned."

"And how is that?"

"We treasure here. She is a saint on earth. Do you know what that means, Roman?"

The centurion looked into a pair of icy-cold blue eyes, and there was nothing there to see but death and hate. He shook his head.

"Then find out, Roman," the man in blue said softly.

There was little that Berenice missed. She had the ability to hear and digest two conversations at once. She picked out bits and pieces, sorted them, filed them; yet continued to be a charming and gracious hostess. Among other things, she noticed Menahem's confrontation of the Roman. Guests were leaving, and she bid them farewell—but Shimeon should have been at her side. His brow furrowed, he was talking to Caleb Barhoreb, a small man with a clubfoot, perhaps the most articulate and powerful voice in the Great Sanhedrin, a great nephew of the Ba'as Hacohen, whom she had met fifteen years ago during the last week of his life. Intense, brilliant, dynamic in his use of power, Caleb Barhoreb was of both the bloodline nobility and the merchant aristocracy, a first cousin of Phineas Hacohen, who was now head of the House of Hakedron, and a dedicated follower of the teachings of Hillel the Good.

Berenice caught Shimeon's eye. He nodded, and then he joined her. They stood together by the door then, bowing, saying the polite and necessary things as the guests left—until in a moment of respite, Shimeon managed to say, "I hope you are not too tired, my dear."

"I'm never too tired when a reception goes well—only when it goes badly."

They bid farewell to the high priest and his two followers, to Niger, the strange war chief of the nomad Jews in the land of Gilead and in the trackless desert to the east of Gilead, and to Habin Judaicus, a leader of the Jewish community in Rome. Another interval:

"Florus demands a meeting tonight."

"With whom?"

"Caleb Barhoreb," said Shimeon, "myself—you."

"He's an animal. He's drunk anyway. Tell him we're tired."

"He's not drunk. I told him we were tired. The little swine said that the walls of Rome would crumble if every Roman citizen who was tired forsook his duties."

Again they paused for farewells. The crowd was definitely thinning out now.

"We are not Roman citizens," Berenice said wearily.

"He is. We are his Jews—remember, my love?"

"No, I don't remember, and I am sick to death of this city, Shimeon. Yes, of this High Place, with its unending intrigue and crosscurrents and undercurrents—and—no, no, we are not his Jews, not you and me. We are Galileans, and if we must belly crawl to Rome, let us be someone else's Jews, not his. I want to go home, Shimeon."

"In good time, when the session of the Sanhedrin is over. Meanwhile, there is nothing I can do about this. His requests cannot be set aside. We will meet with him."

"But why me?" Berenice asked.

"I don't know, but like most Romans, I am sure that he is somewhat confused as to your status. Are you queen of Chalcis or queen of Galilee or queen of Israel or queen of Shimeon or what?"

"Only of Shimeon," she smiled.

"Then he's probably after money, and you're still the richest woman in Isreal."

Shimeon spoke in jest, but he turned out to be bleakly correct.

The guard of four legionaires who had accompanied Gessius Florus were squatting on the steps of the palace and dozing when Berenice ushered out her last guest; and the legend that the legionary dies who dozes on guard duty went with him. One of the legionaries still awake cocked a leg and passed air. His hard, crude fart awakened the others, who made some conversation in their bad Latin, which could not run three words without some reference to male or female sex organ.

Berenice turned back to the house and joined the men in Shimeon's workroom, a pleasant room where he conducted business, saw patients, or did his writing when they were in Jerusalem. Only now it was fewer patients and more of everything else.

Darkness had fallen by now, and the room was lit by half a dozen lamps and full of what was to Berenice the warm and familiar smell of olive oil. Gessius Florus sprawled on a couch. He had kicked off his sandals and made himself comfortable, one foot drawn up on the couch so that he could pick at his toes. Caleb Barhoreb stood leaning against Shimeon's worktable, and Shimeon himself sat stiffly on a small bench. Barhoreb came erect and Shimeon rose as Berenice entered, but Florus did not move, only looking at her fully and frankly, like a slave buyer examining the merchandise before him. Shimeon drew an armchair out for Berenice, and she seated herself and said without more ado,

"I tell you, Procurator, that I have had a very full day, and if you think that a reception for half a thousand people is a game played for pleasure, why, try it. Myself, I am exhausted—and if whatever you have in mind will take time, I must excuse myself."

"No time at all," Florus replied, smiling without parting his lips. He got to his feet, went to the table, where a sand glass stood, and turned it over so that a thin stream of sand began to run. "One glass—fair enough?"

"We're waiting, Procurator," Shimeon said.

Back on the couch, Florus picked at his toes and said, "I can't afford to give receptions like this. It would bankrupt me. I can't even afford to carry out the common and necessary duties of an administrator. It's a pittance that's paid to a procurator. The fact is that I am in debt up to my ears. I try to be understanding, patient, and just. Above all, just—and that's not terribly easy with Jews. But everything bogs down under my obligations. I should not be pressed to think about money, morning, noon, and night—and my debts. It's a constant state of temper, and that makes for poor judgment. You don't want that. Do you know that I had to borrow to come here from Caesarea?"

"How much money do you want, Procurator?" Caleb Barhoreb asked quietly, evenly, his voice under severe control.

"Ten talents," Florus said flatly, staring at his toes.

Both Caleb and Shimeon looked at each other and then bleakly at Berenice.

"We gave you a talent four months ago," Caleb said. "Three weeks ago we sent you ten thousand silver shekels. Even a cow cannot be milked four times a day."

"Jews are not cows," Florus replied, spreading each toe, one after another, staring at the flesh between them.

"I think," said Shimeon, "that the procurator is amusing himself at our expense."

"Am I?" Florus did not look up.

"You can't be serious."

"I am not amused. Why are you amused, Nashi?"

Shimeon shrugged. "Because that is an impossibly large sum of money. It's the ransom of an emperor. It would take months to raise a sum that size."

"Months?" Now Florus looked up. "I was thinking of tomorrow. I suppose I could wait another day."

"And where do we find this money?" Caleb asked. "You say tomorrow. Where do we find the money by tomorrow?"

"I am only a Roman," Florus said. "You are Jews. It is your business to find money. The queen here is the richest woman in the world."

"What nonsense!" Berenice said. "Do you think that I could lay my hands on ten talents in two days? If you do, Procurator, you know less about the ways of the world than I would have expected."

"Are you pleading poverty?"

"No, Procurator—not at all," Berenice had no intentions of diminishing herself in his eyes. He worshiped wealth; then let him be impressed with her wealth. "I can raise ten talents. It would take a little time, and it would mean selling a number of things that I own. I do not keep chests of coins in anticipation of such moments as this. In fact, I could raise ten and another ten and another ten to boot—and I would not be poor, Procurator, far from it."

Florus had let go of his toes now. He was staring at Berenice, his expression mingled with greed and awe.

"But I have no intention to do so, Procurator. None. I owe you no money. I am the titular dowager queen of Chalcis, and I am responsible only to the Emperor at Rome. I am not impressed with you and your demands—"

"Berenice!" Shimeon cried.

—"no, no, Shimeon. Let me finish."

Gessius Florus was on his feet now. Barefooted, short, and round as a dumpling, his hair thrusting up in all directions, his face glowing with deepening color, he puffed out his lips and snapped,

"Yes, Nashi—let her finish! I would not miss a word she has to say!"

Berenice-also rose, towering over the procurator, and said quietly, "I repeat that I am not impressed. You have no power over me, Procurator, and may all your gods help you if you or any of your people lay a finger on me or mine. I am not a Judean, and this is not my city, and I am no stranger in Rome. Not one shekel would I give you—not if I were rich as Croesus, with all the wealth of Lydia in my coffers. Let me add this—"

"Enough!" Shimeon cried, but Caleb gripped his arm.

—"others have made a religion out of hating Jews and looting them. They are dead and forgotten. We are still here, Procurator." With that, she swept from the room, leaving the three men silent behind her.

Shimeon and Caleb remained silent, waiting. Florus breathed deeply until he had himself under control, and then he said. "I want the ten talents tomorrow. Before I leave Jerusalem. Take them out of the temple treasury."

"That's impossible, Procurator," Caleb said. "You know that. I speak in your own interests. The Temple's treasury is sacred—"

"Except to the priests, who dip into it like a bottomless well."

"We won't argue that. But this is not a happy or easy city. Such an action could explode it."

"My legionaries will handle any explosion your Jews can make."

"Procurator," Shimeon said, "would it hurt to give us a little more time? In the past, you have made demands and we have met them. We are not unreasonable."

"Tomorrow," Florus said.

Berenice was awake, sitting on her bed meekly, her long legs drawn under her, hardly daring to look at Shimeon while she asked him what had come of it. He shrugged and said that nothing had come of it, except that Florus wanted his money out of the temple treasury.

"I made a fine display of myself," Berenice said.

"No. It changed nothing."

"He thought I would offer him the money."

"I suppose so."

"Should I have?"

"And next time—and the time after that? You were right. He has no power over you. Well—we shall see. I am tired, Berenice—I feel old and tired tonight."

"You are the nashi. We are celebrating," she pleaded. "My husband is a prince over all of Israel—and don't be angry with me. Let me be proud."

"I am not angry," Shimeon said, "only very tired."

In bed, she tried to hold him in her arms, but he turned away. She lay there sleepless, telling herself that all would be well when they left this place and went back to Galilee.

Berenice finally slept, but fitfully, and in the hour before dawn, she was awakened by Shimeon's movements. He was already dressed, and by the time the first red edge of the morning sun topped the desert hills to the east of Jerusalem, his messengers were out calling for an assembly of the Great Sanhedrin. Berenice went to the kitchen, where a red-eyed, sleepy Gabo was scolding the servants, complaining that the milk was sour and telling a fruit vendor at the back door that she would see him crucified, did he ever again dare to sell her tainted figs. Dropping onto one of the benches at the long kitchen table, Berenice gave the orders for Shimeon's breakfast. "Is there sour dough?" she asked. "I want him to have hot bread. And warm the milk for him, Gabo." "It's sour." She brought Berenice a wooden tub of sour dough, and Berenice began to work and shape the bread. "Then find sweet milk. Where is the milk vendor?" "Dead, I hope," Gabo snapped. "And the oven isn't hot enough—unless he waits for the bread. Does he wait?" The cook, a hugely fat Jebusite, pleaded with Berenice that he was not master even in his own kitchen.

"I say the stove is hot enough," he said. "But she—that one—that devil of darkness—"

"I'll tear your gonads off, so help me! If you have any, you fat capon!" Gabo shrilled.

"Do you hear? Lady Berenice, do you hear? Is that the way to talk to a man in his own kitchen? Or is it my kitchen? That devil of Benjamin is destroying me. Destroying me. Give me the bread. You will have hot bread. I say so. I pledge so."

Gabo spat in disgust and went for fresh milk. Berenice, bearing a platter of fruit, went to the breakfast room. The slaves were already at work in the great reception hall, cleaning away the debris and leavings of the celebration of the night before. As she passed, Berenice heard them talking. "Ten talents," said one, and another corrected this, "Eight talents—I have it on authority," "Seven, eight, ten talents—do you know what I would do with ten talents?" And another one, an older woman said, "Empty-headed fools— you'll drink your own blood for the trouble that will come of this. Trouble. That's what it means when the Romans ask for money."

In the breakfast room, Berenice put the fruit on the sideboard and prepared the basin of water and the white linen towels for Shimeon's hands. He came in a few minutes, held out his hands—why was she always surprised at the size of his hands, not the hands of a scholar or jurist, but the long-fingered, strong hands of a woodcutter?—and she laved them from a ewer. He said his blessing to the Almighty softly, "—who maketh the fruit to grow in the field—" She held out the linen and he dried his hands.

"About last night and the procurator's demands," she said. "I heard the slaves talking as I came in here, Shimeon. They were arguing about the amount."

"What? How could they possibly know?"

"You know what slaves are."

"I don't want that out. It's like pouring oil on the city and lighting it. I'll talk to them."

But as he left to do so, Berenice sighed and shook her head. It would not help. The word was out, and nothing could bottle it again.

By noon that day, the story of Gessius Florus and his demand was all over the city. The amount—as the story was related—varied from five talents to twenty-five talents; but consistently the story had him pleading his debts and obligations before Berenice and Shimeon. Berenice belonged to the people of Jerusalem, so far as they were concerned, and they were possessed of three singular things that were not to be duplicated elsewhere on earth, namely: Yaweh, His Temple, and the saintly Berenice. They had ceased even to think of a time when Berenice was perhaps not so saintly, and if there was an act of charity that Berenice was responsible for—and there were many—there were ten for the one that were added to the apocrypha, and which had no other basis than the fertile imaginations of the creative taletellers. After all, was she not an Esther come to life and walking among her own folk? So the very fact that Florus should dare whimper his demands to Berenice added fuel to the flames.

Also, out of the reception had come a story of unspeakable insult offered to the queen—the Roman had laid his hand against her breast, openly and insultingly. What Roman? No one knew exactly, but obviously Florus. The stories were woven and unwoven, but the children were not content with stories.

By noon, the morning classes were over. The thousands of children who had crouched in the courtyards of the city's synagogues while the teachers—Levites they were—paced back and forth, listening to the chanted verses of the Torah, listening for any variation in the pronunciation of the *holy tongue*, the ancient ritual Hebrew, punishing instantly and severely with a blow from the cedar wands they carried—these thousands of children were suddenly released and poured into the streets of Jerusalem. From six to thirteen years of age, they were bold, wiry, and insufferably insolent. They feared nothing and mocked everything that was not Jewish, and as they poured through the streets they whipped off their ritualistic stocking caps—the dashing cap that Judah Maccabeus first wore—held them out, and screeched, "Alms! Alms! Alms for Florus!" Thickening and mispronouncing the Latin word, which someone had supplied, the roar became *Shtipem–Romus–Florus!"* They made it into a singsong cadence that was presently echoing from thousands of throats. And joining in the spirit of the occasion, adults began to drop copper coins and even a silver shekel or two into the outstretched hats. Once the game had turned into the reality, the aimlessly circulating swarm of children began a motion toward the Praetorium, which was in the Palace of Herod in the ancient quarter of Zion. Men and women laughingly joined the procession, which a few moments later poured into the great plaza of the Upper City Market. The fruit and vegetable and oil vendors there looked up questioningly, to be met with the cadenced cry:

"Shtipem–Romus–Florus!"

Across the plaza, the palace front was in the Greek style, a deep portico of fluted columns, dark in its shadow; and now, from that shadowed darkness, Florus emerged and stood at one end of the portico—and almost as if he materialized them magically, there appeared behind him a full maniple of legionaries, one hundred and twenty in full armor, carrying scutum and naked Spanish sword, but not pilum. And behind them, still in the shadow and invisible, stood a second supporting maniple.

It was at this moment that Berenice appeared at the head of the marble staircase that led from the market plaza to the Temple. She took in the scene with a single swift glance—the crowd of children and adults pouring across the plaza and halted suddenly by the clockwork precision of the maniple that marched forward from the portico; the crowds behind them, unaware, and forcing them forward; the sudden screams of women and children mingling with the derisive scream of "Alms for the Roman Florus!" At one side of the market plaza, across from where the vendors' carts were stationed, there was a line of the finest villas in Jerusalem, magnificent homes of some of the oldest and most revered families in Judea, built thus to take advantage of the splendid view in the rear and from their roof tops. The afternoon sun struck the plaza just in front of the houses; children played there; mothers watched them. Now these too churned into a screaming effort to escape the death that marched from the portico across the plaza. And from the end of the portico, Florus watched.

Berenice leaped down the stairs, keeping close to one wall to avoid the people streaming by her to escape; and then she was in the plaza and running toward Florus. But already the maniple had mixed with the children and the feckless adults who had joined them, and still children poured into the plaza. At least two or three thousand children were there already, churning in a screaming, terror-stricken mob—and into the center of it the maniple charged, the Spanish short swords weaving like the warp and woof of a loom, the shriek of death all over Jerusalem.

Behind the carts, Berenice raced across the plaza; she had not run like this since she was a child—and as she took the last few steps that brought her to where Florus stood, he was watching her and grinning. Her plea came through her gasping intake of breath:

"Stop it, Procurator—in God's name, stop it!"

"Whose gods?" he smiled. "Yours? Mine?"

"They're killing children!" she cried. "Children! Look there—infants! Do you make war on infants?"

The second maniple was marching out of the portico now.

"The more glory to Yaweh," he yawned.

"Please, I beg you."

"One begs on one's knees—even queens."

She could not hear him; he could not hear her—so great was the shriek of horror and terror that rose over the plaza.

"On one's knees!" he shouted.

Weeping, she fell to her knees and embraced his legs. Behind the vendors' carts, hundreds of people who had taken shelter watched this. Weeping themselves, they saw the woman they considered their queen and the queen of all Israel kneel and embrace the legs of the procurator and beg him for mercy.

Florus tasted it and rolled it on his tongue. He tasted it long and with pleasure. Casper Ventix, the young centurion, had paused to watch. The second maniple was now killing—without passion, without zest, simply killing whatever was alive and in its way, killing as a machine kills.

"Centurion!" Florus shouted.

Ventix walked toward him slowly.

"Move when I call you!"

"I hear you, Procurator."

"Where's the Tubicen?"

"There—Procurator." He pointed to the other end of the portico, where a man leaned on a five-foot-long trumpet.

"Have him sound the recall."

"I hear and obey, Procurator," he said, his voice lazy and

buried in insolence—and just as slowly and lazily, he walked across the portico to where the Tubicen stood. A moment later, the recall echoed across the plaza.

Berenice rose, "Thank you, Procurator," she said.

"Time enough later for payment," Florus nodded, grinning. He was vastly pleased with himself. His was not the kind of mind that measures the future or weighs the consequences. He had revenged himself and turned the scream of Jewish mockery back upon itself and humbled a woman who despised him. He felt a sense of achievement.

Looking back, remembering, Berenice always had difficulty in piecing together that day—as did others; for it was an infamous day, a day of separation between past and future, a day when a furious sickness was born, if such hatred be a sickness. Joseph Benmattathias was in the Temple when the worst of this day took place. Being beyond question of priestly blood, he had certain privileges he was never loath to exercise, and while the Great Sanhedrin debated in one room of the Temple, he made notes of their arguments and conclusions in another room, putting together bits of information, surmise, and gossip that was brought to him by the Levites. This was essential to his being; and he could no more refrain from the narration of existence than he could from breathing. If he had been a Greek, he would have already styled himself a historian, but among the Jews—who unreasonably demand that a historian be divinely inspired—he gave himself no titles and contented himself with an endless search for the actuality of event. People knew this; it was of his nature; and he questioned Berenice very carefully afterward, pointing out that such horror must be provoked. He strained himself to be objective and neutral.

"I saw so little," Berenice replied. "I was pleading with Florus."

"I know, I know. We all know And he heeded you."

"Did he? Or was he tired of the bloodshed—or afraid?"

"Oh, he heeded you. No question of that. He sounded the recall, and when the troops returned to barracks, he went with them. He will never again walk alone in the streets of Jerusalem—or with much less than a legion around him. But what did you do then?"

"I walked across the plaza," Berenice told Joseph, frowning, trying to think beyond the stillness of the place. "It wasn't still," she said, "because people were screaming wih pain. But it seems like stillness when I think about it."

"Only the dead and wounded were there then?"

"In the center of the plaza," Berenice said. "There were unwounded people—Jews I mean—at the sides, at the street openings, on the staircases, by the villas—but not in the center. There were only the dead and the dying, and they were like heaps of cloth, all over, all over—so many—"

Some things she would never forget. She would never forget that. She would see things far more horrible, far more terrible—but different. At her feet were three little children, two girls and a boy, their bellies split, their guts on the pavement. She walked, and the blood covered her toes—the pool of blood an inch deep and growing where there was a timeworn depression in the plaza, and the bodies lay here and there and everywhere. The Roman troops had been marvelously efficient, a mother dead with her child clutched in her arms, and then the child dispatched with a sword-thrust, as if life of any kind was an affront to the clockwork soldiers who had marched out of the portico, and in another place was a pile of bodies, seventeen in all, piled one on the other—and how had that happened? The wounded pleaded with her—

Shimeon found her kneeling by the side of a twelve-year-old boy, holding an artery together so that the flicker of life she had discovered in him should not go out. With needle and thread he sewed the boy's wound—and then as he went on, working with the other physicians, Berenice remained with him, helping, holding flesh together for him to stitch, tearing all of her overdress into bandages and much of her underdress, for the blood that covered her from head to foot was cloak enough for modesty. The plaza was full now. The evening shadows were lengthening, the looming Temple casting its darkness upon them, and men with torches lit the plaza so that the doctors could work and so that mothers and fathers could find their children among the dead—and so that whimpering children could find their mothers and fathers. Death played no favorites here. The rich and noble ladies who were of the bloodlines of David and Mattathias and Aaron and Herod had died alongside of the common Israelites and Jebusites of the city—and within sight of their own villas.

When the bodies were counted, the toll was as follows: of grown men, fifty-nine, of grown women, one hundred and fourteen, of boy children, two hundred and six, and of girl children, three hundred and nineteen. This is aside from those who died later.

There was no quarter, no street in Jerusalem where there was not weeping that night. Washing the blood from her aching and tired limbs, Berenice heard the weeping, and Joseph Benmattathias heard it, too, where he was making his own notes on what happened.

It was nighttime, and Shimeon and Caleb Barhoreb and Phineas Hacohen and the former high priest, Hanan Hacohen, had gone to meet with the Procurator Gessius Florus as a deputation from the Great Sanhedrin. He had summoned them and they had decided that the wisest course would be to meet with him and speak with him. Hour by hour the excitement and rage and frustration of the people grew—and how it would burst forth and what would be the result of such an explosion no one could say; but it seemed to Shimeon and others—men who kept their heads and tried to weigh consequences—that if Florus could be persuaded to leave Jerusalem with his legionaries and go back to Caesarea for a while, the Sanhedrin might quiet the city and bring order and common sense as a means of dealing with the future.

Meanwhile, at her table and in the light of two smoking lamps, Berenice wrote a letter to her brother, Agrippa, who was in Alexandria at the invitation of the Jewish community there, undergoing a tiresome round of ceremonial dinners and receptions. She had set down all the events of this day and the day before, and now she wrote:

"—So now we sit in a city of grief, you you must not think me cruel or inured to suffering if I say to you, my brother, that I wish this were it and this Rome's price from us. We are a people not unuse to death and tragedy, and at this moment—or so I feel—such a price, bitter though it is, would not be too much. But the price is never ours to post, is it? And what happened today, if I read the signs aright, is only the beginning. Still, it is not yet Rome against Israel, but Israel with its own dagger in its heart—the House of Hillel facing the House of Shammai. I am terribly afraid of events that cannot be reversed, of action taken that cannot be ever put right, of words said that cannot ever be recalled—and in the end of a series of events that will inexorably lead to war with Rome and to the destruction of all that we are and all that is Israel.

"There is a man here in Jerusalem now, my brother, named Menaham Benjudah Hacohen—a Galilean whom you may have heard about—who is the leader of the dreaded Sicarii. They say that three thousand of these fanatical killers are in the city now—and who is to deny the rumor? There is no way of distinguishing them or identifying them, but those in Jerusalem who are identified with the House of Hillel are terribly nervous. What has happened to us that we should raise up in our own hearts such a breed as these Sicarii? Menahem himself I have met. He came all unbidden to my reception, tall, thin, with icy-cold blue eyes that burned with hate, and dressed all in the pale blue of Levi, as if proclaiming his priestly blood.

"I am told that in an argument at the reception in honor of Shimeon—he was voted nashi, and I must pass so lightly over so great an event—this Menahem took my part against an Roman officer. Why, I do not know, unless anything that includes hatred of Rome concerns him. Whether this had anything to do with what happened today, I do not know; but as I said before, this is a city of fear—and not fear of the Romans. What happened today was ghastly beyond belief, but it was also a piece of the monumental idiocy that has guided these procurators for so many years now. Florus destroyed himself today. He may not yet be aware of that, but it is a fact. So it is not Rome that the people fear at this moment, but the forces that Rome is unleashing. It is even said that each of the Sicarii has been instructed to select a victim—or else that Menahem has assigned victims from his list. You cannot fight this. One of these assassins stands beside you; he strikes with his knife—and it is done. Nor will the House of Shammai utter one word in condemnation of them. There are over twenty Zealots in the Great Sanhedrin, but Shimeon tells me that under no circumstances will they denounce the Sicarii. In fact, the whole party of the Zealots are rather proud of the Sicarii—a kind of twisted, unstated pride which they voice only to each other, as, for example— 'Murderous, swine, killers, devils out of hell, but they do the job they do, those Sicarii. They've put the fear of God into the Romans. You may argue with their methods, but you have to admit that they get results.'

"So it is that the ultimate negoation of all the teachings of Hillel the Good has arisen among us—and may even take control of all the destinies of Israel, if such half-wits as Florus pursue the course on which they have embarked; and it is even doubtful that when this horror we have spawned is released, Rome will be needed—and if needed, it will not be to begin but only to complete our destruction.

"I cannot tell you how I feel or what is happening inside of me. What I saw and went through today would have been as much as a Jew should be asked to endure—yet the background is even worse. Do you remember what I was, brother, in those days before I first laid eyes upon the House of Hillel? That was sixteen years ago, and Israel has been gentle enough to forget and they made a saint of me because they had suffered too long and too much under the just and implacable shadow of Yaweh. They wanted a woman of flesh and blood, a mother image, a Demeter who was not a blasphemy, an Esther who was not a legend, an Ashtarte who was not a whore—all these things they wanted, and I was none of them, but I existed and they chose me; and for sixteen years they have reverenced me—or perhaps what they made me a symbol of. And of course they forgot. But I did not forget. I shall never forget that cruel, cold, warped and unhappy creature that was Berenice. I shall never forget the pain of a shrunken soul, the fear of a child who could not love—and shall I forget that Hillel washed me clean and gave me a rebirth, a second life? Am I the only one who learned the secret of love from the House of Hillel, the secret of understanding, of peace, of charity—or are there not thousands of Jews who were shaped by the teachings of this saintly man? All of my existence is predicated on this—that thou shalt love thy neighbor as thyself, that this is the whole Torah, the soul and being of the Torah. Thus I married my husband. Thus I lived with him and became one with him. Thus I try to atone for the past in the way that Hillel taught, by doing what I can to ease the pain of this earth.

"And now it is to be swept away, destroyed, and replaced by that easy and invidious doctrine—the doctrine of kill. Kill what you do not like. Kill what shrinks your pride. Kill what has hurt you. Kill and kill and kill—and all wrongs will be righted, all sores healed. Is that the Roman doctrine—man's doctrine—our doctrine? I don't know, but oh, my brother, you are needed here. Now. Come here. I don't know what you can do, yet whatever you can do must be done. So come to us here at Jerusalem."

Berenice rarely slept until Shimeon came to bed with her, and nights without him were for the most part nights of sleeplessness. Now she lay in the dark until she heard his step, and she realized that simply from the sound of his step she knew of his whole being, whether his spirit was high or low, whether he was in a condition of hope or despondency and whether he came to her with love or without love. Now, as softly as he walked, his step was a step of dejection. She called to him quietly, "My love—Shimeon?"

He sat down beside her. "It would have been better if we had children, Berenice—"

Her voice choked. "You never reproached me before—I saw those children today, God help me."

"I don't reproach you."

"The Almighty makes a womb fruitful or barren—"

"My beloved, you misunderstand me," he said to her, stroking her hair and brow gently. "It is not out of want or need or desire that I spoke but of a fullness, too much—too much. Our love for each other is too much—"

"How can love be too much?"

"How? Don't you know? We are like one soul in two bodies. For fifteen years we have never been away from each other. Tell me, my beloved—what will be with you if I am slain?"

"I won't talk about that," Berenice answered with annoyance. "There is enough real grief and no need to imagine more. Tell me what passed with Florus."

"What should pass with a madman?"

"Always the Jew," she smiled. "Always the answer that is a question. Why is Florus a madman?"

"When the gods visit a madman—"

"And I will quote Euripides to you, but another time. What did Florus say?—may he be damned and cursed for eternity!"

"No sorrow, no apology, no shame. His manhood stiffened like an erect penis, and suddenly you have the feeling that under his round little belly is a weapon of pride and eagerness. You know what makes the Roman soldier so feared, Berenice? When he is attacked, he goes back and down on one knee, raising that huge wooden shield of his. He is a very little man, by and large. You will recall reading in Caesar's stories of the wars in Gaul how the barbarians always referred to the legionaries as 'the little men.' True with them, with us, with others—little men. He raises his shield, and the barbarian towers over him with spear or ax or sword. And then with that short Spanish word of his, the legionary thrusts up into the barbarian's groin—into his penis and gonads—that is the death wound of the Roman, from underneath with a tiny knife, into the manhood—so on a battlefield where Rome has conquered, the men lie apparently unwounded, except those cut down from behind, and Rome has the satisfaction of making a eunuch of the world. War is an orgy for Rome, and Florus was trembling with sex; he smelled sex; the room stank with the smell of his emission—the whole, monstrous slaughter of the innocents had been a sexual debauch for him, and he could not tear himself loose from it. Twice, just the memory aroused him to a point where he had to excuse himself, to come back stinking even higher of his sex—"

"No, no," Berenice cried. "A man is a man—"

"You should know better!"

"What will he do?"

"Already he has sent to Caesarea for two more cohorts of troops—a thousand men. They will be here in three days, I imagine, and he wants honor done to them. He wants them to be greeted by cheering, loving Jews. He wants flowers strewn in their path. He wants five hundred virgins appointed to embrace them—"

"Yes, he's lost his senses—"

"God help us!"

"What did you tell him?"

"We mollified him. We told him we would attempt to

satisfy his demands. In other words, we lied to him. He was itching for defiance. His testicles had tasted blood, and he wanted nothing so much as an excuse to pick up the slaughter where he left off."

With Shimeon and a dozen other members of the Great Sanhedrin, Berenice went up to the temple elevation, to the Court of the Nokri, where they would have a clear and uninterrupted view of the Antipatris Road, along which the two cohorts would march to enter Jerusalem at the Damascus Gate. It was a day like so many days in Jerusalem, cool, crisp and clear, the air as brittle as crystal and as sweet as wine, and the visibility so perfect that not only the Mediterranean but miles of Israel in every direction were visible. On a day like this, it was very easy for Berenice to comprehend why her ancestors had believed that God dwelt in the High Places—and Yaweh here in this ancient High Place that was hallowed by a thousand years of unbroken history. She had that singularly Jewish feeling of a memory that went back to a beginning before the beginning—a feeling that always filled her with emotion and even a sense of fear.

All over the city, men, women, and children had chosen places where the view was unobstructed—not to watch the Roman cohorts enter, but because the city was filled with hate and resistance to the notion of a thousand more legionaries to buttress the occupation forces. From her vantage point so high, Berenice could see them—on the city walls, on the outer Wall of Herod, on the second wall, on the Akra and perched over the Fish Gate, on roof tops and packed onto the terraces of the Maccabean Palace, with children everywhere sitting on tower tops, on ornaments, in the embrasures of the First Wall and even on the temple walls—where they perched in defiance of the curses and warnings the Levite temple guards flung at them. Outside the city, on either side of the Antipatris Road, stood the delegation of Jews who had gone to bid the cohorts welcome; but they were not virgins. Far from it—as Berenice could see even from her vantage point—they were all men, tall, lean men who in the very manner of stance and walk proclaimed the party they belonged to.

Berenice pointed this out to Shimeon. "Zealots, aren't they?"

Shimeon nodded. "Probably Sicarii—"

"What will come of this, Shimeon?"

He shrugged.

"We see each step," Berenice said. "We anticipate each step. And still we let it happen."

"I can do nothing. We deal with a madman."

"And who does he deal with?"

"He brought it on himself."

"But where does it go?" Berenice demanded. "Florus is one man. We revenge ourselves on him—but at what cost, Shimeon? We put a city of half a million people on the scale? Or did I never learn at the House of Hillel that vengeance is for the Almighty—if He should will it?"

"Look—there they are," Shimeon said, and pointed to where the cluster of Roman standards topped a hill about a mile from the city wall. "I can do nothing, Berenice—nothing."

No one could do anything now, Berenice realized. Events were in motion that had been set to motion a long time ago, and now movement everywhere was toward the climax. It must have only now occurred to Florus that his relief cohorts might walk into a trap they could not handle, and from the Praetorium across the city he dispatched two maniples, or four hundred men. The men passed on the double through the Phasael Gate in the Old Wall, which brought them to Herod's wall near the valley gate. Inside Herod's wall, they proceeded at a fast trot toward the Damascus Gate, by which the relief troops would enter the city.

It was a strange scene that Berenice watched from the temple elevation. On the one hand, the thousand legionaries from Caesarea were moving at parade march toward the walls of Jerusalem—unaware that anything untoward was either happening or scheduled to happen. They had been summoned against the possibility of trouble in the city; but trouble in Jerusalem was a constant of the world they and their fathers and their grandfathers had inhabited. On the other hand, the four hundred legionaries inside of the city wall were racing toward the Damascus Gate, very well aware of trouble; and now there descended upon this group, from walls and housetops, a rain of rocks and bricks, slates, building stones, arrows, and javelins. On every roof top there in the low city where the working people, the water carriers, masons, carpenters, potters, and weavers lived, there was a cluster of men and boys, bows bent and loosed without hurry or fear, javelins poised and then discharged against a sheltering Roman shield ten feet below. The Romans tried to cover themselves with their big shields, but the rocks smashed the shields; the javelins pierced the shields; and the arrows sought out the flesh that showed. Faster and faster ran the Romans as their initial wariness turned to panic, and they left behind them a trail of the dead and dying, the four hundred becoming three hundred and then two hundred and then finally no more than forty or fifty bleeding men to make a half circle of their shields alongside the Damascus Gate, fighting desperately against the mass of Jews who slowly closed in around them.

The wild shouting of the battle hysteria that had overtaken the Jews was picked up across the entire city and was heard by the two cohorts on the Anitpatris Road—who were now approaching the city gate. Berenice could see, even at this distance, how their precise step began to falter, how the soldiers glanced from side to side, trying to assess the meaning of the noise from the city and the intent of the Jews who had been waiting to receive them and who were now closing in on them from either side. An officer on a white horse spurred down the road, shouting at the Jews and lashing at them with his whip. Berenice could not hear his words at this distance, but she could well imagine him ordering the Jews back with all the delicacy of language a Roman officer commands— and then someone threw a rock and the officer fell down from his horse. Half a dozen legionaries broke ranks to rescue him, and from the other side the Sicarii closed in, knives drawn, ripping aside the Roman shields and coming in close, body to body with their razor-sharp, deadly knives. The other officers raced their horses toward the front of the column, shouting for the gates to open. The column broke in two, the front half toward the gate on the double and the latter section cut off and surrounded by the Sicarii. Then the gates were open, and the head of the column plunged through and the latter half wrenched itself loose from the grasp of the Sicarii and ran wildly toward the gate, all order and discipline forgotten. Of the thousand in the two cohorts, about seven hundred managed to enter the gate—the rest lay dead and dying on and alongside the Antipatris Road.

Berenice was no stranger to scenes of violence; she lived in a time and place where violence was very much the order of the day, and only a few days before she had witnessed the slaughter in the Great Plaza. But this was new—this thing of standing calmly and safely on the high mount of the Temple and watching, through the clear and sparkling air, a desperate fight to the death taking place no more than a few thousand feet from where she stood, a beginning less than two thousand feet away and an ending no more than three hundred feet below her. From beginning to end, she watched all of it.

The Roman relief column, pouring through the gate, joined forces with the handful left of the group that had raced there from the Praetorium. The centurions shouted orders for discipline and for a reconstitution of the ranks; shields were raised; the Romans began to move—but they were adrift now in a sea of Jews. From all over the city Jews poured

248

toward the Damascus Gate—and the Romans became an island in that shouting, enraged mob. The shout went up to the heavens and lay upon the city.

From the Damascus Gate to the Citadel of Antonia—a stone warehouse alongside the temple elevation and guarded by ten legionaries—was less than a quarter of a mile; but it took almost an hour for the Romans to fight their way there—and all along the twisting way their numbers dwindled. Almost two hundred reached this shelter—two hundred out of the original fourteen hundred, and this only by dint of discipline and desperation.

The royal horse troop had accompanied Agrippa on his ceremonial visit to Alexandria, and now they rode with him from Alexandria to Jerusalem. There were three thousand men in the horse troop, and in plain fact, aside from the Levite temple guards, whose ancestors had defended the Temple for hundreds of years, these three thousand horsemen were the only trained and disciplined body of professional soldiers in all of Israel. It is true that eight hundred Jews served the alabarch of Alexandria as an armed guard and that there was a city guard of four hundred in Chalcis, but the former were volunteer sons of good family and the latter a citizen service. A generation ago, the Emperor Claudius had disbanded all Jewish military forces, leaving only the ceremonial guard of horsemen for young Agrippa and the Levite temple guards, and there had been no armies in Israel since that time—except for the Roman legions of occupation. But this was less unnatural than it might seem, since Israel itself had changed over the past century, breaking out of the narrow confines of Judea and Galilee, until the Jewish lands and cities spread from Egypt to the Black Sea and along the coast of Africa even to within sight of Spain—lands and cities won not by conquest but for the first time a combination of trade and the teachings of the saintly Hillel, by conversion and persuasion. Nor, during the twenty and more years of Agrippa's kinghood, had his horsemen ever been in battle or performed more than police duties.

As in Alexandria, half of his troop were the sons of good families, younger sons, adventurous sons who enjoyed the peacock effect on women of a glittering brass cuirass and a fine helmet topped by white and blue plumes. After the Parthian fashion, they were heavily armed—short cavalry bow, sword and lance, and round bull-hide shield. They carried as their standard the golden lion of Judah on the pale blue background of Levi and they all rode white horses. They made a wonderful spectacle at parades and celebrations, but Agrippa was understandably doubtful over their usefulness in a war. In any case, considering what the news out of Jerusalem was, he decided not to lead his men into the city—where some accident might touch off an incident between them and the Zealots—but to stable them outside of the walls and enter Jerusalem by himself. Berenice, aware of the same danger, rode out from Jerusalem alone and met him half a dozen miles away, on the Bethlehem Road. It was a strange meeting, for Berenice, aching to be embraced by this man who had been father and mother as well as brother to her, had to restrain herself in the sight of the troops and kiss his hand most formally, saying with equal formality, "I welcome you, my royal brother, and may the Almighty visit you with fortune." Then she told him that she had made arrangements with Phineas Ba'as Hacohen of the House of Hakedron to stable the horses; he would also provide a flatland where the troopers might pitch tents. From the Idumean shepherds south of Bethlehem, she had purchased fourteen hundred fat sheep—which would be ample to feed his men, even if their stay was a long one. At Hakedron, they had been baking bread for three days, and four thousand loaves were waiting. And she had purchased five hundred skins of wine at the market in Jerusalem.

Deeply impressed, Agrippa thanked her, but she said. "Yes, brother, I can work miracles with bread and meat, which money buys very easily—but not with the hearts of men. God help me, I am so afraid."

"We will work it out," Agrippa said.

"I don't know. This isn't Galilee, and this city is not Tiberias. Do you know what the Sicarii are?"

"I have seen something of their work."

"Have you ever looked into the eyes of one of them? Do you think a Jewish madman is better than a Roman madman?"

"Anger blows off, like a punctured bag," Agrippa said. "Florus did a terrible thing, and he paid the price for it. An eye for an eye, and a tooth for a tooth. That isn't my doctrine, but there it is, and so the scales are balances. Is Florus dead?"

"He's very much alive," Berenice said. "Locked up in the old Palace of Herod—the stone part—with a cohort or so of legionaries. The rest of them are in the tower of Antonia."

"Good—then with him out of the way, we can calm down the hotheads. Water on fire—that's what I say."

Berenice shook her head hopelessly. Her brother had not the vaguest notion of what had transpired and what could transpire in Jerusalem.

Shimeon, pacing back and forth, shook his head and said that in his opinion, it would do no good for either Agrippa or Berenice to talk to the people of Jerusalem.

"Events move," he said. "Things change, people change—cities change."

They were met in the House of Hakedron, the king of the Jews in Galilee, his sister, the queen of Chalcis, and the nashi over all Israel, Shimeon Bengamaliel, who was the head of the Great Sanhedrin. With them, there was Phineas, the Ba'as Hacohen, who was the head of the house now, and Joseph Bengorian, the Judean prince reputedly the wealthiest man in Judea, and Anan Benanan, who was once high priest, eloquent, a poet in his own right and blood kin to both the House of Herod and the House of Mattathias, and Gideon Benharmish, the old man who was the head of the

House of Shlomo in Tiberias, and who had come down from Galilee to be with the king.

"What are you saying Shimeon?" asked Benharmish. "Are you saying that these events cannot be reversed—?"

"By words?"

"Words, reason."

"I don't know. I don't know. But for Berenice and Agrippa to go in there—I don't know how they feel about the king."

"You think they would harm us?" Agrippa asked quietly. "Why, Shimeon—tell me. I know I haven't been the best or the wisest king to rule over the Jews, but I have been at least the first king to acknowledge the way of Hillel the Good. No man has been tortured or murdered by my order, and there is no terror where I rule. I walk in the streets of Tiberias like any other man, and if a Jew sees me, he nods and bids good morning to Agrippa Benagrippa. My armies have ravaged no lands—and if I rule without genius I also rule without hate."

"You rule by virtue of Rome," Shimeon said, halting suddenly and thrusting a finger at Agrippa. "There is the rub—because"—he flung his arm in the direction of Jerusalem now—"there is a city that nourishes itself with hatred of Rome."

"Which leads us where?" Bengorian demanded.

"Face that, Shimeon," said Benanan. "Hatred of Rome—that is a state of mind. We talk of something else, not simply a state of mind. We talk about twelve hundred Roman legionaries who were slain by our people in Jerusalem—"

Caleb Barhoreb limped into the room in time to hear the last of this, and he denied the label "our people." "Sicarii," he growled. "They were murdered by the Sicarii."

"No—we cannot use the word murder, not in the light of the slaughter of the children. That was murder—foul and unforgivable murder; but what followed was an act of hatred and revenge—and this is not"—turning to Shimeon—"this is not a city that ever embraced Hillel. This is a city of Shammai, and it is a city of the Sicarii because the people approve of the Sicarii and shelter them—not only because they fear them. And as for the death of the Roman soldiers, it was not only the Sicarii. Every hand was raised against them. I saw women, gentle, sweet women—Jewish women bringing down legionaries with rocks." Benanan paused and took a long breath. Then he continued,

"I don't know, Shimeon, how they would react to the king. But I do know this—there is no Jew who would ever harm a hair upon Berenice's head. Let them go into the city and plead. It's a straw. But if we don't grasp at straws—"

"We will be at war with Rome," Benharmish finished. "I tell you, my friends, that we have made a profession of hating Rome—but what a luxury hate is. It is so hard to reason and to understand."

They were looking at Berenice now, who had listened to all their talk and heard it ringing as hollow as a bell, and she said to them, reaching out for her brother Agrippa's hand,

"The bitter truth of it is, as you gentlemen well know, that my brother and I rule over nothing except a shadow permitted by Rome. Yet that is not wholly the case. We rule over a cherished memory of the Jews, and howsoever we place ourselves we cannot cover over the fact that we bear the bloodlines of David and of Solomon Bendavid and of Mattathias and of Judah Benmattathias as well as those of Herod. If we have no power, we have at least an obligation, and we will not have anyone tell us whether or not we can enter a Jewish city. We will do so tomorrow, and without fear."

That night, Berenice lay in bed in the room given to them at the House of Hakedron, sleepless and silent, as she had been silent through the evening—and almost at a point where she could bear it no longer when Shimeon spoke to her and asked her directly what lay between them.

"A wall I think," Berenice said. "I never believed it could—"

"What makes it?"

"You do, Shimeon," Berenice said.

"I love you. That's all I can say, my beloved."

Then she resisted him no more, but lay in his great arms, trying to find answers to all her fears and doubts in the strength of him, the smell and manhood of him.

In the morning, sunlight and the hot wind from the south. The House of Hakedron lay five hundred feet below the city wall, a thousand feet below the top elevation. Berenice said to Gabo, "I dress like a queen today." Gabo was growing old all too quickly. She was always pregnant with someone's child; she was petulant, sharp-tongued, and each year she took additional liberties. She flatly told Berenice that she was a fool. "You are no Judean. What do you know of the south?" "I know the kind of brown ape the south breeds. Namely, yourself. I should have boiled you in oil when I had a taste for such things." To which Gabo replied, "Just as they all overdo your saintliness now, so do you overdo your wickedness. You never boiled anyone in oil, and I am not afraid of you, and why don't we go back to Galilee?" "Oh, put out my clothes and stop chattering," said Berenice.

She chose her clothes thoughtfully and with attention to symbols. Perhaps no people in the world put such stress on symbols as did the Jews—and they were quickly and emotionally responsive to symbols. On her golden slippers, Berenice wore the sign of the cherubim. They were graven images, but of a singular and inviolate kind, as were the lions of Judah or the snake of Levi. They bespoke the Holy of Holies—the innermost of sanctuaries. For an underdress, Berenice chose pale blue silk. If Menahem could presume to wear the color of Levi, she could claim it, just as she claimed the blood-red of Judah in her overdress, heavy red cotton with the lion motif woven in and out of it in gold thread. Her costume was bold, bright and barbaric, and she braided her hair to match, two thick red braids that lay upon her shoulders. She wore no rings for the legend that Deborah had rejected rings as witchcraft, and on her left arm above the elbow, she wore a golden bracelet with the holy injunction:

*Thou shalt love the Lord thy God with all thy heart
and all thy soul and all thy might!*

Attired in this manner, she entered the room where
Agrippa waited for her—with Shimeon and the Ba'as Hacohen in attendance—and all three men were struck dumb by
her appearance; only the Ba'as Hacohen coming forward,
bowing low and taking her hand to his lips, that he might, as
he put it:

"Pay homage to a queen in Israel."

She thanked him, and told them, her husband included,
very formally, "We go to Jerusalem now, my brother and
myself, the two of us alone. We will see you there."

"You won't wait?" Shimeon asked her.

"What is there to wait for, Shimeon? For the Sicarii to
grow tired of murder? No—either I am a Jew and there are
Jews in Jerusalem, or I have no desire to go on living. I am
not leaving you—not you, my husband—nor any of you.
Come behind us, if you wish, but remain at least a mile
behind us. Whatever we will do today—well, my brother and
I must do it alone."

Shimeon nodded. "Very well—as you say." Then they
stared at each other, Berenice unreal, like a painted piece of
sculpture in her glittering sandals and shining clothes, Shimeon with his broad shoulders sloped; and suddenly Berenice realized that his hair was turning gray. A gray hair here
and there—that had been the progress of the year; now he was
gray suddenly. She went up to him and placed the palms of
her hands against his bearded cheeks. There was a special
and particular feeling from the hair on a man's face, her
husband's face; half a shudder, half the flame of desire filling
her with shame, as she realized that she could have been a
grandmother had her children lived. She was not of a time
where women grew old or even into their middle years with
beauty; yet she was in all the vigor and beauty of youth.

"Nashi," she said softly to Shimeon. Agrippa and the Ba'as
Hacohen moved away so that they could speak in privacy.

"Nashi," she said, "I used to dream that there would be a prince in Israel—not like the kings we remember but a prince like Gideon or Judah Benmattathias, and he would sit on a golden throne and rule with the wisdom of Solomon and the mercy and compassion of Hillel. Because I am really an unpleasant and proud woman who took great pleasure in the fact that she was once a queen. But queen of Chalcis is very little, believe me—this is different. You are nashi over Israel, and the Great Sanhedrin. I think that in all the world, a man could stand no higher."

He shook his head.

"I speak the truth."

He shook his head again hopelessly.

"Well, this is no farewell, my beloved. We will be together this evening in Jerusalem."

Then Berenice left with her brother. The gates of the wall that surrounded the House of Hakedron were open, and as Berenice and Agrippa walked through—on foot toward Jerusalem—the men who had met the night before gathered in the gateway to watch them. In the field where the horse troops were encamped, there was a flurry of motion as the soldiers pressed forward to look at the strange sight of the king of the Jews walking on foot with his sister, on the road that led from the House of Hakedron toward Jerusalem, and shepherds, too, stared with gaping mouths as they cleared the road of their sheep and goats. But there was no sound, no voice raised, and they walked on, the House of Hakedron dropping behond them and the mighty walls of the city looming up ahead.

Here there were Sicarii stationed as outposts on the road, for the Sicarii held the gates to the city and manned the approaches. They stared at Berenice and Agrippa, and one or two of them took a step toward the pair—only to be halted by the disdainful green eyes of Berenice. Green eyes, red hair, blood-red dress and pale blue underdress—she walked like no woman they had ever seen—these lean and ragged

desert assassins. Berenice had a good opportunity to see the
Sicarii now, look at them, study them—and they were very
much of a type. Unwashed, emitting the stale, dry odor of
men who never washed, long of beard and hair, burnt
brown, even black by the sun, they had the look of fanatics,
the wild irresoluteness of madmen; and as she watched them,
Berenice thought of the House of Hillel and the gentleness,
the aura of love that seemed to hang over it there among the
green and golden Galilean hills. The aura of hate here was
equally strong. She said to her brother, "They are not seen by
you, only by me." "I hide behind your skirts, then."
"Brother, brother," she said, "this is ours too, our
unclean—for we have raised this up out of Israel as much as
we raised up the House of Hillel. We will try to comprehend
it before we fight it. There are three thousand of them here
in Jerusalem. They hold the city, the approach, the gates
—because they are the only ones here who know their
minds, their aims and objectives." "And what are their
objectives?" "Death," Berenice answered him.

Two of the Sicarii barred their way. They wore their long
knives openly now, two knives with crossed handles. They
wanted no shields. Yaweh was their shield, they proclaimed.
They put their hands on their knives and they barred the way,
and from every direction people whose homes and work were
outside of the city walls came running. The walls around the
gate were equally crowded.

"You know who we are," Berenice said quietly.

"But what are you?"

"This is the king of the Jews, and I am his sister," Berenice
said. "I am also the wife of the nashi. So this is what we are,
and lay a hand upon us, assassin; and see how Jews will
choose between the Sicarii and their king."

The Sicarii haed waited too long, and the decision was
made for them. In the old days, it had been said of Berenice
that her eyes were not those of a human but of a devil; still
now, in anger, her eyes were not something easy to face, and

the Sicarii stood aside. Berenice and Agrippa walked on. By the time they stood before the city gates, a crowd of over a thousand people had gathered around. The Sicarii were in front of the gate, and they manned the towers above it; but there were more people than Sicarii; the walls were packed with people, and as those in the city threw up their questions, those on the walls shouted down:

"It is the Queen Berenice and her brother, Agrippa."

From inside the walls, they shouted, "Open the gates!" The cry was taken up—by more and more, until it was a commanding roar heard quite clearly at the House of Hakedron. Meanwhile, the people in the crowd, poor people mostly, very poor people, shepherds and charcoal burners and peasants who scraped a living out of a few olive trees planted in the inhospitable soil, pressed closer, not daring to touch Agrippa, who stood tall and slender and silent, wearing a robe of the royal purple, beard and hair curled, and on his head a pale blue cap of Levi; but they were drawn toward Berenice as toward a magnet. A woman bolder than the others dropped on her knees by Berenice and kissed her hand. The woman wept, and the weeping became contagious. Other women picked up stones and hammered at the gates, and when the Sicarii tried to push the women away, they spat wildly in the faces of the assassins. Then the gates were unbolted and opened.

The crowd opened up a path for Agrippa and Berenice, and they walked forward into the city. Berenice had decided that she would lead Agrippa up into the plaza of the Upper Market—an area large enough to hold half the population of the city in a common assembly—and it was toward there that they now walked, through streets that were packed with people—not to see Agrippa, but to shout back to others, "It is Berenice—our queen. The queen of the Jews has come back to the city." They pressed around her and followed her. Berenice had not realized the magnitude that her action in the plaza had taken on; but now they would have it that no child in the city was alive but by virtue of her plea to Florus. They wanted it that way. They needed her desperately, for all the skies had turned dark and dismal and were closing in upon them, and they needed the refuge of the mother. It was right and proper that she should be so tall and improbably beautiful and clad in the burning red that was an old and holy color, as it was right that her hair was red; for the red hair was as ancient as the Jewish memory. Who did not know that Aaron's hair burned like fire? Moses himself had been touched by the red finger of God. "Let Levi be red," said the Almighty, red with blood, with anger, with holy fanaticism—and among the temple guards, who were Levites, one in three was red, and as they came to the great open plaza of the Upper Market, the Levite guards leaned over the temple wall to watch, their burnished spearheads in a long line. Half of the population of the city was in the plaza now, and more were pressing to find the approaches, and each of the Sicarii was pinned by citizens of the city, pinned so tightly that knife and mind were impotent. From the roof tops of the two stone citadels where they were imprisoned, trapped and under siege, the remainder of the Roman cohorts also watched the enormous assembly come into being.

Agrippa climbed onto a ledge of stone, and then bent to draw Berenice up after him. The hands were gentle, tender as they handed her up. The king and his sister were alone— no guards, no seneschals, no dragging servitors, handmen, handmaidens, no trappings—only the two of them with a quarter of a million people around them; and Berenice felt pride and contentment. If she did no more, it was still fitting that at least the line of Herod had achieved this, to stand alone and unprotected and secure among their own people.

Agrippa raised his hands for silence, and Berenice felt her own heart tighten with anxiety. Could he do it, control this, make himself heard, find words for this vast throng?

Silence came. Silence over everything, the upturned

faces, the people packed on the rooftops, the guards lining the wall of the Temple, the trapped Romans in their stone redoubts.

"I also honor my sister," Agrippa said, "for she taught me the way of Hillel—"

The silence was deeper. Jerusalem was not a place committed to the teachings of Hillel. Here Shammai the vengeful ruled, and out of every ten men in the crowd, eight were Zealots, passively or aggressively.

"—and so I came here," he went on, speaking clearly and simply, "not to make war but to make peace. There have been great war chiefs who were kings in Israel. I am not one of them. I hate war and I hate death. I will go to the Romans, and I will be a voice for you, not to plead out of fear but out of the pride that was the soul and essence of Hillel. I think I can make peace and avert war. I think that perhaps I can put a finish to the terrible things that the procurators have done here in Jerusalem. I only plead with you for time and for patience. I think that Gessius Florus misjudged many things—you, your anger, the strength of his cohorts, and the patience of the Emperor Nero. I know the emperor, and he will hide his face in horror when he hears from my lips and from my sister's lips and from the lips of Shimeon Bengamaliel, your nashi, what Florus unloosed here in Jerusalem. The Romans are not like us, but war with the Jews is the last thing they seek. Who would profit by such a war? Jerusalem would become a tomb, Israel a place of death and woe; and will it comfort us when the mothers of Rome weep? There is no honor to be gained from such a war, not for us, not for the Romans. The Romans will move heaven and earth to avert such a war—and we, too, must spare no effort. In the Almighty's name, I give you my sacred oath that I will make an honorable condition of peace, or I will die in the attempt. Will you believe me? Will you?"

Silence again, so long and painful that it cut into Berenice's heart like a knife.

"Will you?" Agrippa cried, and this time the crowd roared,

"Yes!"

"Will you wait?"

"Yes!"

"Will you be patient?"

"Yes!"

Berenice was weeping. A dam had broken, and she stood before them now, her breast racked with sobs, the tears rolling down her cheeks.

"Why does the queen weep?"

The question came from a thousand throats, a ripple and roar of sound. Why? Why? Berenice held up her arms for silence; still she could not control the weeping. She fought to find her voice and use it, and then she said, "For joy. Only for joy." But not loud, and only the front ranks heard her. They passed the words back, and by repetition they became a thunder. "For joy." Now there was no woman and few enough men in the great assembly who remained dry-eyed.

For Berenice, personal gratification mingled with a mystical sense of fulfillment in terms of the covenant—the very ancient covenant that the Almighty Yaweh had made with Moses, the first of the prophets: that He, the Almighty, would bring to Israel the sponsorship of everlasting peace. And so from prophet to prophet it had been nurtured, had grown and matured into that simple statement, "And they shall beat their swords into ploughshares." Was this not it? Had not the lions of peace fought with the jackals of war and beat them down? And could this not be the beginning of the element of man—in which the saintliness of Hillel and his house would envelop the world? Was not a whole city delivered out of the maw of bloody vengeance?

And this mystical knowledge of fulfillment mingled with the gratifying and personal triumph of her brother. In its own time, every slander, every canard had been preached about herself and her brother. Because his life had failed in terms of women, because his tall, powerful, and totally demanding father had left him a legacy of impotence that neither he nor anyone else in his time understood—because he could not marry as much as he might desire to marry—because of all these things and the murky cloud of obscurity in which they functioned, there was erected a structure of his relationship with his sister, which even her increasing presence as the mother of Israel failed entirely to dispel. Agrippa had grown into his middle years as a tall, thin, stooped, and very gentle man. His lack of ambition was balanced by a sense of pity— which turned into compassion as bit by bit he absorbed the teachings of Hillel. He was a strange king, one who fought no wars and made no enemies, a soft-spoken king who somehow had avoided all arguments and disputes. His adolescent boasting of his feats with women, his inane and childish drinking, his fits of senseless cruelty—so like his sister's—all these had vanished by his twentieth birthday. He became an old man in his young years, and now, although he was only turned forty, he gave his subjects the impression of endless years of gray-streaked maturity. When he walked in the streets of his beloved Tiberias—often and alone and un-guarded, for none bore him ill-will—his people greeted him simply as the Adon Agrippa.

Sometimes Berenice felt pleasure at his lack of formality and at the curious respect and regard his people bore for him; but at other times, sensing the fear and loneliness that per-vaded his existence, she felt an overwhelming sense of pity and sorrow. But now that had changed. What an act he had performed! How simply courageous it was! And how blind-ingly successful! Even Shimeon, who had never entirely respected Agrippa or overcome his concealed contempt for his background, even Shimeon looked at Agrippa with new eyes and new respect—as did the dozens of men and women who had come to Berenice's palace to congratulate Agrippa, to embrace him and to acknowledge the fact that there was a king in Israel once again. Weeping like a child, Phineas, the Ba'as Hacohen, embraced Agrippa and kissed him on the

mouth and on both cheeks; and Anan Benanan, supposedly
the wealthiest man in Jerusalem and once high priest, wept
over Agrippa's hand and, on one knee, pledged fealty to him,
even though Benanan was a Judean and under no legal
obligation to Agrippa. Caleb Barhoreb, that ugly and imperious little aristocrat, bowed before Agrippa, kissed his hand,
and then proclaimed to all the company, "What a time this
is, and what men are raised among us! Is it not the time that
the Almighty promised us? For here before me is such a king
over Israel as Hezekiah was, and under the same roof there is
his sister, the blood of Mattathias with the blood of Herod,
and spoken as a saint and loved as a mother by all Israel, and
her husband, Shimeon, who is our nashi. Shall the hand of
God write more clearly than when He makes Hillel's own
beloved grandson nashi over us and His disciple a king?"

Berenice pushed through the crowd and stopped him.
Now she was afraid. "No, no," she told Caleb, "you talk like
a fool. It angers the Almighty when men talk like you are
talking." The little man was hurt, and she had to soothe him.
"Ah, Caleb, I honor and respect you—but honor must be
calculated. The Almighty is jealous of honor accorded to
others." "That is not what Hillel taught." "There are true
things," Berenice pleaded, "that are older than the things
Hillel taught. Does your own bloodline teach you nothing?
Do you think the God of Horeb is dead and only the God of
Hillel lives?" She was choking and on the point of tears, and
she tore free from the crowd, pushed through it and away—
and then caught her husband's glance. Shimeon was on the
other side of the room, alone with Joseph Benmattathias,

She crossed to them, slowly and afraid, for her husband's
face was bereft of any triumph or joy, and his eyes were full of
death.

"Tell her," Shimeon said hoarsely to Joseph.

"My cousin, Aba," Joseph Benmattathias said dully, "rode
a horse to death here from Caesarea, so I have news that no
one else has yet. In Caesarea, the pagans rose up against the

Jews. The Roman troops did nothing. They had heard the news from here of the defeat in Jerusalem, and they lifted no hand to protect the Jews—who were without arms and defenseless and only a fifth of the population of the city—"

"I know how many Jews are in Caesarea," Berenice burst out. "Tell me what happened there."

"They closed the gates," Joseph said, "and they began a slaughter, and they did not stop until every Jew in the city was dead. The Roman troops stood by and watched, and the pagans—"

"Pagans—pagans—what pagans?"

"Egyptians, Syrians, rabble, bastards of five nations who call themselves Greeks—you know Caesarea—"

"All the Jews?"

"Men—women—children—I think only my cousin escaped, because he was on the wall, and he watched from there, and then he dropped off the wall and stole a horse and got away. But he said that before he left, the streets were ankle-deep with blood—"

"O—my God, my God," Berenice cried, and then she sank down on the floor with her face in her hands. Shimeon bent over and raised her in his arms, and with her in his arms he walked out of the room. Joseph remained to talk to the guests, who, having seen Berenice crumple to the floor, gathered around him now.

Each thing begets another, and there is no beginning and no end except for a single man or woman; and this was something that Berenice came to know. She could not find a beginning. She could not go back in time and say to herself, "Here or here or here did this begin." What forces had brought her father, the great King Agrippa and the bosom and blood companion of the Emperor Claudius, to the conclusion that Rome and Israel could not inhabit the same world? Whatever they were, the forces were there, and by now she had learned that they were implacable. She remem-

bered how when she had first read Thucydides' history of the
Peloponnesian War, she was so hugely depressed by the
sense of tragedy, of irreversibility that emanated from its
pages. The Greeks understood and accepted that implacabil-
ity of cause and effect, but the Jews resisted it. The Greek part
of her education and training accepted the murder of her
father. What alternative did Claudius have? The Jewish part
regarded it with horror. In the plaza, when the children were
being slaughtered, Florus had made a bargain with her. He
would halt the slaughter and she would give her body to him,
so that he could mount her with his little sagging pot belly
and ride supreme over the queen of Israel. A Jew would
comprehend her action, weighing it against the lives of the
children she had saved; a Greek would not—nor did she feel
better or worse that Florus was pinned down in the Palace of
Herod; it made no difference; the children were saved. The
implacable and inevitable had been set aside.

In this, the Jews were apart from all the world—in this
defiance of all the tributes and implacabilities of fate; and
possibly for this reason more than any other they were never
tolerated, only hated or loved. Either the pagan turned
Jewish endured circumcision if a man, and embraced all that
was Jewish—or the hatred of Jews became a chronic disease
of his existence. The pagan lived in a world where defeat was
accepted, where poverty and ignominy and slavery were
accepted, where every turn and caprice of fate was
accepted—and where every opportunity for lust, conquest,
thievery, or enrichment was also accepted. For this, the Jew
despised him; and knowing he was despised, he hated.

Hillel said love; and in Caesarea twenty thousand Jews
perished in a single day. This hammered in her head; it tore
at her head and beat at her skull. And it beat at the city too.
Berenice could almost hear it, like a vast drumbeat pounding
at the heart of the city—and the city became very quiet. The
city wept. In any or every street of the city, you could hear the
sound of tears.

The next morning, Berenice went up to the high roof tower of her palace—a pinnacle that rose above the temple court. Shimeon was already there, and when Berenice had joined him he said to her,

"I think they will try to take the temple enclave today."

"Why?"

"They must control the city. We are at war with Rome."

"Oh—no, no!" Berenice exclaimed. "Not from you—I will not hear that! Are my brother's promises nothing? We said that we would go to Rome and make peace."

"Too late," Shimeon said softly but with profound sorrow.

"Why is it too late?"

"I have not declared war on Rome," Shimeon said. "This city has—"

"The Sicarii!"

"You make too much of the Sicarii," Shimeon said impatiently. "Not the Sicarii—but the Zealots, the House of Shammai—and that means more than half of Jerusalem."

"How do you know? Have you counted? Have you asked? Have you gone to the people, to every one of them, and said to them—who are you for? For Hillel? Or for Shammai?"

"After Caesarea?"

"Do I ask you to do it? I only say that you have not done it—so how can you say who is for what? Of course Shammai moves. Shammai shouts! Shammai roars! Shammai has a sword in his hand. You see the sword—you respect it, you heed it. But Hillel—what is love to shout? There is no sword in the hand of Hillel."

"My dear, good wife," Shimeon said, "you have gone to places I have never been."

"Why, Shimeon? You were my teacher. You were a physician—so it is with the sons of Hillel, they must learn to heal—and you healed. What has happened?"

"I don't know," Shimeon replied, "because it is happening. How can I tell you why or what the end will be? Look there!" He pointed to the street that paralleled the temple wall. "It's happening, isn't it? Can I stop it?"

She followed his hand with her eyes. "You're the nashi, aren't you?" And he said bitterly, "The nashi—yes." They both stared now as the street filled with Sicarii bearing ladders. As the ladders were raised against the temple wall, another group of Sicarii dashed up the broad steps that led to the Temple, where one of the gates stood open.

Inside the walls, the temple guards leaned on their spears, and all was right with the world so far as they were concerned. In the Court of the Gentiles, a deputation of sheep herders from Idumea moved slowly, gingerly, staring about them at this legendary wonder that they were finally seeing with their own eyes, and in the inner court a group of five priests argued and gestured. Shimeon cupped his hands and shouted. He had a strong, deep voice, and the sound of his shout was like a physicl violence against Berenice's ears. In the Temple, at least the sound if not the words was heard, and one of the priests pointed to Shimeon and Berenice. The others bowed, accepting this unusual means by which the nashi asked for attention. He shouted again, and the Levite guards bestirred themselves, and now the first of the Sicarii topped the wall, and one after another they straddled the wall, knife in hand, knife in teeth—and then they leaped down, inside of the temple compound. The Levite guards ran toward them, spears leveled, and now the other band of Sicarii poured in through the open gate. They raced across the court, screaming an awful war cry, their demeanor not that of men but of devils, their knives cutting at the air in anticipation of the flesh. The Idumeans turned to flee and then went down before the knives, beheaded, disemboweled. The Levites tried to rally, but they faced the madness of dedicated and monstrous fanaticism. They leveled spears against screaming men who impaled themselves, yet lived to kill the Levites who held the spears. Other Levites raced from the inner court, to go down under the weight of Sicarii leaping from the walls, and then the Sicarii poured into the inner court. The priests tried to escape, but the Sicarii cut them down, sliced flesh from their bones, disemboweled

them. The Sicarii did not know these priests or have hatred
for them or reason to destroy them; but the priests were alive,
and the Sicarii were insane with the lust to kill and the need
to kill. They existed to kill, and this was a moment in which
the truth of their existence was revealed to them—and so they
killed. They poured through the Temple, killing everything
that moved. They cut down the Levite guards to the last man.
They killed priests and they burst into the Holy of Holies,
screaming out the name of God in the ecstasy of their
madness, and from where he had attempted to hide himself
they dragged out Hananiah, who had been high priest only a
while ago, and they cut him to pieces there upon the Ark of
the Lord.

Much of this Berenice saw, and more of it was told to her
later; but she no longer reacted with shock—with all the
outer adornments of horror. One thing had followed
too quickly upon another; a kind of bleak desolation had
began to overlay her sense of compassion.

Twenty-four hours later, Jerusalem had been split in
half—or in three parts, depending upon how you saw it. The
temple complex on the eastern border of the city was held by
the Sicarii, who straddled the walls and filled the night air
with their keening prayers. The northern half, or Lower
City, was held by the Zealots under the leadership of a man
whose father had been hacked and sliced to death by Sicarii.
His name was Elaezar Benananias, a Zealot by conviction
and thereby of the Houe of Shammai in belief and
philosophy; but by birth out of the bloodline of Aaron and
thus entitled to style himself, if he so desired, Adon Elaezar
Benananias Hacohen; and thereby a prince of Israel out of
the oldest bloodline on earth. In addition to this, he came out
of a family both wealthy and important—his father had been
high priest over Israel, Hananiah Hacohen. His father's
body, disemboweled and cut to ribbons, lay in the inner
sanctuary of the Temple, and only bit by bit did the proof
come to him that his allies, the Sicarii, had slain his father.

The southern half of Jerusalem, or Upper City, walled off

from the rest of Jerusalem, a mighty fortress in its own right and containing Berenice's palace and the Palace of the Herods, too, and most of the noble buildings of the city, was held by the nashi, Shimeon Bengamaliel. With him were four hundred and eighty-seven Levite spearmen, who had been in their barracks in the Maccabean Palace when the Sicarii attacked, and now these spearmen held both the double and triple gates that led from the Upper City in to the temple complex, and also the Xustus Bridge. The walls facing the Lower City were held by a hastily raised militia of about ten thousand men whose homes were in the Upper City—but how they would react if attacked by the Zealots and whether they would kill their fellow Jews to hold the Upper City from the Zealots remained to be seem. Shimeon himself was dubious, as were most of the members of the Great Sanhedrin, most of whom had made their way into the Upper City. After some discussion of the matter, Shimeon went to Agrippa, who was with Berenice on the roof of her palace. They had been doing nothing—simply sitting there through the hours and waiting. But for what they waited, Berenice did not know.

Without any preliminaries, Shimeon came to the point and told Agrippa that he wanted him to go down to the House of Hakedron and bring back with him into the Upper City the three thousand troops of the horse guard. "There is no problem yet," Shimeon said. "I have checked at the Fountain Gate and at the Gate of the Essenes, and we hold both gates securely—and there are niehter Zealots nor Sicarii in sight. I will send twenty of the Levites with you on horseback, and you can be back here with your troops before the sun sets."

Agrippa shook his head, smiling bitterly. "No, Shimeon—you want soldiers, and you mistake me. My horse guards are no more soldiers than I am a valid and real king. We are both fakes. They have never fought anything, and they know less about fighting than I know about being a real king. Most of them are the spoiled children of wealthy

Jewish families, and if the Sicarii should shout at them, they will not stop spurring their horses until they are back in Galilee."

"Still, they wear armor and they know how to hold a lance and stand in a straight line. That's all I need. God help us if it comes to more than that, if Jew turns his sword against Jew."

"And isn't that precisely what will happen if Agrippa brings his horsemen into the city?" Berenice asked.

"No. No, I can't believe it—"

"Then what future have you, Shimeon?" Berenice asked. "I ask you in all sincerity—and tell me, tell me truthfully—for what there still is between us, Shimeon."

"Still is? No, Berenice, I love you with all my heart. I never loved you more."

"And I love you—and we sit here talking like that, and the world comes to its end. Shimeon, what will you do?"

"Hold the Upper City as long as I can—and pray to the Almighty that Benananias comes to his senses. What else can I do?"

"What are his senses? What do you mean? Are we at war with Rome? And Florus—do we kill him or let him go? Will we have the blood of a procurator on our hands? That is something Rome never forgives."

"I let him go," Shimeon said tiredly. "I let him go two hours ago. I took him myself to the gate and put him to horse. He will reach Caesarea before the twenty thousand Jews are buried!" His voice rose. "Yes, Berenice—I am a man and a human being and a Jew, and I have violences and hates and passions—and I could have killed that lousy bastard with my own bare hands. But I didn't. I let him go—"

His voice broke. He spread his arms hopelessly, and then Agrippa rose and said quite matter-of-factly, "I will go for my men, Shimeon. Understand me—you should have commanded me. I wish you had. I am king of sorts in Galilee, by the tolerance of Rome. But you are nashi because the Jews so made you, and by leave of no one—and my prince as well as

Berenice's. I don't know what is wrong with us. We are being called upon for greatness. In the Bible, God speaks and man responds. God commanded Gideon to be great, and Gideon was great. I think that in the same way, He commands us, but I don't know what His commands are and there is no greatness in me." His shoulders were bent as he left them, and when he had gone, Shimeon said,

"It's true. Where is greatness—in me? In Agrippa? In Elaezar and his Zealots? In those monsters—the Sicarii? In you, my wife, I see greatness. What shall I do? Shall I say, Shimeon is no longer nashi; make his wife nashi over you. Because she has greatness. Oh, what nonsense. But what should I do, Berenice?"

"Why do you ask me? You know what to do. Make peace—force it—command it! You are the nashi. No one will raise a hand against you. Be what you are, Shimeon the grandson of Hillel."

"Too late," Shimeon said.

"Why? Why?"

"I suppose," Shimeon said, "I suppose because I have lost my faith in peace."

Before dark, Agrippa led his three thousand horsemen into Jerusalem, and in the last rays of the setting sun the Zealots in the Lower City saw the long line of brazen breastplates, burnished helmets and long, iron-tipped lances parade on the walls of the Upper City. The people of the Upper City were encouraged by the magnificently armed young men, who made such a splendid sight as they rode up into the great plaza, and no one thought to speculate on the possibility that such handsome soldiers were perhaps the worst in the world. There were three thousand of them, and—apart from the few hundred Levites, indifferent soldiers at best, and the remnants of the Roman cohorts, trapped in their fortress towers—these three thousand were the only body of disciplined and professional soldiers in Jerusalem. Also, they wore body armor, which not one Jew in twenty possessed, and body armor always impressed civilian militia.

The Upper City housed the priesthood, the wealth, the merchants, the professionals and the bloodline nobility of Jerusalem. There were three quarters of the fine houses, the palaces, the great villas, the counting houses, the warehouses, the huge olive-oil cisterns, and the wine cisterns—the new schools, the synagogues, many of which were devoted to the teachings of Hillel, the theater and the great Maccabean Palace. At the same time, the population of the Upper City was much less than the population of the Lower City, fewer in numbers, less militant, and almost without those dedicated and fanatical fighting men who called themselves the Zealots. If it had come to a pitched battle between the Lower City and the Upper City, Shimeon had no doubt who would conquer. The Upper City might hold out against the Zealots for a week or five weeks; but sooner or later it would succumb, and if that were to happen, the blackest pages of Jewish history would be written, brother against brother, father against son.

But it did not happen. A day went by, and then another day, and then a third, fourth, fifth, sixth, and seventh day—and then the Sabbath dawned. There was no attack, not even by the Sicarii. Zealots were posted on guard all the distance from the Valley Gate to the wall of the temple enclave, hard, somber men who fingered their terrible bows—those ancient Jewish weapons made of layers of laminated ram's-horn—counted their arrows, sharpened their curved knives, but did nothing. Almost shoulder to shoulder they stood in a line half a mile long, and silently they faced the line of Galilean boys in their brazen armor—and silently, the horse guards faced them. On both sides the injunction was given that no words be uttered, no taunts, no jests, no curses—and both sides obeyed. Thousands of men and women and children of Jerusalem came and stood behind the Zealots, staring at the beautifully caparisoned Galileans, but no one was allowed to pass through the line of Zealots. And then it was the Sabbath.

Two hours after sunrise on the Sabbath, Elaezar Ben-ananias, the leader of the Zealots and the titular head of the House of Shammai, pushed through the line of Zealots and walked to within twenty feet of the wall of the Upper City. He was dressed simply yet splendidly in a robe of pale blue, wide-sleeved and ankle-length, and he wore on his head the symbolic red stocking cap of the Maccabees; his costume almost identical with that one of Menahem had worn to Berenice's reception. For a while he stood in silence, arms akimbo, staring at the wall and at the Galileans who manned it, then he cupped his hands about his mouth and cried out:

"Up there—whoever commands, I would speak with him! I am Elaezar, captain of the Zealots!"

A few minutes, and then a tall young man came striding along the wall, stopped, facing Elaezar, and asked civilly enough what he could do for the captain of the Zealots.

"Go to the nashi and tell him it's time we spoke to one another face to face, the way two Jews should, and an end to this nonsense of Jew against Jew. Tell him to open a postern for me, and I will go in to him and his home."

"With how many guards?" the young officer demanded.

"Alone, I say. Now go to the nashi, because I will not stand here on the Almighty's Sabbath and bicker with you."

A little while later, the Demeter Postern—so-called because it was used in the old times by those who secretly worshiped the mother-god—was opened, and two of the splendidly armed Galilean troopers led Elaezar through to Berenice's palace. A tremendous crowd had gathered from the Upper City to attempt to read something of their fate in Elaezar's manner, but all they saw was the Zealot's fascination with the horse soldier's armor. Elaezar had become very armor-conscious during the past several weeks, and now he could not keep himself from fingering the cuirass of the man beside him to test its thickness and estimate its weight. There were any number of questions he would have liked to ask the young man, such as how it felt to wear the armor in intense heat and whether the weight of it had a debilitating effect— but the relationship of station hardly permitted it, and Elaezar walked along in silence.

At the palace, Elaezar was taken to a rather small room Berenice and Shimeon were both fond of and where they spent many hours. This room was open to a spacious balcony that could be closed off with cane blinds; but when the blinds were drawn open, the balcony commanded a magnificent view of the sere mountains and lonely wadis of the South. It was a noble view from a noble site, and enviously Elaezar admitted as much. Here a table covered with a white cloth had been spread with fruit and wine and sweet cakes and a loaf of bread wrapped in a napkin. Shimeon asked Elaezar to be seated, unwrapped the flat disk of bread, and said to the Zealot,

"Will you break bread with me—or do you come out of hatred?"

"If we are going to talk, Shimeon," Elaezar replied, leaning forward and tearing a piece from the bread, "then let it be like two sensible adults and not like a pair of street urchins who decide that one of them is of the House of Shammai and the other of the House of Hillel. Shall we say that we are both of the House of Israel?" He bit into the bread then.

"I like that," Shimeon nodded.

"The bread is good."

Shimeon broke off a piece for Berenice and another for himself. "It's the bread of life and not the bread of affliction," Shimeon said as he poured wine for them. "Good bread and good wine—and love and companionship. That makes for a life that could be a good deal worse."

"Well, Nashi," Elaezar smiled, "I find it hard to disagree with that kind of thing. But I also find it difficult to talk about matters which we must discuss with a woman present."

Berenice smiled at this, and he added, "Even so beautiful a woman as the queen."

"She is my wife," Shimeon said, "but more than that, my companion. We have been a long time together, dealing with this and that and some of it not unimportant—so it would be rather odd, wouldn't it, if I were to ask her to leave us that we might discuss the future of a city with which she is very intimately related. Unlike you, Elaezar, I have no bloodline of any consequence; I am an Israelite and no more, and I know that since I am nashi and the grandson of Hillel as well, this sounds like inverted snobbery of the worst sort; but I only mention it to make a point. If you go from here, from this palace, you walk on the road of Jonathan past the Palace of Helena and the Palace of the Maccabees to the Palace of Herod alongside the wall rebuilt by Shimeon Benmattathias, the watchtower reared by Agrippa, the fountain given to the people by his wife, my wife's mother—need I go on? What you have to say, say it here, and as you suggested before, we will all try to be sensible and adult."

"All right," the Zealot nodded. "I begin by saying this, Nashi—no wheat is made from flour, only bread. What is done is done, and there is no use bawling over it. Do you agree?"

"Well, that's one of those questions, isn't it?" Shimeon shrugged. "What do you want me to say? That there is no going back?"

"That we are at war with Rome."

"Oh? My wife doesn't think so."

Elaezar looked at Berenice, who said, "I think, Elaezar Benananias, that as far as the House of Shammai is concerned, we have always been at war with Rome."

"Perhaps—"

"I don't think so. No—Rome doesn't want war with the Jews."

"Do you agree with the queen?" Elaezar asked Shimeon.

"No—not entirely," Shimeon said. "I think we are at war. After what happened in Caesarea—well, I don't know what else. If the Romans will not protect the Jews in Alexandria, in

Damascus, in Sidon, in Tyre, and Antioch and Sardis and Tarsus—and in twenty other cities, then they will have to protect themselves, and that means the involvement of the Jewish lands, Idumea and Judea and Galilee—and Samaria too, if the Samaritans should decide that they are Jews or at least closer to Israel than to Rome. But what such a war will come to, this I don't know—except that if one half of Jerusalem fights the other half to the death, it will not have a chance to come to very much."

"Now I tell you this," Elaezar cried, driving a clenched fist into his open palm, "such a war must be fought—if not today, next year or in five years or in ten years—for this earth is too small for Israel and Rome. And what is Rome? A city? A nation? A pack of mongrel pagan bloodlines pretending to be a people—and not much more. I say that Israel is stronger than Rome, and I say that Israel will prevail!"

"And I say," Berenice told them, rising, "that you are both talking nonsense—such incredible nonsense that it makes me sick to listen to you!"

Both men stood up to protest, but Berenice, her green eyes flashing, cowed them and informed them that she would say her piece, just as they had said theirs. "Because from here on, only the men will talk in Israel," Berenice said. "And I will say what I must—and then I will go. But I tell you this—God help you!"

"I don't think, Berenice—" Shimeon began.

"No—no, Shimeon—let me talk, and I will tell you something about Rome. This Rome which you have such contempt for as an adversary has a standing army of half a million men. In all Israel, the only force of trained soldiers, armed and armored, that exists is my brother's troop of horse guards—three thousand of them. One Roman legion consists of twice that number, and at this moment ninety-four Roman legions are in existence. And do you know what a legionary is? He is enlisted for twenty years, and for twenty years he knows nothing but war—he drills for six hours every day. Will you invade Rome? Is that what you plan?"

"We are Jews, and this is our land, and here we will fight," Elaezar said angrily.

"Naturally. And since Rome maintains a fleet of over seven hundred warships and Israel not one warship, even the thought of a Jewish invasion of Italy is a dream. But if you should wipe out every legion Rome possesses, as Hannibal came close to doing, still Rome would raise up half a million more men—but you are talking to each other as men, not as children. Then talk as men and give me leave to go!" And with that, Berenice angrily left them.

Later, when Shimeon entered her bedroom, he had to pass by Gabo who was filling chests with clothes; and in the bedroom he asked his wife whether this meant that she was going away.

"You called me your compaion before in front of the Zealot," Berenice said, "and I think that was the best thing anyone ever said about me—that a man like yourself and I could be not only lovers but companions who needed each other and leaned on each other. But what now, Shimeon? I can't stay in this place. It is filled with the voices of death and violence, and if I remain here, I shall have to stuff up my ears or go mad."

"As bad as that?" Shimeon asked, a note of helpless woe in his voice.

"Sit down, Shimeon. Tell me what the Zealot wanted—and tell me, does he know whether his father is alive or dead? Rumor had it that the Sicarii murdered the old man in the Temple, in the Holy of Holies on the altar of God."

Shimeon pulled over a stool and seated himself, and watching him, Berenice felt herself swell with grief and nostalgia. The way he moved, in that awkward manner of an overlarge man, and the awkwardness contradicted by the competence of those large, long-fingered, and beautiful hands. It occurred to her that never in her life had she seen anything as beautiful, as clever and dextrous as her husband's hands—and she could close her eyes, if she would, and remember those hands over a decade and a half, hands that made love, cherished, caressed, healed, comforted, put together what was broken, smoothed away pain and stanched the flow of blood—and now the hands touched her knees gently:

"Berenice?"

She shook her head, hard and firmly. "No. We must talk about this, Shimeon."

"All right," he sighed. "We will talk about it."

"I asked you about the rumor."

"Elaezar heard it. He doesn't know. Nothing from his father. The Sicarii still hold the Temple, and they will permit no one to enter the complex."

"Why did he come to you, Shimeon?"

"To make common cause for the war and the defense of Jerusalem. Don't misjudge him. He's a brave and a dedicated man."

"But not brave enough or dedicated enough to find a way for the Jews to live. His specialty is death. I must learn to bow down and worship those who are brave in the commission of death."

"What a way to talk!"

"It's the way I feel—so I talk that way. What else did he want?"

"He wants me to command," Shimeon said abruptly.

She shook her head slowly, studying him, wondering—and realizing now that all things come to an end. "I don't understand you, Shimeon. No—I don't even think my guesses have any point."

He reminded her bleakly that he had never known her to guess wrong. "You became a woman too late," he said—and she realized it was the first deliberately cruel thing he had ever spoken to her. "I should have married a woman who was a woman, and if she were stupid as a cow, she would at least be what a woman should be."

But now she couldn't be angry; her heart was breaking for

him, and she thought, "Poor Shimeon—poor Shimeon—in the end they bought you so cheaply—a shred of glory hanging on an old stick, and you walked out of the House of Hillel and closed the doors behind you, and never a look back." But aloud she only said,

"And what does he mean, the Zealot, when he asks you to command?"

"To lead the people, the war, the defense of Jerusalem if it comes to the defense of Jerusalem."

"I see. But you are not a soldier, Shimeon. You're a physician."

"I am nashi."

"Yes, you are nashi. What else, Shimeon? I think you should tell me all. Will he place himself under your command?"

"What I said before was cruel and unnecessary," Shimeon said.

"It was necessary to you, and it was not cruel to me, and I have no desire to talk about it, Shimeon."

"You never forget and you never forgive."

"My darling," Berenice said, very gently, "there is nothing to forget and nothing to forgive you for. I asked you whether Elaezar would place himself under your command?"

"Yes, he agreed to."

"All the Zealots, their secret armies, their hidden weapons?"

"Yes."

"And the Sicarii?"

"We did not discuss the Sicarii."

"Oh? Just in case the profession of murder should not be discarded?"

"No, damn you!" He shook his head grimly. "I am sorry, I am sorry." He reached out his arms toward her.

"No, Shimeon—we can't feel love and tenderness with our hands until we have talked about this and discovered whether there is any of love and tenderness remaining between us. I am not angry, and I don't want you to be angry."

"There were other things we talked about," he sighed.

"Yes, of course," she nodded. "And he must have made demands too."

"Not so many. He wants Agrippa and the horse guards out of the city and back to Tiberias—which is just as well. They have served their purpose. He wants all Roman legionaries remaining in Jerusalem to leave, from both the Palace of Herod, on our side of the wall, and the Tower of Antonia in the Lower City. He wants Florus out of the city—well, that's done—and that is about it. In return he will place the entire city and the entire Zealot force under my command. It is a gesture of great trust on his part, a surrender of power he already holds—"

"Unless he unites the people, no one holds any power," Berenice interrupted. "So look at the entire picture before you make him your benefactor."

"Why do you hate him so?"

"I don't hate," Berenice said. "I stopped hating many years ago, Shimeon. But this is a man who stands for death. I am against death, Shimeon."

"All men die."

"Yes, in their appointed time—even as I could die now in misery and shame, to hear you giving me the argument that all men die. Is that why you went into every pesthole between Antioch and Alexandria and risked your life—and mine, too, if the truth be told—to try to save the lives of people stricken and dying? Because all men die? God help me that I have lived to hear this!"

"Berenice, you twist the meaning of every word I say."

"Do I? And if you accept and become a captain of armies—is that meaning twisted too? Have you accepted?"

"I told him that tomorrow I would give him my answer."

"Shimeon?" She allowed herself to hope, and her voice shook with it.

"Yes?"

"Shimeon, leave with me today. If there are ten thousand or fifty thousand or a hundred thousand people here in the Upper City—and in the Lower City too who feel as we do, them let them come with us—and we will lead them out of the slavery of Shammai as Moses led his people out of the slavery of Egypt." Her voice rose with excitement. "We can do it. And I can feed them—and offer them a place of refuge in Galilee. I have money enough for that—" And then, as she watched his face, her voice died away.

"You would reshape the whole world with dreams of goodness—"

"Common sense."

"No. Such things are not done, Berenice."

"But wars are."

"It will not be the first war Israel fought for freedom and independence."

"Yes, drag out all the war words, Shimeon. Comfort yourself with them. Remind me that two hundred years ago, the Maccabees threw off the yoke of the conqueror—or do I know it out of my own bloodline, for I am kin to Yannai the Great, who was spawned out of the line of Mattathias, and my great-grandfather was Herod the Great, who was spawned out of the bloodline of Antipater; and two more deliberate and terrible devils than these never ruled over any people. So I will not become enchanted with these new words of yours. I know the words that your grandfather Hillel spoke when he said, 'Who diminishes himself diminishes me, and who diminishes another diminishes me. And when a man dies, a part of myself also dies, and as mankind is lessened, so is the Lord God Almighty lessened. For the death of one man is the death of all men, and the pain of one man is the pain of all men. And is prayer is an exultation of the Almighty, there is a higher exultation than any prayer, and that is the saving of a human life. For he who saves a human life performs the holiest work of God and he takes a life, whatsoever be the reason, circumstance or justification, denies God and degrades all men. And if a spear is a force and a sword is a force, they are nothing and less than nothing, before the force of love. Love they neighbor as thyself; there is the whole law, and all the rest is commentary.' Or am I misquoting? Or have I learned poorly in the House of Hillel—learned the word life where death was intended?"

"Berenice, what do you want of me," he pleaded.

"I want you to come with me away from here."

"And desert my people?"

"And you don't desert them when you take up the sword?"

"I am the nashi—and you want me to slink away, to hide myself?"

"I want you, my beloved, to do what is the hardest thing in the whole world for a man of character and decency to do—to state that you will not take up the sword—that you are the grandson of Hillel, and upon you the House of Hillel rests."

Berenice watched Shimeon as he sat and stared at the floor, his shaggy, graying head supported by the palms of his big hands. Yet she knew what his decision would be, and when he told her, she nodded wordlessly. When he left her, she wept. Before nightfall, together with her brother, the horse soldiers and her maid Gabo, she left Jerusalem to return to Galilee.

In the weeks that followed, Berenice learned the details of what had transpired in Jerusalem—so far as Shimeon was concerned—after she had left. She learned how Menahem Benjudah Hacohen, the leader of the Sicarii, had a vision in which—as he put it—God made him high priest. It was thought that then he dressed himself in all the colorful and ancient vestments of the high priest and began the ceremonies of sacrifice in the Holy of Holies, within the Temple.

But exactly what went on in the temple complex, no one ever knew, for the Sicarii held the place. They threw over the walls, into the Lower City, the bodies of the priests and Levite temple guards whom they had murdered, among them the body of Elaezar's father. It was not merely that these bodies—seven of them were of important and noble Jews of priestly descent—were obscenely and outrageously mutilated; but the treatment of the dead in such a manner, violating the injunction of immediate burial and casting the corpses into the street from a height, was so alien to Jewish thought and practice that within hours after it was done no voice could be found in Jerusalem to defend or apologize for the Sicarii.

The Sicarii alone were undisturbed in their righteous and pious self-justification. About half of them held the Temple. The rest pushed into the synagoguges, shouldered the rabbis aside, and set about the conduct of the prayer, swaying and wailing as if over-taken by the prophetic seizure—or else they preached to a congregation that sat imprisoned by the threat of the naked, razorsharp weapons they carried. They styled themselves as the voices of the House of Shammai; they referred to their leader, Menahem, as the Prince of Righteousness who had set his face against the Evil One, the betrayer of Israel, the enemy of Yaweh—namely Hillel. To oppose them was to invite their anger and inflame their righteousness, and when irritated, they killed. During the ten days they held the temple complex, they murdered sixty-seven Jews on the streets of Jerusalem.

When Elaezar came back to Shimeon for the nashi's answer, he, Elaezar, had already learned of his father's murder and had already seen his father's body. Stony-faced he demanded to know what Shimeon had decided.

"As you wish," Shimeon nodded, "but with a single condition."

"What condition?"

"I want the Sicarii destroyed," Shimeon said, letting go of the last card that bound him to the House of Hillel. "Root and branch, I want them dug out and cut down. I want no prisoners and no trials and no judges—but they must die as they live, by the sword. Every one of them."

"Every one of them," Elaezar agreed.

A few hours after this, the assault on the Temple began, and the very unexpectedness of the attack carried the place. So secure were they in their self-appointed role of judge and executioner over Israel that the Sicarii made no attempt to guard the walls with more than a token handful of men. As for the gates, once they were barred, the Sicarii forgot about them, simply taking it for granted that nothing could stir the mighty bronze and gold portals. But the temple gates gave under the first blow of a battering ram carried by a hundred Zealots, and at the same time, five hundred ladders were raised against the temple walls. Zealots swarmed into the area by the thousands, and the Sicarii were cut down almost before they knew what was upon them. As they lived they died—violently and without mercy, impaled on spears or cut to pieces by the swords of the furious Zealots.

Elaezar himself led the party into the Holy of Holies, and when all resistance had been cut down, Menahem alone was left, tall, lean, wildly impressive in his ancient vestments, and gold breast-plate with its attached Urim and Thummin moving slightly as he breathed deeply. He faced the Zealots with one upraised arm, demanding,

"Who is responsible for this—to come here where I commune with the Lord God of Hosts?"

"I am," Elaezar replied shortly. At that moment, Shimeon entered the Holy of Holies, and took his place alongside of Elaezar.

"You I see, Elaezar Hacohen!" Menahem cried. "But who is this Israelitish cur"—pointing to Shimeon—"who defiles this place?"

"Cut him down!" Shimeon shouted to the Zealots who were crouched around Menahem.

"I am the holy one!" Menahem screamed, flinging himself toward the altar, where the razor-sharp knife of sacrifice lay. "I am the preached of righteousness, the hand of God, the keeper of His kingdom!" He whirled to face them, the knife in his hand, and the Zealots speared him as he stood thus, one spear driving through his golden breastplace, another spear transfixing him from behind and a third spear into his groin.

Yet he remained alive, staring with undiluted hatred at Shimeon and Elaezar until he died.

By nightfall of that day, all the Sicarii in Jerusalem were dead. They were hunted through the city like rats. Men, women, and children joined to drag them out of their hiding places. They were slain in cisterns, in sewers, and in the pulpits of the synagogues. They took refuge on roof tops, where they were spitted and feathered by the Jewish bowmen. They hid wherever there was cover—and wherever they hid, they were found.

It was during these hours that the remnants of the Roman garrison in Jerusalem were released by Shimeon's orders and told to leave Jerusalem immediately and march to Caesarea. He was unaware of the fact that Elaezar had given orders that all the gates of the city be closed until the Sicarii were destroyed—and that he had assigned a hundred bowmen and a hundred spearmen to guard each gate. The Romans, released from the Palace of Herod and the Tower of Antonia, marched into the streets of a city that was tasting blood and half mad with hate. No sooner were they seen than the people closed in about them, with their bows and improvised spears. A rain of rocks came from every housetop. Covering themselves with their shields, the Romans raced in close order for the Valley Gate, leaving a trail of dead and wounded behind them—and at the gate they impaled themselves on the massed points of the spearmen. The Romans fought well and desperately, but by nightfall they as well as the Sicarii were dead.

All night long, carts loaded with corpses rumbled through the streets of Jerusalem down to the valley of hell, where five thousand men worked through the night digging graves. Sicarii and Romans, stripped of clothes and weapons, were thrown together into the mass graves.

Shimeon watched it—watched the bodies, bleached by death, degraded by death, being disposed of. Under the light of hundreds of flaming torches, the scene was terrible and loathsome—and as Shimeon observed, he was bereft of the last shred of his pride. At least he could comfort himself with the thought that Berenice had returned to Galilee; but with nothing else.

Finally, he turned back to the city—a city free at last from Romans and Sicarii alike.

"My dear and beloved wife," Shimeon wrote to Berenice, "it is now five months since we have seen each other, and I compose this letter and send it to you in a mood of lonely and bleak desperation. How dreary and pointless life has become; and how ironic that so many should point to me and say, There is the nashi, who leads his people. How wonderful life must be for him!

"Hardly. As to the three letters you sent to me, I received them all and your messengers were good and faithful and discreet. No fault should be found with them. The fault is rather inside me, in my heart, which has in all truth become the heart of a stranger. How could I have answered your letters? What could I say? When you spoke to me, I heard the voice of the saintly Hillel. Better that you had reproached me than to forgive me—for in your eyes my sin is the only true sin that any man can commit, the taking of human life, whereas in the eyes of a world nourished by blood and drunk by blood, I am Shimeon the Patriot. God help me, they have struck coins, and on one side of these coins it reads: SHIMEON, THE PRINCE OF ISRAEL. On the other side, IN THE FIRST YEAR OF OUR REDEMPTION. So it is neither an apology nor an act of contrition that I indulge here. I do not ask for your forgiveness, but for just a shred of your respect. I want you to know that I, Shimeon, your husband, have not fallen prey to the music of the idiots—the music of death that is called glory. I live with it, but my eyes are open, and if I act the falsehood in my very existence, I still know the truth.

"Now I must write to you, because of certain rumors being spread by our erstwhile friend and admirer, Joseph Benmattathias Hacohen. Without going into endless details and complexities of the matter. I must explain that Joseph and I are politically apart. He esteems himself highly and opposes me on every point—and since he considers himself an expert in affairs military, he has developed a sneering and superior attitude that is quite unbearable. It has served, however, to impress sufficient of the Sanhedrin to win him the command of great captain in Galilee and other Jewish lands in the north, where he will head our forces.

"Of course, you know me well enough to wonder why I should engage in these personal hostilities—or why under any circumstances I should pit myself against such a person as Joseph. I might well answer that this business of war is constantly a struggle for power, not against one's enemies but against one's own party and friends—but that would be short of the truth. The plain truth is that Joseph has appointed himself historian, not only of our times and this war in which we are so deeply entrapped, but of every human being who shares the responsibility of Rome's anger. He makes notes endlessly, asks questions, and hands down his own decisions which then come alive as rumors; frequently enough, damaging and heartless rumors. Thus it has come to my attention that there is a process of denigration directed toward your name and reputation. It is being said, under Joseph's tutelage, that all the good and gentle acts attached to your name are inventions—that you are of the House of Herod in its worst sense. I know how little this will impress you and how small a value you put on questions of reputation—just as I know better than any other that you have never engaged in any action for the sake of glory or reputation.

"But since Joseph realizes that any stones cast in my direction might ricochet and damage him, he has added to the rumor the fact that we were never truly married or man and wife, but myself only a tool of you and a victim of your charms. Oh, I know how ridiculous this must sound—but all I have left is the love I bear you and the memories of the years we spent together. I am writing to you to plead with you to ignore such rumors if they reach you and to know always wherein is their origin.

"I have faced Joseph with these things, and so great is the change in me that I could have killed him with my bare hands. (Do all men who live with war and death turn into animals?) But he denied everything, and I could prove nothing. In any case, I do not desire to further the divisions in our ranks; there are enough.

"I am sure that you have heard all the details of the defeat of Cestius Gallus, the proconsul of Syria. I imagine he was a dull and stupid man, and I can almost feel sympathy for the Romans—in their need for hundreds of administrators—knowing how difficult it is to find even a handful of intelligent men in an entire nation. You will remember old Vibius Marsus, Gallus' predecessor. Fat, heavy, slow as he was, he understood Jews and respected Jews. There is where so many of our enemies make their mistake; and when Cestius Gallus decided to restore Roman order in Palestine and to march down here to Judea and teach a lot of unruly Jewish civilians a lesson they would not forget, he despised us and paid the price for despising us.

"In war, I am learning, there are nothing but lies—as if the truth and war were utterly inimical, and this display is like strong wine, each liar supporting the next. My colleagues now insist that Gallus come down from Syria with thirty thousand soldiers—when I know very well that there never were thirty thousand Roman troops in Syria. If Gallus had five legions with him when he marched to Judea to punish us, the outcome might have been very different. But he had only three legions, and they were thoroughly indoctrinated with the fact that there were no trained soldiers in Judea and that Jews were an unruly people who fought chaotically with tiny knives. As if there existed a more terrible weapon anywhere than the Jewish horn bow with its cedar shafts!

"So Gallus came down on us with the effrontery of a fool, marching his men in a column a mile long, as if they were on the Appian Way, drums beating, horns tooting, standards flying—as if they had only to parade into Jerusalem. At Gabaoth, a mile to the north of the city, Elaezar and his Zealots were waiting. They had two hundred Levite spearmen with them, and the Levites were half crazy with chewing erg-batha, and while the Zealots made a roof over the Romans with their arrows, the Levites faced the Roman front and drove onto them with a solid phalanx of spears. The entire head of the Roman column was wiped out, perhaps six hundred men, and if Gallus had not been able to bring up a few hundred horsemen, his army might have been destroyed then and there. As it was, Jews having a historic uneasiness in the presense of horses, the Zealots fell back into the city. They lost less than thirty men in that first engagement.

"For all of his great losses, Gallus still managed to behave like an idiot, and brought up his legions and attacked the city wall in the area of Herod's Gate. The Jewish archers stood on the wall and laughed at them and brought down the legionaries with their arrows. Finally, Gallus lost his nerve and began a retreat to the north.

"Laughing and mocking at them, the Zealots threw open the gates of the city and poured out after the Romans. Over twenty thousand bowmen followed the Romans. I rode after them, and saw some of it myself. On every hillside, every cliff, every mountain—on the sides of every wadi, the bowmen stood and loosed their arrows at the Romans.

"The Romans fled by the way of Ram and Gophna in the direction of Antipatris, and every mile of the road was carpeted with their dead. At Bethloran, the Zealots trapped them and tried to seal the pass, but Gallus broke out, and that night he rasied a barricade across the road and the valley and left five hundred legionaries to defend it—while the rest of his men shed their shields and heavy weapons and marched on the double all night long—to the safety of the walls of Antipatris. But the five hundred he left behind were trapped and wiped out to the last man, and the Zealots brought the Eagles of the Legion back to Jerusalem as trophies.

"I write all of this, not to boast, but that you may understand the mood of defiance and certainty that prevails here in Jerusalem. We have destroyed an entire Roman legion, six thousand legionaries dead on our soil, and we have captured their standards. Not since the time of Hannibal has such a shameful defeat been inflicted upon Rome—and by no soldiers but only by half-armed Jews. Whom could I convince, even in the Sanhedrin, that we were victors not over Rome but over the arrogant stupidity of Gallus? No one. There are no sober minds left. The mood is that we can defeat the entire world—and soon enough we will have the world against us. I know now that Rome will never rest until Judea pays the price for this—and yet I command. My dear and beloved wife—I am lost. There is no way back, no way out, for I will not desert my people. The House of Hillel has vanished for me. As if it never existed.

"But to my dying moment, my love for you will not lessen. Perhaps we will never see each other again, for I think your will is so strong and firm that you will not come to Jerusalem—and as for myself, I have accepted the fact that here I will remain and die—even as everyone who remains in Jerusalem must die. I see this so clearly now, and when I walk through the streets—empty because you are not beside me, empty for me, but filled with people—my heart breaks for the knowledge that I am of the company of the dead. How well the Greeks understood the knowledge of the dead and the world of the dead—a place of everlasting gloom and despair. This is what Jerusalem has become for me—and in spite of the wild confidence of the people with their victories over handfuls of Romans, I think that under all they, too, sense the implacable end.

"What terrible thing have we done that the Almighty should take this revenge upon us? That He should punish us, not with His hate but with our own—so that a whole nation decides to die? Yet from the very first time I heard the teachings of the House of Shammai—I knew that the destination was in darkness. We are almost there. My dear and beloved Berenice, forgive me."

PART FIVE

Titus Flavius Sabinus Vespasianus, commander, to Ber-enice, Queen of Chalcis:

"Greetings, and I write to you with no ease, and not to command you either, for I know full well what anguish and misery these events at Jerusalem impose upon you although I an uncertain as to how much information you have as to what goes on in the city. I also know with what distaste you receive my compliments and my assurances of regard, re-membering only too well how poorly my advances went when I was at Tiberias. So be assured, dear lady, that I write to you because I feel a heavy and unavoidable obligation to do so, as you will understand if you only bear with me and read to the end of this message.

"Believe me that the events at Jerusalem have brought no joy to me. Neither duty nor obligation are necessarily pleas-ant. I could have reduced Jerusalem two years ago, when I first entered Judea with my army. I am not boasting, but only stating a grim fact of war. But in my eyes and considerations the lives of my soldiers come first—and when I saw that the Jews were destroying each other, I made a difficult if cold-blooded decision. (I pray you to believe that I speak of the decision, not of myself. I am not a cold-blooded man. I do not imagine all men love you, Berenice. The fact that I do, boyishly perhaps, but truly—this speaks something for my nature.) I decided then not to attack Jerusalem, but to ring it round and wait until the Jews inside the walls had destroyed each other or so weakened each other that they could offer no hard defense to my legionaries.

"I am no Jew hater. I have said this. I repeat it, and I will repeat it again and again, so many times as the occasion may require. In fact, I have always been in awe of your Temple and Yaweh, that ancient God that has no being nor substance nor definition in form. My Greek friends say that this Jewish concept of God is the most sublime that mankind ever devised, and I have no reason or desire to contradict them. And if that is so, can one escape the feeling that the frightful, almost indescribable events that have taken place in Jerusalem these past two years are in some measure Yaweh's punishment? Can you imagine civil war inside a besieged city—two years of awful civil war? First it was war between the Zealots and the people in the Upper City who wanted to come to terms with Rome, and finally the Zealots broke into the Upper City and put to death every man, woman, and child in the families of peace. Then the Zealots split—a fanatical section of them demanding that every suspect Jew—suspect of desiring peace with Rome—be put to death. This faction opened the gates and let twelve hundred Sicarii from the Dea Sea region into the city. For five weeks, bloody war raged between these Sicarii and the ultra-Zealots against the moderate Zealots. Then the Sicarii opened the gates and let in an army of Idumean Bedouins, the so-called Jews of Herod. The Idumeans fought both parties of Zealots and finally the Zealots combined to destroy the Idumeans. So it has gone, month after month after months of unspeakable warfare inside a great walled city—and never a night that I have lain down to bed without hearing the faint screams of horror and pain from inside Jerusalem. Is it any wonder that we have begun to believe that even your God wills this?

"I had planned to wait another year—and by then this city would be a tomb, a charnel house of self-inflicted horror—but word from Rome changed my plans. My father there has staked his reputation as emperor upon a swift conclusion to the war in Judea, and he commands me to reduce the city immediately.

"I need not tell you that one keeps no secrets here. No sooner had I decided to proceed against the city than I received a message from one Shimeon Bargiora—who leads the largest party in Jerusalem, a combination of ultra-Zealots and Sicarii who number about twenty thousand. No one appears to know too much about Bargiora—some say he is of the Sicarii and some say he is not—but all are agreed that he lives on the edge of madness, a huge, powerful man with a violent and terrible temper. Much is said about Roman cruelty, but I can tell you that for three days in a row, this Bargiora hanged from the wall a hundred men a day—men of the peace party.

"In his message Bargiora claimed that he holds in chains in a prison cell in Jerusalem one Shimeon Bengamaliel, whom he also claims is your wedded husband as well as a grandson of that Rabbi Hillel whom Jews all over the world venerate so highly. I know that the name Hillel is not uncommon, but Bargiora states specifically that this is the grandson of that man whom Jews call the Hazaken, and who is spoken of among you as 'the saint' and also as 'the blessed of the Almighty.'

"I know of your distaste for this Joseph Benmattathias Hacohen, who shed hs allegiance to the war party once we had captured him. He has become a sort of Israelitish image of repugnance, but it is not my place to judge or moralize but only to bring the campaign here to a successful conclusion, that I may return my legions to Italy. Joseph has been invaluable as a translator, historian and encyclopedist of Jewish custom and usage. He is also a biographical dictionary of sorts, for he either knows or pretends to know every person of blood or importance in all the Jewish cities. I asked him about Shimeon Bengamaliel, and while Joseph grants that he is in all likelihood the grandson of Hillel the Good, he was distinctly dubious concerning Bargiora's claim that this man is your husband. Mind you, my dear lady, I am striving to maintain an objective position—to help you if I can in any way. I find that when Joseph desires to be obscure, no one can be more obscure; when he desires to be devious, he is a master at the art, and I cannot obtain any assurance that this Shimeon Bengamaliel is not your husband, but neither will he offer an opinion to the effect that the man is wedded to you.

"In any case, Bargiora warns me that if I move to reduce the north wall of the city, he will put Bengamaliel to death—and there he makes a pointed reference to you, that the blood of a man you love will be on my hands. I cannot take such a threat lightly. Bargiora demands that you enter the city. If you do, he guarantees your safe conduct and pledges himself to allow you to talk freely with Shimeon Bengamaliel. I do not know exactly what he is up to; but I suspect that he desires to make some exchange of prisoners or something of the sort. If that is so, and if you desire me to, I will exert all my energies to gain the freedom of Bengamaliel, whether he be your husband or not. I do this out of regard for you—a regard, a love that is not returned but which is strong enough to endure.

"So I send you this message. I left in Tiberias two fast chariots with the best of my horses and drivers, and if you should desire to come to Jerusalem and accept Bargiora's offer, they are at your disposal. I will make no move against Jerusalem until I hear from you concerning your plans."

Tiberias to Jerusalem, by the Samaria Road, was eighty-five miles in a foot-by-foot and mile-by-mile measure. In actual distance measured by travel time, it was much further. Traveling south, the road was fairly level and good as far as Sythopolis, wretched between there and Jacob's Well, passable to Bethel, and well kept under Roman repair between Bethel and Jerusalem. Grades varied; ruts varied; and the wheel quality was capable of tremendous variation: but even at best, travel in a Roman chariot was incredibly uncomfortable. Though the chariots were broad and spacious, drawn by two horses, they had no springs and no seats. The passenger could stand or crouch at the floor of the vehicle, where a few cushions supplied a minimum of comfort; but in either position the ragged jolting never ceased.

Berenice bore it grimly and silently; in the second chariot, Gabo whined and complained and cursed the Italian driver in Aramaic, and when they stopped to rest or eat, she pleaded with Berenice to give up the notion of going to Jerusalem. Gabo was aging too quickly; she was old and querulous; and if it were not that Berenice could not face the thought of some young and empty-headed slave girl being her companion, she would have left Gabo at home. For herself, it was comforting to listen to Gabo's whimpering complaints. She could deal with that and become fretful and provoked with it, and thereby direct her thoughts away from what awaited her in Jerusalem.

It was too easy to think of Shimeon. First, for a whole year, she had thought only of Shimeon; day and night and night and day—and she lived for the few letters he sent her. But no one can go on like that, and presently there was the last letter, the last word by mouth, the last rumor—and then nothing. "What of Shimeon?" There was no answer to that question. Jerusalem had become a vast, silent prison—yet no prison is escapeproof. People escaped from Jerusalem, and all those who escaped came eventually to Tiberias. Each month that the unspeakable and cannibalistic warfare within Jerusalem continued, the population of Tiberias increased. In the space of a year it doubled, and thousands stood in line for the bread dole of Berenice. But when those who had escaped Jerusalem—men and women and children hidden months in cellars, in cisterns, in hollowed-out piles of rubble—when those were questioned by Berenice, they had no answers. "What of Shimeon Bengamaliel?" But how could they answer? They were hidden. By night, they let down a rope over the walls. Or else there were Sicarii who were corruptible within their corruption, and for a price, they let the fugitives out through a postern. That is—some they let out and others they murdered for their gold or silver or few hoarded shekels that would buy freedom.

And then, finally, the Romans put the city under siege and closed it off—and then no more refugees from Jerusalem came to Tiberias. The horror that Jerusalem had become was turned upon itself—and a terrible silence surrounded the screaming, pain-wracked city.

Since then, there had been no word at all of Shimeon. Elaezar Benananias was dead; that she had heard with certainty. Bargiora had hurled his body over the walls with a proclamation pinned to it: "Thus to all priests!" Other news too; it was the season for death in Jerusalem. The House of Hakedron had been burned to the ground. Phineas Hacohen, whom they called the Ba'as Hacohen, was dead—slain by the Sicarii. His cousin, Caleb Barhoreb, the last of the oldest bloodline in all Israel, was beheaded by order of Bargiora—his head displayed on a spike from the walls. Of the seventy members of the Great Sanhedrin, Berenice had heard the names of over forty who were murdered—but never the name of Shimeon. Then she had heard of a single act of mercy on the part of Shimeon Bargiora: he had allowed two hundred and forty-two children, orphaned by the murder of their parents, to leave Jerusalem, and eventually almost all of these children arrived in Tiberias—where Berenice and her brother made a palace available for them and provided food for them and people to take care of them. Presuming on the fact that Bargiora could at least have pity for children—although many said that he released the children to save food and to spare himself the blood curse of killing them—she sent a message to him, pleading that he give her some word of the fate of her husband. But whether this message ever reached Bargiora, she never knew. The Romans were already closing every road into Jerusalem—

and soon after that, the Romans put the city under close siege.

After that, the months of silence, month after month while the memory of Shimeon grew ever dimmer—and then the Roman commander, Titus, came to Tiberias. She remembered the first time she saw him, not tall—so few of the Italians were tall—but well formed, like a Greek athlete, a short, straight nose, deep brown eyes, a wide, sensuous mouth, black, curly hair, close-cropped—twenty-eight years old and so strangely without arrogance, two vertical lines between his heavy, dark brows marking him with a sort of patient despair, as if all his days were destined to be spent in hopelessness. He stood and looked at her, stared at her— until, provoked and embarrassed, she turned on her heel and left the room.

After that, the months of silence, month after month with you—hopelessly, idiotically in love with you. I don't like it. It's an uneasy state of things."

"It's nonsense," Berenice declared flatly. "How old is he? Twenty-eight—twenty-nine? I've passed my fortieth year. I am old enough to be his mother."

"Well—hardly. You'd be an improbably young mother to have birthed him. Anyway, you are still a very beautiful woman. I doubt whether he knows how old you are."

"Tell him. I have no intentions of conducting a love affair with a Roman. You might also tell him that I am married and that my husband is in Jerusalem."

"Oh? No, sister—I will tell him nothing of the sort. For one thing, it is highly unlikely, even impossible that Shimeon should be alive. I loved him, honored him, respected him—and I leaned on him, so I certainly do not wish him dead. But no leader in his party remains alive. No, Shimeon is dead, God help him, and may he rest in peace. Will you at least be charming?"

"No," Berenice said. "No, I will not. Also, I have my hands full, and a day is not time enough to do what I must do.

Ask your Roman friend whether he will feed and shelter the homeless Jews he created?"

"The fact is, Berenice, that he's been most un-Roman about the whole thing. He's burned no houses and murdered no people. He's a most peculiar Roman—"

"A most peculiar Roman," Berenice said to herself now, crouched in the jolting chariot, her face covered that she might not breathe in the cloud of dust raised by the horses on the dry roads. "Peculiar Romans—peculiar Jews—in a peculiar and senseless world. And is Shimeon alive? Do I dare hope that he lives—or will the hope be as fruitless as all else? Yet why would Bargiora say he lives if he doesn't? What point to a stupid, meaningless invention?" And then, again, and again, the realization, "He is alive. He must be."

Down from Galilee and into the lowlands of Samaria, and as Berenice looked at the rich and verdant countryside, it seemed almost inconceivable that only three years ago war had raged all through this area. Almost no signs of war were left. The crops waved in the soft breeze; the peasants worked in the fields; and caravans of donkeys and camels moved goods through a peaceful countryside. Occasionally there were the ruins of a villa, burned to the ground, and most likely the owner dead and gone and no one to rebuild. And in a single instance, a walled town—Tabalee by name—reduced to a pile of shapeless ruins, clothed already in dust and overgrown with green weeds. But all in all, it was a prosperous and industrious land—southern Galilee, and northern Samaria—the old hatred and strife between Jew and Samaritan washed away in the terrible purge that had swept over the land. Berenice remembered with pity how ten thousand Samaritans—binding old wounds and declaring themselves to be Jews—set out to lend their aid to Jerusalem. It was a foolish and childish gesture, yet strangely noble; and ill-armed as they were, strangers to war, the Romans cut them to pieces and wandering bands of Sicarii that had scourged the borders of Judea destroyed what was left of them.

It also occurred to Berenice that this properous and untouched condition of the land might in good part be due to the role Joseph Benmattathias had played. She had never known a man who perplexed her more than this Joseph. Still only thirty-three years old, his life and actions had become such a web of strategems, falsehoods, plans, schemes, betrayal, and double betrayal that the man himself somehow disappeared behind the structure he was constantly erecting. With one foot in the war camp and the other in the peace camp, he had talked the war chiefs into giving him command of the Jewish forces in Galilee—where the Roman army first moved to halt the rebellion. Once in command, Joseph retreated, betrayed, escaped, dodged, threw victory away when the possibility of victory appeared, accepted defeat where there was no necessity for defeat, and finally entered into a suicide pact with forty desperate Zealots in a cave of the last defense. Somehow, the forty Zealots had carried out the pact—and Joseph had survived, to turn up as a special and privileged prisoner of the Romans, expert on all things Jewish and personal aide and adviser to the Roman command.

He was brilliant enough, Berenice admitted to herself, clever and adroit beyond belief—but to what end? Did he have a plan? Was there meaning or purpose in the endless structure of deceit that he erected? Why had he told Titus that there were doubts concerning her marriage with Shimeon? Was it already so in the history he purported to be writing?

These and other thoughts accompanied Berenice on the jolting, dusty ride to the borders of Judea. They stayed a at Jacob's Well, at the villa of Joab Baromar Hacohen, a Samaritan olive grower of priestly blood, knit to the Hasmonean line by a thread of blood and memory—a friend of Agrippa and eager to please the royal house. He was a small, anxious man, unsuited for the times he lived in, and torn with worry each time his wife or one of his seven children stepped out of the house. Five times in the past seven years, his house had been attacked by the Sicarii. Each time he bought them off, and each time they thoughtfully refrained from burning his villa—on the simple proposition that one did not kill the goose that lays the golden eggs.

"At least," he said to Berenice, "this will mean an end to the Sicarii—for we were coming to a point where there was no law in Palestine except the law of the Sicarii. I would be a prosperous man today—had they not bled me dry over the years. Well, I can endure it; they will take gold and oil from me and I survive, but from the peasant they take the last measure of meal, the last sack of barley—and then the peasant does not survive."

"Will we find them south of here?" Berenice asked.

"In any case your chariots can outrun them. But the Romans have cleaned them out for the most part. Yet I would not go south of here if I could help it, Queen Berenice. You will see terrible things."

"I must go," she said.

They were on the road before sunrise, the Roman drivers muttering at the way the Jewish lady drove them. They had a long day's journey before Jerusalem, and Berenice desired if possible to reach the city before nightfall. South from where they had spent the night, the road was in excellent condition for a stretch of over ten miles, and they covered that distance by sunrise—and then went on at a slow pace until an hour before midday, when they rested the horses. When they set out again, the landscape had altered radically. This was grazing country, but Berenice saw no shepherds, no sheep, no goats. The land was bare, desolate, abandoned—and every tree had been felled, every olive tree, every fruit tree. Every house they passed here had been destroyed, either wholly or in part; whether it was a shepherd's hut or some great country villa, it was seared with flame, collapsed, abandoned. Only in one place near the road, a stone fortress tower still stood, garrisoned by Romans, and here they were stopped and questioned. The centurion in command at this tower dispatched ten mounted men to accompany them, and with the Roman horsemen taking up the front and rear, they drove through the empty streets of Bethel, a town desolate and deserted, the stink of fire and decay hovering over it.

From Bethel to Jerusalem the land was deserted and desolate, the only movement Roman cavalry patrols. The fields were fallow, the houses in ruins and ashes, and the trees felled. Berenice saw swift, moving shapes that she mistook for dogs. "Jackals," the driver said. "I saw them last year, lady. There are more now."

As they came in sight of the high, walled rock of the city, Berenice understood why ever tree within twenty miles of Jerusalem had been felled. At a distance of about eight hundred yards from the walls of the city the Romans had built their own wall. The outer walls of Jerusalem measured something over three and a half miles, the wall the Romans surrounded it with almost six miles—of rock, ditch, and palisade—miles of olive trees, trees that had taken a thousand years to reach their maturity, and now split and upended in a ditch. It was a terrible, awesome, and heartbreaking sight—overwhelming in concept, the wall marching over mountains and into deep valleys—and awful in all of its implications. There were forty-three gates in this wall, every one guarded. Not a dog, not a mouse could leave Jerusalem now.

Or enter Jerusalem either—unless the Romans willed it, as Berenice realized as her chariot drove onto the road the Romans had built on the outside of the wall. Already the sun had dropped below the hills, and now everything was in shadow, the Roman legionaries shadowed as they stared curiously at the tall, red-haired woman in the first chariot and the small, dark woman in the one that followed it, the wall throwing its long somber shadows, the legion camp with its shadowed streets—and only light upon the walls of the city above them, walls blazing brilliantly, the gold and white and blue Temple like a glittering torch in the last light of the setting sun.

Titus came to her—to the pavilion which he had prepared for her, a great tent the size of his own and divided by drapery flaps into four rooms. He had furnished it with what he could lay hands on—some couches, beds, chairs, a table, and two beautifully made Egyptian chests containing an assortment of jewels and dresses. Nothing in the tent was Jewish, and that, Berenice reflected, was very much like this most peculiar Roman. He must have sent to Egypt and Caesarea for the furnishings. Servants were waiting to provide for her comfort—water for a bath, rose water then to refresh her, fruit and bread and wine and cheese, simple food he had learned was her preference. He had, Berenice reflected, learned a tremendous lot concerning her. Like some Roman legate entering a new and unknown territory, he had been curious, thorough, and workmanlike.

Now he came to her, himself and alone and on foot, waiting a full three hours before he presumed to impose himself upon her. She lay on a couch, resting now, having bathed and changed her clothes and had a glass of wine. She had no desire for food. She told Titus to enter, and he passed through the flap and stood looking down at her in the light of the smoky lanterns the Romans used.

"You look rested, my lady, Berenice," he said.

"Somewhat—yes."

"Was everything provided for? I mean, I tried to anticipate your wants—as much as a man like myself can comprehend and anticipate the wants of a woman. Such a woman as you."

"Everything," Berenice replied.

"Well—I'm pleased. At least with that. Do I appear foolish? I mean, it seems to me that I stand here and mumble and make very little sense—"

She smiled now, thinking to herself how likable and utterly improbably this young man was, the first son of the Emperor of Rome and someday emperor himself if the fortunes of war spared him, yet as soft-spoken as if he had neither command nor power. She was also very tired, and when she realized that it was the first time she had actually smiled at him, she wondered at himself. Her whole being existed in the fact that she would soon see Shimeon, speak to him—and also in its reverse. Shimeon was dead, and she would never see him again.

"No—you make sense, and you have been kind and thoughtful," Berenice said. "If I seem terse, it is because I am nervous and ill at ease—and I suppose a little sick with fear and anticipation."

"I can understand that," he nodded.

"Can you? Do you know—this man is my husband, if he lives. Regardless of what Joseph says."

"I suspected as much."

"Why?"

"I am interested in you—that is no secret. I ask questions. I would be a fool to rely entirely on Joseph. Wouldn't I?"

"I have nothing to say about Joseph Benmattathias," Berenice answered. "He is of no interest to me."

"I think he's in love with you," Titus said, casting the stone to the water and watching the ripple.

"Titus Flavius," Berenice said flatly, "the truth is that no one is in love with me, and in this cruel and awful moment, it is more of hurt that compliment. I am no young woman, regardless of what you may choose to think—but forty-two years old. That's very old."

"May all the gods forgive me if I have hurt you in any way!"

"Don't talk that way—please. I am a Jew, and you are a Roman, and we are both of us here before Jerusalem. Whatever they are in there, whatever they have done, they are Jews."

"Even if the man Bargiora speaks of is your husband?"

"Yes."

"And I suppose nothing—no argument, no reasons can prevent you from going into Jerusalem."

"You can prevent me," Berenice said tiredly. "I am one woman—so you know that you can prevent me."

"I spoke of arguments."

"If you will allow me to, Titus Flavius, I want to go up to Jerusalem as soon as there is dawn light tomorrow."

"I will not prevent you."

"Thank you," Berenice answered him. "You are a good man—I think a very good man—which only confuses me and troubles me. Sometimes I have also felt that I am a good person, and that too confuses me, and I suppose the final judgment on us will not be of ourselves but of such a man as Joseph Benmattathias. There was only one man in my life whom I loved and trusted, and I thank you with all my heart for allowing me to go to him."

"And if you should be thanking me for allowing you to die with him?"

"If that must be—"

"I heard so much about you," Titus said uncertainly, "and it was always in terms of a very complex and difficult woman. Then why do I find you direct and simple?"

Berenice shook her head, and then Titus left her. She was grateful for that, since she could no longer hold back her tears, and she had no desire to weep in front of him. She lay on the couch then, weeping, and presently she fell asleep. Gabo came in and covered her and removed her sandals and tucked the quilt under her feet against the chill of the night air—all the while clucking and complaining with annoyance. Berenice was never certain whether Gabo, who was now the mother of seven children, had come to tolerate her, endure her, or perhaps love her.

The hour before dawn, the trumpets sounding, the drums beating, and the rhythmical tread of thousands of leather boots falling into line, place, maniple, century, cohort, and legion. The noncommissioned officers shouting their orders, the ripple of Latin names on the roll call, the sharp, authoritative tread of the centurions, and then the single tread of one centurion to the tent entrance:

"Queen Berenice?"

She had been awake for hours, waiting—yet not to go to a

funeral. She had dressed carefully, aware of herself, as ever—the underdress of pale blue and the overdress of blue only a few tints darker, and around her head, holding her still flaming hair, a simple gold band with the lion rampant of Judah. Whatever she was going to, let them see that no one had more right to the royal and sacred colors, or to the symbol of the royal house. Whatever her fate, she would not conceal her bloodlines nor deny them.

The centurion, a boy in his early twenties, caught his breath as she stepped outside of the tent. Like all others who shared the gossip of the camp, he had heard that his commander was enamored of an elderly Jewish lady. Now, seeing the elderly Jewish lady face to face, so early in the morning, he understood the nature of his commander's entrapment.

"I am instructed to take you through the wall, Queen Berenice—you understand me? My Aramaic is very poor."

"I speak Latin," Berenice replied.

"Well, you do. If I may say so."

"What is your name, young man?"

"Hermanius Bracus."

"Then let us go, Hermanius Bracus."

"If you should desire refreshment?"

"I need nothing, Hermanius Bracus. You were told to take me through the wall. Do so—please."

His every instinct was to be courtly, yet all the small pieces of flirtation that he would have used with a Roman matron—and she was a matron, no matter how often he looked at her and caught his breath—fell flatly on the wall she had erected about herself. She could not be reached.

Or perhaps one would have to go back many years to reach her; for now, as they walked along the wall the Romans had erected, Berenice was thinking of the time she had been in Jerusalem—back to so long ago, when they bore her father's casket here, and again when she and Shimeon came down from the North to go to the copper mines in the desert, and again and again, time after time, herself and Shimeon like

309

companions who knew each other so intimately that each anticipated the thoughts of the other, and that was to be forever; but here was Shimeon like a dim vision already, and man's memory and love was a fraud and a swindle.

These and other things she remembered, and as they walked the Roman soldiers stared at them silently—having been warned that the price of any jest, any insult, any coarse word flung at this woman might well be the speaker's life. The first light of the morning sun touched the towers of the city, the tall spires of the Temple, and Berenice, looking past the crazily leaning Roman wall, remembered how she and Shimeon would greet the morning sun up there—on that height, where Yaweh's eternal altar stood. She remembered other things, and said suddenly,

"Centurion, is Gessius Florus here with the army?"

"No, my lady, he is dead."

"Oh? How did he die?"

"I don't remember all the details," the centurion said, "but it would seem to me that it was an attack of indigestion. Wasn't he a short, fat man? A bit of a glutton—?"

With what ignominy were the mighty fallen, Berenice thought, and how little of nobility or grandeur was there in any of it! She had always had a sense of something sexually barren about men with swords, as if the tool of death in hand replaced the tool of life hanging limply and meaninglessly. Well, that was a woman's thought, and so many women could not understand strutting. They all strutted now—these men of the sword, as if the presence of a beautiful woman among them poured forth a torrent of admiration in which they bathed. Even the young man beside her, with his polished armor and his fine white shoes and gloves, even he strutted in admiration.

She saw Joseph Benmattathias, tall, healthy, his hair combed, his short beard trimmed and curled, wearing a long blue robe embroidered in gold with a hem of six-pointed stars. A full head taller than the legionaries around him, slim and elegant, his presence broke in on Berenice's reverie, and suddenly there was no meaning or purpose in anything—not in her being here and not in any foolish hope that Shimeon lived.

He bade her good morning, eying her keenly and setting aside any anticipated rebuff by saying, "I will not trouble you with my thoughts or advices at this moment. Queen Berenice. I know what ordeal confronts you. I am here simply to wish you well." He spoke in Aramaic, and she realized that he did so to have her reply in Aramaic—if she were disposed to insult him or cut him down. Then the Roman soldiers would not understand and he would maintain face. She did not reply but walked on, marveling at the workings of the man's mind, remembering that first time he had explained to her how a man might exist with one foot in each of two different and opposed camps. But in that he was no way so different from most men—and could not the same be said of Shimeon? But Shimeon struggled in the murk of events; he tore his heart out with each step he took, and because he was a man of compassion, every step of his experience was a betrayal of one sort or another. For Shimeon, life was impossible; every choice was of necessity the wrong choice, and his broad shoulders bore all the ridiculous luggage that the male of the species had devised, courage and honor and loyalty and devotion—only all of it inverted, and the courage was no courage, the loyalty to all that was unreasonable and unspeakable—

"Here, Queen Berenice."

They were at the gate. A guard of legionaries stood there and they opened the city for Berenice and the centurion. He pointed to the space between the two walls, and, facing them, the Damascus Gate in the wall that her great-grandfather had built, and for the rebuilding of which—at least in part—her father had paid with his life. A few men on the walls—and nothing else, and nothing in the no-man's-land between the two fortifications; and all of it in the deep shadow of early morning.

"I must leave you here, and you must go on alone," the

centurion said, repeating by rote what he had been told, and
wondering why, if his commander was so enamored of this
woman, he was not here. "That was their condition, that you
come out of the wall alone and go across the space in between
alone. I am sorry. But there is nothing between the walls to
frighten you—"

"You need not worry about my fears, Centurion."

"I meant that there is nothing Roman out there—but what
there is from the Jew's side, I don't know. I am told not to
question why you are—"

"Then don't question why, Centurion. And now I thank
you for your aid and courtesy." With that, Berenice left him
and walked on toward the gate to the city.

She did not look back, but she could not avoid looking
ahead of her, and this small piece of road between the two
walls was no pleasant place to walk. It had been fought over
too much. Here the Idumeans had fought, and here the
Sicarii had hacked down a party of men and women who had
attempted to feel the city. Here too, the Zealots had fought a
pitched battle with four cohorts of legionaries, when the
Romans first made their approach to the city—and here,
eventually, the Romans would make their final assault on the
city, pushing their great siege engines in front of them. But
now, already, the road stank with death. There was no dust
on this piece of road, for its surface was cemented with
hundreds of gallons of blood; a black surface of dry blood that
the vultures pecked at angrily, drawn by the smell and frustrated by the product. But there was better eating for the
vultures in the rotten flesh that lay alongside the road, carcas-
ses of horses and donkeys and camels, dead jackals, and dead
men too—skeletons picked clean and others that bore half a
coat of stinking flesh.

It required all of Berenice's control not to retch, not to
double over in a spasm of sick horror, not to cover her mouth
and nose, not to race back to the protection of the Roman
wall—but she knew that she was being watched, and she told
herself, "I will not be afraid, and I will not let them see me

shrink from any of this. This is the game of men. This is the pleasure they call war. I will not vomit and weep over what men do."

More and more people appeared on the walls, until they were crowded with a solid rank of people as far as the eye could see in either direction. The Damascus Gate opened now to a crack of about two feet, and a man stepped through, a big, broad-shouldered man, with a cadaverous, bony face and a flaming scar down one cheek to his chin. He was dressed in full armor, brazen cuirass, arm pieces, brass greaves, and plumed Roman helmet, and he wore sword and dagger but carried no shield. Watching him, his manner, his fierce, bold strut, the fixed, stonelike expression on his face, Berenice guessed that he was Shimeon Bargiora, the leader of the city now—a war man who had no existence before the war, no existence that anyone knew of, no family, no youth, no past, even as he himself disrupted and wiped out his future. He was a creature of war. Some said he was of the Sicarii; others said that he was a Zealot; and still others held that he was an Idumean Bedouin; but identity as such made no difference. His identity was with death, and even when he stood still, he gave the effect of a man in violent motion, plunging; and hate was a part of this motion. He walked in an aura of hate that was almost noble in its defiance of everything.

He stood outside the gate, waiting for Berenice, and when she was almost up to him he nodded, so that the white plumes in his helmet swayed back and forth, and he said to her,

"You are the queen of Chalcis?"

"Yes."

"Is it true that you are the wife—or were the wife of Shimeon Bengamaliel, who was the nashi?"

"I am his wife," Berenice nodded. "Is he alive?"

"He's alive, and I will take you to him. I am Shimeon Bargiora. I command the city."

"I know who you are," Berenice said.

"You know what you hear of me. Outside, talk is cheap—and the rumor mill never stops grinding." His voice was harsh, grating, angry, and now that she was close to him, Berenice saw a tic in his cheek, just over the ugly scar. Without the scar, he would have been a handsome man, for all the high-boned, death's-head quality of his face.

"I came here to see my husband," Berenice said.

"I know that, lady. You came—and you will go. We are here. We are committed here."

"I know that."

"Do you? Really—do you?" He stepped close to her, fingered the silk of her overdress, sniffed at its perfume. "Where did you bathe this morning, Queen Berenice? You smell like the flowers of Eden. Forgive me—that wall has ringed us around for months. We are starving to death inside, and dying of thirst too."

"You said you would take me to my husband."

"Ah! So I did." And then, brusquely, "Come along!" And without more ado, he strode through the gate. She followed him. The sun was up now, blazing down with its rich morning heat, still tempered by the chill of the night air—that miraculous combination of heat and chill that made Jerusalem's one of the finest climates in Palestine.

Inside the gates there was a circle of soldiers, well armed and well armored with Roman weapons and armor, and beyond them a silent crowd of people who were alive yet dead—this was Berenice's first and immediate impression—living dead, people so thin, so emaciated that they had lost all resemblance to ordinary men and women and children, people who watched her out of sunken eyes and pleaded without words. They stayed back quietly, beyond the reach of the soldiers who fell in on either side of Bargiora and herself and marched with them. Other soldiers closed the gates behind them, while still more soldiers were dropping down from the walls, on ropes and wooden ladders, that they might see this legendary woman at close range—commenting

314

about her hair and the look of her, "A hundred years old—the devil she is!" "And I tell you she's a witch." "A witch—a bitch, it's all the same." They were well fed, these soldiers, not fat but not skinny either, lean and tight but by no means emaciated.

Bargiora led Berenice toward the old wall and the Fish Gate, and when the people saw that she would be gone in a moment, one of them, a man, cried out and reminded her that she had fed the hungry once. "We die of hunger, Berenice!" he cried out, and a soldier shouted at him, "Then get on with it, and the sooner the better."

"They don't fight—they don't eat," Bargiora said shortly.

"Do you want the women to fight?"

"If a man fights, his wife eats. There is no Sanhedrin to sit in judgment and divide the few rotten baskets of bread that remain. There isn't enough food for all. The fighting men must live."

"Why?" Berenice asked quietly.

"To defend the city."

"And then?"

"We live now—not then," he snapped. "If your heart must bleed, my lady, why not let it bleed for these soldiers who will die for their God and their city—and for their holy Temple."

"My heart bleeds," she whispered. "It bleeds enough, Bargiora—so don't tell me for whom."

"People like you," he began in anger and disgust and then shook his head and swallowed his words. "Come on, lady."

They walked on. A woman sat on the street, and her husband lay there, his head on her lap, pillowed. But he was dead. She wept for him, but only the tears made a difference; she was as yellow and emaciated as he was. Three children sat naked in the street, their bellies swollen, their bones protruding. A woman crawled past on her hands and knees, half naked, her flat dugs hanging down before her, dragging on the ground as she forced the bony frame that had been her body to move. A man and woman walked slowly, blindly, supporting each other.

"God in heaven," cried Berenice, "let them live! Let them out of the city and I will see them fed. I swear it."

"There are more important things than life."

"What?"

"That house of God." He pointed to the Temple.

"That house of God is empty," Berenice whispered, and in sudden anger, Bargiora cried,

"Will you blaspheme? By Yaweh, I will see you—"

"What will you do, Bargiora?" she asked drily and nastily. "Tell me what you will do, Bargiora. I came here by your word. I see you as a murderer—let me hear you as a liar!"

"No—I won't lose my temper over you. No. You—you're as much of a Jew as Titus."

"Yes? And are you a Jew, Bargiora?"

He shook his head and clenched his lips—and whatever might have followed was interrupted by the appearance of a mongrel dog out of a gaping doorway—a yellow dog with a half-eaten human hand and forearm clenched in his teeth. When he saw the approaching group of soldiers, he paused warily, looking around for an avenue of retreat. But already his way back into the door from which he had emerged was blocked. A soldier covered it as Bargiora cried,

"Get him! Kill him!"

Two of the soldiers hurled their javelins, but the yellow dog was an old hand at survival; he would have to be to remain alive after two years of siege. He watched the javelins and dodged them. Then the soldiers closed in, and the dog twisted, turned, and evaded. He dropped the arm in the process and suddenly darted away. Just as he seemed to be making good his escape, one of the soldiers picked up a cobble and threw it, catching the yellow dog on the side of the head and cracking his skull. In a moment, they were on him, and one of the soldiers had gutted the dog, ripped out its insides, hooked it onto his javelin, and continued to march with the carcass over his shoulder. "We eat meat tonight," another said.

When Berenice stared in horror at Bargiora, he shrugged and said, "We have a dispensation. We fight in the Almighty's name. Whatever will keep us alive is permitted."

"Even what has eaten human flesh?"

"Remain with us for a while, my lady. You will become less discriminating, I assure you."

They had passed into the Akra, climbing higher and higher, and now they entered the Upper City through the ancient Ephraim Gate. The gate iself, however, was new and improvised onto the charred remains of the old gate, and on either side of the gate, the wall had been pounded down and subsequently repaired. As they entered the old City of Zion, Berenice had the feeling of a place already conquered—and, looking around her, she could feel almost concretely the despair and desolation of the place. In the Lower City, there were people—sick, starving, and enervated people, but people nevertheless—men and women and children; but here there were no women and no children. The men were soldiers, poorly armed but all with weapons and most of them near the gates and the temple area; as they proceeded into the Old City itself, there was no one, only the ruined houses, gaping walls, burned interiors and roofs—the great mansions and villas, gutted, ruined, ransacked, and looted as if the Romans had already been through this place and abandoned it. Only the Temple itself remained inviolate, shining in the morning sun.

"Where are the people?" Berenice asked Bargiora, knowing what the answer must be.

"People? What people?"

"A hundred and fifty thousand people lived here in the Upper City," Berenice said.

"Oh? That may be—and I will tell you that a good many still live here. They stay tight in their holes—just as a half a million more in the Lower City prefer the darkness of their bolted chambers to the good light of day."

"Tell me, Bargiora—how many have died here in the city?"

"It's war and people die."

"How many have you murdered?"

"Now, damn you to hell, Berenice—I will not be spoken to that way—not out of that sneering, aristocratic manner of yours. We have proved here that the aristocrat dies as easily as the common Israelite."

"But the aristocrats got out of the city, didn't they, and you've been practicing the way of death on others—on common Israelites and common Jebusites. How many, Bargiora? And how many are left?"

"More left than I can count, I tell you that. I have been most patient and most tolerant, my lady—"

"No," said Berenice, "you don't know the meaning of patience or tolerance. You need me, Bargiora—you need me a great deal, don't you?"

The Palace of Herod was the prison, a great, looming, ugly pile of a building, tasteless, a long veranda of square pillars, a kind of parody of the Grecian style. Half the building had been destroyed in the inner-city fighting, but the fortress part of it, built out of mighty blocks of red stone, was untouched. How many memories it recalled to Berenice! When her father had been king he had held court in this building, which his grandfather had erected, and again from the steps of this building, Gessius Florus had directed the attack against the children, the slaughter in the plaza. There was nothing gentle or beautiful about this building—it was of the nature of the city, a city without parks or green places, a city of stone wherein for a thousand years one fortress had been built upon another, as if it had somehow been foredoomed to die as it was now dying, and forewarned of its impending doom.

"Here," Bargiora said, pointing to it, "the Romans made their praetorium—but we drove them out just as we drove out the sniveling descendants of your great-grandfather, who built the place—"

"You didn't drive me out," Berenice said, "and when I left Jerusalem, I had never heard of the name Bargiora. And if you would know something about my husband, he is no aristocrat and never needed to boast a bloodline; for he was out of the blood of Hillel the Good, and that is something you would hardly understand."

"I understand Hillel—which is simply another word for cowardice and treason—and believe me, my lady, when we have driven out the Romans, we will go up into Galilee and scourge it of Hillel as you scourge a house of rats. So now, close your trap and come with me. Your husband is in there."

It took all his control to hide his fury now as he led Berenice into the building, his soldiers around him and other soldiers lighting the way with flaming torches. Berenice saw that all effort to maintain the building had been abandoned; it had not even been primitively cleaned for months and months. Filth and rubbish lay everywhere; the glass windows were smashed and the decorations had been torn down, whether by Jews or Romans she did not know. They went down two flights of stairs into the subcellar, where the dungeon was—and then along a passage where the air was thick and sickening with the smell of human defecation. There were the doors of the prison cells, and from behind each door the pleading and whimpering of lost souls. With each step it was more difficult for Berenice to control herself, and when at last they stopped in front of a door, put the key in the lock, and opened the door, she was numb with the effort of beating her body and mind into submission. The cell was black until the glare of the torches lit it, and then, by the light of the torches, she saw a man sitting on a wooden bench, covering his eyes with his hands to protect them from the light. He was naked except for a filthy loincloth; his body was covered with scabies and running sores; his hair was long, white, and tangled in a mass of lice, dirt, and excrement—as was his beard; and he muttered inanely against the light, "—blinding me with it—take it away. Or is the sun rising? That would be something, the sun rising in here—" Other words that were meaningless to Berenice, and as he muttered, spittle drooled from his lips.

Berenice realized that a person dies more than once, and that the dying is more awful than death. The man on the bench was Shimeon; she knew immediately, and inside her something died, and because it was dead she did not scream or weep or whimper or plead but simply went over to him, placing herself between his face and the light of the torches and raised his face to her, whispering to him, "Shimeon, my beloved, my heart—Shimeon, I am with you now."

He uncovered his face, which was scarred from beating and covered with open sores, and he looked at her with eyes that saw nothing.

"Shimeon?"

"I am hungry," he said.

From behind her, Bargiora said harshly, "Bring him food—bring him bread and wine and raisins. The best!"

Berenice pushed his hair aside, bent and kissed him. "It will be all right, my beloved."

"What is my name?" he asked her. "What is the name you called me?"

"You are Shimeon, the nashi—who is prince over Israel, who is prince of all the Jews in all the world, wherever they may be. And this they know. They know—"

Shimeon giggled foolishly, stared at his hands, flexed his fingers.

"Enough!" Bargiora said, and two of his soldiers pulled Berenice back. The moment she ceased to be a shield against the light, the naked man on the bench covered his eyes again—and then mercifully darkness covered all of them.

Outside, in the warm sunshine of the Mountain of Zion, as the Upper City was called, with the cool wind blowing from the sea, Bargiora said to Berenice, "Are you satisfied that he is Shimeon the nashi?"

"He is my husband," Berenice said.

"Believe me, you are a strong one, Queen Berenice—or do the stones weep more easily than you do?"

"I want to talk about why you brought me here, Shimeon Bargiora. Nothing else concerns me. My life is what I believe, and in the House of Hillel there is no vengeance. Vengeance is to the Almighty—and may God help you, Bargiora, when He evens the score!"

"I make no apologies to you or God."

"What do you want of me?"

"No—it's what you want of me," Bargiora said. "You want your husband, don't you? He lives. A month of good food, rest, and sunshine, and these months in Jerusalem will pass out of his mind. Life is easy for the rich, and they say you are the richest woman in the world. No one looks good in a prison cell, but cleaned up—"

"You have no shame," Berenice whispered.

"We are not here to discuss shame or pride or loyalty. I could have some arguments on that score. We are here to discuss your husband's life. Do you want him to live?"

"Yes."

"Any price?"

"Any price you ask," Berenice agreed. "But what is gold to you? You have the temple treasury—more gold than any man on earth owns. What can I pay you?"

"Not gold. I want life—for my men and for myself because I lead them."

"Can I give you life?" Berenice asked bleakly.

"I think you can, lady. It is no secret that Titus is enamored of you—and I would guess that he is enamored, as all Romans are, of the House of Hillel, which carries no sword or spear to annoy them. Does he want the grandson of Hillel to die? Does he want your hatred? And does he want Jerusalem—as it is or battered into rubble and burned as a pyre? Because if he comes to take this city from us, we will fight him on every street and on every wall and he will pay a price he doesn't dream of—if he ever takes the city. And he knows that."

"What do you want?"

"I want his sacred word that he will give me safe conduct out of this city—myself and ten thousand of my men. In return, I will open the gates of the city to him."

"Ten thousand?" Bernice wondered. "What ten thousand? There must be thirty or forty thousand men on the walls of this city. Do you mean ten thousand Sicarii?"

"Sicarii! Sicarii! I hate that word—it's your word, a rotten lying, Roman word! Who are the Sicarii? Men too devout to abandon their God? Men who believe in the sacredness of the Temple? Men who pray morning, noon, and night, making the Law a sign as frontlets between their eyes? Men who would die before they sullied the purity and holiness of Jewish blood with the filthy blood of pagans! These are what you call the Sicarii!"

"And if Titus allows you to leave the city, you will release my husband?"

"Let Titus give me his word, and I will release the nashi."

"You will take his word?"

"I will take your word—and I will wait one day, no more. Our food is going. One day."

Berenice sat on a chair in that high and spacious tent that was the praetorium of Titus Flavius. With Roman thoroughness, the legionaries had laid down a hewn-rock and mortar pavement to make a great square in the middle of the enormous camp, and in the center of this square was the commander's tent, striped gold and white, and on one side an altar of worship in a black tent, on the other a court of justice in a red tent. The room in Titus' pavilion where Berenice sat was thirty feet by twelve and held a table, three chairs, a couch, standards, weapons. Titus himself paced back and forth, talking softly and with an intensity that verged on desperation:

"What do you ask me? Don't believe that I haven't thought to myself that one day you would come and ask me to help you. To do anything for you—so I could say this is concrete. This is real. I am not an empty-headed and emotional Italian who has fallen madly in love with an older woman. Before God, I am no boy. I am thirty years old—and I have seen all that a man can see in thirty years and retain his sanity. And three years of that damned city—three years of that city, so that there is no night I don't dream of it and wake up shuddering and sweating. Do you think I am not human? Do you measure us all by scum like Gessius Florus? I wanted you to come and demand—Titus, do this for me! And then you come with the impossible."

"And you have no guilt?" Berenice demanded. "No responsibility? Don't talk of casting gifts at my feet. I am not asking for gifts. In a way I am simply asking for justice. You can sneer at Gessius Florus, but he was your puppet. Your own. Why did you send him here? And before him, Fadus. Tiberius Julius. Cumanus. Felix. Festus. Albinus. All of them *your* procurators—and they have torn our hearts out and twisted our souls out of shape—"

He stopped pacing, turned to Berenice, his hands stretched out: "What do you expect? There are procurators—men who give up their home and country and language and city, for money! Only for that. The quick road to riches, and most often they are scum. I admit it. But I was not responsible—not my father. We did not appoint these men. Listen to me—do you know what Rome is? I mean in the sense of order as opposed to anarchy? In the sense of law as opposed to greed and fanaticism?" He flung an arm in the direction of Jerusalem. "Think about what is happening in that city! Think of what has happened there over the past three years! In the name of what? Freedom? What kind of freedom, that makes Jew kill Jew in this bloody and indescribable fratricide? In that city alone, more Jews have been murdered by Jews than all the lives taken by every rotten and gold-hungry procurator we have sent here in a hundred years. And is it only Jerusalem—or a whole world willing to put itself to death? Our way isn't perfect. We are faced with governing the whole world, and we don't know how. I admit that. But we have imposed a system of law and order, and we are in motion, and we cannot stop, and we cannot let go. We have a tiger by the tail, but we also have the strength to tame that tiger. Right or wrong—I can't decide that. I was given something here that neither of us made—"

"My husband is Hillel's grandson. He is also the prince-elect of all Israel. Released, free of those madmen in Jerusalem, he can raise up Israel to a new future. We don't threaten Rome. Our kingdom is Hillel's kingdom—"

Titus shook his head. "I know what Hillel teaches, and I know what Shammai teaches—and in the end Shammai always wins, doesn't he? Shammai has the sword in his hand, and by all the gods that be, the sword is deeply persuasive. I have heard of a sect that preaches not unlike your Hillelites. They have a prophet called Joshua, and they put aside the sword, but I see no talent among them except for death—because the sword defines the truth."

"No!" Berenice cried.

"My dear, my dear," Titus said softly, coming to her now, "ask me something that is possible. That city was half for Hillel and half for Shammai—and where are the Hillel people today? Dead—or like your husband. And now you ask me to let Bargiora and ten thousand of his Sicarii march out of those gates to freedom. How can I without betraying my father, Rome—and every soldier in my army? And what of the Zealots left in the city? Will they surrender if the Sicarii go? I think not, and I will still have to reduce the city. But while I am doing so, Bargiora and his army will go up to Galilee, and I tell you that if they ever enter Tiberias, they will kill every man, woman, and child in that city. They don't fight Rome, Berenice—that is why they want safe conduct out of the city. They fight Hillel—face it. Face it. And then tell me, am I not right?"

Berenice looked at him, and wondered how it felt to be a

Roman and to know so easily and surely what is right and what is wrong. For herself, she only knew that she had failed—her life had failed and her beliefs had failed. She had loved a man and failed at that too.

They waited until the full shape of the sun rose above the Judean hills on the following day, and then they threw Shimeon's body over the wall of the city. Titus sent a hundred men to bring the body to Berenice, but they were driven back by a storm of arrows and rocks—none of them killed, sheltered as they were by their heavy wooden shields, but willing enough to go back; and watching them, Berenice found herself asking herself coldly enough, "Why should they die for a Jew's body?"

She stood by the gate of the Roman wall, watching, and Titus stood next to her, and then she said, "I am going to my husband."

"No—I forbid you—" Titus began. Berenice looked at him coldly, and he bit off his words. She walked past the panting legionaries who had run out to the Jewish wall and back, and they turned away, not to meet her glance. But she cared nothing about whether their cowardice shamed them or not—they had no reality to her at this moment, these small, dark men, with their rank smell of sweat-soaked leather and their scatological Latin patois. The only reality in her existence was that broken body at the foot of the city wall, and she walked to it now, not deigning even to glance up at the men on the wall. The shouting and catcalling that had marked the abortive Roman attempt died away now, and an almost palpable silence settled over the no-man's-land between the two walls.

Berenice was dry—dry, with her heart tight and shriveled; and this sense of dryness, this feeling of dryness more profound than grief and beyond grief pervaded her. She knelt above Shimeon, who lay on his face, and she turned his body over. He was not the weight he had been once—the body had starved for so long—yet he was heavy with the added heaviness of death. Cut, bruised, his limbs broken, his skull smashed—still there was in his death-being what Berenice knew and loved, and suddenly all the memories came crashing upon her, her first meeting with him as he tore down the blinds in her room, their strange courtship, his missions to the sick, his gentleness with the sick—as he said to Berenice once, "A sick person is like a child, helpless, defenseless—and it gives me a sense of the father that is the truest thing in my life, and I suppose that is why I can live contentedly with no children of my own."

More and more memories; they threatened to explode her, to tear her into tiny shreds, to smash her mind into chaos and blindness; and she said to herself deliberately and coldly, "No, Berenice—you are past indulgence, and these memories are the purest indulgence. There are many things that must be done before you can afford to scream your way into madness, and first you must bring Shimeon home."

Home meant Galilee; she had already decided that; and now she knelt by the body and tried to raise it—and failed and let go. She stood up, looking up at the walls, and cried out:

"What are you up there? Are you Jews? This is the body of your nashi, and I will bear him home to Galilee if I must do so on my own back. Is there no Jew with courage enough to help me?"

At first there was no response. Then Berenice heard them shouting on the other side of the wall, and then a scream of pain and the clash of iron on iron—and then a moment later a postern opened and three men dashed through and stood panting outside the wall. Berenice looked up, and there was Bargiora above her and his men all along the wall. They stood with arrow and javelin poised—waiting his order.

The three men approached her, dirty, skinny men, girded with swords and some rusty plate armor. They didn't look like much, and they didn't speak, but lifted Shimeon's body up in their arms.

"If we take this to the Romans, Queen," one of them said, "they will kill us."

"They won't."

"That's your judgment, lady," said another. "We will help you, but give us a fair chance to live."

"Bear him beyond arrow shot—and the Romans will help me."

They carried Shimeon's body halfway toward the Roman wall, and set it down there, and then one of them said, "We could not have prevented his death, Queen Berenice, but that doesn't wash the blood from our hands. The nashi is like a saint in heaven, and he sits at the side of Moses and at the side of God—and we all share his murder. The Almighty knows that, and because the mark of Cain is upon us, the Almighty will do what He must do. What is left in that city will die, and we die with it—and God willing, the Jews will never know the like of us again. We have all made a pact with death, and we only desire to live that we may die. Don't hate us, Queen Berenice—pity us. Pity us."

Berenice wept now, not for her husband, but for these three skinny, nameless Jews who now turned away from her and walked hopelessly back to their doomed city. The dam opened, and as she wept, she was saved.

Could he help her? Could he do anything for her, Titus desired to know? Even in the largest sense, he had failed her—could he help her now?

There were things she needed. She needed a coffin of plain wood, and he said it would be ready within the day. She needed plain white linen for a winding shroud, and she needed spices to pack the body with, so that it would bear the trip to the north. All of this Titus promised. It was a small matter, and it was done for her.

She washed the body herself. It was laid out in her tent, and she refused the services of the Roman embalmers, who had studied their craft in Egypt and who swore to her that they could preserve the flesh of Shimeon for a full eternity, whatever that might mean. Berenice was not interested in preserving his flesh for an eternity—and it was an abomination to a Jew for the flesh to be cut after death. The man she had loved was gone. The body was nothing; she honored it only because it had been his, and because it gave her a sort of surcease from despair to do these things. So she cut away his rags, washed the flesh clean, washed the hair and beard and combed them. Because he was an Israelite, the most common clay of the Jews, without blood or gens to matter, she could dispense with ceremony. The Roman soldiers helped her to wrap him in the linen winding sheet and lay him in his coffin, after which the spices were packed all around him. During these tasks, Joseph Benmattathias came to the tent to offer his condolences. Berenice nodded. She could not trust herself to speak to him.

Titus provided a wagon for the coffin, and he offered a guard of honor to ride with them, but Berenice refused it and said that she and her slave, Gabo, would travel alone. Gabo had been a source of help and strength; they had become closer than ever before; and as she had done several times in the past, Berenice offered her manumission. As always, this led to tears and great emotional distress on the part of Gabo, and Gabo said that it was a cruel thing on Berenice's part to bring up the subject now—with the body of the nashi lying there in his coffin.

Titus attempted to insist that Berenice travel in the manner that a queen should, but Berenice was not easily moved—and she tried to make him understand that she was less a queen than a Jew, and that as a Jew she could travel in Palestine on foot and no one would look askance at her.

"And you intend to go from here to Galilee in that cart—with the body?"

"With my husband," she replied, "and Gabo will be with me."

"But you cannot!"

"But I can," she said.

They left the following morning, Berenice and Gabo, driving a team of mules that drew a wagon bearing a coffin. They left at the break of day, and a few hours later Titus ordered the first assault on Jerusalem.

The news ran ahead of her, and all the way through northern Judea, through Samaria and into Galilee, the people came to the roadside to watch silently as the queen of Chalcis drove by in a wagon drawn by a team of mules. Two women were in the wagon, and behind them a coffin covered by a pale blue cloth; and such was the curious nature of people that even though a great city was experiencing its last mortal agony only a few miles to the south, it was not for the city that the Jewish peasant wept, but for this red-haired, green-eyed woman who was taking the body of her husband back to Galilee—for the pathos of the queen who lowered herself thus, and of the nashi—that most noble title on all the earth—who lay dead in the coffin.

Berenice thought of this, and the more she thought about it, the more her heart and her mind returned to that strange massive city of rock and its wild, half-insane defenders. Hurt and pain and remorse and pity churned inside of her. Can one weep for one man when a hundred thousand must die? Yet the people who came to the roadside to stare silently and to weep silently knew that Jerusalem was dying. Even in Samaria, they knew full well that the city of Yaweh was perishing and that soon enough His Holy Temple would be in flames. Thousands of Samaritans had gone into the city to fight for its life. They had put aside or forgotten that ancient hatred of Israel for Judah, and they had become Jews again so that they might join in that Jewish fratricide which had repaved the streets of Jerusalem with flesh and blood. Those Samaritans would return no more—and who had killed whom, no one knew. Death stalked the treeless hills of Judea, and it was for this that the people wept. Already, by the time Berenice's lonely wagon drove across the lowlands of Samaria, Titus had brought his great battering rams up to the city's wall. The Jews poured out of the city, and from morning to night a wild and awful battle raged around the battering rams. But even the death-hungry Sicarii could not drive back the iron maniples of the Romans; and there, that first day of the attack, half of the Sicarii died—and with them died the life of the sword and the god of the sword, that keen-edged phallic god that took worship by ripping the cover of a man's guts—the iron penis that made his sexual union in death. In all the history that man knew to that time, no great city, no mighty city of teeming, uncounted thousands had ever died the way Jerusalem would die, utterly, totally, every human life extinguished or removed from it, every building crushed, gutted with fire, sown with salt, and sealed with blood. But neither would any other people see so quickly and completely the murderous bastard of the old gods that was called war.

If it was the beginning of Hillel's victory, then the whisper of that beginning was unheard. Neither Berenice nor any other man or woman could bridge the countless centuries that lay ahead, and she only knew what she knew. It was the season of death, and people wept.

But in Galilee, it also appeared to be the season of life. The Passover was only days away, and the air was sweet as honey with the cool winds of springtime. The newly sown crop had begun to break ground, and the rich fields showed a delicate veil of yellow-green. The cedars swayed in the wind and filled the air with perfume, while in the distance the mountaintops had not yet shed their white caps of snow. Everywhere, the peasants were making their dwellings ready for the blessings and purity of the Passover, and whosoever could afford white lime dressed their dwelling places and their barns and their walls in shining coats of white. In Galilee you would not know that Jerusalem was dying; here the signs of war were gone; and the Jewish population, swollen by a quarter of a million refugees from Judea, was entering a period of prosperity unmatched in all its past.

And in Galilee, the House of Hillel still stood in its peaceful valley—unchanged, and here Berenice came with the body of Shimeon Bengamaliel, the last nashi of Israel, the last prince of the Jews, not in a land or place or city, but all the world over the prince and liege lord of all who belonged to the body Israel. He was the last. There would never be another.

The House of Hillel rejected tombs and considered funerary cults and the worship of the dead an abomination. Hillel himself had said, "Man's concern is with life, and he must live his life not with his eyes upon death but with his eyes brightly fixed upon eternity, for life is his eternity and the riddles of death are not for him to solve but for the Almighty's whim—" The riddle remained. There was always a riddle at the core of what Hillel taught, for he plucked at life and in life there are no final answers, only a path from question to question.

Berenice thought of this as she stood with the rest of the family and some servants and slaves on a hillside above the farm compound and listened to the voice of Shimeon's brother. A grave had been dug in the small cemetery where the blood of Hillel was buried, and now the box containing Shimeon's body was being lowered into the grave. "What shall I say of a good man?" asked Hillel Bengamaliel, Shimeon's brother. "He is voiceless. But if he had a voice, would he not proclaim, 'I am for myself? I am for myself—thus it is at the root of all that the saintly Hillel taught. But is it simple to ask, ask Hillel asked, 'If I am not for myself—who is for me? And if I am only for myself, what am I? And if not now—when?' Oh, my brother, Shimeon—there are no mysteries, only eternity. It takes patience to be a man and more to be a Jew—and there is no judgment here for one who was strong and good and capable of love."

Then he prayed, while they put dirt into the grave. He was only forty-nine years old now, this brother of Shimeon's, even as Shimeon would have been only forty-seven, but he seemed older than that to Berenice, his shoulders bowed with a great weight. When he had finished with the prayer, he came over and kissed Berenice; but his mother, Sarah, tiny, wrinkled, ancient in her woe, stood by the grave keening and weeping out her grief. Berenice did not weep now, and when Hillel's wife, Deborah, kissed her, Berenice said, "Don't pity me. I was like a empty bowl of dry, chipped clay, and he filled me full." Now Gabo joined the old woman. In the manner of the Benjaminites, Gabo rubbed dirt into her eyes and hair and filled her mouth with dirt, screaming it out. Then she cast herself on the grave, twitching and beating her head with her clenched fists. Hillel looked at Berenice, who said, "Better take her away. She doesn't know anymore. She loved your brother, and when love or hate hurts them, they can become mad. I wish I could." Then Hillel told his slaves and they took Gabo away, but her hysteria was contagious, and many others were weeping and keening now. Hillel led them back down into the valley, but when he saw that Berenice remained by the grave, he returned to her.

"What kind of stone will you cut for him?" she asked Hillel.

"Did Shimeon ever say anything about that?"

"Only that a single stone should cover both of us—a plain stone."

"You are a young woman—what a way to talk!"

"Forty-two. That's not so young, brother; but this is something I want very much, to lie here. He will rest in peace here. He suffered such pain. Can I tell you what the Sicarii did to him? And tell me this, brother—is it true that your grandfather, Hillel, himself was a friend of Shammai?"

"Yes," Hillel nodded. "They were friends. They loved each other."

"And Shammai was a gentle person?"

"A good rabbi—very courteous, very gentle. Never would he permit bars or locks on the doors of his house, lest by some accident a hungry or tired man should be turned away—"

"And from this to the Sicarii in less than a hundred years?" Berenice wondered.

"Yes."

"Why—why? Why did they torture Shimeon and starve him and destroy him and rob him even of his soul and his pride—in the name of Shammai? Why did they turn Jerusalem into hell in the name of Shammai?"

Hillel shook his head miserably. "It's no use to think about these things, sister."

"Only tell me—or must I think about them every hour of my life!" She went close to Hillel now, staring at him, measuring him. "Or don't you know?"

"I know."

"Then tell me."

"Because above all," Hillel answered slowly, "Shammai taught to hate and to fear. No man was his brother. He shared blood and God with the Jews, and he would share his bread with the pagan, but he would kill his daughter with his own hand before he gave her in marriage to one who was not a Jew, and he would kill his son with his own hand if he saw him eat meat from a pagan's table. So what was his life worth and what was his gentleness worth and what was his charity worth? Could he ever ask, 'If I am not for myself—who is for me?' He was never for himself. He shriveled his own soul, put blinders on his eyes, and made love a thing your parcel out on a grocer's scale—and in the end, he was the inheritance of the Sicarii. It was natural—what else could have happened? If you believe that God is something that lives in a box called an ark in a gold-plated temple on a hill in Judea, and that He can only be placated by burnt offerings and that He is a creature of whim, stupidity, and superstition—well, if you believe that God is of that Nature, and this was very much what Shammai believed, and that He exists only to enrich the party of priests, and that a thousand men must perish before one sight of Him or His Temple is tolerated— well, if you believe this kind of senseless mind-gibberish, than the Sicarii are the natural end product of your teachings. You see, Shammai was always righteous. Hillel was never righteous. There was the whole difference."

Days passed, and Berenice remained at the House of Hillel. She had no plans, no thoughts about the future, no dreams, and no hopes—only memories. Gradually, the sharp edge of her pain was blunted and it became possible to think of Shimeon without agony in the tightening of her heart. She did little. At first she would go each morning to the new grave on the hillside, but she soon found that it gave her neither comfort nor inspiration. Wherever or whatever Shimeon was, or whether he was not, he was surely not in the clay that had been buried, and she was in no mood to bury her sorrow in the worship of the dead. It was better to turn to the living, and when she sat at the edge of the shade of the ancient terebinth tree and watched the children being taught by Hillel, his own son, Gamaliel, among them, she was as close to a sort of dulled contentment as she would ever hope to be. Often she wondered about the persistence of this school, generation after generation of children sitting under the great live oak and listening to the gentle wisdom and wise tolerance a certain rabbi had taught almost a hundred years before. From all over the world some of these children came, sent by parents who wept to part with them; and again they would go to every corner of the world to teach others what they had learned and to begin the shaping of a landless, nationless, sprawling thing called Jewry and based on the astonishing proposition that one should love his neighbor as himself—for thus taught Hillel; and Berenice, sitting quietly, working on some piece of embroidery or sewing a seam and sometimes alone and sometimes with Deborah and Sarah and younger women and suckling infants around her, would hear a thin, squeaking voice telling by rote what might or might not be understood years hence, "Who hurts man diminishes me and who slays man slays me; for the Almighty having given life, man has yet to find an adequate reason to take it away—" Squeaking voices committing to memory the nobles sentiment man had as yet proposed, and then fleeing from the task of it to play and shout and be children—and watching them, listening to them, Berenice would ask herself over and over,

"Why did we have no child, no flesh, no seed to be planted again?"

She found herself listening freshly, wonderingly, to those piping voices, "And if I should offer a burnt sacrifice? But Hillel answered this pious man thus, 'Should you never offer a sacrifice and never speak a prayer and even deny the Almighty Himself, yet live with love and with charity, I tell you that you are keeping the law—' "

Did it have meaning? Or was this the ranting of haplessness and hopelessness? The children sat under the terebinth tree and Jerusalem was dying. Each day word came from Jerusalem. Fifteen days after Titus had brought up his battering rams and opened the assault on the Wall of Herod, this northern wall of the city was breached. For four days after that, a terrible battle with no quarter asked and no quarter given raged in the streets of the Lower City—and finally the Zealots and the Sicarii, who had made common cause now, were driven across the Second Wall and into the Akra.

The reports were confused and very often contradictory. No one entered or left the city now, and the only information was what filtered through the Romans to their Egyptian and Greek and Samaritan camp followers and camp servants and then through them to the Jews. It was a time when information was not only passed on freely but bought and sold as well by Jews who were desperate to know the fate of friends and relatives in the city; and if there was no news, the sellers were ready enough to manufacture it out of the whole cloth. Thus the word came to Galilee that in the Lower City the Romans had put every man, woman, and child to the sword, that they had killed only the able-bodied men, that they had killed only the women and children, preserving the men for their triumph, that they had killed no one since every single soul had escaped to the shelter of the Akra and from there to the impregnable Upper City and the temple citadel, and that they had taken over twenty-five thousand prisoners. The last was closest to the truth, but it could not be verified.

The battle for Jerusalem went on, and the reports continued to seep into Galilee—and then came word that the Temple, the eternal and indestructible Temple of Yaweh, had been put to the torch and had burned to the ground—nothing being left of it but the scorched foundation stones. The defenders had retreated from the temple area into the Upper City, which they had sworn to defend to the death. Already almost a hundred thousand prisoners had been taken by Titus. The city was in flames, a pillar of smoke hanging over it so high and dense that it could be seen from as far away as Samaria—and red at night with the flames of the burning city. And still the Upper City was defended.

Then it was August, and word came that the Romans had breached the wall of the Upper City and had set it aflame. The end was now in sight.

And still, at the House of Hillel the sun rose and set each day over the unchanging and bucolic setting—and each day the children sat in the shade of the terebinth tree, intoning the sayings of the sage.

Jerusalem was dead. Barring Rome itself, the most populous, the most strongly defended, and the proudest city on all the earth had perished. The unconquerable had been conquered; even if it had destroyed itself, ripped out its own gut, and cut its own throat and bled itself until every street was a river of blood—still, if there were ten thousand left to defend its walls against a million, its conquest was no small feat. The

Jew was dead, and wherever the Roman looked in all the earth, there was no one to oppose him. And with the city died Yaweh, the angry old God of the mountain, Yaweh of the tabernacle, Yaweh of the ark, Yaweh of the Temple— Yaweh who had plucked the noblest Jews down from their concept of an invisible and formless Eternal and had charged them, "I am Yaweh, your God, who brought you out of Egypt to be my own chosen people. I am the just God, the angry God, the God of fire and war, of thunder and lightning, of vengeance and memory, the God of Horeb, of all the high places and ancient beginnings, of the burnt offering, the flesh offering, the foreskin and the stink of the sacrifice, I am your God—and no other Gods will you have before me." So He had charged them over a thousand years—but now no more. His Holy Temple lay in ashes and molten metal, and even His name—Yaweh—would gradually fall into disuse among a people who would see Him in their homes, their hearts, and their synagogues, but no more on a hill in Judea. The Romans celebrated; twice had they been threatened by cities—once by Carthage and now by Jerusalem, and twice they had destroyed the cities that threatened them. They were full of pride.

And the Jews celebrated differently. They said the Kaddish, the ancient prayer for the dead. Wherever the news came, they gathered together, in homes and in synagogues, and they said the prayer for the dead. They said it at the House of Hillel. Berenice gathered with all the others under the terebinth tree, and as the setting sun touched the western hill, they spoke in unison, men and women and children, "Increase and make holy His mighty name in this world which is His creation as He willed it. May He build His kingdom in your lifetime, in your good days, in the lifetime of the House of Israel—quickly and soon."

They said Amen, and then they wept. The whole world was weeping, Berenice felt. It was one thing for a city to die; it was another thing for a city to murder itself. When the Rabbi Hillel Bengamaliel, leading the service, said to them, "The

Zealots are dead. We will pray for them," Berenice could abide it no longer. Many things she would do, because the only meaning life had for her was the meaning the House of Hillel had given to it, but she would not pray for the Zealots and she would not mourn for the House of Shammai.

She walked away, and no one tried to halt her. This at least was her privilege. She walked away and up the hillside to where Shimeon was buried. But again, as before, this brought her none of the peace or comfort she yearned for.

Agrippa came to the House of Hillel bringing three men with him. One was Anat Beradin, the wool merchant and onetime sponsor of Polemon, the king of Cilicia, who had died almost eight years ago. Beradin was old, past seventy, but dry and sound as a nut and alert, with clear eyes and a clear mind. The second of the three men was Gideon Benharmish, who was the head of the great House of Shlomo, who ruled over an empire of fishermen from Alexandria to Tarsus and whose ships with their Phoenician crews traded from Caesarea to Cornwall. And the third man was Jacobar Hacohen, that strange, round-faced, pale-eyed Jew of mysterious antecedents, who admitted to no paternal name yet insisted that three quarters of his bloodline was priestly, and who had once been the greatest Jewish banker in Jerusalem—and perhaps in the world. He had departed Jerusalem before the civil war broke out, being of the party of Hillel, and had withdrawn his resources too. He was a stony-faced angular man, past sixty, with a haughty eagle's beak of a nose. It was said that there was no city in the civilized world where he could not immediately command half a million shekels on demand.

These three men came with Agrippa to see Berenice. They were welcomed as all were welcomed who came to the House of Hillel; and then in the shade of the terebinth tree they were given food and fruit and cold wine—and then left alone with Berenice and her brother-in-law, Hillel. They had already offered their sympathies and condolences to Berenice, and now Jacobar Hacohen said to her,

"We must understand, hard though it may be, that a city has died—not a people, only a city. True, a great and ancient and holy city, but still only a city—"

"Only a city?" Berenice raised a brow. "Is it only a city that dies? I shed no tears over brick and stone or even over the Holy Temple, for we of Hillel are not taught that God is a thing that can live in a temple—or be worshiped there; but I was in Jerusalem while it was dying—I was there. I tell you, Jacobar, people died. Not a city."

"If I express myself poorly—"

"No, no, no," said Benharmish. "We must understand each other—because there is no disagreement. If we don't mourn with every word, it is because the present necessity is not for mourning but for something else. May I say something about Jerusalem?"

"Please," Berenice agreed. "Please. And if I appear churlish, it is only because I have been so long alone, with no companions except my grief."

"We have all made companions of grief," Beradin nodded.

"All right," said Benharmish, "we will talk to the point of Jerusalem—not as priests or prophets, nor politically nor in judgment. We leave that to others. Specifically, we are men of affairs, and your brother, Agrippa, called us to him precisely because we are men of affairs. We have each of us been of some service to him in the past, and perhaps now, together, we can still effect something—"

"That is well put," said Jacobar Hacohen. "Do you see, Queen Berenice? I am better with numbers than words, and you must not have a sense of indignation about me."

"I have no sense of indignation about you," she replied gently. "I was petulant, that's all. I frequently am." She touched Benharmish on the arm. "Go on, old friend."

"All right. Now there is a situation in Jerusalem that we

must approach as men of affairs. Mind you—there are no certainties in what I say, but I think my figures are realistic and make sense. Other figures are very unrealistic and make little sense. Firstly—what was the population inside the walls of Jerusalem when Titus began his direct attack on the city? A million? Nonsense! There never were a million souls in Jerusalem—not if they slept ten to a room could the city have held a million. I would guess that its normal population—if such a city as Jerusalem was has a normal population; and I put this in terms of the tens of thousands who constantly come and go—well, a normal population of four hundred thousand. Then it increased—well, say, to half a million when the civil war in the city began. During the civil war, a hundred thousand left—escaped or somehow made their way out of the city. During the two years of the civil war another hundred thousand perished from violence, disease, starvation—leaving three hundred thousand to a quarter of a million when the city was attacked. I think the lower figure is more nearly accurate—and of these I estimate that at least a hundred thousand perished in the fighting of the past few months, killed by the Romans most of them, and others by Bargiora—who is now a prisoner in the hands of the Romans. And what does this mean? It means that in his slave pens and in the slave pens of his Greek and Syrian dealers, Titus holds captive perhaps a hundred and fifty thousand Jews."

He paused to let his words sink in, looking from face to face, and then continued softly, "Gentlemen and Queen Berenice—we Jews have been accused of arrogance to a fault, perhaps not without reason. We despise too many things that the pagans hold dear or sacred, but of the fact that we despise funerary cults—of this I have never been ashamed or apologetic. Since we came out of Egypt, fourteen hundred years ago, we have turned our eyes and our thoughts away from that accursed nation that is obsessed with the worship of death and the dead. We do not worship the dead—or feed them, or sacrifice to them, or brood over them. Our obligation is to the living—and only with the living are we concerned. Our problem is no longer those who perished in Jerusalem—but those who survived. Those are Jews who live and suffer. Each of us here had relatives in Jerusalem. Of the House of Shlomo, there were fourteen in Jerusalem, my youngest brother, his wife, my cousin and her husband, an old woman, a great-aunt, and children—the rest were children. How many are alive? I don't know—but who is alive must be saved. They are our responsibility, and no others will lift a finger to help Jews. Do you agree?"

No one disagreed, and then Benharmish turned to Jacobar Hacohen and said, "You have thought about this?"

"A great deal," Jacobar replied. "Last week, a slave was sold in the market at Tyre. Tyre is a very interesting and important market, for it provides immediate shipment by water to Italy, Africa, Phrygia, and the islands and mainland of Greece. Quick, cheap shipment. This particular slave was twenty-three years old, male, healthy, ungelded. He was bid and sold at the normal price—eight hundred and twenty sesterces. This, mind you, was a field slave with no house talents, no trade or cooking or ability for management or teaching. Illiterate. But quite strong, well fed, with all his teeth. Now our Jews will not be well fed and not so desirable and the market will be cluttered and very bad. So let us say, all things considered and including the fact that a good-looking woman fetches a very nice price indeed—well, let us say five hundred sesterces per person. To do the arithmetic quickly, averaging the price of a talent of silver at this moment in—if you wish, seven cities where markets are maintained—and calculating in the Attic talent, not the Judaic talent, then we have the possibility of purchasing fifty slaves for a talent-weight of silver. Or gold, as you see our potential—and over all—well, if I were to accept Benharmish's estimation of the number of slaves, which I believe is somewhat inflated—we would require three thousand talents of money—gold or silver, that is an equation of the two metals; and that is providing we can keep our intentions a secret and find a sufficiently trustworthy pagan front to bid at our behest—" His voice trailed away, and he shook his beaked, craggy head in sober doubt.

"You mean to buy the captives," Berenice whispered.

It had taken on the air of a conspiracy, and Agrippa replied, talking as softly, "Exactly."

"There is no such sum of money," Hillel said sadly. "How I wish there were. It's impossible."

"Oh no—not at all," Benharmish said flatly.

"You see, my dear Hillel," Beradin explained, "you are right, and you are also wrong. If we were Romans, we could throw up our hands in despair and admit that such an amount is impossible to raise. I doubt whether Titus will realize anything on the slaves, once the dealers are through cheating him. He will have a great deal of loot, but only a fraction of it will accrue to him—and that sum will be at best less than a hundred talents. The Romans are poor merchants, poor businessmen. Essentially, they are looters— looters on a scale never known before; and in this is the seed of their ultimate fate. You cannot operate an empire on robbery as a first principle. Their knights, their merchants and businessmen, are always puzzled as how to make a distinction between trade and thievery. But when you are a thief, your profits flow to the fence who is your middleman, and the Roman nobility—as they seem to style themselves, proud as peacocks over a bloodline that goes back three generations—this nobility is always begging, always in poverty. No—they could hardly raise three thousand talents on short notice. They have not learned yet that if you buy a city and sell it at a nice profit, you do better than the robber who burns it and then attempts to loot the ashes. Like all who disdain commerce, they are inordinately greedy, and since they only consume, they have no credit."

"And we have?" Benharmish snorted.

"I think so," Beradin nodded. "Don't you, Jacobar?"

"It's not easy," the banker said. "Just don't believe that it's easy—or that there isn't many a wealthy Jew who won't see those poor devils in hell before he'll part with a shekel."

"I'll part with everything I have!" Berenice cried. "Surely my wealth is a thousand talents!"

"Indeed, Queen Berenice," the banker agreed, "and much more, I am sure. But your wealth is not in talents of precious metal—is it?"

"I have palaces, land, jewels—and gold too."

"But is there a market for palaces at this moment? A quick sale means a poor price—or no price at all. Someone who desires to sell a palace must be prepared to wait a year or five years for a buyer—or to give it away."

"Then what?" Agrippa asked bewilderedly. "I had often thought that my wealth is enormous, but when you state the practical and immediate need of three thousand talents—I just don't know. I always keep two or three talents of gold on hand—you know, you can hire ten thousand mercenaries for at least three months with that much gold. And immediate—just how immediate?"

"Now," said Benharmish. "Now. That's how immediate."

"Now look here," Jacobar told them, "there is no need for panic on the part of anyone—because we will raise the money." And turning to Berenice, "And as for you, my dear, may the Almighty bless you. We will not sell your houses and your land. But if you wish, we will mortgage them."

"Mortgage them?"

"Yes—by that, I mean that I can put them up as security. Let us suppose that you have a palace worth twenty talents. I will go to a certain friend of mine and say to him, lend me ten talents and I will secure the loan with a palace belonging to the Queen Berenice—a palace worth twice what I lend you."

"But if you should fail him, and I can't sell the palace for ten talents?"

"Then you will mortage it to someone else. No need to sell it ever. The value is locked into it—and you can mortgage it again and again, paying off one with another, providing you have the cost of the mortgage itself. But what of you?"—turning to Benharmish. "Surely the great House of Shlomo can raise a thousand talents."

"Of fish, yes—of gold, no," Benharmish growled. "You don't mortgage ships, because no one will lend you a shekel on that kind of security. Yes—yes, I could raise a thousand talents—give me a year to do it. And let me tell you this, Jacobar—Croesus himself could not go into his treasure house and weigh out a thousand talents. Nor could Vespasian, the emperor. Nor could Titus. Nor can this particular Jew. I can do something—give me thirty days, and I will pledge you two hundred talents, give me sixty days, and I will pledge you five hundred."

"A moment ago, you said now. Immediately—now."

"I said it."

"What can you do now?"

"I will have a hunred talents of bar and money tomorrow—perhaps a hundred and fifty. Our house in Tarsus and Chalcis will send another hundred—enough to buy a kingdom."

"Or twelve thousand Jewish slaves, maybe fifteen thousand. What about you, Beradin?"

"Now?"

"Tomorrow—the next day—a week?"

"I am a merchant. I don't accumulate gold, I use it."

"We all use it. How much do you have on deposit—five hundred talents?"

"Two hundred—three hundred if you include silver and property. But it's spread among fifty cities between here and Nicaea—over three thousand miles of camel road."

"Then borrow."

"With what security?" Beradin demanded. "I have no palaces or plantations—"

"You have your good name."

"Thank you," Beradin said caustically. "So I will borrow ten talents on my good name—no, no, we are going about this the wrong way, Jacobar. I can recall no occasion where the speedy raising of such a sum was required—and we sit here, a handful of Jews, and attempt to think it into being. No. This must be an effort of all the Jews the world over, Italy and Spain and Greece and Egypt, not to mention Anatolia. And let me tell you something else, if you will. There is no market for a hundred and fifty thousand slaves; and who is to say that there are not two hundred thousand of them? No market. If they are worth three thousand talents at a depressed price—where is that money to come from to go into the slave market? You don't buy slaves with promissory notes. You need gold or silver coinage—and there is no such amount of coinage available—if indeed in circulation. We sit here as rich men and estimate our wealth. I have no faith in Jacobar's proposition for mortgaging property. Who will lend on such property? Jews. So we take it out of one pocket and put it into another. Do you know what I think?"

"All right," the banker snapped. "What do you think?"

"I think that as soon as the major slave dealers—the really big commission merchants—can come to some agreement among themselves, they will fix a price and a number. I mean that if they set a price of seven hundred sesterces, then—to grasp at a figure—they will propose a market of fifty thousand souls. This will give them an opportunity to select the very best specimens, and all the rest will be slaughtered, crucified, sold in the games, put to death for the edification of the crowds."

The others shook their heads.

"No?" Beradin asked. "I think you had best face it. Who ever heard of a hundred and fifty thousand slaves in the market? Did they ever do it with the Germans or the Gauls or the Spanish—and who is to say that they love the Jews more? No, I am afraid we are very much the hated ones. Yes—yes, I agree that eventually we can put our hands on a sum of money to add up to three thousand talents—and it will mean that every Jewish community in the world must be involved. But meanwhile, either we act or we will never need the money."

In the silence that followed Beradin looked from face to face. Only Berenice responded, and she nodded and said, "I know what you mean."

"I am not intruding or gossiping when I say that I know he loves you. This does not impugn you. No secret has been made of it."

"I know."

"Or that you do not love him."

"I will do what I can," Berenice said. "What I can— because I am not like a servant of myself, and I don't know what I can do."

"The important thing is for him to stay his hand—give us time."

"Time for what?" Berenice asked.

"To reach the big slave dealers—to make our agreements with them and to set the whole process into motion. We talk about it glibly, but I think that the redemption of these captives will be the biggest thing that our people have ever undertaken. We are old men, we three, and soon we will go away from here, and I for one would like to make something like this to be remembered by. It would not be the worst thing a man could do."

Titus came to Tiberias. He came with four hundred legionaries, leaving his main force at Jerusalem, where there was work to be done. A city is not turned into a graveyard easily. The dead must be buried and the living taken away. The walls must be leveled, and there were miles of walls in Jerusalem. The ashes of the Temple had to be sifted, literally mined, for the gold and silver that had melted in the flames and for the precious jewels. Certain important tokens of victory, such as the great Menorah and various significant costumes, manuscripts, and ornaments had to be catalogued and packed for transshipment to Rome—and in this the cooperation of Joseph Benmattathias was invaluable; which provided Titus with a reason for not bringing Joseph with him to Tiberias. There was also a vast amount of loot that had to be itemized and distributed—and enormous payments to be made to the chandlers who had kept the Roman army provided with food, wine, and cloth and metal during the years of war in Palestine. So great were these costs that it was questionable whether the army would have any profit to speak of after the reduction of Jerusalem. The financial situation was quite desperate, and Titus, who had no understanding of finance, no head for figures, and a mistrust of all matters relating to money, was happy to leave these matters to his aides and go on to Galilee and Berenice.

For Berenice, the beginning of this period was a sort of muted nightmare. She swore an oath to herself that she would do what was necessary, whatever had to be done. If it saved one life, she was repaid. She thought about these matters for endless hours and finally came to the conclusion that it was no privilege of hers to choose how or why. What was needed was needed.

A banquet was needed—a banquet to welcome Titus, the son of the Emperor of Rome, the conqueror of Judea and Jerusalem, the commander of the army; and for seven hours Berenice performed the role of hostess at this banquet. Then there was a water procession, ten great barges on the lake, a chorus of young girls to sing, nets of flowers trailing in the water, handsome young men to draw the oars, and a thousand torches to light their path as darkness fell. She sat beside Titus and answered his questions and spoke gently and politely. There was entertainment in the great hall of the palace. And in the streets, self-styled prophets spoke with voices, screamed of the day of judgment, and denounced Berenice as the whore of ages, her brother as the immortal enemy of God.

The display of wealth and pleasure bored Titus as much as it bored Berenice, and finally he said to her, "Berenice, you are a Jew, and an exceedingly sensitive one. Why are you doing all this?"

"Because eventually, I will make a request of you."

"Then make it now and enough of all this. Whatever reputation we Romans have for overeating and overcelebrating and overdrinking, rest assured that there are a good many of us who find it tedious beyond description. As a matter of fact, I eat very little—only one meal a day, in the Greek manner—and mostly I am quite satisfied with a little bread, a few olives, and some wine. There is nothing that gets on my nerves more than one of these endless, wretched banquets—unless it is a display of dancing girls or some such similar idiocy. I am a very powerful man, Berenice—after my father, the most powerful in Rome—yet I sit transfixed and speared by these merciless entertainments. So go ahead and make your request, I beg you."

"You took a great many slaves in Jerusalem."

"Yes—almost two hundred thousand. But some are very sick, very weak, and many of these will die."

"Where are the slaves?"

"They are being transported to Caesarea, where they will be penned."

"I am told that perhaps half of them or more will be slain to keep the price up."

"So I understand. I am not too familiar with these things."

"I ask only that you order the dealers not to kill any slaves for ninety days."

"Berenice, we have contracts with the dealers. I can't interfere."

"You can interefere with anything on earth," Berenice said. "You know that."

"You were told to make this request of me?" Titus inquired.

"Asked—not told. Asked, because people believe that you

feel something for me and would not deny me so small a matter as this."

"And what do you feel for me, Berenice?"

"It would do no good to lie, would it?"

"No."

"Then don't force my hand—"

"Yet you force mine."

"Not that way," Berenice said. "You call me a Jew—so I ask this as a Jew."

Titus shook his head. "You amaze me—I mean, I never meet a Jew who does not fail to amaze me. All right, Berenice—not as man to woman, but as Roman to Jew, I agree. There will be no killing of prisoners for ninety days— except what is necessary as some token of punishment in Rome. We have taken Shimeon Bargiora and the men around him. They will die."

"You would have to be an extraordinary man to allow them to live."

"Don't cozen me, Berenice," he said, smiling. "I have none of your powers of forgiveness, neither do I worship you god, Hillel."

"He is no god, only a plain man who died a good many years ago."

"Whatever he was or is, I am not of his persuasion. I granted your request, Berenice. Now, please—no more banquets."

He kept his word and better, for the following day there came to him a delegation from Alexandria, pleading for the right to expel the Jewish population of that city, and to seize all Jewish property—and for Roman troops to expedite the matter. Angrily, Titus replied that if the Jewish population of that or any other city was in any way molested, he would raze the city to the ground if he had to, to find those guilty and to punish them.

In spite of the very important and pressing matters that

demanded his presence in Rome, Titus remained in Tiberias; and Berenice, who knew that he remained there only to see her, to be with her, left the city early one morning and returned to the House of Hillel. Her brother-in-law said to her, "This is as much your home as mine, Berenice, but when all is said and done, it is only a house in Galilee and in itself no answer. I have known you many years now—and I know you by my own judgment. You are an unusual and a great woman—and a very beautiful woman, and you cannot hide here. We are too bereft in Israel, and we have too few great people left to us."

"I am tired," Berenice said. "I want only to rest."

"Yes, this is a good place to rest, but I think it is more than weariness. You know that he will follow you here."

"When he talks to me," Berenice said, "I don't hear his voice. I hear a wall of pain out of the South that drowns out every noise and murmur in the universe."

"Jerusalem is something that Titus will bear for eternity—regardless of how you judge him. Let the Almighty judge him. Do you think that it would have been any different with Jerusalem had there been no Titus? Is it a virtue when Jew kills Jew?—because I can tell you this, Bargiora's hands are dyed redder than Titus'."

"This is our country and they came here—"

"They are conquerors. We have played that game in the past, and there is no joy or reward out of it. There are always conquerors—for so long as the sword is the ultimate law, the world is a jungle. At least the Romans make it less of a jungle."

"And you are ready to forgive?" Berenice demanded.

"Berenice, Berenice," he said, "when Shimeon died, I became the head of the House of Hillel. What is our way? Do we condemn or forgive? Do we sit in judgment? Do we choose the Zealots above the Romans—because the Zealots are Jewish? The Zealots murdered my brother, Shimeon, and believe me, I loved him deeply—yet right now eight

Zealots are hidden here on our place, where we shelter them and feed them. And let me tell you this—that if the Zealots had triumphed, and fleeing Romans came to us for shelter, we would not have turned them away."

"I understand that," Berenice said. "Where I am not myself involved, I can be as clear about matters as you are. But where I am involved—"

Then she admitted to herself that she was involved—otherwise, why did she remain here at the House of Hillel? Jews there were in a dozen cities who would have sheltered Berenice and risked their lives and their homes to do so; but she remained here a few miles from Tiberias, and all too constantly her thoughts turned to the boyish, open face of the emperor's son. She grasped at her own soul and tore it to shreds in guilt and despair. How long was it since Shimeon's body had been flung from the walls of Jerusalem? Hardly five months—yet her thoughts could dwell again and again on a man twelve years younger than she was. Yet for her Shimeon had been dead far longer than five months—or had he been? Or had she deserted him?

She sat with Deborah one day, and her sister-in-law reminded her of how much she could do in this awful moment if she did command the love of Titus. Berenice said, "That's a fraud, and I will not have it." "Because," said Deborah, "you see any course you take hurting Shimeon—yet Shimeon is dead and beyond hurt." "No," Berenice argued, "I see in myself the same chaos that is outside of myself, a world without reason or meaning."

Her brother-in-law tried to help her, but specified that it was not easy to be with Hillel. "It makes for doubt and we live with doubt. If you want certainties, Berenice, you must go elsewhere."

"Can you live always with doubt?" Berenice wondered.

"How else?" Hillel asked her. "If you read the Scriptures—particularly in Kings—you will see that in the old days our ancestors created a structure of reason by reversing cause and effect. If a king's army was destroyed, it meant that he was wicked and thus God judged him. If a city fell, it satisfied some bloodthirsty whim of the Almighty. But we've gone beyond that. Hillel went beyond it, and we cannot go back. Jerusalem fell because men did wrong—and it's no affair of ours to try to fit it into some tremendous scheme of things. Now men are captive. A Roman loves you—and I think you yourself are intrigued by him—and because of this many poor and suffering people who would otherwise die may live. Your conscience is a bit of a luxury too—if the truth be told. All conscience is. Guilt is a great lever for evil and a poor guide for conduct. Do you remember that Hillel said, 'If a stranger is hungry, feed him to satisfy his hunger and not your pride.' It is one thing for dignity to be proud, but when virtue is proud it becomes almost indecent."

Titus came alone to the House of Hillel. Early one morning, he came alone on horseback, turned his horse over to the slaves at the stable, and then stood in the shade of the mighty terebinth tree, looking curiously around him.

From inside the house, Berenice saw him, but waited, and watched her brother-in-law, Hillel, go to greet him, and then children gathered around to stare at his man so curiously attired in a tunic of white and gold, with high white boots buckled in gold and a cloak of pale yellow over his shoulders. But then her patience broke; she could wait no longer, she went to meet him, and he held out his hand to her quite easily and naturally and said,

"So here I am, Berenice, I came unbidden. Shall I go away?"

"Then I would really know shame," Berenice smiled, "for you would be the first one ever turned away from the House of Hillel, and for this my brother here would never forgive me—although he forgives me in all else." There were disclaimers and protestations then and bits of embarrassed sentiment. Deborah could not stand aloof, and she was presented to Titus. "How strange," Berenice thought, "that the conqueror of Jerusalem should stand here and chat with us—the blood still wet on his hands." But she was thinking, she realized, in clichés and platitudes. There was no evidence of villainy about Titus. Young, strong, handsome, and healthy—it was almost impossible not to like him, and Berenice recalled the stories she had heard about him, his scrupulous sense of justice, his innate decency, and the manner in which his legionaires adored him.

A slave brought cold white wine, and Titus drained a goblet Hillel poured for him. "Your wine is the best wine in the world," he told them. "But I suppose you know that."

"We Jews have too much that is best—or that we believe is best. It invites envy and hatred. We permit people to admire what is ours, but we are loath to admire what is another's."

"I think the commander would like to see our place here," Berenice said, "so if I may take him away, I promise to bring him back when the tables are set up." The others agreed, and as Berenice led Titus away, she specified a rescue from philosophy. "Unless you came here for that?"

Titus shook his head.

"Well, here in the House of Hillel we are more like Greeks than we like to admit. We talk a great deal, but we never answer questions. We only enlarge upon them."

"And this is the House of Hillel," Titus said. They were at the gate to the enclosure now, and he stared at the rambling country villa with its great live oak. "A Galilean farmhouse. You know—that is hard for me to understand, Berenice. The House of Hillel is something that encompasses the world. I can remember as a young man in Rome, evenings when the conversation held for hours on the subject of the House of Hillel—bitter arguments, devotion, dedication, hatred; yes, and young Romans swearing that there was no other way to live but the way of Hillel, and through so many years the House of Hillel wherever you went, in Greece, in Africa—yes, in Spain too—and here—this."

"What did you expect?" Berenice asked him. "Some great palace—some incredible mausoleum?"

"I hardly know."

As they stood there at the gate, children ran past them to take their places under the terebinth tree, for the school to begin. More and more children, until almost a hundred of them sat crosslegged upon the ground.

"That," Berenice said, "is the House of Hillel—an old farmhouse and a place to teach children. There is the whole mystery."

She led him through the gate now, and they walked on the dirt road that led up the hillside out of the valley.

"Is it a religion?" Titus asked.

"No—we are Jews. We have no need for any other religion."

"Then what is it—only a school? But no school is the life basis for people—and when you say you are Jews—believe me, Berenice, I did not want the Temple to burn. I tried to save it—and yet it went up in flames, whether by the hands of Romans or Zealots, I don't know. But it burned, and now Yaweh is dead. Seen or unseen, He is dead, and His Temple is no more. So what do you mean when you say that you are Jews? That you have no need for any other religion? All people need the gods."

"Perhaps. But our God never lived in the Tmple—not in the sense that you mean."

"You supported the Temple."

"Yes—because it was an old thing, and we are a very old people."

"And what was Hillel? One of your prophets?"

"No, only a man. A teacher. What we call a rabbi."

"And what did he teach?"

"Ah," she smiled, "everything at once. If it's there, the Roman must know about it."

"How beautiful you are when you smile," Titus said. "Always, with every movement and motion of yours, there is beauty, as if the essence of your being was to create it—but when you smile—"

"You talk well of such things."

"Not because I have had practice, believe me," he said, almost with annoyance.

"Ah, now—and why does that hurt, Titus Flavius? You are a great and powerful figure, and you are young and good to look on, and yet it hurts you if an old Jewish woman suspects that you have spoken to others of beauty and love."

"An old Jewish woman—is that how you see yourself, Berenice?"

"No," she admitted. "That's a pose. I looked at myself in my mirror today. I looked at my face and my body—and the age is within me, if not on the surface—"

"Do you always answer truthfully?" he broke in.

"You asked me what we teach. We teach that."

"And what else?"

"To love thy neighbor as thyself."

"Yes, yes," Titus agreed. "I heard that. I heard it in Rome and in other places, and it's remarkably persuasive for a piece of nonsense, and it travels."

"Then what I believe is nonsense?"

"No—no, I don't mean that, and you know it, Berenice. I mean that these are impractical things. Your House of Hillel can survive in a world where Roman legions maintain law and order and stability—but not by loving our neighbors. By teaching them a decent respect for order—"

"We could argue that forever, Titus Flavius."

"Yes, I suppose so. And your creed is not to fight—ever?"

"Our creed is no rigid creed, and we are not an order from which we expel people. We try to teach an act of civilization—I know of no other way to put it. Some of us will not kill under any circumstances; others feel differently. Myself—"

"You are a woman, Berenice, and therefore this does not become your problem."

"No? And yet I took two lives once—snuffed them out with as little compunction as you put out a candle. Shall I tell you? I haven't spoken of these things in years."

"Only if you wish—"

"I don't know why I should want to, any more than I know why I desire you to understand me—ourselves, our ways—or what that farmhouse down there in the valley means, what it means to a people like ourselves who just saw our city die and our Temple die; and we remember how Isaiah wept, and he said, 'If I should forget thee, O Zion, may my right hand lose its cunning.' Now we are all weeping, for something is over and finished. I had a palace there on the Mountain of Zion, and every morning I would awaken in the moment before dawn, and dress and hurry outside to the plaza, so that I could see the sun rise over Jerusalem and see the Holy Temple turn to gold and look down at the wonderful shadows of the Judean hills—you have seen how they are etched out in burning contrasts of black and yellow—and my whole being would throb with joy because I was a part of this ancient and holy city and all its somber grandeur and breathtaking beauty—and now it is gone, perhaps forever gone, not your doing, Titus Flavius, but you and myself part of its death—and what is left to the Jews but this villa we call the House of Hillel, and this must be all things to us now, our temple and way of life and our hope too. Do you understand me?"

"I am trying to," Titus nodded.

"I wonder sometimes how much I comprehend, who I am, or what—and then I talk like this, because it is not very often I find someone to talk to—the desire of course, I mean to talk—and a long time ago, the Emperor Claudius had my father murdered. He believed, and with some reason, that my father plotted against him. My brother, Agrippa, and I knew who had killed my father, but we picked some poor hapless priest whom we disliked and he was put to death for a crime he never committed. And again, a few weeks after this, a soldier tried to make love to me. Poor boy, he was only enamored of me, and blundering with the excitement of touching a royal princess, and he did no more than that, only to touch me, and I had him beaten to death. This defined my life; this was the being and morality of the House of Herod, where Agrippa and I had been raised, and I remember it, the bleakness of infamy, the awful boredom and depression of wickedness, the hopelessness of cruelty and the utter emptiness of a life devoid of love. That is the whole history of the Herods and perhaps of the Julians, too, and it's nothing to live for; so such houses make a process of dying their existence—do you know what I am trying to say, Titus Flavius?"

"I think so—in part. Tell me, Berenice, what did the House of Hillel give you then?"

"Life."

"We all live."

"But to taste its sweetness, there is a privilege."

"My father is emperor," Titus said thoughtfully, "but the only sweetness I have tasted in this life is the sight of you."

"Ah—no. Surely more than that."

"Are you happy now?" Titus asked her.

"Happy? What a strange question to ask me. My husband lies buried a few paces from here, you know how he died. Our holy city in ruins—my people weeping—"

"You don't weep. I saw no weeping at the House of Hillel."

"We teach a way of love—not sorrow."

"And you love? Now?"

"Yes," Berenice replied.

"Whom?"

"Many people and the memory of many people. A great many people. It is something you learn, and then you live a little better, a little easier."

"Do you love me?" Titus asked her.

"I don't know. It must be said that Titus destroyed

Jerusalem. What else can be said?" They stood facing each other now, and Berenice reached out and touched his face—and then her hand fell. Titus moved not at all. "You are very gentle," Berenice whispered. "I prayed to the Almighty that He would let me know about you."

"Perhaps He will," Titus answered her.

They stood on the hillside above the farmhouse in the little cemetery where Shimeon lay buried, and Berenice watched the Roman. In all things, he was tentative. He looked at the grave and asked her what kind of a man Shimeon was.

"Tall and slow. He spoke slowly and moved slowly. You had to know him, otherwise he would appear slow-witted, because he was tender and gentle, the way you are. But he was not like you—he could not command, God help him. He would not have taken Jerusalem. He would have left it, had he been in your place."

"But he would have been a Roman," Titus reminded her. "Had he been in my place—he would have thought as I do. And why did they kill him, Berenice?"

"You saved that question, Titus Flavius," Bernice said. "What will you do to me with that question?"

"I could never do you harm. But neither is it easy to do you good. I would have to understand you first, and you would have to understand me. Do you know why they killed him?"

Berenice nodded, tears welling into her eyes in spite of her efforts to remain cold and objective. "I know why they killed him. He became tired of death—too quickly. How I pleaded with him not to remain there in Jerusalem! But he had become proud. In all his life, he had never been proud in this way—because he was a simple man, a plain man, what we call an Israelite, which means one out of the common mass, without noble ancestors or bloodline. Do you see?"

"The Flavians are that way—no noble ancestors or bloodline, out of the common nothing."

"So he became proud, and pride is a disease. He stepped

into the man's game—the game of death. My people, my city, my land, my honor, my courage—all the war words, all the filthy, prideful words that have made my people's history a history of blood and slaughter unending for a thousand years. He forgot Hillel for a little while, and when he remembered it was too late. Because of the Sicarii—death is life, and they can make no distinction between the two—and so they murdered Shimeon and Shimeon's friend and every other man I knew and loved in Jerusalem—every one of these they murdered. Yet we weep for them. Why? You are a stranger among us—tell me why?"

"We are a part Sicarii, I suppose," Titus shrugged.

"You know—they became proud of their Latin name," Berenice said. "All other things Roman they hated but the name. The men of the knife. They gloried at that. The men of death. You know, before the war, we would hold great assemblies of all the people in Jerusalem on important issues, but the Sicarii would circulate in the assemblies and those who voted against what the Sicarii desired would feel that knife, and then when the assembly was over, there would be forty or fifty bodies on the ground. So presently, we held no more assemblies. We elected high priests, but if the Sicarii disagreed they would murder the priest. Murder became their sole statement—because they felt so surely that they were the voice of God. They were the holiest of the holy, the most orthodox of the orthodox. No one prayed more than they did. No one more carefully observed every minutia of the Law. No one was more pious—or more righteous. So righteous that they pre-empted the right to practice death."

She was weeping now, without restraint, nor could she restrain the words as they poured out of her:

"So you see, my lord, Titus Flavius, I speak the truth when I speak at all—and I say that this city had to perish. Part of me died with it, and I will mourn for Jerusalem all my days—but I will not wish it to be otherwise. God willing, we will not take up the sword again. Let other nations kill and be killed—I think we Jews will fight no more."

"I am afraid not, my dear Berenice," Titus said. "No one in all the world has the courage to live without the sword."

They climbed higher, to where the cedars grew, and then they sat in the shade on the sweet-smelling sod under the trees, and the cool wind from the west caressed them.

"This is a good place," Titus said, "beautiful and old, and nowhere in the world are there such trees as these."

"They are very old—as old as time, our legends say, planted by the hand of God when time began. The Greeks say that this is nonsense, but I like to believe it. To us they are holy trees, and out of these trees, my great-grandfather built the Temple."

"Yes—and it went up like a torch," Titus nodded.

"The wood burns easily—and the smell is good. And if you like our land so well, Titus Flavius, stay here."

"You ask me to?"

"Yes, I ask you to."

He turned, sprawling on his stomach, his legs flung out behind him, and he rested his chin on his hands and stared at her.

"My asking you won't keep you here—"

"You, Berenice," he said, "are like this place—with those strange green eyes of yours and your hair the color of cedarwood—long-limbed, like the wood creatures that the Greeks worship; and I would give my life to stay here with you—but I am Vespasian's son, so even if I laid down my life to make a bond, they would return my body to Rome."

"You love him, don't you?"

"My father?"

"My father was a king. I never loved him."

"But I learned to love Vespasian before he was ever king," Titus said. "He was everything to me, mother and father and nurse and teacher, a simple man—so very simple—and out of poor, plain people. The kind of Roman they never send overseas to govern. No, we send out our scum, and they lie and conspire and kill for the privilege of being sent out as procurator or proconsul—because that way is the short road to riches. And this lust for wealth, for money and more money and still more money is the disease of Rome—and it will be the death of Rome too. But my father never had this disease and he never taught me it. He taught me other things."

"What king of things, Titus Flavius?" she asked him.

"To measure a man—or a woman. To look at a woman like you—and to know her worth. And believe me, Berenice, I have never looked at a woman this way before. In one thing we are the same. I don't lie either, not because I am a follower of Hillel, but because I have been taught this way—and I say that you are the only woman in my life. Yes, I have had women and I have sickened myself with lechery and drink—it was expected of me, but I have not loved as a man loves a woman. I waited, but I waited with great certainty, and that is why when I saw you, I knew. I love you, Berenice—I love you as much as a man can love a woman. You are twelve years older than I am—granted. I don't close my eyes to that. But it makes no difference. Twenty, thirty years, and still it would make no difference. You are all of woman that I desire—the loveliest, the wisest—and there is no other. And there will be no other for me ever again. Nor am I such a fool as to fail to see that you don't hate me—that you look at me with some fondness, some good feeling. Admit it!"

"I admit it, Titus Flavius."

"I don't press you. By all the gods, I do not press you. Let the wounds heal first. The past is too close. I am patient."

"Patient—patient—do you think time ever stops? What will you wait for?"

"For your love."

"While I grow old and dry? I am already barren. As the old wives here say, my womb is cursed—just as the whole House of Herod is cursed. There is no more seed, only my brother and myself to grow old and dry and finally to perish. So what will you wait for, Titus Flavius?"

"My own destiny. I can no more avoid it than I can avoid the death that awaits me somewhere along my road."

"Ah, that is Roman talk—and we Jews believe in no such destiny. When the Almighty put man on earth, He left it to man to make his own destiny. We plot our own road and mostly our own death too. So don't talk to me about death. You are too young, too vital—and some day you will be Emperor of Rome, and you must have children who are the flesh of your flesh—"

"Berenice," he interrupted. She paused and looked at him. "Berenice," he said, "let me decide what my own destiny must be. I am no boy. I command an army of eighty thousand men here in Palestine alone, and as my father's legate, I command half the world. I can call into being great fleets and great armies—simply by my word or my seal. I have the power of life and death over millions. I have led my men into many battles and I have seen great nations and cities fall beneath my blows. Of course, I am boasting in a most disgusting manner, but I don't know how else to impress upon you the fact that I am aware of my own thoughts and my own needs—and that I know my own mind. It is three years since I first met you, and in that time nothing has happened to change my original observation, namely that you are a beautiful and wise woman. I love you. I am patient—but I love you deeply, very deeply."

He spoke formally, a man much tutored in the art of speech, articulate, but also the victim of his voice and its power; in his eyes there was something else, something pleading that touched Berenice in spite of all her resolution. Titus drew himself up beside her and lightly caressed her face. She shook her head. Then he kissed her gently, but she saw that he was trembling and fighting to control himself, and she drew away from him and got to her feet. He rose and faced her, staring at her for a long moment, and then he took her in his arms. She didn't resist, but neither did she feel desire or passion; yet the pressure of his hard-muscled body, the smell of him, the close male smell that she had almost forgotten, and the strength of his arms around her—all this had its effect. Still he let go of her and stood away.

"When the wounds heal," he said.

She was summoned to Caesarea by an urgent plea from Gideon Benharmish and Jacobar Hacohen—and they said for her to bring jewels and whatever gold she could lay hands on. The urgency resolved into a cheap and wretched piece of blackmail. Two Syrian and three Egyptian slave dealers— who had an option on eight thousand Jewish captives, mostly virgin girls between the ages of six and thirteen—had chanced upon some rumor to the effect of a Jewish syndicate being formed, a rumor re-enforced by Titus' injunction about the slaughter of slaves. Now they announced that they intended to march their slaves across the northern shore of Sinai to Alexandria—a long and arduous march, and one which would exact a large toll from such a group, even if they were well fed and in the best of health. But these five dealers had spent their money on options, and the only way they could continue to feed their slaves was to sell them off; however, there were no customers. Everyone knew of the tremendous number of Jewish slaves to be offered and everyone knew by now that Titus had rejected all pleas to lessen their numbers and keep the price up. Dealers and buyers had come from all over the world to the main slave markets of Anatolia, Greece, Palestine, and Egypt, but no one was buying. Everyone was waiting for the prices to break—for slaves to be cast on the market for a pittance—and desperate, these five dealers had evolved their plan. They spoke to someone who spoke to another—and finally it found Benharmish, who still maintained warehouses in Caesarea. Flatly these dealers said:

"Either buy these eight thousand slaves or we will walk them and starve them to death. We will not wait."

There were no Jews left in Caesarea to spell out the

situation or analyze the motives of these men or the worth of their threats. In the great massacre of half a decade past every Jew in Caesarea had been slaughtered; it was a city Jews hated, avoided, and coupled with a malediction. The brothers Philip and Cadmus Bargora Hacohen, two very wealthy Alexandrian Jews who dealt in Chinese jade and practically had a monopoly in it, had come up to negotiate some business loans with Jacobar, the banker. They knew the slave dealers—that is, the Egyptian ones—by reputation as an unsavory and desperate lot who would do anything for money, and they persuaded Jacobar and the others to deal with them. Then the slave dealers fixed the price at one thousand sesterces per slave, on the grounds that these were virgins, young and desirable. The figure thus arrived at was at once incredible and impossible, eight million sesterces, but the agreement was made, and the five slave dealers became both rich and Judophile at once. The brothers Philip and Cadmus turned in all the jade they had with them, and Jacobar turned in the substance of the loan he would have made to them. Benharmish raised a million sesterces personally—still they had to turn to Berenice. In the warehouse of Benharmish in Caesarea, where they met, she opened a jewel casket to reveal pearls, diamonds, and rubies to the value of three and a half million sesterces. She bore also a note of demand from her brother, Agrippa. Still they were short, and Berenice left by ship for Alexandria, with Jacobar and the Bargora brothers to raise the rest of the money. Meanwhile, the slave children were moved quietly, in groups of ten or fifteen, to Galilee. All of Berenice's villas and palaces on the lake there had been set aside as staging areas for the slaves—and there began the vast operation of feeding and caring for the slaves, of moving them then to other cities, to Greece and Italy and North Africa—wherever there were Jewish communities large enough to accept them, integrate them, and return them to an existence of hope and work. It was a complex and vast operation, frequently inoperative, seemingly hopeless, yet somehow stumbling along in the face of food shortages, in the face of the growing dislike of the Galilean Jews for the Judean Jews, in the face of the continuing discord, quarrels, and hatred among the Jewish captives—slaves and manumitted—still Zealot against Hillel and Sicarii against both.

On the coasting galley from Caesarea to Alexandria, Berenice relaxed, lay for hours on a couch under an awning, and enjoyed the attention and converation of those three worldly men—the jewel merchants from Alexandria and Jacobar Hacohen, the banker. Gabo, older, even more petulant, frequently seasick, let Berenice know that she trusted no Jew who made his home outside of Israel—and what right had such to style themselves Jews? Yet she crouched within hearing distance when Philip Bargora told his incredible tales of a trip he himself had made across the top of the world to the land of a slant-eyed people with yellow-brown skins, where there were a thousand walled cities and where armies mounted on elephants fought each other. His mixture of truth and fantasy enthralled Berenice, and the witty and knowledgeable talk of all three of them shortened and enlivened the trip. It was almost as if time had not passed at all when the swift coasting galley shipped oars and slid slowly alongside the docks at Alexandria.

So it began, and then for a long time to follow there was little rest for Berenice. In Alexandria, a message from Titus that had fled after her in a galley speedier than hers reached her: "And now, my beloved Berenice, I find that I can put off my return in Rome no longer. My mind is as filled with you as my heart—and in that I, who can have everything else the world may provide a man, cannot have you, is a lesson in humility, a habit I have never considered a virtue. Yet I said I would be patient. We are both of us persons, my beloved one, very much persons, and strong and willful and with much to do. I know what you do—be assured that I will feast little and make merry less. Already the polite set in Rome look upon the Flavians as a dour and brooding lot, little given to dancing a jig when the piper pipes; and I am afraid I shall do little to alter that reputation. I shall think of you and send my messages to you when I know what corner of the world you currently inhabit, and if you should think of sending me a word of greeting on some occasion, I shall burn sacrifices to all the gods that be, including your angry Yaweh, who has such little reason to bless me. But no freedom from my love, my regard, my desire to serve you shall ever be yours."

So in Alexandria, at a meeting of the most influential Jews in the city, Berenice looked from face to face—wondering what they would say if they knew how closely her thoughts followed a Roman almost young enough to be her son. What did they think of her in any case? And yet she hardly cared—it was of so little importance what anyone thought of her. The Alabarch was dead. Philo was dead. And the Berenice who came down to Egypt then, so long ago—was she also dead?

"So we say now," Berenice told them, "that this is our salvation, that we will raise up out of the ashes of Jerusalem not the dead but the living—"

They were tense, tired, defensive, these Alexandrian Jews. No longer were they the driving, moving power in the city. No longer was Alexandria their city. Day and night they faced a hostile population, and the alabarch among them, one Casper Shamo Hacohen, said to Berenice and Jacobar:

"What is our debt to Jerusalem? What happened in Jerusalem set off a riot here, and many Jews died—and we lost millions in sesterces in property—burnings, looting, destruction. Jerusalem turned the pagan mad, and he is not yet sane. And what was Jerusalem? Shall we weep for a monster like Bargiora? Already they are hailing him for a hero. Shall we weep for him and his Sicarii?"

"No," replied Berenice simply, "we do not ask that. Yet if you weep for him, I will weep with you. He murdered my husband, the nashi, yet I will weep for him—because we made him. We Jews made him, yet God placed upon us an obligation to make something better. I will ask you to weep for something else—for eight thousand slaves, most of them little girls, whom we must buy out of death quickly, quickly—"

Then she told them the story.

"This is madness—eight million sesterces," said one of them.

"The legends of Jewish wealth in Alexandria are of the past," the alabarch insisted.

"It was God's will that Jerusalem fell," a third said.

"We know what took place in the walls," said a fourth.

"God help me, I am ashamed to be Alexandrian!" Cadmus Bargora cried. "I know you. Lie to the queen if you must—not to me. I know you and you and you and you and you"—directing a finger at each. "We talk of life! Do you put a price on human existence? Her husband was the grandson of Hillel. Hillel! It is told that when Hillel died a river of tears flowed out of Alexandria. All the tears? Are none left?"

In Alexandria the money was found to complete the purchase of the children, but the game had spread and now there was a crisis in Antioch. From Antioch, Berenice went to Rhodes, where eighteen thousand Jewish slaves had been brought. The ninety days were almost past, and she wrote to Titus in Rome; but as it turned out her letter never reached him. Anat Beradin joined her at Rhodes with word that Jewish captives were being slain at Salamis and starved in Tyre. The Jews of Rhodes had put together a purse of four and a half million sesterces; yet it was not enough, and Beradin pledged four tons of wool and twelve thousand sheep on various ranges in Anatolia to the pagan bankers in return for another three million sesterces. As a double pledge, he assigned to these bankers his gold reserves in various cities— and Berenice was convinced that it meant his ruin. When she spoke to him, Beradin shrugged his shoulders.

"I am seventy-three years old, Berenice. The game is

done. You heard the old legend about how the angel of death whispered in one's ear seven months before he claims him—"

His premonition was correct, and Berenice heard the news of his death before the year was out. But meanwhile, she had the sensation of one who builds a wall of sand against the sea and then attempts to stem its collapse with bare hands, rushing from here to there. She felt that the whole world was well aware of this particular Jewish madness; that having first provoked an insane and suicidal war with Rome, they were now trying to buy a whole nation out of bondage. With Jacobar Hacohen she traveled to Athens, where a wealthy Greek slave dealer said to them, "You Jews have this business of bondage and freedom on the brain—the way that you preface everything with the recollection that your Yaweh brought you out of bondage in Egypt. You are not the first people to go down to defeat. When Rome broke the back of Greece, she took a quarter of a million slaves in a single week and killed half of them. There it is—life and death, war and peace, freedom and bondage; it is the substance of existence, and you might as well accept it. Now let me tell you this. I am a rich man, and I don't need the money—but let me tell you that everyone in Athens and everyone in every other city, if my guess is right, is laughing at you Jews. It has become the short road to riches. Get hold of a dozen Jewish slaves, and these rich Jews will pay what you ask—anything. Madness! What are these Jewish slaves? Cutthroats! The scum of Judea! What are they good for? Who will buy Sicarii? This world is pretty rotten—but a cult dedicated to murder is still more than one likes to take, even as a bargain. If you would only stand clear of this for a few months, we will wash out the adult males. Then you can buy the children and the women at a fair price."

In a way, Berenice decided, by his own lights and his own manner of thinking, he was not too wrong. With tough, iron-covered guards, she walked through one of the slave pens in Athens were the men were kept, half-starved, filthy-bearded Jewish soldiers who looked at her with silent hatred and then spat a malediction onto the ground she trod. Yet it made no difference, and when Jacobar had managed to bring together in Athens rich Jews from Nicopolis and Corinth as well as Athens, and a handful of noble Spartans too—who thought of themselves in good measure as Jews through an eternal blood brotherhood—Berenice wept as she spoke to them.

Nicodemus Kractus, a Spartan who operated olive groves of considerable size in Arcadia, said that while he would not quarrel with the purpose of the queen of Chalcis, they could not continue in this mode of desperation, nor could they expect men of substance to bankrupt themselves in the cause of the Jewish captives. Even in Sparta, he reminded Berenice, the Sicarii evoked disgust and horror—and so nightmarish were the tales of the internecine warfare in Jerusalem before the Roman attack and of the murders done by the Sicarii that most people were poorly disposed toward the cause of the captives. All too many felt that their present condition was a just judgment.

"I am not here to argue the directions of divine justice," Berenice said, "nor distinctions of guilt. We are determined to save as many captives as we can."

"Exactly," Kractus nodded. "But Athens is hardly the place to undertake this decisively. The great Jewish wealth is centered at Rome, as we all know—but that is not enough. Either we get the support of the emperor or his son, Titus, or most of the slaves will be dead before half the money is raised. I think, Queen Berenice, that we must turn to Rome.

Melek-ak was a folk hero of the Semitic people who lived on the coast of Palestine. In the dawn of time, it was held, at the very beginning of beginnings, Melek-ak was filled with lust for a woman, and, seeing Tyros, the daughter of the mother-god, walking on the beach, he set off after her. Never before had he caught Tyros, who was remarkably fleet of foot for a girl, but on this occasion the nymph's attention was diverted by a dog with a purple muzzle—and that moment of diversion cost Tyros her virginity. Being a wise maiden—and wise even when no longer a maiden—Tyros ensnared the large-muscled demigod who had raped her and demanded in return for her maidenhead a cloak of the same purple that stained the dog's muzzle. It was only fair, the nymph argued, for through the beauty and unusual color of that stain, she had lost what women profess to value but are so eager to part with. With this request, Melek-ak, who had not formerly been noted for intelligence, displayed rare deductive intelligence and traced the purple dye to shellfish the dog had been crunching, namely the banded murex and the spiny murex—and so began what was to remain for uncounted centuries one of the prime business monopolies of Jew and Phoenician. At first, a thousand years before Berenice's time, it had appeared that the supply of murex on the Palestinian coast was unlimited, and though only a few drops of the precious fluid—colorless when it emerged from the shellfish but turning pruple on exposure to sunlight—were available from each mollusk, the mollusks were so abundant that no one could imagine that some day they would be exhausted. Not only did King Solomon wear the purple, but he clothed his women in purple and hung purple drapes from the walls of his palace. The Jewish caravans carried bolts of cotton and linen dyed purple even to the far-off cities of India and the Punjab, while the Phoenician galleys bore the purple cloth to every corner of the known world. A Phoenician-Jewish network of dealers and dyers, based on the precious murex, covered the whole Mediterranean basin; and when suddenly it was realized that the mollusks on the Palestinian coast were rapidly disappearing, Jew and Phoenician joined forces to begin a systematic search of the beaches of the world, across Africa, around every mile of Spain, and down the Atlantic coast of Africa for more than a thousand miles—in search of the shellfish that was more precious than gold; for as the murex became increasingly rare, the price rose and rose.

Meanwhile, Rome had come into the political and military ascendancy—and Rome chose the purple as the symbolic representation of its power and majesty. At first the purple toga was commonplace in Rome, Jews settling in Rome and setting up dyeing vats there—until Rome became the cloth-dyeing center of the world. But then, as the purple became increasingly difficult to produce, the purple toga was replaced by the purple stripe—and then, suddenly, Augustus forbade any but the members of his own house to wear the purple; and he placed an injunction upon the Jews who controlled the purple that hereafter no purple was to be sold anywhere in the world but at Rome—and there only to agents of the imperial house.

Thus the history and wealth of the House of Barona, where Berenice went as a guest of the head of the house, whose name was David Barona Judaicus Purpureus—a small, gentle, white-haired Jews, mild in manner, devout, a follower of Hillel, and perhaps one of the richest men in the world. For over five hundred years, his family had been a leading force in the exploitation of the murex, and not only did he own dye factories in Rome, but he had eleven plantations on the African coast, where the murex was cultivated and farmed. That Berenice would come to him in Rome was inevitable; equally inevitable the fact that he would insist that she remain at his house, a very large city house at the edge of the Jewish quarter, where an apartment of rooms was set aside for her pleasure. While Barona was one of the very few Jews granted Roman citizenship, he was essentially a very simple and modest man—overwhelmed at the honor done to him by the fact of Berenice as his guest. It was many years since Berenice had been to Rome—and during that time, she had become a sort of legend to Jew and non-Jew alike. Her astonishing beauty, apparently invulnerable to the ravages of time, her strange and striking green eyes, and her red hair, still unstreaked by any touch of gray or white—made her an object of attention and discussion from the moment she stepped off the Greek galley that brought her to Ostia; and this, connected with the fact of servants and baggage, marked a woman of importance and wealth. By the time she had arrived at the House of Barona, the city was buzzing with the news that Berenice, queen of Chalcis and princess of the ancient houses of Herod and Mattathias was in Rome and at the home of the Jewish millionaire, David Barona.

Barona had thoughtfully asked only the slightest of social amenities from Berenice, the merest words of peace and greeting with his wife, his very old mother, his five children, three of them married. Of the grandchildren, eleven stood quietly in the background, staring with wide eyes and open, speechless mouths at this very tall, very beautiful woman whose blood, they knew, went back to Judah the Maccabee and his father, and beyond them to the great King David and then beyond David into the dawn of time of the mighty priest and wonder-worker, Aaron, who was the brother of Moses. They asked no genealogical proof, these children, but stared at Berenice as if she were the living proof and embodiment of God's choice of Israel.

"We will talk tomorrow, Berenice Basagrippa," the old man, the head of the house, said to her. "Tonight, rest in your rooms, and I will have food and refreshment sent to you. I take a liberty, my dear—a liberty of intimacy, because I am much older than you. Never did I imagine that my house would be blessed with your presence. I am fortunate and rewarded."

For all of her weariness, Berenice was touched, and tears came to her eyes as the old man kissed her hand. He led her himself to the apartment that had been provided for her. "I know why you are here," he told her, "and I have invited people to meet with us tomorrow. I will not fail you."

The apartment provided for her was magnificent—as indeed the entire house was. Even very wealthy Romans would

build four or five stories of income-producing rental apart-
ments over their town houses; Barona was one of the very few
who kept a great, multi-storied mansion exclusively for his
own use—a kind of extravagance that was sourly put by the
Romans to the uncountable wealth of Jews—and within this
mansion, the quarters assigned to Berenice made her own
houses in Galilee seem almost austere by comparison. There
was her own limpid pool of water to bathe in if she desired, or
simply to contemplate a pillared gallery around it, a reception room of her own with a ceiling twelve feet high, a suite of
three bedrooms, and a room for writing, study, or contem-
plation: all of this furnished with taste and without thought of
cost.

As Berenice walked slowly through the place, she listened
to Gabo's bitter complaints about the cold weather, the damp
air and the distance from Galilee: "And do I ever see my
children again?" Gabo wanted to know. "Or are we here
forever? Of course, it's all right for you—but I have children
and I have grandchildren—and there isn't a word of sensible
language spoken here, only that Latin gibberish, and I might
as well be dead."

It made no impression upon her when Berenice pointed
out that this was not only the largest city in the world, but the
center of the world's government, culture, and excitement;
she went on complaining and whining. Berenice bathed.
The pool was filled with warm, sweet water, slightly per-
fumed, and equipped with a total plumbing system of silver.
You turned the taps on and off, as water was needed, fed
water through the mixer, had a clean flow always, and let the
used water out through the silver mask over the drain. The
pool was tiled with green marble, its fixtures in the shape of
dolphins, herrings, and sea horses. As Berenice bathed,
turning lazily in the water, she thought of how in all of
Galilee there was no bath like this; and then, thinking of
Galilee, she thought of the lake, its milk-warm water, swimming there as a child with her brother, Agrippa—and other

things, too, as she left the bath; wrapped herself in a robe, and calmed Gabo, who came running in breathless to announce that he was here.

"Who?"

"Who do you think, foolish one? Titus."

"Well, he must wait. Look at me—look at my hair! And this wretched robe! He must wait."

"He won't wait," Titus said, from the door to the bath. "It is exactly four years since I first saw you—and I'll wait no more."

He strode across the floor of green marble tiles and then he took her in his arms. She didn't resist now. She lay in the hard, wide cradle of his arms like a child come home.

To be touched by a man, stroked, caressed, awakened, brought back to life and awareness; this was more than she had ever dreamed could happen to her again. It cut through guilt and fear and wonder—and she was a woman, filled with all the knowledge of a woman, her body alive and full of music and fire and response. The touch of Titus' hands, his fingers, his mouth, his tongue, and the pent-up need of his love, the rigid demand of it—all of this was terrifying in her want of it, her need of it, and the confrontation of herself that was unavoidable. In the pulsing joy and agony, the doubt washed out. "I love you," she told him, calling upon God not to be her witness but her executioner. "May God destroy me, may my soul burn in all the fires of hell—but I love you, Titus—I love you more than life itself." "And will your God punish you for this?" "My God is an angry God," she wept, "and you came into His land with your sword and your torch and you burned His holy city—" "But you told me that all lands were His. And I will tell you something, Berenice—"

It waited, and he made love to her. He traced out her long, copper-skinned limbs, her wide hips, her wide shoulders, the beautiful, youthful curves into her groin—the carved planes and angles of her face, the great silken flood of her red hair,

"This is such a woman as there is nowhere else—and I will love you forever, Berenice, and cherish you—" Passion flooded her. He lay by her, and she clutched his naked body, and he was child and man and necessity and the breath of life and being.

She slept for a little while. She opened her eyes, and he was there, and she asked him, "What were you going to tell me, my beloved?"

"Ah—let me remember. We spoke of God's anger. Yaweh will not forgive me, but I made me a pledge to the God of your Hillel. I will be emperor some day, and I pledged to Him that when that day comes, I will make a garden of justice and beauty out of all the world that Rome rules. I will repay Him for giving me Berenice. I will repay in a world where fear and hunger have been banished, where all men live and work in peace, and where war is only a memory. I tell you I will do this because with you beside me, I can do anything. Anything."

Berenice smiled at him as she would have smiled at a child. He was a child—her own beautiful youth given to her to recreate her youth. He was filled with youth-strength, and he would pour this youth-strength into her. And between them, they would do anything, anything—

He was sleeping now, and she lay next to him and looked at him, and then she too slept. The first light of dawn was coming into the room when he awakened her, and again he touched her and awakened the wellspring of her life and being.

Lying back, her eyes closed, she heard his soft plea.

"Yes."

"Speak it."

"I love you, Titus Flavius."

"And you will be my wife?"

"If you wish."

"Have I ever wished otherwise?"

"Ever? Ever is too long."

"Not for us, blessed Berenice. For us, it is ever and always—our own eternity."

"You are so young, Titus Flavius—so young, and this city of yours is so young, and your people so young—"

"I will be as old as time for you."

"Ah? And what will that solve?"

"There is nothing more for me to solve. I have you, my beloved. So I have everything. I have life and I have eternity."

"You are really an amazing man," Berenice said. "I have never known you to do a cruel thing or a thoughtless thing, or to speak a cruel word, and you are as gentle as any man I have ever known, and—"

"And yet I am a Roman," Titus agreed.

"Yes."

"And you are a Jew—and doesn't your Hillel teach that God has a purpose and a plan? So we are Jew and Roman joined finally, and if it is true that your bloodlines go back three thousand years to time's beginning, is it not highly proper that they should find their haven here in my arms?"

"Oh, what ego! What arrogance!"

"Yes—because we shall rule the whole world, you and me, Jew and Roman joined together finally for man's golden age. Doesn't this poor, beaten old world deserve it?"

"Your dreams are too beautiful for me to upset them."

"My dreams will be the hard facts of history. Only, don't leave me, Berenice. Without you, I am nothing. I swear by all the gods that be that I am telling the truth—without you, I am nothing. But with you to support me, to love me, to caress me, to give me some worth in myself—with this, all things are possible. So promise me that you will never leave me."

She didn't answer for a while, and then she said, "For as long as you want me to remain with you, I will. I promise that."

The following day, David Barona made no mention of

Titus' visit. The best part of the day was given over to discussions with the leading men of the Jewish community—and out of seventeen men who attended, twenty-two million sesterces were pledged, either as a gift or as a sum to be raised within sixty days. Not all of it would be raised in Rome, or even in Italy; certain men would embark immediately for Africa and for Spain; but the pledges were secure, and the money would be raised—and now, at last, the final step in the enormous financial effort was in sight. Here, too, Berenice found herself changed. She was not pleading for money. She was demanding it, quietly, gently, but demanding it nevertheless—with a kind of firmness she had never considered herself to be capable of, and the men responded to her.

That night, she dined with Barona and his family—and they were utterly charmed and captured by her directness, her simplicity, and her great beauty. To people raised in luxury in Rome, where every woman who could afford it painted her face, rouged her lips, powdered her cheeks, and framed her eyes in heavy gobs of red-black outline and shadow, the sight of this Galilean princess, unrouged and unpainted, was exciting and unbelievable—and in Italy, where most men were quite short and the women shorter, her height and breadth of shoulder marked her as one apart, foreign and mysterious. The children of the house worshiped her with their eyes; the little girls attempted to walk as she walked, to hold themselves as she held herself.

After dinner Barona took her aside and said, "I think, my dear, that there are one or two matters we must discuss. Not our visitor last night. That is not my concern and in any case, it is something that I have known about. But concerning the slaves, you must understand this: Vespasian, the emperor, took over a throne where not the least among a number of pressing problems was finance—in other words, the near bankruptcy of the Empire. No, don't look so surprised—the Romans have only the most primitive concept of finance, and their scheme of balancing a budget is to balance enormous expenditures with equally enormous international looting. Eventually they will pay for this and pay an awful price, but for the moment they are able to step out of each crisis into the next. Now, when Titus began his siege of Jerusalem, Vespasian, at his wit's end for money, pledged two hundred thousand Jewish slaves to the big dealers and took option money to the extent of five million sesterces. We want to preserve the lives of the captives until sufficient funds are raised, and the only way to do this, I think, is to satisfy the dealers that you will not bring undue pressure on Titus to ruin them. In other words, we must, I think, meet with them. I hate to do this, my dear. These are not Jews or like the Jews you met here today. These are not even like Romans. These dealers are very wealthy, but they are the lowest of the low, the scum of the earth. So if you feel that you cannot—"

"I will meet them," Berenice said.

The following day she met with these slave dealers in their common room at the slave market at one end of the Circus Maximus, gross men, wealthy men, but mixed breeds barred from citizenship and from the baths and unwashed as in protest, foul of smell and foul of tongue, addressing her as "Jew-woman," though they knew well enough who she was. Barona watched her as she dealt with them, never for one moment losing her composure, controlling herself and talking to them firmly but without hostility, as if she were dealing with a group of truculent children. Gently and firmly she induced them to part with the options, and when the meeting was over each of them bowed to her. There were seven of them. They kissed her hand one by one.

In his litter on the way back to his house, Barona said to Berenice, "Do you know, my dear—I think you are the most remarkable women I have ever known. Through the years, I have heard much about you, and none of it measured up to the fact of yourself. I am seventy-six years old, so I can say things that would be impermissible in another man; also I have a prior claim. For when your father lived in Rome and was in desperate need of funds, I gave him credit to the extent of eighty thousand sesterces—"

"I never knew that. I must repay you," Berenice said.

"Child, child—the money was repaid thirty years ago, and money is nothing, nothing at all. In the end there is only one thing that matters, and that is Israel and its destiny along the road that Hillel marked. May I talk frankly?"

"I think we should both talk frankly," Berenice said.

"Exactly, for it seems to me that we need each other. Now it is common talk that Titus adores you—but tell me this, will you be content as his mistress?"

"No, I will not," Berenice answered flatly.

"Good, good," he nodded, rubbing his hands together with pleasure. "I am glad you said that. As sure as the Almighty is, my child—this is ordained. Have no regrets, for this is no ordinary man—this Titus. I think I know as much about him as anyone, and you see that he comes and goes freely in my house. I tell you, he is sober and wise and just, and when he puts on the purple, there will be a new era for the world. Now answer me straightly—did he ask you to marry him?"

"Yes."

"And you agreed?"

"Yes—and no. I need more time."

"Well, nothing is simple. I don't think he can marry you before he becomes emperor."

"Why?"

"Isn't it plain? Because we are Jews, my dear—and because the hatred of Jews is becoming both a fashion and a passion in Rome.

"But why?" Berenice asked. "I lived here as a child—and there was no hatred of Jews then. I don't think the people here had any real notion of what a Jew was."

"Well, they do now. A great deal has changed since then, and they know very well what a Jew is now—a Jew being someone who is apart from the dole, who lives quietly and decently, who remains sober and manages to eat with such restraint that he is not obligated to vomit up his excess food each evening, who does not destroy his children at birth— and who most dangerously converts Romans. Over the last five years, here in Rome, we have had eight hundred converts from Roman families—from the best families, if I may say so—and the men endure all the pain and indignity of circumcision to become Jews. And each year the number increases. Rest assured, my dear, we are envied and feared and hated, and that too increases constantly. I don't think that Titus could marry you without risking the throne—I don't think that he should until the throne is his."

"Isn't that for Titus to decide?"

"Now you are angry at me. But I am trying to make you understand what Vespasian will decide—and Titus will obey him. You see, my dear Berenice, a man loves a woman, a woman loves a man—this is within a framework, and the framework is the world. We are playing for the largest stakes in all time—for I tell you this: if ever Rome and Israel were joined together, then a new age would begin for mankind. Yes, I have dreamed of that—but until now, there has been no possibility. Now it is at least possible. Only don't press him. Let it be in his own good time."

To this, Berenice was silent, absorbed in her own thoughts and suddenly desperately lonely for Galilee.

But it was to be a long time before she saw Galilee again. The vast effort in which the Jews of all the world had joined was now coming to fruition. The gigantic sum of money was being raised, and in every important city of the Mediterranean basin, agents were quietly bidding for and purchasing Jewish slaves. But in Rome the slaves were most numerous, the effort largest; and here, too, was located the central bank, to where the major part of the money was directed and from whence it was dispensed. Jacobar Hacohen and Gideon Benharmish—his House of Shlomo had a warehouse at

Ostia and ships based there—joined Berenice in Rome, bringing with them Phineas Hacohen. He had been recorded as among the dead in Jerusalem, but had turned up subsequently in the slave market at Antioch and had been purchased for a token fee of twenty sesterces, being then almost dead with hunger and disease. Now, four months later, he was still thin, slow in his step, and humble at the fact that twenty sesterces had been his price in the markets of men. While his own fortune was gone, he was the last survivor of the ancient House of Hakedron and the grandson of the legendary Ba'as Halcohen and therefore a potent force in the effort. It was at his urging that Spain was chosen as the destination for most of the manumitted slaves.

Not only were the Palestinian members of the syndicate uneasy at the prospect of thousands of Zealots and Sicarii bought out of slavery and returned to Judea to nurse their hate and their dreams of revenge, but the Romans let it be known that at the first sign of substantial numbers of ablebodied men being returned to Judea, they would intervene and halt the traffic entirely. At the moment, because of Titus' support, the Roman authorities were standing aside, allowing the manumission to continue as a private process between the Jews and the slave dealers. For this reason, it was decided to ship as many of the Jews as possible, that is, adult men and women and their families, to Spain and to southern France—spreading the orphans and widowed women among the Italian, Greek, and Galilean Jewish communities. In Spain there was no trace of anti-Semitism; Jewish synagogues and communities had flourished in the coastal communities for hundreds of years; and thousands of Spaniards had been converted to Judaism.

Still there were a hundred matters to be arranged, and the support of the Jewish community leaders in Spain had to be won. For this reason Berenice made two trips to Spain. On the first trip she was absent from Rome for three months; and when she decided to make the second trip, Titus refused to accept so long a separation and went with her—leaving quietly so that only a handful of his intimate friends and of the Jews in the syndicate knew that he had left for Spain with Berenice.

Now a year and a half had passed since the death of Shimeon—and almost five years since she had parted with him in Jerusalem. The pall which had been upon her through all that time seemed suddenly to lift. She felt young, footloose, and amazingly happy. Never had she been the recipient of the kind of devotion Titus offered her; never had she been so long and so intimately connected with a man as lighthearted as Titus, as open-faced, and as unfalteringly optimistic. And never had she felt so certainly that her presence on earth was useful and important.

Most astonishingly, Titus was apparently happy to stand in the background and observe her. Except for Benharmish's son, Enoch, no one on the galley knew Titus' identity—only that he was a wealthy and highly placed Roman—and so it was in Spain, too, where Berenice was greeted with an adulation that verged on worship. Apparently he was delighted with this. Berenice had wondered whether he could sit back and watch and observe without jealousy and without uncertainty, and she was pleased to find still another aspect of him that she had not known of.

Then they returned to Rome overland through the gardens and valleys of northern Italy, taking ship from Spain to Cisalpine Gaul and traveling south from there by chariot. And it was out of the flush of joy and certainty of this trip that Titus decided to present Berenice to his father. But that went poorly.

In the great palace of the principate Berenice felt dwarfed. The public buildings of Tiberias could be set in the hallways here and yet leave enough room to pass. And the hawk-nosed, hard-faced man called Vespasian, who sat behind his desk and examined her, did nothing to ease her feelings.

"So you're the Jewish princess my son has lost his head

over," the emperor said flatly, his voice harsh and nasal. "Well, you're not the old witch they say you are, and I doubt whether you're old enough to be his mother, which is something else they say. Still, you're a Jew, and I can't say that I like Jews. I'm plain-spoken about things; that's something you'll have to get used to."

"It's a habit, and maybe not the worst one in the world," Berenice replied. "But it's nothing I have to get used to. You see, I am equally plain-spoken, Imperator, and I never confuse rudeness with the truth—so I can take your ways with women or I can leave them alone. As I wish."

Out of the corner of her eyes, Berenice watched Titus, whose mouth was twitching and who had to control himself visibly to restrain his mirth. Vespasian swallowed and roared and asked Berenice who the devil she imagined she was to talk to him like that? She replied that he knew very well who she was; and then he turned to Titus and demanded:

"Did you bring her here to irritate me? Don't I have enough troubles as things are? I never found a Jew I could trust—not even that wretched Joseph Benmattathias who cozened his way into our bosom and now calls himself Flavius Josephus—and why should I trust this one?"

"Why indeed?" Berenice asked him. "Only that you're the father of a man I care for."

"How old are you, woman?" he snapped.

"That, Imperator, is of concern only to myself and to Titus. And further, do not address me as *woman*. My ancestors were priests at Jerusalem and kings of Megiddo when Rome was a circle of mud huts inhabited by brutes who had not yet learned to weave cloth or even to smelt copper. And as for this meeting, I think that I at least have had sufficient of it—and if you will permit me, I should like to go."

Hours later, when Titus met her at the House of Barona, he was still unable to control his mirth. "My whole body aches from laughing," he told her. "By all the gods, I have not laughed like that in years."

"Did your father laugh?" Berenice asked him.

"He is furious. In all truth, if he was not out of the hardest, meanest peasant stock in all Italy, he would certainly have a stroke. Let him stew. He deserves to. Was ever a man put down so brilliantly and neatly!"

"That's enough!"

"What?"

"I do not wish to discuss it any further," Berenice said, and then Titus realized that she had been weeping.

"But why?"

"I did not think it particularly humorous," Berenice said. "How old am I? Is that the current gossip all over Rome—how old is this Jew witch? Is that what I am here for? I tell you this, Titus, I am sick and tired of your Rome, and I have had enough of it—"

But he closed off her protests with his embraces, and when they lay in bed, making love to each other, her hatred of Rome melted away. As did her plans for returning to Galilee.

"You are as young as the new morning," Titus whispered to her, "and as old as the truth—"

Titus went to Greece. He had expected to return in weeks, but he was away almost five months; and back in Rome a few days, he was ordered by his father to Africa. Now Berenice sat in front of her mirror, conscious for the first time in her life that her face was changing. A few slight wrinkles. A single white hair that she angrily plucked out. She lay for hours in her rooms, while beauticians applied mudpacks to her face and body and then gently massaged cream into the wrinkles around her eyes. Never before had she given a thought to her appearance; blessed with beauty, she had never questioned it, never doubted it. Now she was filled with doubts and even more filled with mistrust of herself. What had happened to her? She was becoming short of temper, querulous, angry too easily. She tongue-lashed Gabo until Gabo fell into a fit of hysterical tears; and then, conscience-stricken, Berenice attempted to comfort her. Gabo turned up to her mistress a tear-streaked face that was suddenly old—old, and that pierced Berenice to her heart. Wasn't Gabo only a year older than she was? And now Gabo was a small, dark, wrinkled woman with sagging dugs and nests of creases to bed her eyes, complaining forlornly,

"Is it right to talk to me like that? I love you so—and for a whole lifetime I served you and followed you everywhere, even to the ends of the earth and even to this pagan place which is the true Edom, the vanity of vanities and cursed by the Lord God—and always a slave—"

"No, no, no," Berenice begged her. "I manumitted you years ago."

"Then I made myself a slave. Did you ever thank me? I have children—"

"But they are well taken care of, Gabo," Berenice pleaded. "I shelter them in the palace in Tiberias and they are fed and clothed and schooled."

"Don't I have feelings? Don't I wish to see them?"

Berenice threw her arms around Gabo. "Anything—of course, you must go to see them. And I will find a swift ship for you and money, and you will bring them wonderful gifts from here, dresses for the girls and fine tunics and shoes for the boys—"

Now Gabo burst into tears and swore that she would die before she ever permitted herself to be separated from Berenice. And Berenice thanked her. "Oh, I am so lonely, Gabo. I am so lonely. I am so afraid here—"

"Come home with me, mistress. We will go back to a Jewish land—to a place where the God Yaweh can look down on us and keep us. Does He even know that we exist here, with these dark and ugly Roman gods?"

"Gabo, Gabo—there is only one God and He is everywhere."

"In Israel, yes, because Yaweh would destroy any other gods. Just as He destroyed the gods of Canaan in the olden times. But what can Yaweh do here?"

Go home—it was a dream. She said to Barona, "I am so lonely for Israel—"

"Because Titus is away? But that is only natural, my dear. Now listen to me—I know how long it has been—"

"Can anyone know how long it has been?" Berenice asked him. "Once, when we had the mission to the Jewish captives and there was meaning in my life because so many thousands of poor people had to be saved—once it was different. But when that was over, time became a river, and I floated on the river wishing half of the time that I could sink into it and drown."

"And yet you love Titus."

"Do I? I don't know. Sometimes—it seems to me that I love him so much that I cannot face life without him. Other times I am simply indifferent and unable to comprehend my relationship to this young man."

"Isn't that only natural?" Barona asked her. "Please, believe me, Berenice Basagrippa—and remain here with me only a little longer. Let me tell you what I have heard. I heard that Vespasian is mortally ill. They have had doctors from Greece and from Egypt, some of the most renowned physicians on earth, and they all agree that there is little or no chance for a recovery. In other words, the emperor is dying, and tomorrow or a month from now, as God wills, Titus will be emperor of Rome. Has he not sworn that he will make you his empress?"

"So he said," Berenice agreed.

The days and the weeks passed, and Vespasian still lived. Titus returned to Rome, but there was so much intrigue, so many problems surrounding the dying emperor that Berenice saw little of Titus. And when he did come, he was perturbed and distracted. As if a wall had come into being between them.

"Do you want me to go away?" Berenice asked him. "Back to Galilee—because you must say so if you do. You must tell me. I cannot remain here without your love."

"If I could only tell you how much I love you."

"What then, Titus? What then?"

"How can I tell you, Berenice? People hate me, fear me, envy me; it's part of being what I am, and you don't escape it. I have a brother, Domitian. I have cousins, stepbrothers, friends, enemies—and more who might be either one. Already, I am the Praetorian prefect. Two years ago, my father made me his colleague in the Imperium. A year ago, he gave me tribunician authority. I have power—too much power, and enemies, too many enemies. I have enemies who hate you even more than they hate me."

"Why should they hate me?"

"Because I love you, and because you are a Jew. They hate me for loving a Jew—and they hate you for being a Jew. They hate me because I turned a deaf ear to all their pleading that I drive the Jews out of Rome and dispossess them of all their property in Italy. Our curse is wealth, my darling, and our sickness is a lust for it; and now we have the new sickness of lusting for the wealth of the Jews. Why not kill them? Why not destroy them?"

"Yet you are Titus. They will never forget that."

Yet within three months after Vespasian died, they forgot that Titus was emperor—or hoped that as emperor he would ignore such things; and twenty armed men attacked the House of Barona. Berenice had just left her rooms to go down and join the family at their evening meal, when the assassins burst into the house. The entrance to her apartment was on a marble landing, about nine feet above the magnificent reception hall; so from where she stood, Berenice could look down the whole length of the reception hall to the front door, into the dining room on her right, and into passageways on her left that led to the kitchen. Gabo was coming from the kitchens with a bundle of Berenice's clothes, which she had steamed over the great stove, and the assassin in the lead cut her down with a single stroke of his sword, almost severing her head from her body. At that moment, Barona's daughter entered the room, leading her two children, one by each hand, and she paused and screamed. The second assassin ran her through, and two others ran after the children, cutting wildly at them. Brought by the screams, Barona and two of his sons ran into the reception hall, and they were murdered there on the spot. At the same time, half a dozen of the assassins raced down the length of the reception hall to the stairs to reach Berenice—who was apparently the focal point of their attack and the underlying reason for it. When she leaped back to the shelter of the door to her apartment, they flung swords and daggers at her, and though one of the swords skipped into the doorway, she was untouched. She slammed the door behind her and managed to throw the bar into place just as the body of the first of the assassins to mount the stairs hurtled against it. The door quivered but held. In a moment, all of them were fighting the door, hurling their weight against it and cutting at the panels with their swords. For the moment it held—but for how long? And if it did hold, how long before one of them exhibited intelligence and realized that there were other ways into the apartment— windows, balconies?

When the door continued to hold up under their blows, they stopped—and now, too, the terrible screams from beyond the door had stopped, which could only mean that the members of the House of Barona were dead, unless some of them had escaped. Leaning against the wall next to the door, Berenice was sick with what she had seen. Her first reaction over, she felt that it made no difference whether she lived or died. If they broke down the door now, she knew that she would make no effort to escape—that she would accept whatever fate awaited her. She was past caring, and suddenly she felt weary, so inexpressibly tired and exhausted that the effort of standing erect was too much for her. She sank down to the floor and crouched there, waiting for the assassins to make their way in through the windows or to devise some sort of battering ram that would smash in the door.

She waited, and time passed, and suddenly there was a wild shout, a clash of iron against iron, more shouting, more sound of weapons, screams of pain, roars of rage, and then a metal-shod hand hammering at the door.

"Berenice! Berenice—do you hear me?"

It was the voice of Tutis, and yet it could not be. He called to her again. Someone was attacking the door with an ax. Blow after blow, and it began to splinter. Berenice saw the axhead come through, Then a hole was made and enlarged, and a hand came through the flung the bar out of its socket. Titus leaped into the room, two Praetorians following with bared sword. He looked around him wildly for a moment, and then he saw Berenice—to whom it was all like a senseless dream. She watched him come to her and raise her up; only when his arms were securely about her did she begin to sob, deep, hard sobs that racked her whole body.

"We have the queen—she's safe!" one of the Praetorians was shouting.

Holding her up, Titus led her through the broken door, his arm like a rigid band of iron behind her and around her; and from the landing outside of her apartment, she looked down on an abattoir. The entire floor of the reception room was covered with blood and bodies, the men and women and children of the House of Barona—not a single one of them spared. (Berenice discovered afterward that a servant had escaped to give the alarm.) And with the Baronas, the bodies of a dozen of the assassins. Two of the assassins were held now by Praetorians; the others must have escaped.

"What have you got from them?" Titus demanded.

"Nothing yet."

"Well, take them home with you—and see whether hot irons and cold tongs may not loosen their tongues. Don't spare them. I want to know who is behind this, and I don't care whether those bastards live or die. Only keep them conscious, I want them to plead for death."

"Hasn't there been enough death?" Berenice whispered.

"No—hardly, my dear. We balance such things on bitter scales, and I loved and treasured this old man Barona and his flesh and blood. It will take a while to balance the scales."

But the assassins died, and the scales were not balanced; it was Titus' decision that Berenice should go to a villa he owned in Cisalpine Gaul, where she would be safe, where twenty Praetorians would be detailed to guard her—while Titus dealt with the cabal in Rome, which had apparently begun its campaign against him with the decision to murder her. He was not alarmed about the plotters; every Imperator faced that when he took office, and he was certain that he could deal with them, given time. But he was alarmed about Berenice's safety—and he was firm on the question of Gaul. No one would know where she was; the Praetorians would sell their lives, if need be, in her defense, and the moment this menace had been dealt with, he would bring her back to him.

She allowed herself to be convinced by his arguments. For herself, she would have preferred to return to Galilee, but she was no longer able to do what she desired or preferred. The spring, the mettle, the vibrancy had gone out of her. She wrote to her brother, Agrippa:

"Suddenly, I am old—if constant weariness means old age; and I feel so often that I have seen too much. A person is supposed to live a single life, and then return it to the Almighty when its time is over. But I feel that I have lived far more than one life, and perhaps this is my punishment. For I think I have sinned enough to warrant punishment. Agrippa, my brother, what am I to do? The dream of becoming Empress of Rome has worn very thin indeed—and if it ever does come to be, I think it will come without love. I no longer love Titus—if, indeed, I ever loved him—and that is something I do not know at all. But I did love David Barona Judaicus Purpureus—David, the son of Ona, the Jew of the purple. How foolish these pompous Latin names sound when you translate them! I loved him because he was sweet and gentle and wise and practical in the ways of the world—oh, how many Jews like him have I known! And then to see him and his entire seed murdered so cruelly, on my account; as if I myself had wielded the steel that cut him down! That I will never forget. Every night since then I wake up moaning and in a cold sweat, living through that terrible incident once again. How strange that in spite of the fact that I was won over to the House of Hillel, I seem to have lived with nothing but violence, war, and murder and the death of those I loved most! And now the House of Barona is finished, its long and ancient line brought to an end. How sorrowful! So for this good old man, for the dream he cherished of our royal house and line joined to the Imperium of Rome—for this man and his hopes, I will do as Titus begs me to do and go to his country place in Gaul and wait there for him to send for me.

"It will not be an arduous trip, for Titus is providing me with a comfortable galley, which will not only take me to Gaul but will be anchored at the mouth of the River Arno for my use when I desire it—and he is supplying me with trusted body servants—now that poor Gabo is dead, and you must cherish her children always—who will supply my every want. I stress this because I must not give you the feeling that Titus has changed. No. The change is in me, not him; and he remains as gentle and wise as ever. Already, all Rome is talking about the golden age he has ushered in. There are reforms every day. He has released thousands of people unjustly imprisoned, and he very pointedly absents himself from the hideous gladiatorial games. I would guess that the great majority of the people adore him, and everyone says that never before has Rome had an emperor so fair and wise and levelheaded. Of course I am deeply flattered that he not only considered me beautiful and desirable, but wise and judicious as well—but such flattery and self-adulation is poor meat and bread.

"Do you know what is most lacking in me? The spark of youth—and it seems to me that there is nothing in the world I desire more than to go back to Galilee and sit by the lake and listen to the songs of the fishermen as they plant their nets and watch their torches by night—oh, my soul aches simply to say it; for who knows that I will ever again see that beloved place. For so long, Israel was simply a word to me, an amorphous word overused by sentimental people. But now when I heard the word Israel, my eyes fill—

"So now I bid you farewell. I go to live for a while at least in a strange and distant land, where snow falls in the wintertime and where the inhabitants are little more than skin-clad barbarians who speak a tongue that is strange and rough and who have never heard the word Jew. Yet perhaps that is what I want now. Certainly, it is no joy for a Jew to live in a pagan land—where every pagan looks upon him with fear or ignorance or envy or hatred. So if I cannot go home, best that I go where Jews are neither known nor hated. I send you my love, brother. Think well of me."

She lit the candles and made the blessing, thanking the Almighty who brings the Sabbath. By her reckoning it was the evening before the Sabbath, but how certain could she be that her reckoning was to be depended on? It always seemed to her that somewhere along the way she had lost track of the days—skipped a day here, forgotten a day there. And this was hardly surprising, since one day was precisely the same as another. Well, God would forgive her, and had not the saintly Hillel preached that the least of men was more important than the Sabbath, since the Sabbath was only a memory of God, whereas man was a living reminder of him?

So she lit the candles and spoke the words of the old blessing, noting that while she had always been reasonably pious in her behavior as a Jew, she had never been overly respectful of ritual. It was only now, with no other Jew within a hundred miles, no Jew to speak to, to exchange a word with, that she had come to depend upon the comfort of the ritual. Hillel had small praise for the ritual, but then Hillel was never alone.

And she was alone. Sometimes a whole day went by without her speaking a single word—except to the servants who took care of the operation of the villa. At least the servants and the Praetorians spoke Latin. The local population of skin-clad, long-haired, long-bearded natives, unwashed, unkempt, and rank with that strong, sour smell that was the common property of peasants everywhere, had a tongue of its own—not a single word of which was intelligible to her; and she was at least initially amused by the fact that she who was so fluent in Greek, Latin, Aramaic, Punic, and old Hebrew, and who could make herself understood in Egyptian and Arabic, should here he rendered mute by this barbarous, guttural speech.

The Praetorians were not unwilling to temper her loneliness. Did Titus imagine that they were not men—these soldiers who had been detailed to guard her? Their eyes spoke. Their whispered comments to each other spoke. Their talk to her spoke more than words. "Only give us a chance," they intimated without ever saying it. "We'll show you that the Imperator is not the only man. It's a risk—a man's life, but you are worth it, lady." Or was this her imagination—her own new prayer for the preservation of her charm and beauty? So long as the Praetorians desired her, she could not be growing old. Or was the desire a product of her own imagination?

A letter from Titus said, "Only be patient, my beloved one—and it will be soon, I promise you that, much sooner than either of us had expected. I know that it is cruel to keep you penned up in so lonely a place, but almost anywhere else your life would be in danger from day to day. This way, at least I know that you are safe, and I console myself with the thought that soon, soon an empress will sit beside me so wise and gracious and lovely as Rome never knew before. I look for that moment from day to day now, and when it comes, I will send to you a centurion of the Praetorians named Lucillus Juvan. He is a man in whom I have great trust, and you must trust him and he will bring you back to my side."

So the letter from Titus read, and after that weeks went by and there were six more letters and each of the six was much like the next—and the dispatch of Lucillus Juvan was predicted. The centurion in command at the villa said to her,

"I know you dine alone each day, my lady. If the loneliness bites too deep, I can offer myself as a dinner companion. With a circumspection, believe me, that my beloved master would entirely approve."

She thanked him and declined; but had that been the entire sum of his meaning? Had he said no more than that? More and more poorly she slept, waking twice, three, four times in a night—lying sleepless for hours. In the morning, there were circles under her eyes, and the fretwork of tiny wrinkles was more pronounced. Of the four body servants Titus had sent with her, one was an expert masseuse and another had worked for years in a beauty salon. She had massage and cream treatment daily, but time would not stand still or retreat.

Almost daily there would be another white hair in her head. It did not gray gradually, as with most hair; instead the fierce red color turned immediately to white. Day after day she plucked these white offenders forth—until one day she stopped in horror. Was her hair thinning—or was it her imagination? Quickly, frantically, she parted her tresses, her heart hammering with fear. But it was true, and now she recalled how more and more often her comb was tangled with hair. She had believed that the hair was breaking off, as it did when it was young and healthy. But how could she reject the evidence of her eyes? Her hair was thinning. And what now? Should she pluck out the white ones? The thought of it made her skin crawl with horror. She had seen bald women—

She who had never thought of beauty before was now obsessed with it. During the endless days of loneliness, she had somehow worked out the postulate that only through her beauty could she be rescued from this isolated and wretched place. Without her beauty, Titus would reject her—and condemn her to live and die here in this hated spot.

She awakened one night from a nightmare in which she was the murderer of Gabo. Then she wept for Gabo. In the morning, the servants came, and she exploded at them: "Get out of here! Leave me alone! I don't want you—I want Gabo!" An hour later she was herself again, and she was apologizing profusely to her servants.

But how long, she asked herself, before she reached a point of no return? How long before her perceptions went awry—now that nightmares were becoming a regular occurrence? Less and less was she able to sleep. Outside her bedroom door there was a small garden, and she would take to going out there during her sleepless nights when the weather was mild. She would walk in endless circles, hoping to tire herself— and these would be the times for fantasy. Why doesn't that centurion come here now, she would ask herself? Why doesn't he find me here? Grasp me? Even attack me? It would mean that I am wanted, that I am a woman—that I still retain some vestiges of desirability and beauty. And what would I do? I don't want him—or any man, so what would I do? And do I want Titus?

But everything has its termination, and one morning as she sat toying with her breakfast, one of the servants entered to announce that a man called Lucillus Juvan had arrived by chariot on the road from Rome, and he was waiting to see her.

Afterwards, Berenice could not remember what this Lucillus Juvan looked like. He had no appearance in her memory, no face, no clothing to identify him, only a voice—a very even, low-pitched voice which said, in answer to her excited demand—was he from Titus?—and her trembling, pleading expectancy:

"Yes, madam."

"And what word does he send me?"

"No word, madam, for he sits among the gods, and the gods do not talk to mortal men. Titus Flavius is dead. Seven days ago he came down with a burning fever. A day later, he died—and knowing what you meant to him, knowing that he would want no other to bring you word, I took to the roads and raced here. I wish I came with better tidings—as I had always hoped to."

By noon of that same day Berenice felt that she would be able to talk without fighting desperately for control of her voice and her senses. She went to the mirror to straighten her hair, and there she looked at a ravaged face. Could it be the result of only a few hours? The deep hollows under her cheekbones, the dark circles under her eyes, and quivering upper lip with the tiny wrinkles feeding down into it—and the eyes, the strange, wonderful green eyes that had now lost their luster and were framed in a network of lines—could all this be the result of something she had heard only a few hours ago? Did beauty flee in that manner? Was age and decay the matter of a moment?

"We are both dead, Titus," she whispered—and the banality and cheap drama of the thought struck her like a blow, and she whispered, "Forgive me, my beloved—I am alive and you are dead—dead, my beloved and beautiful youth, my king of equity and justice; and where are the thrones where we would sit side by side and make a new Jerusalem that would be the whole world? Gone, all gone, and this life is a farce and fraud, Titus Flavius, a game we play so briefly, and it has no sense or meaning, only a road coming from nowhere and going nowhere—and the gods—oh, I am so tired of the gods, my darling, just as the ants must be tired of the men who walk upon them and crunch out their lives without thought or reason—"

Enough, she thought. Titus is dead, and I am alive.

Then she sent for Lucillus Juvan.

"Did you love him?" she asked.

"I loved him and he trusted me."

"Did he have pain?"

"You know what fever is, madam. It burns—but not pain that one cannot endure easily. It brought him death, which is, I suppose, the worst pain of all."

"Was it natural?" Berenice asked evenly. "Did he die of a natural fever, or was he poisoned?"

"They began to speak of poison the moment he took ill, and they will go on talking about it, but I know of no poison that could create such a fever. I was with him about five hours before he died, and he was like a furnace. No, madam, he was not poisoned. Who would want his death? It could only profit Domitian, his young brother—and the boy loved Titus Flavius—envied him, yes, but loved him too."

"Did he speak to you of me?"

"Yes, madam—believe me."

"What did he say?"

"What could he say? He could not give you money—he never solved the financial problems that beset him, and he knew you had all the money you could spend."

"I don't care about money!"

"And I knew he loved you—he knew that, and he told me to do whatever can be done for you—whatever you ask. The galley has been kept here. You may stay here—he gave you this villa—or go where you wish."

"I want to go home to Galilee in Israel," Berenice said. "That's all I want now. So if you would have them make the galley ready for the sea trip, I will leave. Whenever they are provisioned. I have only one desire now—to go home."

The captain of the galley was a Greek named Philo Menelae, an old sailor, a worldly man and aware of what went on in the world of the Mediterranean. He knew who Berenice was, and he did her the grace of leaving her alone, and ordering his officers to respect her privacy. In any case, Berenice was not much of an attraction to them. They looked at her and saw a tall, painfully thin, aging woman who possessed at best the ravaged remains of what might once have been beauty. Only the red hair conformed to the legend of Berenice, and even that was changing rapidly.

One morning, daring to look at herself in her tiny pocket mirror, Berenice saw the white had spread through the roots of most of her hair. Now it would grow in, but it meant little and she cared little. She tried to remember her age—was it fifty-two or fifty-three years? Or fifty-four years? Why was it so hard to think, to remember?

Day after day she sat on the afterdeck of the galley, a striped awning over her head, and tried to remember the many things that one should remember. But it was not easy. She spoke to no one. Sometimes, for hours, she would stare at the shore line slipping by in the distance, for this was a swift, coasting galley, never out of sight of land; and then her sight would blur and she would develop a headache. Never in all her life had she known a real severe headache—and these frightened her. Seeing that at times she was discomforted, the Greek captain made overtures toward her. Could he help her? Was there anything that she needed? She would shake her head—and wonder what he meant. What could she possibly need that this Greek might provide?

He came to her one day to point out the white towers of Tyre in the distance, as they raised the Phoenician coast. "See the height of them, Queen Berenice. Even taller than the apartment houses of Rome, and better built, if the truth be told. One winter I had an apartment in Tyre, seven stories high, a great climb—but I was younger then—and the view from the window once you got there was something to talk about, you may be sure. And the climate—I tell you, Tyre has a beautiful climate. But who am I to be telling you that, Queen Berenice? You know Tyre better than I do."

"A little, shipmaster—what little I remember." But the sight of Tyre had set her heart to racing. She felt one of those flushes beginning—the flush of old age and the loss of womanhood, as they called it—yet she could not contain her excitement.

"It's the weather of that coast that calls me. God save me from your Roman winter—ugh. It destroys. Now here—"

"Shipmaster?"

"Yes, my lady?"

"Can you put into Ptolemais instead of going on south to Caesarea? It's hours nearer. Is there a dock where you can tie up?"

"Of course, madam—of course. I have a cousin there—half Syrian, half Jewish, half Greek—three halves? Too much. Anyway, I have a cousin there who owns a dock."

"And can you hire me a litter, a four-man litter? I don't want to be in the town at all—but to stay here and go directly from the deck on the litter. I am very tired, I am afraid—very tired and not so well. My hair is turning white. Did you notice? It was red when I came on board—was it not?"

"Red as fire, Queen Berenice. Why, the moment I saw you coming down to my ship, I remembered the hair. I saw the hair, and I said to myself, there is the beautiful queen of Chalcis. But you have so much luggage—"

"Send it to Tiberias—at your pleasure." With a sudden gesture, she wrenched a gold crescent bracelet from her wrist. "Have this, shipmaster. You have been good and kind."

"No, no, no"—holding up both hands in protest, shaking his head until his curly ringlets waved like small snakes. "No, you are too good. My ship is under hire to the Flavians, who pay me well."

"I want you to have it, shipmaster."

"If you insist, my lady," he said, taking it and pressing it to his lips, "I will accept it, not as payment, but as something to remember you with and to give to my children, may your years be long and blessed and may your God, Yaweh, be merciful to you. I have great respect for Yaweh and Jews. I will hire you the best litter in Ptolemais."

The galley master picked up the pace of the oars, and the ship raced forward. And three hours later, they rounded the point to Ptolemais, backed water, and floated gently in to the docks.

Berenice had imagined that the litter would give her a restful and gentle journey up through the hills into Tiberias; and she had even anticipated looking through her curtains at the countryside—now in the full flush and color of the October harvest, with the Galilean peasants waist-deep in their lakes of wheat and barley and the rosy-cheeked Jewish maidens singing the old harvest hymns as they plucked the fruit from the heavy trees. Never in all her life had Berenice seen a harvest time like this, the land so fat and fruitful, every corner, every foot of land bursting with crops, the hillsides terraced for additional acreage—and nowhere even a sign that war had ever passed this way. But war was many years in the past, and to the young Jewish boys and girls who worked in these fields, the great war with Rome, and great and futile rebellion of the Zealots and the Sicarii was as ancient as the battles the Bible narrated in Judges and Kings. Among the older ones were those who claimed to remember seeing the mighty Roman legions march past, but even their memories were uncertain and clouded.

Such was the land, and Berenice had anticipated the sight and the sweet smell of it; but the increasing pain of the headaches and the severity of the flushes drew a veil of agony between her and the countryside. In the midday heat, she threw the curtains of the litter aside, but no one who peered into it was moved in terms of recognition. The thin, pain-wracked woman whose hair was discolored and turning white brought no response of memory. So evident was this that Berenice thought of halting the litter and crying out.

"Stop and look at me! I am Berenice—the last queen in

400

Israel! I am Berenice, whom kings adore for her beauty!"

But she did nothing of the kind. She wept a little out of pity for herself, but no more. Not even when they halted for the night at an inn did Berenice reveal herself. She remained in her litter, claiming that she was most comfortable there, and at her request the innkeeper brought her some hot milk and fresh-baked bread. He looked at her and saw nothing familiar—not even when she thanked him for the bread, telling him how good it was.

"Plain country bread."

"The bread of my heart—the bread of my blood," Berenice answered him.

"Well, if you wish, madam." He shrugged and thanked her for the gold piece she gave him. If she desired to pay a hundred times what the bread was worth, it was her business.

She hardly slept that night, and at the break of day, in the first light of the dawn, she awakened her bearers, who had curled up in a corner of the landlord's shed.

"Come, come," she told them gently. "I must be on my way."

They grumbled under their breath for her impatience. It was very well for the gentry to demand this and demand that, treating a litter slave no better than an animal; but for a slave it was another matter entirely. As if she read their thoughts, she opened her purse and counted her money. She had one hundred and twelve sesterces there, and she had the slave stop the litter while she divided all this money among them. "Buy freedom—or what you will." They were gold coins, each worth eleven of silver, and such a small fortune that the slaves knelt in the dust to her and wept and abased themselves, rubbing their foreheads in the dust.

"Enough, enough," she said. "Only bear me quickly—"

The pain in her head was agonizing, but at the sight of their joy, the joy that a little bit of money could bring to degraded human beings, she began to weep; and then the pain left her, and she felt light and happy.

"I am home," she said. "I am so happy to be home."

At first, there was a ground mist lying in the holes and in the valleys, but they mounted a hill, and from the top of it, they saw the whole lay and sweep of the lovely land of Galilee, with the silver glint of the lake in the distance. Or was that her imagination, and no more than a layer of mist in the valley?

"Do you know Galilee?" she asked the slaves.

Ah yes, they did. They knew it well. Again and again their master hired them out over the roads and traces of Galilee.

"Do you know where the House of Hillel is?"

Ah, they did, they did. Who was there in all of Galilee— no, in all of Israel who did not know where the House of Hillel was? It lay blessed in a valley of benediction, and it was a place where they could pause and rest on their way back from Tiberias, because a slave was treated like a man there. And there would be food for them, and in the heat of the summer sun, shelter in the shade of the great terebinth tree.

"Then bear me there quickly," Berenice said, "and we will reach there by noontime and you can lie and rest in the shade of the terebinth tree. But quickly!"

"With winged feet," they replied, and at a steady trot the bearers carried her on.

They were good men, she decided, and when the good man ran, not even the Angel of Death could run faster. How lighthearted she felt, and so happy that she wept a little with her pleasure.

And at last they were there, and they measured the breast of the hill and came down into the valley, where the old, sprawling Galilean farmhouse lay in the noonday sun. At the gates Berenice stopped them.

"I must walk in," she said. "I must not be carried in."

They helped her out of the litter, but when she tried to stand erect her knees bent, and she would have fallen had not the bearers leaped to help her. "Forgive us for touching you," they pleaded, and she told them, "You are my brothers."

Leaning on their shoulders, she walked with them toward

the terebinth tree, where servants were setting up the long tables for the midday meal. They saw her coming. The children saw her coming. Hillel, Shimeon's brother, saw her coming and he knew her. His wife, Deborah, saw her coming and recognized her. And the old, old mother of Shimeon, still alive, saw Berenice coming.

They ran to her, but Shimeon's brother reached her first and embraced her, weeping—and the others gathered around, weeping. But for Berenice, the pain began again, and she managed only to whisper.

"I think, brother, that I am dying. All the way from Italy, I fled the Angel of Death, but I am home. I must lie down, not inside, but under the tree. And then you must send for Agrippa."

"I will send for him, but you will not die," Hillel said.

Each time she opened her eyes, her vision was too blurred for her to comprehend what she saw, and the pain was very intense. But then as before, the pain departed, leaving her very weak, and her vision cleared and she saw the man bending over her. Time was trying to trick her, she thought. His face was lined, his hair and beard gray, but she knew immediately that it was Agrippa; and when he touched her face, she seized his hand, kissed it and clung to it.

"Brother—brother—"

"Now you are home, sister mine, and you will rest and become well—and all the old times, the lake and the forest, and then we'll sit at night and listen to the fishermen sing—"

"Yes," she whispered.

"You were away too long."

"Too long, and I found nothing—and then I did not know what I sought."

"You will tire yourself."

"No. I am not tired any more, brother." She felt a tiny motion of his hand. He is leaving, she thought. "Don't go away—"

"I stay here now, sister. Always. We will grow old together, and talk about all the things we have seen—"

"Poor brother. He's angry—such childish, foolish anger."

"Who?"

"Yaweh—because they drove Him from the high place. But I don't care. Brother, I don't care any more, because there's no meaning and no purpose, only the senseless, childish anger. And I hate this cold, wretched place—and the peasants with their smell, and the centurions."

"Sister—"

"Where am I?"

"In the House of Hillel, under the terebinth tree."

"That's a good place to be," she agreed, as simply and gently as a child. "I am tired now, and I want to sleep."

That night Berenice Basagrippa died—in her fifty-fourth year. They buried her on the hillside next to her husband, Shimeon Bengamaliel, the grandson of the sage who is remembered as Hillel the Good. In time the gravestone was carried away or sank into the ground, and so the grave was unmarked and become one with the ancient soil of Galilee in Israel.

There are a lot more
where this one came from!

Don't Miss these Ace Romance Bestsellers!

_____ **#75157 SAVAGE SURRENDER** $1.95
*The million-copy bestseller by Natasha Peters,
author of Dangerous Obsession.*

_____ **#29802 GOLD MOUNTAIN** $1.95

_____ **#88965 WILD VALLEY** $1.95
*Two vivid and exciting novels by
Phoenix Island author, Charlotte Paul.*

_____ **#80040 TENDER TORMENT** $1.95
*A sweeping romantic saga in the
Dangerous Obsession tradition.*
